SEPARATE BEDS

SEPARATE BEDS

LaVyrle Spencer

G. P. PUTNAM'S SONS
NEW YORK

This is a work of fiction. Names, characters, places, and incidents either are the product of the author's imagination or are used fictitiously, and any resemblance to actual persons, living or dead, business establishments, events, or locales is entirely coincidental.

G. P. Putnam's Sons
Publishers Since 1838
a member of
Penguin Group (USA) Inc.
375 Hudson Street
New York, NY 10014

PUBLISHING HISTORY
Jove paperback edition 1985
Separate Beds appeared in *Three Complete Novels*
published by Random House Value Publishing, 1991.
Putnam hardcover edition 2003

Library of Congress Cataloging-in-Publication Data

Spencer, LaVyrle.
Separate beds / LaVyrle Spencer.
p.   cm.
ISBN 0-399-15131-1
1. Parenthood—Fiction.   I. Title.

PS3569.P4534S46   2003   2003043223
813'.54—dc21

Printed in the United States of America
1   3   5   7   9   10   8   6   4   2

This book is printed on acid-free paper. ♾

Book design by Jennifer Ann Daddio

With love to my husband,

DAN,

the best thing that ever happened in my life

Dear Reader,

Separate Beds was first published in 1985, a different time from today in many ways. Though the conflict surrounding the characters is timeless, some aspects of the drama are products of their time. Today some young readers might ask, Were there really homes for unwed mothers? Yes, there were. Did pregnant women not realize it was harmful to drink alcohol during pregnancy? No, we did not. And could a man truly be denied admittance to the bar because he'd fathered a child out of wedlock? Unbelievable, but absolutely true back then. Also, in the eighties contraception was considered a woman's job—thus the opening conflict of this novel. We smile now at the modes of dress described, and at the idea of a new mother's staying in the hospital nearly a week after having a baby, but that's how it was in that era, and everything from fashions to morals have taken a decidedly different turn in the intervening years. So read it for what it is: a piece of fiction set in a period a little different from now, yet not so different at all, because human emotions and needs do not change. We all crave love, and most of us want a lifetime commitment to go along with our babies. For Catherine and Clay, the road to achieving this together is what makes *Separate Beds* a satisfyingly emotional story.

To my readers of old, thank you for your many requests that I write again. Retirement, however, is a splendid arrangement, and

I have no plans to resume writing. I still spend time with family, and entertaining, and gardening, and going to Maui in the winters. Life couldn't be better.

LaVyrle Spencer
Stillwater, Minnesota
February 2003

SEPARATE BEDS

ONE

Circumstances being what they were, it was ironic that Catherine Anderson knew little more of Clay Forrester than his name. He must be rich, she thought, scanning the foyer, which revealed quite clearly how well-off the Forrester family was.

The deep side of the expansive entry opened into a sprawling formal living room of pale yellows and muted golds. Above was a great crystal chandelier. Behind her, a stairway climbed dramatically to the second story. She was faced by double doors, a console table whose cabriole legs touched the parquet as lightly as a ballerina's toes and a brass accent lamp reflected by a gilt-framed mirror. Beside her stood an immense brass pitcher bursting with an abundance of overpoweringly fragrant dried eucalyptus.

The pungent stuff was beginning to make her sick.

She turned her eyes to the massive carved oak entry doors. The knobs weren't shaped like any she'd ever seen. Instead, they were curved and swirled like the handles of fine cutlery. Acidly Catherine wondered how much handles like those must cost, to say nothing of the pretentious bench, on which she'd been left. It was lush brown velvet, armless, tufted—the kind of absurd extravagance afforded by only the very rich.

Yes, the entire foyer was a work of art and of opulence. Everything in it fit . . . except Catherine Anderson.

The girl was attractive enough, her apricot skin and weather-streaked blond hair having a fresh, vital look. Her features bore the strikingly appealing symmetry often found in those of Scandinavian ancestry—the straight nose and fine nostrils; shapely, bowed lips and blue eyes beneath arched brows of pleasing contour.

It was her clothing that gave her away. She wore a pair of heather-colored slacks and shirt that spoke of brighter days long gone. They were homemade and of poor fabric. Her trench coat was limp, frayed at hem and cuff. Her brown wedgies were made of artificial stuff, worn at the heels and curled at the toes.

Yet her clean, wind-blown appearance and fresh complexion saved Catherine from looking disreputable. That, and the proud mien with which she carried herself.

Even that was slipping now, the longer she sat there. For Catherine realized she'd been left like a naughty child about to be reprimanded, which actually wasn't far from the truth.

With a resigned sigh, she dropped her head back against the wall. Vaguely she wondered if people like the Forresters would object to a girl like her laying her head against their elegant wallpaper, supposed they would, so defiantly kept it there. Her eyes slid shut, blotting out the lush elegance, unable to blot out the angry voices from the study: her father's, harsh and accusing, followed by the constrained, angry reply of Mr. Forrester.

Why do I stay? she wondered.

But she knew the answer; her neck still hurt from the pressure of her father's fingers. And, of course, there was her mother to consider. She was in there, too, along with the luckless Forresters, and—rich or not—they had done nothing to deserve a madman like her father. It had never been Catherine's intention to let this happen. She still remembered the shocked expressions of both Mr. and Mrs. Forrester when her father had barged in upon their pastoral evening with his bald accusations. They had at first attempted civility, suggesting that they all sit down in the study and talk this over. But within moments they understood what they were up against when Herb Anderson pointed at the bench and bellowed at his daughter, "Just plant your little ass right there, girlie, and don't move it or I'll beat the livin' hell outa you!"

No, the Forresters had done nothing to deserve a madman like Herb Anderson.

Suddenly the front door opened, letting in a gust of leaf-scented autumn air and a man whose clothing looked like the interior decorator had planned it to blend with the foyer. He was a tapestry of earth tones: camel-colored trousers of soft wool, European-cut, sharply creased, falling to a stylish break upon brown cordovan loafers; sport jacket of subdued rust and camel plaid, flowing over his shoulders like soft caramel over ice cream; a softer shade of rust repeated in the lamb's-wool sweater beneath; an off-white collar left casually open to foil a narrow gold chain around his neck. Even nature, it seemed, had cooperated in creating his color scheme, for his skin bore the remains of a deep summer tan, and his hair was a burnished red-gold.

He was whistling as he breezed in, unaware of Catherine, who sat partially shielded by the eucalyptus. She flattened her back against the stair wall, taking advantage of her sparse camouflage, watching as he crossed to the console table and glanced through what must have been the daily mail, still whistling softly. She caught a glimpse of his classically handsome face in the mirror, its straight nose, long cheeks and sculpted eyebrows. They might have been cast in bronze, so flawless and firm were their lines. But his mouth—ah, it was too perfect, too mobile, too memorable to be anything but flesh and blood.

Unaware of her presence, he shrugged off the stylish sport coat, caught it negligently in the crook of one wrist and bounded up the stairs two at a time.

Catherine wilted against the wall.

But she stiffened again as the study door burst open and Mr. Forrester stood framed against the bookshelves within, his slate-gray eyes submerged below craggy brows with a formidable expression, his anger scarcely held in check. He wasted not so much as a glance at the girl on the bench.

"Clay!" The invincible tone stopped the younger man's ascent.

"Sir?"

The voice was the same as Catherine remembered, though the formal word of address surprised her. She was not used to hearing fathers called *sir.*

"I think you had better step into the study." Then Mr. Forrester himself did so, leaving the door open as yet another command.

Had the circumstances been different, Catherine might have felt sorry for Clay Forrester. His whistling had disappeared. All she heard now was the soft shush of his footsteps coming back down the stairs.

She squeezed her rib cage with both arms, fighting the unexpected flood of panic. Don't let him see me! she thought. Let him walk right past and not turn around! Yet common sense told her she could not escape him indefinitely. Sooner or later he'd know she was there.

He reappeared around the newel post, shrugging once again into his sport coat, telling her even more about his relationship with his father.

Her heart beat in the high hollow of her throat and she held her breath, the stain of embarrassment now coloring her cheeks. He stepped to the mirror, checked his collar and his hair. To Catherine, for the briefest moment he seemed vulnerable, being watched from behind that way, unaware of her presence or of what awaited him in the study. But she reminded herself he was not only rich, he was degenerate; he deserved what was coming.

He moved then and her image became visible in the mirror. His eyes registered surprise, then he turned to face her momentarily.

"Oh, hi," he greeted her. "I didn't see you hiding back there."

She was suddenly conscious of the frightful thud of her heart, but she carefully kept her face placid, giving him no more than a silent, wide-eyed nod. Never having planned to lay eyes on him again, she was not prepared for this.

"Excuse me," he added politely, as he might have to any of the clients who often waited there to do business with his father. Then he turned toward the study.

From within came his father's command. "Shut the door, Clay!"

Her eyes slid closed.

He doesn't remember me, Catherine thought. The admission made her suddenly, inexplicably want to cry, though it made no sense at all when she'd hoped he'd walk right past like a stranger, and that was precisely what he'd done.

Well, she berated herself, that *is* what you wanted, *isn't it*? She summoned up anger as an antidote to the tears that Catherine Anderson never allowed herself to shed. To feel them threatening—and here, of all places!—was unspeakable. Weaklings cried! Weaklings and fools!

But Catherine Anderson was neither weakling nor fool. The circumstances might appear otherwise just now, but in twenty-four hours everything would be far different.

From behind the study door Clay Forrester's voice exploded, "Who!" and her eyes came open.

He doesn't remember me, she thought again, resigning herself to the fact once and for all, straightening her shoulders, telling herself not to let it matter.

The study door flew open, and she affected a relaxed and unconcerned air as Clay Forrester confronted her framed in that doorway, much as his father had before. His eyes—gray, too—impaled her. His scowl immediately told her he didn't believe a word of it! But she noted with satisfaction that his hair now looked finger-combed. Pushing back both front panels of his sport coat, hands on hips, he challenged her with those angry eyes. He scanned her summarily, allowed his glance to float down to her stomach, then back up, noting her detached air.

She suffered the insolent way his gaze roved downward—like a slap in the face—and retaliated by pointedly studying his full, lower lip, which she remembered quite well, considering the brevity of their association and the time that had lapsed since. But, knowing virtually nothing about him, Catherine decided she'd best take care in dealing with him, so she carefully remained silent beneath his scrutiny.

"Catherine?" he asked at last. She expected to see his breath, the word was so cold.

"Hello, Clay," she replied levelly, maintaining that false air of aloofness.

Clay Forrester watched her rise, slim and seemingly assured. Almost haughty, he thought, but certainly not scared . . . and hardly supplicating!

"You belong in here, too," he stated tersely, holding that implacable stance while she gave him one extended look that she hoped appeared cool. Then she walked past him into the study. Antagonism emanated from him. She could nearly smell it as she passed so close in front of him.

The room was like a storybook setting: pre-supper fire burning on the grate, stem glasses half full upon polished tables, book-lined walls, an original Terry Redlin wildlife oil on the wall behind a leather love seat, soft carpeting underfoot. Masculine yet warm, everything about the room spoke of an interrupted coziness, which was precisely why Herb Anderson had chosen this time of day to make his appearance, when he figured all the Forresters would be home. His exact words had been, "I'll get them rich sonsabitches when they're all holed up together in that fancy brick mansion, wearin' all them family jewels, and we'll see who does the paying for this!"

The contrast between Clay's parents and Catherine's was almost laughable. Mrs. Forrester was ensconced in a wing chair at one side of the fireplace. She was shaken, yet extremely proper, feet crossed at the ankles. Her clothing was impeccable and up-to-date, her hair done in a tasteful coiffure that made her features appear youthfully regal. Upon her shapely hands glittered the magnitude of gems Herb Anderson derided.

Ada Anderson, in the matching chair on the opposite side of the fireplace, picked at a slub of her bargain-basement coat, keeping her eyes downcast. Her hair was mousy, her shape dumpy. Upon her hand was only a thin gold band whose apple blossom design was worn smooth from years of hard work.

Mr. Forrester, double-vested in well-tailored business gray, stood behind a morocco-topped desk that held several leather-bound books in a pair of jade bookends worth as much as the entire Anderson collection of living room furniture.

Then there was her father, decked out in a red nylon jacket boasting the words *Warpo's Bar* on its back. Catherine avoided looking at the bulging beer belly, the bloated face, the ever-present expression of cynicism that perpetually claimed the world was out to beat Herb Anderson out of something, when actually it was the other way around.

Catherine stopped beside her mother's chair, conscious that

Clay had stopped behind her. She kept a shoulder turned away from him, choosing instead to face his father, easily the most formidable person in the room. Even his position behind the desk was strategically chosen to connote command. Understanding this, she chose to confront him on her feet. Her own father might swear and carry on like a drunken sailor, but this other stern adversary was by far the greater threat. Catherine sensed the man's total control, sensed, too, that should she face him with a hint of challenge on her face it would be the worst possible mistake. He was the kind of man who knew how to deal with hostility and defiance, thus she carefully kept them from her countenance.

"My son doesn't seem to remember you, does he?" His voice was like the first edge of November's ice on a Minnesota lake—cold, sharp, thin, dangerous.

"No, he doesn't," Catherine replied, looking at him squarely.

"Do you remember her?" the father snapped at his son, daring it to be true.

"No," answered Clay, raising Catherine's ire not because she wanted to be remembered, but because it was a lie. She hadn't really expected the truth out of him anyway, had she?—not once she'd suspected he had enough money to back up any lies he chose to tell. Still, his answer rankled. She turned to find him nearer than was comfortable and accosted him with blue eyes that rivaled the frost in his father's.

Liar! Her eyes seemed to shout, while he smugly perused her features, then cast a glance over her blond hair and saw the fire create sundogs on it, dancing behind her that way. And suddenly he recalled it backlit by fireworks.

Oh, he remembered her all right. . . . Now he remembered her! But he cautiously kept it from showing in his face.

"What the hell is this, a frame-up?" he accused.

"I'm afraid it isn't, and you know it," Catherine replied, wondering how long she could maintain this feigned calm.

But then Herb Anderson jumped in, yelping and pointing. "You're goddam right it isn't, lover boy, so just don't think—"

"You're in my home," Mr. Forrester interrupted explosively, "and if you want this . . . this *discussion* to continue, you will control yourself while you are here!" There was an undeniable note of sarcasm in the word *discussion*; it was obvious Herb Anderson didn't know the meaning of the word.

"Just get busy and make lover boy here own up, or, so help me, I'll squeeze the truth outa him like I done outa her."

Something slimy seemed to crawl through Clay's innards. He glanced sharply at the girl but she remained composed, her eyes now on the desktop, where whitened knuckles were depressing lustrous leather.

"You will remain rational, *sir*, or you and your wife will leave at once and take your daughter with you!" Forrester ordered.

But Anderson had been waiting all his life for his ship to come in, and this . . . by God! . . . was it! He turned to confront Clay nose to nose.

"Let's hear it, lover boy," he sneered. "Let's hear you say you never laid eyes on her before, and I'll make you the sorriest lookin' mess you ever seen in your life. And when I'm done, sonny, I'll sue your old man for every goddam penny he's got. Rich bastard like you, think just because you got a few bucks your kind can go around screwing everything in skirts. Well, not this time, not this time!" He shook his fist under Clay's nose. "You're gonna pay up this time or I'll be hollering rape so fast it'll make you wish you was a fag!"

Mortified, Catherine knew it was useless to argue. Her father had been drinking all day, getting primed for this. She'd seen it coming but could do nothing about it.

"Clay, do you know this woman?" his father demanded grimly, pointedly ignoring Anderson.

Before Clay could reply, Herb Anderson pushed his face near his daughter's and sneered, "Tell him, girlie . . . tell him it was lover boy here knocked you up!" Instinctively Catherine drew away from the disgusting smell of his breath, but he reached out and grabbed her cheeks and rasped, "You tell him, sister, if you know what's good for you."

Clay stepped between the two. "Now, wait a minute! Take your hands off her! She's already pointed the finger at me or you wouldn't be here." Then, more quietly, he added, "I said I don't know her, but I remember her."

Catherine flashed him a warning look. Actually, the last thing she wanted from Clay Forrester was noble self-sacrifice.

"There! You see!" Anderson made a motion like he'd slapped a trump card on the desktop. Mrs. Forrester's face quivered. Her husband's showed the first sign of defeat as his lips fell open.

"You're admitting that this woman's child is yours?" Claiborne Forrester exclaimed disbelievingly.

"I'm not admitting any such thing. I simply said I remember her."

"From when?" Claiborne insisted.

"This summer."

"This summer, when? What month?"

"I think it was July."

"You *think* it was July! Hadn't you better do more than *think?*"

"It was."

A look of gloating turned Herb Anderson's face more detestable than ever.

"July what?" Claiborne pressed on, facing the calamity head-on, in spite of his growing dread.

"July fourth."

"And what happened on July fourth?"

Catherine held her breath again, embarrassment for Clay making her acutely uncomfortable now.

"We went on a blind date."

The room grew church-silent. Catherine sensed everyone counting off two and a half months since then.

Claiborne's chin hardened, his jaw protruded. "And?"

Only the soft hiss of the fire spoke while Clay considered, his eyes briefly lighting on Catherine. "And I absolutely refuse to answer another question until Catherine and I speak alone," he ended, surprising her.

"You, Clay Forrester, will answer my question here and now!" his father exploded, rapping a fist on the desktop in frustration. "Did you or did you not have relations with this woman on July fourth?"

"With all due respect, Father, that is none of your business," Clay said in a tightly controlled voice.

Mrs. Forrester put a trembling hand to her lips, beseeching her son with carefully made-up eyes to deny it all here and now.

"You say this is none of my business when this man threatens to bring a paternity suit against you, and to ruin your reputation along with mine in this city?"

"You've taught me well enough that a man makes his own reputation. As far as you're concerned, I don't think there's anything to worry about."

"Clay, all I want is the truth. If the answer is no, then for God's sake, quit protecting the girl and say no. If it's yes, admit it and let's get it over with."

"I refuse to answer until she and I can talk privately. Obviously we were both left out of any earlier discussion. After we've had a chance to talk, I'll give you my answer." He gestured to

Catherine, motioning her to follow, but she was too stunned to move. This was one turn of events that was totally unexpected!

"Now, wait just one goddam minute there, sonny!" Herb Anderson hissed. "You ain't gonna go skipping out on me and leaving me lookin' like some jackass don't know which end is up! I know *exactly* what your game is! You take her outa here and pay her off with some measly couple o' hundred bucks and shut her up and your problem is solved, huh?"

"Let's go." Clay made a move to pass Anderson.

"I said, hold on!" Anderson stuck his pudgy fingertips in Clay's chest.

"Get out of my way." Some grim note of warning made Anderson comply. Clay strode toward the door, curtly advising Catherine, "You'd better come along with me if you know what's good for you."

She walked toward Clay like a puppet, even while her father continued his tirade at their backs. "Don't you get no ideas about givin' her the money to get rid of the kid either, you hear me! And just see to it you keep your hands offa her, lover boy. She better not have no more complaints or I'll have the law down on you before the night is out!"

Face scorching, insides trembling, Catherine followed Clay into the foyer. She assumed he would lead her to another room of the house, but instead he stalked to the front door, flung it wide and ordered, "Let's take a ride." It took her off-guard and rooted her to the parquet, quite involuntarily. Realizing she hadn't followed, he turned. "We've got some talking to do, and I'll be damned if I'll do it in the same house with all of our parents."

Still she hesitated, her blue eyes wide, mistrusting. "I'd rather stay here or go for a walk or something." Not even the blazing color in her cheeks softened him. Her hesitation only made Clay more unyielding.

"I'm not giving you an alternative," he stated unequivocally, then turned on his heel. From the library came the sound of her father's voice, badgering the Forresters further. Seeing no alternative, she finally followed Clay outside.

TWO

A silver Corvette was parked now in the horseshoe-shaped driveway behind her family's sedan. Without waiting, Clay yanked a door open and got in, then sat glaring straight ahead while she tried to quickly measure the risk of going for a ride with him. After all, she knew nothing about him. Did he have a temper like her father? Was he capable of violence when cornered this way? What would he do to keep her from making trouble in his life?

He glanced back to find her looking balefully over her shoulder at the front door as if help would step through it at any moment.

"Come on, let's get this over with." His choice of words did little to reassure her.

"I—I really don't care to go for a ride," she stammered.

"Don't tell me you're afraid of me!" he taunted with a dry laugh. "It's a little late for that, isn't it?" He started the engine without taking his insolent eyes off her. She moved at last, only to realize, once she was in the car, that there was one eventuality she hadn't considered. He'd kill them both before this was over!

He drove like a maniac, throwing the car into gear and careening down the brick driveway while manicured shrubbery blurred past the windows. At the road, he scarcely braked, changing gears with a screech and a lurch, then tearing at breakneck speed through a maze of streets that were unfamiliar to her. He slammed his hand against a cassette that hung in the tape deck, sending throbbing rock music through the car. She couldn't do anything about his driving but she reached over and lowered the volume. He angled her a sidelong glance, then stepped a little harder on the gas. Obstinately she wedged herself into her seat and tried to ignore his childish antics, deciding to let him get it out of his system.

He steered one-handed, just to show her he could.

She sat cross-legged, just to show him she could.

They sailed around corners, up curving hills, past strange street signs until Catherine was totally lost. He took a sharp right-hand curve, gunned his way into a sharper left, flew between two stone gate markers onto gravel where they fishtailed before climbing into a pocket of wooded land. The headlights flew across a sign: PARK HOURS 10:00 A.M. TO—but the lights moved too fast for Catherine to catch the rest. At the top of the last incline they broke onto a parking lot surrounded on all sides by trees. He stopped the car much as he'd driven it—too fast! She was forced to break her forward pitch with a hand on the dash or sail through the windshield!

But still she stubbornly refused to comment or to look at him.

Satisfied, anyway, that he'd managed to budge her from that damn uppity cross-kneed pose, he cut the engine and turned to her. But he remained silent, studying her dim profile, knowing it made her uncomfortable, which suited his purpose.

"All right," Clay said at last in the driest of tones, "what kind of game are you playing?"

"I wish it were a game. Unfortunately, it's very real."

He snorted. "That I don't doubt one bit. I want to know why you're trying to pin the blame on me."

"I understood your reluctance to answer with our parents present, but here, between just the two of us, there's no further need to play dumb. Not when we both know the truth."

"And just what the hell is the truth?"

"The truth is that I'm pregnant and you're the father."

"I'm the father!" He was in a high state of temper now, but she found his shouting preferable to his driving.

"You sound slightly outraged," she said levelly, giving him a sideways glance.

"*Outraged* isn't the word for me right now! Did you really think I'd fall for that kangaroo court back there?" He thumbed over his shoulder.

"No," she answered. "I thought you'd flatly deny ever having laid eyes on me and that would be the end of that. We would go our separate ways and take up our lives where we'd left off."

Her unruffled detachment took some of the wind from his sails. "It's beginning to look like I should have."

"I'd survive," she said tonelessly.

Baffled, he thought, She's an odd one, so composed, almost cold, unconcerned. "If you can survive without me, tell me why you created that scene in the first place."

"I didn't; my father did."

"I suppose it was entirely his idea to storm our house to-night."

"That's right."

"You had nothing to do with it," he added sarcastically.

At last Catherine grew upset, losing her determination to remain unruffled. She whirled sideways in her seat and let him
have it. "Before you say one more thing in that . . . that damn-
ably accusing voice of yours, I want you to know that I don't
want *one damn thing from you! Not one!*"

"Then why are you here, picking the flesh from my bones?"

"Your *flesh*, Mr. Forrester?" she parried. "Your flesh is the last
thing I want!"

He pointedly ignored her double entendre. "Do you expect
me to believe that after all the accusations that have been hurled
at me tonight?"

"Believe what you will," she said, resigned again, turning
away. "I don't want anything but to be left alone."

"Then why did you come?" When she only remained silent,
he insisted again, "Why!"

Obstinately she remained mute. She wanted neither his sympathy nor his money nor his name. All she wanted was for tomorrow to hurry and get here.

Antagonized by her stubborn indifference, he grabbed her
shoulder roughly. "Listen, lady, I didn't—"

She jerked her shoulder, trying to free it from his grasp. "My
name is Catherine," she hissed.

"I know what your name is!"

"It took you some time to remember it, though, didn't it?"

"And what is that supposed to mean?"

"Let go of my shoulder, Mr. Forrester, you're hurting me."

He dropped his hand, but his voice zeroed in, slightly
singsongy now. "Oh, I get it. The lady is feeling abused because I
didn't recognize her right off the bat, is that it?"

She denied him an answer, but felt herself blushing in the
darkness.

"Do I sense a little contradiction there? Either you want recognition from me or you don't. Now which is it?"

"I repeat, I don't want anything from you except to be taken home."

"When I take you back, it'll be when I'm satisfied about what I'm being threatened with."

"Then you can take me back now. I'm not threatening anything."

"Your mere presence in my home was a threat. Now let's get on with what you want for a payoff . . . that is, if you're really pregnant."

The thought had never occurred to her that he'd doubt it.

"Oh, I'm pregnant all right, make no mistake about that."

"Oh, I don't intend to," he said pointedly. "I don't intend to. I mean to make damn sure that baby is *not* mine."

"Are you saying you really do *not* remember having sexual intercourse with me last Fourth of July?" Then she added in a satirically sugary tone, "You'll notice I do not mistakenly call it making love, like so many fools are prone to do."

The dark hid the eyebrow he cocked in her direction, but it couldn't hide the cocky tone of his voice. "Of course I remember. What does that prove? There could have been a dozen others."

She'd been expecting this sooner or later, but she wasn't expecting the anger it evoked, the way she simply had to fight back, no matter how degrading it was to have to. "How dare you say such a thing when you know perfectly well there weren't!"

"Now you're the one who sounds outraged. Promiscuous females have to be prepared to be doubted. After all, there's no way to prove paternity."

"No proof is necessary when it's the first time!" She smoldered, wondering why she wasted her breath on him. Without warning the overhead light came on. In its beam, Clay Forrester looked like she'd just thrown ice water on him.

"What!" he exclaimed, genuinely stunned.

"Turn that thing off," she ordered, turning her face sharply away.

"Like hell I will. Look at me." Something had changed in his voice, but it made it even more impossible to face him.

The view outside the window was totally black but she studied it as if for answers. Suddenly a hand grabbed her cheeks, the fingers sinking into them as he forced her to look at him. She glared into his surprised face as if she hated every feature of it, gritting her teeth because she didn't.

"What are you saying?" Intense gray eyes allowed her no escape. She was torn by the wish to have him know nothing of her and the equally strong wish to let him know everything. He was, after all, the father of the child she carried.

He stared into her imprisoned face, wanting to deny her words, but unable to. He tried to remember last July fourth more clearly, but they'd had too much wine that night.

"You're hurting me again," she said quietly, making him realize he still held her cheeks imprisoned in his grasp.

He dropped his hand, continuing to study her. She had a face that wasn't too easy to forget: shapely, narrow nose; long cheeks dusted with a suggestion of freckles; blue eyes trying hard not to blink, meeting him squarely now within long, sandy lashes. Her mouth was sullen, but memory flashed him a picture of it smiling. Her hair was shoulder-length, blond on blond, tabby-streaked, its bangs feathered back but falling in alluring wisps onto her forehead. It curled hither and thither around her long neck. She had a tall, thin frame. He suspected, although he could not clearly remember, she was shaped the way he liked his women shaped: long-limbed, hollow-hipped and not overly breasty.

Like Jill, he thought.

Sobered at the thought of Jill, he again fell to trying to remember what had passed between himself and this woman.

"I . . ." Catherine began, then asked with less acid in her voice, "will you turn out that light?"

"I think I have a right to see you during this sticky conversation we're having."

She had no choice but to be studied like a printout from a lie-detector test. She tolerated it as long as she could before turning away, asking, "You don't remember, do you?"

"Parts of it, I do, but not all."

"You struck me as a man of experience, one who'd know a virgin every time."

"If you're asking me how often I do things like that, it's none of your business."

"I agree. It's none of my business . . . but I wasn't asking. I was only defending myself, which I had no intention of doing in the first place. You are the one who seemed to be asking how often *I'd* done things like that, and no girl likes to be called promiscuous. I only wanted to point out that it was undeniably my first time. I assumed you'd have known it."

"Like I said, my memory is a little fuzzy. Suppose I believe you—there could have been others after me."

That brought her anger back in full force. "I have no intention of sitting here and being insulted by you any further!" she spit out. Then she opened the door and got out. He wasn't far behind her, but she stalked off into the dark, her shoes crunching gravel, gone before he could storm around to the other side of the car.

"Get back here!" he shouted into the dark, his hands on his hips.

"Go to hell!" she yelled from somewhere down the road.

"Just where do you think you're going?"

But she just kept on walking. He broke into a run, following her shadowy form, angered more than he could say by her stony insistence that she wanted nothing from him.

She felt his hand grab her arm and swing her around in the dark. "Dammit, Catherine, get back to the car!" he warned.

"And do what!" she exclaimed, turning to face him, fists clenched at her sides. "Sit and listen to you call me the equivalent of a whore? I've taken that kind of abuse from my father, but I certainly don't have to sit still and take it from you!"

"All right, I'm sorry, but what do you expect a man to say when he's confronted with an accusation like yours?"

"I can't answer your question, not being a man myself. But I thought a—a worldly stud like you would know the truth, that's all!"

"I'm no worldly stud, so knock it off!"

"All right, so we're even."

They stood in the dark, unmoving combatants. She wondered if he could be as experienced as he'd seemed that night and yet not recognize the fact of her virginity. He, meanwhile, wondered if a girl of her age could possibly have remained a virgin all that time. He guessed her to be twenty or so. But in this day and age, twenty was old, sexually. Again he strove to remember anything about that night, how she'd acted, if she'd been in pain, if she'd resisted. All he knew for sure was that if she *had* resisted in any way or asked him to stop, he would have. Wine or no wine, he was no rapist!

Giving up, he said cajolingly, "You must have done all right. I never knew the difference."

His chauvinistic remark riled her so swiftly she lost good sense and swung on him, giving him a good one with her knuckles in the middle of his breastbone.

Caught off-guard, he gasped and stumbled one surprised step backward. "Ouch, that hurt, goddammit!"

"Oh, that's rich! That's so rich I could throw up! *I* must have done all right! Why, you insufferable egotistical goat! Telling me *I* must have done all right when you're the one who can't even remember clearly!"

Nursing his bruised chest, he muttered, "Christ, are you always like this?"

"I don't know. This is a first for me. How do your pregnant girlfriends usually react?"

Wary now, he was careful not to touch her. "What do you say we stop trading insults, okay? Let's just forget our sexual histories and own up to the fact that we went out on a blind date and gave each other a little refreshment for the night, and take it from there. You say you were a virgin, but you can't prove it by me."

"The dates will bear it out. The baby is due on the sixth of April. That's the only other proof I have that it was you."

"Pardon me if I seem dense, but since you claim you don't want anything from me, why are you trying so hard to convince me?"

"I'm not . . . I . . . at least I wasn't until you questioned me about there being others. It was a point of self-defense and nothing more." Then, realizing she was beginning to sound more and more entreating, she muttered, "Oh, why do I waste my breath on you!" And she turned down the road again, leaving him with the diminishing sound of her footsteps.

He let her go this time and stood there with one hand on his hip in the dark, thinking to himself that she was the singularly most irritating woman he'd ever met. It was all the more frustrating to think he'd made love to a wasp like that! Then, with a rueful grin, he corrected himself, making it "had sexual intercourse" with a wasp like that. He listened to her footsteps fading away, thinking, Good riddance, lady! But in the end he couldn't let her go.

"Catherine, don't be an ass!" he admonished, hurting her ego further as she hotfooted it down the gravel road. "You're at least three miles from my house, and God knows how many miles from yours. Get back up here!"

The fragrant night resounded with her response: "Up yours, Clay Forrester!"

He cursed, returned to his car and twisted the key so violently it should have broken off in the ignition. The headlights flashed on, arced around, and the Corvette went roaring down the hill, picking out Catherine's belligerent back as she continued to stalk. He roared past her, spraying dust and gravel.

About fifty feet in front of Catherine, at the bottom of the hill, the brake lights flashed on, followed by the interior light as Clay got out again and stood leaning an elbow on top of the open door, waiting. She would have ignored him, but he wouldn't allow it. When she was abreast of him, a hand shot out and detained her. "Get in, you little spitfire," he ordered. "I'm not leaving you out here whether I want to or not. Not at this hour of the night!"

The light from the car limned her angry face as she thrust her lower lip out, beetling her brows in curled distaste. "I must have been crazy to come to your house in the first place. I should have known no good would come of it."

"Then why did you?" he insisted, holding her easily by a forearm, but well enough away so she couldn't punch him again.

"Because I didn't think your parents deserved the likes of my old man. I actually thought by going along with him I could save them from some unpleasantness they didn't deserve."

"Do you expect me to believe that?"

"I don't care what you believe, Clay Forrester! Let go of my arm, dammit!" She yanked herself free, then whirled like a bantam rooster, unable to keep explanations mute. "You've gotten a dose of my old man. It doesn't take very long to get the drift of how he operates. He's mean and vindictive and lazy, and an alcoholic to boot. He'll stop at nothing to get whatever he can out of either you or your parents. I think he's stark, raving mad to go shoving his way into your house the way he did, badgering your family."

"And what does he expect to get out of it?"

Catherine debated, decided she had nothing to lose by being frank. "A free ride."

She could tell he was surprised, for he studied her in the vague light cast from the car, then exclaimed, "You admit that?"

"Of course I admit it. It'd take a fool not to see what he's up to. He smelled money, which he's never had enough of, and it brought out his every greedy instinct. He thinks he can use this situation to make life a little easier on himself. I don't kid myself one bit that it's my reputation he's concerned about. He can harp all he wants about his little girl's loss of innocence and her ruined future. But it's really his own future he's looking out for. He wants to feather his bed till it's as soft as he thinks yours is. I don't really think he believes for one minute he can get you to marry me. I don't even think he *wants* you to. He'd rather have your guilt money, and he'll do everything in his power to get it. I warn you, he's a dangerous man. You see, he believes his ship just came in."

"And none of those thoughts entered your head?"

"I didn't know you from Adam last July. How could I possibly have smelled money?"

"Your cousin Bobbi lined us up. She's Stu's girl, and Stu is an old friend of mine. It follows."

She threw her hands up and paced agitatedly back and forth. "Oh, sure! First I ran a financial check on you, then got myself lined up with you on the *perfect* night to get pregnant, then I seduced you and sent my father in after the pickings." She snorted derisively. "Don't flatter yourself, Forrester! It may surprise you to learn that not every girl who finds herself pregnant wants to marry the man. I made one mistake last July, but that doesn't mean I'm going to make a second by forcing you to marry me."

"If you're innocent, tell me just how in the hell your old man knew who to come to. Somebody pointed him in my direction."

"I did not *point!*"

"Then how did he choose me to come after?"

She suddenly clammed up, turned her back on him and walked around the car, saying, "I believe I will take a ride home after all." And she got in.

He got in, too, leaving one foot out on the gravel so the light would remain on while he grilled her.

"Don't avoid the issue," he demanded. "How?"

"I did *not* give him your name. I refused to tell him anything!"

"I don't believe you. How did he find out then?" Clay saw how she worried her lower lip between her teeth, refusing to look at him.

Catherine willed her mouth to stop forming explanations for his benefit, but she was not the cunning woman he thought, and it galled her to be accused this way.

"How?" he repeated, waiting.

Her nostrils flared, she stared straight out over the dash, but finally divulged, "I keep a diary." Her tone was quieter and her eyelids flickered slightly.

"You what?"

"You heard me," she said to the window on her side.

"Yes, I heard, but I'm not sure I understand. You mean he found it?" It was beginning to dawn on Clay just what kind of unscrupulous bastard her father really was.

"Leave me alone. I've already said more than I wanted to."

"There's a lot at stake here. I deserve to know the truth if that baby really is mine. Now answer me. Did he find it?"

"Not exactly."

"What then?"

She sighed, laid her head back against the seat but continued staring out the window away from him. Then from the side he saw her eyelids slide shut wearily, almost resignedly. Her voice lost much of its agitation.

"Listen, none of this has anything to do with you. Leave it be. What he is and what he did was never supposed to enter into it. I only wanted to keep your parents from paying his demands. That's why I came along."

"Don't change the subject, Catherine. He found the diary and found my name, right?"

She swallowed. "Right," she whispered.

"How did he find it?"

"Oh, for God's sake, Clay, I've kept a diary since I was in pinafores! He knew it was there someplace. He didn't just *find* it, he ripped my room apart until he found the evidence he was always accusing me of. You wanted the truth, there it is."

Something coiled in Clay's gut. His voice softened. "Didn't anybody try to stop him?"

"I wasn't there. My mother wouldn't try to stop him if she

could. She's scared of her own shadow, to say nothing of him. You don't know my old man. There's no stopping him when he gets something in his head. The man's insane."

Clay pulled his foot inside and slammed the car door. He sat brooding, putting it all together, then cradled the steering wheel in both arms, clasping a wrist behind it. At last he looked back over his shoulder at her. "I'm almost afraid to ask . . . what was in it?"

"Everything."

With a small moan he lowered his forehead to the steering wheel. "Oh, God . . ."

"Yes," she repeated quietly. "Oh, God . . ."

"I take it you remembered that night more clearly than I did?" he asked, embarrassed now himself.

"I'm no different than any other girl. It was my first time. I'm afraid I was quite explicit about my feelings and the events of that night."

The silence lengthened and Catherine's composure slipped. It was far more disconcerting having him even remotely sympathetic than having him angry. After some time he sank back against his seat, shuddering a sigh, leaning an elbow high on the window ledge and rolling his face aside to knead the bridge of his nose. The long, strained silence became painted with provocative images that flickered through their minds until at last Clay forced his thoughts back to the present and the unpleasant aspect of her father's threats.

"So he wants reparation."

"Exactly, but whatever he says, whatever he threatens, you must not meet his demands. Don't pay him anything!" she said with sudden passion.

"Listen, it's not just up to me anymore. He's brought my fa-

ther into this, and my father is . . . my father is the most exasperatingly honest man I've ever known. Either he'll force me to pay,
or he'll pay whatever your father demands before this thing is
over."

"No!" she exclaimed with an intensity that brought her near
to clutching his arm. "You must not!"

"Listen, I don't understand you. You've spent the night convincing me you're carrying my baby. Now you beg me not to pay
your father anything. Why?"

"Because my father is the scum of the earth!" Her words
were as sharp as knives, but the knives were double-edged, for
the words she was forced to utter cut her deeply. "Because I've
hated him for as long as I can remember, and if it's the last thing
I do, I want to make sure he doesn't cash in on any good luck
due to me. He's been waiting for years for something like this to
happen. Now that it has, it almost thrills me to be responsible for
his coming so close, then foiling him!"

Suddenly Clay prickled with awareness. "What do you mean,
if it's the last thing you do?"

She managed a sardonic laugh. "Oh, don't trouble yourself,
Mr. Forrester, supposing for a minute I'd commit suicide over
this. That would hardly foil him anyway."

"How then?"

"Depriving him of the payoff money will be quite enough.
You don't know him or you'd realize what I mean. It'll almost be
worth every time he—" But she stopped just short of being carried away by the hate she felt, by the memories she had no intention of revealing.

Clay again began rubbing the bridge of his nose, fighting
against getting involved with her past any more than necessary.
But the vindictiveness she displayed, the abusive way the man

had treated her and spoken to her, the accusations she said her father undeservedly made to her—it was the classic picture of a physically violent man. But to involve himself in sympathy for this woman would be a mistake. Yet even while Clay refused to allow himself to delve any further into her past, what he knew of it was already festering in the dark silence while he grew upset over being embroiled in this fiasco in the first place. It was all so damn unnecessary, he thought. Pinching the bridge of his nose, Clay found he was now beginning to develop a headache.

He boosted himself up and outlined the wheel with his arms again. "How old are you?" he asked, out of the blue.

"What possible difference does that make?"

"How old!" he repeated, more forcefully.

"Nineteen."

He emitted a single sound, half-laugh, half-grunt. "Nineteen years old and she didn't have the sense to take some precautions," he said to the ceiling.

"Me!" she yelped. A quick, smoking anger assaulted her, making her shout louder than necessary in the close confines of the car. "Why didn't *you*? You were the one who had all the experience in these matters!"

"I wasn't planning on anything that night," he said, still disgusted.

"Well, neither was I!"

"A girl with any sense at all doesn't go around looking for sex without being prepared."

"I was not looking for sex!"

"Ha! Nineteen and a virgin and she claims she's not looking for it!"

"You conceited bastard, you think—" she began, but he cut her off.

"Conceit's got nothing to do with it," he ground out, nose to nose with her now across the narrow space. "You just don't randomly go out on the make without some kind of contraceptive!"

"Why?" she shouted. "Why me? Because I'm the woman? Why not you? What was the matter with you thinking ahead a little bit, an experienced stud like you?"

"That's the second time you've called me a stud, lady, and I don't like it!"

"And that's the second time you've called me *lady*, and I don't like it either, not the way you say it!"

"We're getting off the subject, which was your neglect."

"I believe the subject was *your* neglect."

"The woman usually takes care of precautions. Naturally, I assumed—"

"Usually!" she croaked, throwing her hands in the air, then flopping back exaggeratedly, talking to the ceiling. "And *he* calls *me* promiscuous!"

"Now just a minute—"

But this time she interrupted him. "I told you, it was my first time. I wouldn't even have known how to use a contraceptive!"

"Don't hand me that! This isn't Victorian England! All you'd have had to do was open the phone book to find out how and where to learn. Or hadn't you heard—women have come of age? Only most of them prove it by showing a little common sense with their first fling. If you'd have done the same, we wouldn't be in this mess."

"What good are all these recriminations? I told you, it happened, that's all."

"It sure as hell did, and it was just my luck that it happened with an ignorant girl who doesn't know the meaning of the words *birth control*."

"Listen, *Mister* Forrester, I don't have to sit here and be preached to by you! You're equally as guilty as I am, only you're blaming me because it's easier than blaming yourself. It's bad enough I have to tolerate your inquisition without defending myself against ignorance! It took two of us, you know!"

"Okay, okay, just relax. Maybe I came down a little heavy on you, but this could have been avoided so easily."

"Well, it wasn't. That's a fact of life we have to live with."

"Clever choice of words," he muttered.

"Listen, would you mind? Just take me home. I'm tired and I don't want to sit here arguing anymore."

"Well, what about the baby—what are you going to do with it?"

"It's none of your business."

He bit the corner of his lip and asked quickly, before he lost his nerve, "Would you take money for an abortion?"

Her preliminary silence nearly made her reply redundant. "Oh, you'd like that, wouldn't you? Then your conscience would be clear. No, I wouldn't take money for any abortion!"

Long before she finished, he felt like a confirmed pervert.

"All right, all right, sorry I asked." He couldn't tell yet if he was worried or relieved by her answer. He sighed. "Well, what are we going to do about your father?"

"You're so smart, you figure it out." Catherine knew that after tomorrow, when Herb Anderson's pregnant little trump card disappeared, his ship would lose the wind from its sails. But she was damned if she'd tell Clay Forrester that. Let him stew in his own juices!

"I can't," he was saying almost contritely, "and I'm not that smart and I'm sorry I called you ignorant and I'm sorry I called you promiscuous and I shouldn't have gone flying off the handle like that, but what man wouldn't lose his temper?"

"You might be justified if I were making demands, but I'm not. I'm not holding a gun to your head or forcing you to do anything. But neither am I going to sip from your tarnished silver spoon," she ended sarcastically.

"And what is that supposed to mean?"

"It means that maybe my father was right to resent you because you're rich. It means that I resent your thinking you can sweep it all under the rug by an offer of a quick abortion. I'd have respected you more if you'd never suggested it."

"It's legal now, you know."

"And it's also murder."

"There are conflicting views on that, too."

"And obviously yours and mine conflict."

"Then you plan to keep the baby?"

"That's none of your business."

"If it's my baby, it's my business."

"Wrong," she said with finality, the single word stating clearly that it was useless for him to try to get anything more from her. The silence waged war with Clay's conscience while he sat disconsolately cradling the wheel. When next he spoke, the words told more truth than either of them had expected.

"Listen, I don't want that kid raised in the same house with your father."

You could have heard a leaf drop from the blackened branches that drooped above the road. Then Catherine's voice came quietly into the dark.

"Well, well, well . . ."

For answer he started the engine, threw the car into gear and tried to drive away his frustration. Brooding, he drove again one-handed, allowing the car just enough excessive speed, but not too much. She leaned back, silently watching the arch of trees spin backward above the headlights, losing all sense of direction, shutting out thoughts momentarily. The car slowed, turned, nosed along the street where he lived.

"Do you think your parents might still be here?"

"I have no idea. A madman like him just might be."

"It looks like they've gone," he said, rolling past, finding no sedan in the driveway.

"You'll just have to take me home then," she said, then added while turning her face toward her window, ". . . so sorry to put you out."

He came to a halt at a stop sign and sat waiting with feigned patience. When she only continued staring stubbornly out that window he was forced to ask, "Well, which way?"

Under the blue-white glance of the streetlight she noted the effrontery of his insolent pose: one wrist draped over the wheel, one shoulder slightly slumped toward his door.

"You really don't remember anything about that night, do you?"

"I remember what I *want* to remember. *You* remember that."

"Fair enough," she agreed, then settled her expression into one of indifference and gave him a street address and brief directions on how to reach it.

The ride from Edina to North Minneapolis took some twenty minutes—long, increasingly uncomfortable minutes during which their angers diminished at approximately the same rate as the speed of Clay's driving. With verbal combat forsaken, there was only the sound of the car purring its way through the somnolent city with an occasional streetlight intruding its pale, passing glimpse into their moving world. Within the confines of that world an uninvited intimacy settled, like an unwanted guest whose presence forces politeness upon his host and hostess. The silence grew rife with unsaid things—fears, dreads, worries. Each could not be more anxious to part and be rid of this tension between them, yet for both a final separation seemed too abrupt.

As Clay turned a last corner onto her street the car was nearly crawling.

"Whi—" His voice cracked and he cleared his throat. "Which house?"

"The third on the right."

The car rolled to a stop at the curb, and Clay shifted into neutral with deliberate slowness, then adjusted some button till only the parking lights remained on. She was free to flee now, but, curiously, remained where she was.

Clay hunched his shoulders and arms about the wheel in the way with which she was already growing familiar. He turned his eyes to the darkened house, then to her.

"You gonna be all right?" he asked.

"Yeah. What about you?"

"God, I don't know." He lay back and closed his eyes. Catherine watched the pronounced movement of his Adam's apple rising and falling.

"Well . . ." She put her hand on the door handle.

"Won't you even tell me what your plans are?"

"No. Only that I've made them."

"But what about your father?"

"Soon I'll be gone. I'll tell you that much. I'm his little ace in the hole, and with me gone he'll have nothing to threaten you with."

"I wasn't thinking about me when I asked that, I was thinking about you going in there now."

"Don't say it . . . please."

"But he—"

"And don't ask any questions, okay?"

"He forced you to come to the house tonight, didn't he?" His voice was strained.

"I said, no more questions, Mr. Forrester," she said in a distractingly gentle tone.

"I feel like hell, you know, letting you go this way."

"Well, that makes two of us."

The vague light from the dashboard cast their eyes in shadow, but somehow the intensity conveyed itself. She looked sharply away from his face, for she would not be haunted by the conscience-stricken look she saw there. She opened her door and the overhead light came on and he reached out to stop her. Silence fell while the heat of his hold burned through the arm of her coat. She pulled, slowly, steadily, inexorably away from him, turning, straining toward the door. But her neck arched sideways, revealing under the mellow light three purple bruises strung there in a row, each a finger's width apart. Before she could prevent it, the backs of Clay's fingers glided over the spot and she cringed, lowering her jaw into her collarbone.

"Don't!" Her eyes were wide, fierce, defiant.

In a strident voice, Clay asked, "He did that, didn't he?"

Denial would have been useless, admission folly. All she could do was avoid answering.

"Don't you dare say anything sympathetic or sentimental," she warned him. "I couldn't take it right now."

"Catherine . . ." But he didn't know what to say, and he couldn't sit there restraining her any longer. He didn't want to be involved in her life, yet he was. They both knew it. How could she get out of this car and carry his child away into some hazy future without both of them realizing how fully he was already involved in her life?

"Could I give you some money anyway?" he asked, almost in a whisper.

"No . . . please . . . I want nothing of you, whether you believe it or not."

By now he believed it.

"Will you get in touch with me if you change your mind?"

"I won't." She raised her elbow, pulling it by inches out of his fingers until he no longer commanded her.

"Good luck," he said, his eyes on hers.

"Yeah, you too."

Then he leaned over to push her door open, the back of his arm faintly brushing against her stomach, sending goose bumps shimmying through her, radiating outward from the spot.

Quickly she stepped out onto the sidewalk.

"Hey, wait a minute . . ." He leaned across the seat, peered up at her with a curiously sad expression about his eyes and mouth. "I—what's your last name again, Catherine?"

His question swept her with the insane urge to cry, an urge she'd felt earlier in the foyer when he'd failed to recognize her.

"Anderson. It's Anderson. So common it's easy to forget."

Then she turned and ran into the house.

But when she was gone, Clay Forrester folded the arms of his expensively tailored sport coat over the wheel of his expensive sports car, laid his well-groomed head upon them, knowing he would never forget her name as long as he lived.

THREE

The only light burning on the lower level was the lamp on the console table. Reaching for it, Clay caught his reflection in the mirror. A troubled frown stared back at him. *Catherine Anderson*, he thought, *Catherine Anderson*. Not liking what he saw, he quickly snapped off the light.

Upstairs the door to his parents' bedroom suite was ajar, casting a pyramid of brightness into the hall. He stopped, arms akimbo, staring at the floor in the way he was wont to do when troubled, wondering what to say.

"Clay? We heard you get home. Come in." His father moved into the open door. From the shadows Clay studied him, his heavy velour jacket shaped like a short kimono over his trousers. The older man's hair lay in soft silver waves around his healthy face. Momentarily Clay had the desire to grasp his father's neck and bury his face in the silver waves, feel that tanned cheek against his own as when he was a child and came running in for a morning hug.

"I didn't mean to keep you and Mother up."

"We'd be up in any case. Come in."

The ivory carpeting swallowed his slippered steps as Clay followed, to find his mother, wearing an ecru Eve Stillman dressing gown, her feet tucked up into the corner of a powder blue chair of watered silk.

It was like stepping back twenty years. Coming and going in their separate adult pursuits, they had little occasion to cross each other's paths except when dressed in street clothes. Gone now were the impeccable suits, high heels and jewelry from the woman curled protectively into the corner of that chair. Clay again experienced the strange sensation he'd had in the hall. He wanted to bury his head in her lap and be her little boy again.

But her face stopped him.

"We were having a glass of white wine to soothe the frayed nerves," his father said, crossing to fill his glass from a crystal decanter while Clay took the chair that matched his mother's. "Would you like one?"

"No, none for me." Sardonically he thought, Wine, tricky wine.

"Clay, we assume nothing. Not yet," his father began. "We are still waiting for your answer."

Clay looked at his mother's anxious face, at that guardianlike pose that cried out that she didn't want to learn what might be true. His father stood, swirling the wine around and around in his glass, staring at it, waiting.

"It looks like Catherine is right," Clay confessed, unable to tear his eyes away from his mother's shifting expression, her widening eyes that gaped momentarily before seeking her husband's. But Claiborne studied the expression on his son's face.

"Are you sure it's yours?" Claiborne asked forthrightly.

Clay worked his hands against each other, leaning forward, studying the floor. "It seems so."

Stunned, Angela expressed what both she and her husband had been thinking for the past several hours. "Oh, Clay, you didn't even know her today. How can it possibly be true?"

"I only met her once, that's why I didn't recognize her at first."

"Once was apparently quite enough!" Claiborne interjected caustically.

"I deserve that, I know."

But suddenly Claiborne Forrester, father, became Claiborne Forrester, counselor. Silently he took up pacing for a moment, then stopped directly before his son, brandishing his wineglass as he often brandished a finger at a client too quick to admit his guilt. "Clay, I want you to make damn sure you are the man responsible before we take this thing one step further, do you understand?"

Clay sighed, stood up and ran four lean fingers through his hair. "Father, I appreciate your solicitude, and . . . believe me . . . when I first found out why she was here, I was just as surprised as you. That's why I took her out for a ride. I thought maybe she was just some kind of gold digger trying to stake a claim on me, but it seems she isn't. Catherine doesn't want a thing from me, or from you, for that matter."

"Then why did she come here?"

"She claims it was all her father's idea."

"What! And you believe her?"

"Whether I believe her or not, she doesn't want one red cent from me."

His mother said hopefully, "Maybe she's had a sudden attack of conscience for blaming you unjustly."

"Mother," Clay sighed, gazing down at her. How defenseless she looked with her makeup cleansed off this way. It broke his heart to hurt her. He crossed to her chair, reached down to take both of her hands. "Mother, I won't make much of a lawyer if I can't cross-examine a witness any better than that, will I?" he asked gently. "If I could honestly say the baby's not mine, I would. But I can't say that. I'm reasonably sure it is."

Her startled eyes pleaded with her son's. "But, Clay, you don't know anything about this girl. How can you be sure? There could . . ." Her lips quivered. "Could have been others."

He squeezed the backs of her hands, looked into her despairing eyes, then spoke in the softest of tones. "Mother, she was a virgin. The dates match up."

Angela wanted to cry out, "Why, Clay, why?" But she knew it would do no good. He, too, was hurting now—she could see it in his eyes—so she only returned the pressure of his hands. But without warning, two tears slid down her cheeks, not only for herself, but for him, as well. She tugged at his hands, reaching to pull him down and kneel as she held him.

He felt a keen, sharp pain at having disappointed her, a deep welling love at her reaction.

"Oh, Clay," she said when she could speak once more, "if

only you were six years old this would be so much easier. I could just punish you and send you to your room."

He smiled a little sadly. "If I were six, you wouldn't have to."

Her own wistful smile trembled and was gone. "Don't humor me, Clay. I'm deeply disappointed in you. Give me your hanky." He fished it out of his pocket. "I thought I taught you"—she dabbed her eyes, groping for a graceful phrase—"respect for women."

"You did, you both did." Abruptly Clay stood, plunged his hands in his trouser pockets and turned away. "But for God's sake, I'm twenty-five years old. Did you really think I'd never had anything to do with women at my age?"

"A mother doesn't think about it one way or the other."

"I'd be abnormal if I were pure as the driven snow. Why, you and Father were married already by the time he was twenty-five."

"Exactly," Claiborne interjected. "We were responsible enough to put things into their proper perspective. I married your mother first, no matter what my baser instincts advised me while we dated."

"I suppose you'll preach me a sermon if I say things are different now."

"You bet I will. Clay, how could you let a thing like this happen on a *blind date*, and with a girl like that! It might be understandable if you were engaged to the girl or had been seeing her for a while. If you . . . if you loved her. But don't stand there and ask me to condone your indiscriminate sex, because I will not!"

"I didn't expect you to."

"You should have had more sense!" the older man blustered, pacing feverishly.

"At the time sense didn't enter into it," Clay said dryly, and across the room Claiborne's eyes blazed.

"That goes without saying, since you obviously hadn't enough wits to see that she didn't get pregnant out of it!"

"Claiborne!"

"Well, dammit, Angela, he's an adult who *has* used the brains of a child to let a thing like this happen. I expect a man of twenty-five to display twenty-five years' worth of common sense!"

"We each assumed the other had taken precautions," Clay explained tiredly.

"Assumed! Assumed! Yes, you've assumed yourself right into the hands of that obnoxious, money-hungry father of hers with your stupidity! The man is a raving idiot, but a shrewd one. He has every intention of taking us to the cleaners!"

Clay couldn't deny it; even Catherine had said it was true.

"You're not liable for my actions."

"No, I'm not. But do you think reasoning like that is common to a man like Anderson? He wants restitution made for his little girl's seduction and he won't rest till it's made to suit the figure he has in mind."

"Did he mention how much he wants?" Clay asked, afraid to hear the answer.

"He didn't have to. I can tell his mind works best with big, round numbers. And Clay, something else has come up that bears consideration." The glance he gave his wife told their son it was something Angela, too, knew about. "I've been approached by members of a local caucus to consider running for county attorney. I didn't mention it to you because I thought it best to wait until you passed your bar exams and became part of the firm. But frankly it's something your mother and I have been considering quite seriously. I don't have to tell you how detrimental a little muckraking can be to a potential candidate. It won't matter to the voters who the source is."

"Catherine said she has her plans made, although she won't tell me what they are. But once she leaves home, he won't have a leg to stand on as far as a paternity suit is concerned. She refuses to be a part of his scheme."

"Quit fooling yourself, Clay. You're almost a lawyer, and I am one. We both know that a paternity suit is one of the hardest nuts in the bucket to crack. It's not the outcome of a suit I'm worried about, it's the reverberations it can stir up. And there's one more issue we haven't touched on yet." He looked down into his glass, then into Clay's eyes. "Even if the man does decide to back down and cease his demands, there is a moral obligation here that you cannot deny. If you do, I will be far, far more disappointed in you than I am right now."

Clay's head came up with a jerk. "You aren't saying you expect me to marry her, are you?"

His father studied him, dissatisfaction written on every line, every plane of his face. "I don't know, Clay, I don't know. All I know is that I have attempted by both example and word to teach you the value of honesty. Is it honest for you to leave the woman high and dry?"

"Yes, if it's what she wants."

"Clay, the woman is probably scared senseless right now. She's caught between a stranger she doesn't even know and that raving lunatic of a father. Don't you think she deserves every bit of cooperation she can get from you?"

"You've said it for me. I'm a stranger to her. Do you think she would want to marry a stranger?"

"She could do worse. In spite of the thoughtlessness and insensibility you've displayed recently, I don't think you're a hopeless case."

"I would be if I married her. Jesus, I don't even like the girl."

"In the first place, don't use profanity before your mother

and in the second, let's stop calling her a girl. She's a full-grown woman, as is entirely obvious. As a woman, she should be willing to listen to reason."

"I don't understand what you're driving at. You can see what kind of a family she comes from. Her father is a lunatic; her mother is browbeaten; look at the way they dress, where they come from. That's obviously not the kind of family you'd like me to marry into, yet you stand there talking as if you want me to ask her."

"You should have considered her background before you got her pregnant, Clay."

"How could I when I didn't even know her then?"

Claiborne Forrester had the innate sense of timing peculiar to every successful lawyer, and he used the elongated moment of silence now to speak dramatically before he cinched his case. "Exactly. Which, rather than exonerate you, as you think the fact should, creates—in my estimation—an even greater responsibility toward her and the child. You acted without a thought for the repercussions. Even now you seem to have forgotten there *is* a child involved here, and that it's yours."

"It's hers!"

His father's jaw hardened and his eyes iced over. "When did you turn so callous, Clay?"

"Tonight when I walked in here and the buzzards swooped down."

"Stop this, you two," Angela demanded in her quiet way, rising from her chair. "Neither one of you is making sense, and you'll regret this later if you go on. Clay, your father is right. You do have a moral obligation to that woman. Whether or not it extends to asking her to marry you is something none of us should try to decide tonight." Crossing to her husband she laid a hand on his chest. "Darling, we all need to think about this. Clay has said the girl doesn't want to get married. He said she's refused his offer of money. Let's let the two of them settle it between them after everyone has cooled down a little bit."

"Angela, I think our son needs—"

She placed her fingers on his lips. "Claiborne, you're running on emotions now, and you've told me countless times that a good lawyer must not do that. Let's not discuss it anymore at the moment."

He looked into her eyes, which were luminous with emotion. They were large, lovely oval eyes of warm hazel that needed none of the artifice she used daily to enhance them. Claiborne Forrester, at age fifty-nine, loved them as much now devoid of makeup as he had when he was twenty, and she'd used them to woo him. He covered the hand that lay on his chest. There was no need for him to answer. He bowed to her judgment, giving her a reaffirmation of his love with a gentle pressure of his warm palm.

Watching them thus, Clay felt again the security that emanated from them, that had emanated from them as long as he could remember. What he saw before him was what he wanted in his life with a woman. He wanted to duplicate the love and trust shining from his parents' eyes when they looked at each other. He did not want to marry a girl whose last name he'd forgotten, whose home had been fraught with the antithesis of the love he'd grown up with.

His mother turned, and behind her, his father's hands rested on her shoulders. Together they looked at their son.

"Your mother is right. Let's sleep on it, Clay. Things have a way of becoming clearer with time. It lends perspective."

"I hope so." Clay's hands hung disconsolately in his pockets.

To Angela he looked like an overgrown boy in that scolded pose, his hair far from neat. Intuition told her what he was struggling with, and wisely she waited for him to get it out.

"I'm so damn sorry," Clay choked, and only then did she open her arms to him. Over her shoulder he sought his father's eyes, and in a moment the arms of the velour robe were there to rub his shoulders in brief reassurance.

"We love you, Clay, no matter what," Angela reminded him.

Claiborne added, "The proof of it may seem curious at this time, but as the saying goes, love is not always kind." Then, placing his hands once again on Angela's shoulders, he said, "Good night, son."

Leaving the two of them, Clay knew they would remain allied on whatever stand they took; they always did. He had no wish to play them one against the other, though his mother seemed the far more tractable. Their unity of purpose had created such a great part of Clay's childhood security, anything else would have been out of character now. He could not help but wonder what kind of parenting team he and the volatile Catherine Anderson would make. He shuddered to think of it.

Angela Forrester lay with her stomach nestled tightly against her husband's curled back, one hand under her pillow, the other inside his pajamas.

"Darling?" she whispered.

"Hmm?" he answered, fast enough to tell her he hadn't been asleep either.

The words seemed to stick in Angela's throat. "You don't think that girl will go and have—have an abortion, do you?"

"I've been lying here wondering the same thing, Angela. I don't know."

"Oh, Claiborne . . . our grandchild," she whispered, pressing her lips against his naked back, her eyelids sliding shut, her mind filling with comparisons—how it had been when she first fell in love with this man, how elated they'd been when she became pregnant with Clay. Tears sprang to Angela's eyes.

"I know, Angie, I know," Claiborne soothed, reaching behind to pull her body more securely against his. After a long, thoughtful silence he turned over, taking her in his arms. "I'd pay anyone any amount of money if it meant preventing an abortion. You know that, Angie."

"I kn . . . I know, darling, I know," she said against his chest, strengthened by his familiar caress.

"I had to make Clay face up to his responsibilities, though."

"I know that, too." But the knowing didn't make it less painful.

"Good, then get some sleep."

"How can I sleep when I—I close my eyes and see that odious man pointing his finger and threatening her. Oh, God, he's ruthless, Claiborne, anyone can see that. He'll never let that girl get away while he thinks she's the key to our money."

"The money's nothing, Angie, it's nothing," he said fiercely.

"I know. It's the girl I'm thinking of and the fact that it's Clay's child. Suppose she takes it back home to the same house with that—that vile man. He's violent. He's the kind—"

In the darkness he kissed her and felt her cheeks were wet. "Angie, Angie, don't," he whispered.

"But it's our grandchild," she repeated near his ear.

"We have to have some faith in Clay."

"But the way he talked tonight . . ."

"He's reacting like any man would. In the light of day let's hope he sees his obligations more clearly."

Angela rolled onto her back, wiped her eyes with the sheet

and calmed herself as best she could. After all, this was not some reprobate they were talking about. It was their son.

"He'll do the right thing, darling; he's just like you in so many ways."

Claiborne kissed his wife's cheek. "I love you, Angie." Then he rolled her onto her side and backed her up against him, settling a hand on her breast. Her hand crept behind to cradle the reassuring warmth inside his pajamas. And thus they drew strength from each other in the long hour before sleep eased their worries.

It took practiced skill to outwit the caginess of Herb Anderson. He had the sixth sense that inexplicably thrives in alcoholics, that uncanny intuition that can make the hazy brain suddenly work with alarming clarity. The next morning Catherine carefully maintained her customary routine, knowing any small change would trigger his suspicion. She was standing at the kitchen sink eating a fresh orange when Herb came shuffling into the room. The fruit quenched some new taste she'd developed lately, but it seemed to amuse him wickedly.

"Suckin' on your oranges again, huh?" he grated from the doorway. "Lotta good that'll do ya. If you wanna suck something, go suck up to old man Forrester and see if you can get something outa him. What the hell's the matter with you anyway? The way you stood there like some goddam lump last night—we won't get nothin' outa Forrester that way!"

"Don't start in on me again. I told you I'd go with you but I won't back your threats. I have to go to school now."

"You ain't goin' anyplace till you tell me what you got outa lover boy last night!"

"Daddy, don't! Just don't. I don't want to go through it again."

"Well, we're gonna go through it, soon as I have me a coffee roy-al, so just stand where you are, girlie. Where the hell's your mother? Does a man have to make his own damn coffee around this dump?"

"She's gone to work already. Make your own coffee."

He rubbed the side of his coarse hand across the corner of a lip. Catherine could hear the rasp of whiskers clear across the room.

"Got a little uppity since you talked to lover boy, huh?" He chuckled. She no longer tried to stop him from using the term *lover boy*. It pleased him immensely when she did. He came to the sink and started slamming parts of an aluminum coffeepot around, dumping the grounds out, leaving them to stain the sink, wiping his hands on his stretched-out T-shirt. She stepped back as the stream of water hit the grounds and some came flying her way. He chuckled again. She leaned over the sink sideways, continuing to eat the pieces of quartered orange. But, at close range, he smelled. It made her stomach lurch.

"Well, you gonna spit it out or you gonna stand there suckin' those oranges all morning? What'd lover boy have to say for himself?"

She crossed to the garbage can beside the ancient, chipped porcelain stove, ostensibly to throw away the orange peel; actually she could not stand being so near the man.

"He doesn't want to marry me any more than I want to marry him. I told you he wouldn't."

"You *told* me! Hah! You *told* me nothin', slut! I had to search my own goddam house for any fact I wanted! If I wouldn't've had enough brains to go lookin' I still wouldn't know who your lover boy is! And if you think I'm gonna let him get off scot-free, well, sister, you better think again!" Then he fell to mumbling in the repetitive way she'd learned to despise. "Told me . . . she told me, ha! She told me goddam nothin' . . ."

"I'm going to school," she said resignedly, turning toward the doorway.

"You just keep your smart little ass where it is!"

She stopped with her back to him, sighed, waited for him to finish his tirade so she could pretend to go to classes and he'd leave the house in his usual, aimless way.

"Now I wanna know what the hell he means to do about this mess he got you in!" She heard the exaggerated slam as the coffeepot hit the stove burner.

"Daddy, I have to go to school."

Whining, mimicking, he repeated, *"Daddy, I have to go to school,"* and finished by roaring, "You wanna go to school, you answer me first! What's he intend to do about gettin' you knocked up!"

"He offered me money," she answered, truthfully enough.

"Well, that's more like it! How much?"

How much, how much, how much! she thought frantically, pulling a figure out of the air. "Five thousand dollars."

"Five thousand dollars!" he exploded. "He'll have to do better than that to see the end of me! My ship just come in and he wants to pay me off with a measly five thousand bucks? One o' them diamonds in the old lady's rings was worth ten times as much."

Slowly Catherine turned to face him. "Cash," she said, pleased with the greedy light that responded in his eyes, promising herself to remember it and laugh when she was gone. He pondered, scratching his stomach.

"What'd you tell him?" His face wore that sly weasel's expression she despised. It meant the wheels were turning; he was scheming again about the best way to get something for nothing.

"I told him you'd probably be calling his father."

"Now that's the first smart thing you said since I come in here!"

"You'll call him anyway, so why should I have lied to him? But I haven't changed my mind. You can try bleeding him all you want, but I won't have any part of it, just remember that." This, too, was her long-taken stand. Should she suddenly veer from it he would undoubtedly become wary.

"Sister, you ain't got the brains God gave a damn chicken!" he blasted, yanking a dirty towel off the cabinet top, then slapping the edge of the sink with it. But she'd long grown inured to his insults; she stood resignedly in the face of them, letting his spate run its course. "You not only ain't got enough brains to keep yourself from gettin' knocked up, you don't know when your ship's come in! Ain't I told you it's come in here?"

The term sickened her, she'd heard it so often, for it was part of his grand self-delusion. "Yes, Daddy, you've told me . . . a thousand times," she said sarcastically before adding firmly, "But I don't want his money. I'm making plans. I can get along without it."

"Plans," he scoffed, "what kind of plans? Don't think you're gonna sponge offa me and raise that little bastard around here 'cause I ain't raisin' his brat! I ain't made outa money, you know!"

"Don't worry, I won't ask you for a thing."

"You bet your boots you won't, sister, because you're gonna call up lover boy there and tell him to fork over!" He pointed a finger at her nose.

"To whom? You or me?"

"Just don't get smart with me, sister! I been waiting for my ship to come in one helluva long time!" She almost cringed again at the hated expression. He'd built his pipe dreams upon it for so long that he was no longer aware of how often he used the term, nor the shallowness of character it only served to emphasize.

"I know," she commented dryly, but again he missed the sarcasm.

"And this here is it!" He jammed a dirty finger at the floor as if a pot of gold were there on the cracked green linoleum.

"Your coffee is going to boil over. Turn the burner down."

He studied the pot unseeingly while the lid lifted with each perk and the man remained unaware of the hiss and smell of burnt grounds. The girl who looked on felt a sudden despair at the changelessness of the man and her situation in this household. Almost as if he'd forgotten her, he now conspired with the coffeepot, leaning the heels of his hands upon the edge of the stove, mumbling the litany Herb Anderson repeated with increasing fervor as the years crept up on him. "Yessir . . . a long time, and I deserve it, by God."

"I'm going. I have to catch my bus."

He came out of his reverie, looked over his shoulder with a sour expression. "Yeah, go. But just be ready to put the screws to old Forrester again tonight. Five thousand ain't a piss in a hurricane to a rich son of a bitch like him."

When she was gone, Herb leaned over the sink and took up whispering to himself. He often whispered to himself. He told Herb that the world was out to get Herb, and Herb deserved better, by God, and Herb was gonna get it! And no uppity little slut was gonna ace him out of his rightful due! She had her mother's whorish blood, that one did. Didn't he always say so? And didn't she prove him right at last, getting knocked up that way? Just goes to show things come out even in the end. Yessir.

Catherine owed him—Ada owed him—hell, the whole damn
country owed him, if it come down to that.

He poured himself another coffee royal to stop the shakes.

Goddam shakes, he thought, they're Ada's fault, too! But
after his third drink he was as still as a frog eyeing a fly. He
held out his hand to verify the fact. Feeling better, he chuckled
to think how clever he was, making sure old man Forrester
wouldn't want any Andersons tied to his highfalutin' bloodlines!
By the end of the week Forrester'd pay, and pay good to see no
wedding took place between his high-class son and no knocked-
up Catherine Anderson from the wrong side of the tracks.

It took Herb until nearly noon to get his fill of coffee royals
and amble from the house in search of his imminent ship.

From the corner grocery store Catherine watched her father
leave, hurriedly called her cousin Bobbi Schumaker, then returned to the house to pack. Like Catherine, Bobbi was in her
first year at the University of Minnesota, but she loved living
with her family. Her home, so different from Catherine's, had
been a haven for Catherine during her growing-up years, for the
two girls had been best friends and allies since infancy. They
kept no secrets from each other.

Bumping along an hour later in Bobbi's little yellow Beetle,
Catherine felt relieved to have escaped the house at last.

"So, how'd it go?" Bobbi glanced askance through oversize
tortoiseshell glasses.

"Last night or this morning?"

"Both."

"Don't ask." Catherine rested her head back tiredly and shut
her eyes.

"That bad, huh?"

"I don't think the Forresters could believe it when the old man barged in there. God, you should have seen that house; it was really something."

"Did they offer to pay the bills?"

"Clay did," Catherine admitted.

"I told you he would."

"And I told you I'd refuse."

Bobbi's mouth puckered. "Why do you have to be so almighty stubborn? It's his baby, too!"

"I told you, I don't want him to have any kind of hold on me whatsoever. If he pays, he might think he has some say in things."

"But the economics of it doesn't make sense! You can use every cent you can get. How do you think you're going to pay for second semester?"

"Just like I'm paying for the first." Catherine's lips took on that determined look Bobbi knew so well. "I've still got the typewriter and sewing machine."

"And he's got his father's millions," Bobbi retorted dryly.

"Oh, come on, Bobbi, they're not quite that rich, and you know it."

"Stu says they're rolling in it. They have enough that a few measly thousands wouldn't tip the scales."

Catherine sat up straighter, her chin stubbornly thrust out. "Bobbi, I don't want to argue. I've had enough of it this morning as it is."

"Sweet old Uncle Herb on the warpath again, huh?" Bobbi questioned, with saccharine dislike. Catherine nodded. "Well, this is it; you won't have to put up with it after this." When Catherine remained despondent, Bobbi's voice brightened. "I know what you're thinking, Cath, but don't! Your mother made her choices years ago, and it's her problem to live with them or solve them."

"He's going to be in a rage when he finds out I'm gone, and she'll be there for him to take it out on." Catherine stared morosely out the window.

"Don't think about it. Consider yourself lucky you're getting out. If this hadn't happened, you'd have stayed forever to protect her. And don't forget, I'll get my mother to drop in there tonight so yours won't be alone with him. Listen, Cath . . . you're getting out, that's the important thing." She slanted a brown-eyed glance at her cousin before admitting with a grin, "You know, for that I'm not totally ungrateful to Clay Forrester."

"Bobbi!" Catherine's blue eyes held a faint gleam of humorous scolding.

"Well, I'm not." Bobbi's palms came up, then gripped the wheel again. "I mean, what the heck."

"You promised not to tell Clay, and don't forget it!" Catherine admonished.

"Don't worry—he won't find out from me, even if I think you should have your bricks counted. Half the girls on campus would give their eyeteeth to exploit the situation you've landed in and you get a case of pride instead!"

"Horizons is free. I'll be all right." Again Catherine resignedly looked out the window.

"But I want you to be more than just all right, Cath. Don't you see, I feel responsible?" Bobbi reached to touch her cousin's arm, and their eyes met again.

"Well, you're not. How many times do I have to repeat it?"

"But I introduced you to Clay Forrester."

"But that's all you did, Bobbi. Beyond that, the choices were my own."

They had argued the point many times. It always left Bobbi a little morose and crestfallen. Quietly, she said, "He's going to ask, you know."

"You'll just have to tell a white lie and say you don't know where I am."

"I don't like it." Bobbi's mouth showed a little stubbornness of its own.

"I don't like leaving my mother there either, but that's life, as you're so fond of saying."

"Just make sure you keep that in mind when you're tempted to give in and get in touch with her to see how she's doing."

"That's the part of it I don't like . . . making her think I'm running across the country. She'll worry herself sick."

"For a while she might, but the postcards will convince her you're doing okay and they'll keep your old man away from the university. There's no way he'll suspect you're still in town. Once the baby is born, you can see your mother again."

Catherine turned pleading eyes to her cousin. "But you'll call and check on her and let me know if . . . if she's okay, won't you?"

"I told you I would, now just relax, and remember . . . once she realizes you've had the nerve to pack up and leave him, she might just find some nerve of her own."

"I doubt it. Something holds her there . . . something I don't understand."

"Don't try to figure out the world and its problems, Cath. You've got enough of your own."

From the moment Catherine had first seen Horizons she'd felt at peace in it. It was one of those turn-of-the-century monstrosities with seemingly far too many rooms for a single family's needs. It had a vast wraparound porch, unscreened, festooned now with macrame pieces created by the various inhabitants who'd come and gone from the house. A few of the plants in the hangers looked peaked, as if they, too, had been touched by a late September frost like the maples that lined the boulevard. Inside, there was a wide entry hall, separated from the living room by a colonnade painted a yellowed ivory color. The stairway that led off the left end of the foyer took two turns, at two landings, on its way up. A rich, old, heavy handrail with spooled rails spoke of grander days. Beyond the colonnade spread the living room and dining room, like a sunny, comfortable cavern. Colored light filtered through old leaded glass, splashing across the living room like strokes of an artist's brush: amethyst, garnet, sapphire and emerald falling through the elegant old floral design as it had for eighty years and more. Wide baseboards and hip-high wainscoting had been miraculously preserved. The room was furnished with an overstuffed davenport and chairs of mismatched designs that somehow seemed more proper than the most carefully planned grouping would have been. There were tables with worn edges, but of homey design. The only incongruity present seemed to be the television set, which was off now as Catherine and Bobbi stood in the front hall watching three girls clean the room. One was on her knees sorting magazines, one was pushing a vacuum cleaner and another was dusting the tables. Beyond the far archway, a little girl bent over a dining room table that could have easily seated the entire Minnesota Vikings team. Chairs of every namable style and shape circled the table, and so did the little girl, slapping at each seat with her dishcloth. She straightened up then and placed a hand on her waist, fingers extending around to the small of her back, stretching backward. Staring, Catherine was abashed when the girl turned around to reveal a popping, full-blown stomach. The child was no more than five feet tall and hadn't even developed breasts yet. She might have been thirteen years old or so, but was at least eight months pregnant.

A glorious smile broke out on her face when she saw Catherine and Bobbi. "Hey, you guys, turn that thing off. We've got company!" she yelled toward the living room.

The vacuum cleaner sighed into silence. The magazine girl got up from her knees; the one who'd been dusting threw the cloth over her shoulder, and they all came toward the colonnade at once.

"Hi, my name's Marie. You looking for Mrs. Tollefson?" said the girl who looked like her name: very French, with tiny bones, pert, dark eyes, a wispy haircut and a piquant face that Catherine immediately thought of as darling.

"Yes, I'm Catherine and this is Bobbi."

"Welcome," Marie said, extending her hand immediately, first to one then to the other. "Which one of you is staying?"

"I am. Bobbi's my cousin; she brought me here."

"Meet the others. This is Vicky." Vicky had a plain, long face whose only redeeming feature was the bright cornflower blue of her eyes. "And Grover." Grover looked as if she should have learned better grooming habits in junior high home ec class; her hair was stringy, nails bitten, clothes unkempt. "And that's our mascot, Little Bit, playing catch with the dishcloth over there. Hey, come on over, Little Bit."

They were all in various stages of pregnancy, but what surprised Catherine was how very young they all looked. Up close, Little Bit looked even younger than before. Marie seemed to be the oldest of the four, perhaps sixteen or seventeen, but the others, Catherine was sure, were not older than fifteen. Amazingly, they all seemed cheerful, greeting Catherine with warm, genuine smiles. She had little chance to dwell on ages, for Marie took the lead, saying, "Welcome then. I'll see if I can hunt up Tolly for you. She's around here someplace. Have you seen her, Little Bit?"

"I think she's in her office."

"Great. Follow me, you guys." While they trailed after Marie, she informed them, "Like I said, Little Bit's our mascot around here. Her real name's Dulcie, but there's not much more to her than a little bit, so that's what we call her. Mrs. Tollefson's a good egg. We all call her Tolly. As soon as we talk to her we'll get you settled. Hey, have you guys had your lunch yet?"

Whatever Bobbi's preconceived notions had been about this place, none of them fit. The four girls she'd met so far exuded such an air of goodwill and sorority that she felt quite Victorian at what she'd expected. They all seemed happy and industrious and helpful. Following the bouncy Marie down a hall that led to the rear of the house, Bobbi began feeling better and better about leaving Catherine there. They came to a small room tucked beneath what must have been the servants' stairway at one time. It was as comfortable as the living room, only more crowded. It housed a large desk and bookshelves, and a patchwork sofa in shades of rust and orange that gave a homespun feeling to the room. Shutters were thrown back to let the noon light flood in upon an enormous fern that hung above the desk. Behind the desk a woman was searching through the depths of an open drawer.

"Hey, d'you lose something again, Tolly?" Marie asked.

"Nothing important. It'll show up. It's just my fountain pen. Last time Francie borrowed it she hid it in this bottom drawer. I guess I'll just have to wait until she decides to tell me where it is this time."

"Hey, Tolly, we got company." The woman's gray head popped up, her face appearing for the first time from behind stacks of books. It was a flat, plain middle-aged face with smile lines at the corners of its eyes and bracketing its mouth.

"Oh, glory be, why didn't you say so?" Smiling, she said, "Well, Catherine, I wasn't expecting you quite this early or I would have told the girls to watch out for you and bring your things in. Did anyone get your suitcases yet?"

"We'll take care of it while you talk to her," Marie offered, "if Bobbi'll show us where the car is." But before they left, Marie said to Mrs. Tollefson, "I'll be her sister."

"Wonderful!" the woman exclaimed. "I take it you two have already met, so I'll dispense with introductions. Catherine, we usually have one of the established girls help each new girl, show her where things are, tell her how we arrange work schedules, what time meals are served, things like that."

"We call it being sisters," Marie added. "How'd you like to take me on?"

"I . . ." Catherine felt rather swamped by the goodwill, which she had not quite expected, at least not in such immediate displays. Sensing her hesitancy, Marie reached out and took Catherine's hand for a moment. "Listen, we've all been through this first day. Everyone needs a little moral support, not only today, but on lots of days when things get you down. That's why we have sisters here. I rely on you, you rely on me. After a while you'll find out this is really almost a terrific place to be, right, Tolly?" she chirped to Mrs. Tollefson, who seemed totally accustomed to such scenes. She wasn't in the least surprised to see Marie holding Catherine's hand that way. Catherine, who had not held the hand of another female since she'd given up jump rope and hopscotch, was far more uneasy than anyone in the room.

"Right," answered Mrs. Tollefson. "You've been lucky,

Catherine, to be adopted by Marie. She's one of our friendliest residents."

Dropping Catherine's hand, flapping a palm at Mrs. Tollefson, Marie chided, "Oh, yeah, you say that about every single one of us here. Come on, Bobbi, let's get Catherine's stuff up to her room."

When they were gone, Mrs. Tollefson laughed softly and sank into her desk chair. "Oh, that Marie, she's a ball of fire, that one. You'll like her, I think. Sit down, Catherine, sit down."

"Do they all call you Tolly?"

The woman was carelessly dressed and exuded a friendly warmth that made Catherine think she ought to be wearing a cobbler's apron. Instead she wore a pair of maroon jacquard-knit slacks of definitely dated style, and a nondescript white nylon shell beneath an aged cardigan sweater that had long ago lost its shape to that of Mrs. Tollefson's rotund breasts and heavy upper arms. Altogether, Esther Tollefson was a most unstylish woman, but what she lacked in fashion, she made up for in cordiality.

"No, not all of them," she answered now. "Some of them call me Tolly. Some call me 'Hey you,' and some avoid calling me anything. Others don't stay long enough to learn my name. But they are few and far between. Some think of me as a warden, but most of them consider me a friend. I hope you will, too."

Catherine nodded, unsure of what to say.

"I sense that you're self-conscious, Catherine, but there is no need to feel that way here. Here you will deal with keeping yourself and your baby as healthy as possible. You'll deal with making decisions about what to do with your life after the baby is born. You will meet young women who have all come here for the same reason as you have: to have a baby that is being born out of wedlock. We do not force you into roles here, Catherine, nor do we place labels on you or on the decisions you will make. But we do hope you'll spend time considering your future and where to pick up after you leave Horizons. We will need a little intake information for our records. Anything you answer will, of course, remain completely confidential. Your privacy will be strictly protected. Do you understand that, Catherine?"

"Yes, but I may as well tell you immediately that I don't want my parents to know where I am."

"They don't have to. That's entirely up to you."

"The rest of the information . . ." Catherine paused, looking down at the manila card, looking for a blank that said "Father's name" or "Baby's father" or something like that. She found no such thing.

"There is no coercion here of any kind. Fill out only what you want to for now. If, as time goes by, you wish to add additional information—well, the card will be here. These first few days we want you to concentrate chiefly on gaining your equilibrium, so to speak. Decisions about the future can be made in due time. You'll find that talking with all the girls will help very much. Each of them has a different outlook. There may be some fresh ideas that will help you immensely. My best advice is to remain open to the support that they may want to give. Don't shut them out, because they may be asking for your support when it appears they are giving you theirs. It won't take you long to find out what I mean."

"Are they all as friendly as the ones I've met so far?"

"Certainly not. We have those who are bitter and withdrawn. With those we try all the harder. We have—as you'll soon see— one girl whose rebellion at her situation has taken on the form of kleptomania. There is no punishment here of any kind, not even for stealing fountain pens. You'll meet Francie soon, I'm sure. If she steals something of yours, please let me know. I'm sure she will, right off the bat, just to test your reaction. The best thing to do is to offer her some compliment or suggest doing something for her or ask her advice about something. It always makes her return whatever it is she's stolen."

"I'll remember that when I meet her."

"Good. Well, Catherine, as I said before, during the first few days we want you to relax, gain your composure again and get to know the others. I think I hear the girls coming in now. They'll find some lunch for you and show you your room."

Marie appeared in the doorway just then.

"All set?"

"All set," Mrs. Tollefson replied. "Feed this girl if she's hungry, then introduce her around."

"Aye, aye!" Marie saluted. "C'mon, Catherine. This way to the kitchen."

Some thirty minutes later Catherine walked out to the car with Bobbi. They stopped, and Bobbi turned to look back at the house.

"I don't know what I expected, but it wasn't anything like this."

"Anything's better than home," Catherine said with a definite chill in her voice. Bobbi saw the defensive veneer that always seemed to glaze Catherine's eyes when she made comments such as this. A mixture of pity and relief welled up in Bobbi—pity because her cousin's home life had been so painfully devoid of the love to which every child has a right, relief because Horizons seemed as good a haven as possible under these circumstances. Perhaps here Catherine might at last have, if not love, at least a measure of peace.

"I feel . . . well, better about leaving you here, Cath."

The introspective look faded from Catherine's face as she turned to her cousin. The brilliant autumn sun burned down through the balmy afternoon, and for a moment neither of them spoke.

"And I feel good being left here—honest," Catherine assured her. But that guilty look that Catherine had seen so often lately in Bobbi's expression was back again.

"Don't you dare think it," Catherine scolded gently.

"I can't help it," Bobbi answered, thrusting her hands into her jeans pockets and kicking at a fallen leaf. "If I hadn't lined you up with him—"

"Bobbi, cut it out. Just promise you won't tell anyone where I am."

Bobbi looked up, unsmiling, her shoulders hunched up, hands still strung up in those pockets. "I promise," she said quietly, then added, "Promise you'll call if you need anything at all?"

"Promise."

There hung between the two girls an intimate silence while each of them thought about that blind date last July, their many shared confidences of girlhood leading to this greatest shared secret of all. For a moment Bobbi thought maybe this time Catherine would make the move first.

But Catherine Anderson found touching a difficult thing to do. And so she hovered, waiting, until at last Bobbi plunged forward to give her the affectionate squeeze Catherine needed so badly. In a life where love was a foreign thing, Catherine's feelings for this vibrant, bubbly cousin came as close as any to that emotion. And so the hug she returned told a wealth of things, although she herself remained dry-eyed while tears gathered in Bobbi's throat before she backed away.

"Take it easy, huh?" Bobbi managed, her hands jammed once again in her pockets while she backed away.

"Yeah, for sure . . . and thanks, huh?"

And only when Bobbi spun and headed for the car, getting in and driving off without another backward glance, did Catherine admit that she felt like crying. But she didn't. She didn't. Still, she came closer than she had since, at age eleven, she'd promised herself never to allow that weakness again.

FOUR

It was twenty-four hours since Herb Anderson had appeared at the Forrester home with his threats and accusations, twenty-four hours during which Clay had slept little and found it quite impossible to concentrate on the evolution of the law as affected by the McGrath vs. Hardy case he was currently analyzing in Torts II.

Angela heard the car door slam and moved toward the desk where Claiborne sat in his swivel chair. "He's home, darling. Are you quite sure about what we've decided?"

"As sure as it's possible to be, under the circumstances."

"Very well, but must you confront him seated there like some oracle behind your desk? Let's wait for him on the love seat."

When Clay came to the study door he looked haggard. He stood in the doorway scarcely aware of the comfortable fire within the cozy room. He was too occupied with the strain on his parents' faces.

"Come in, Clay," Angela invited, "let's talk."

"I've had a hell of a day." He came in and sank down wearily on the coffee table with his back to them, slumping forward and kneading the back of his neck. "How about you two?"

"Likewise," his father said. "We spent the afternoon out at the arboretum talking. It's quiet out there at this time of year after the picnickers have gone. Conducive to thinking."

"I might as well have stayed home for all I accomplished today. She was on my mind all day long."

"And?"

"It's no different than last night. I just want to forget she exists."

"But can you do that, Clay?"

"I can try."

"Clay," his mother's concerned voice began, "there's one possibility we did not discuss last night, although I'm sure it entered all our minds, and that is that she might possibly get an abortion. Forgive me for sounding like a grandmother, but the thought of it is utterly sickening to me."

"You might as well know, we talked about it," Clay admitted.

Angela felt a quiver begin in her stomach and travel up to her throat. "You—you did?"

"I offered her money, which she refused."

"Oh, Clay." The soft, disappointed swoon in her tone told Clay how it hurt her to hear the truth.

"Mother, I was testing her. I'm not sure what I'd have said if she had agreed." But then Clay swung around on the shiny table to face his parents. "Oh, hell, what's the use of denying it? At the time it seemed like an easy solution."

"Clay," Angela said, as near to scolding as she'd been in years, "I fail to see how your feelings for that child as its father can be any less than ours as its grandparents. How could you think of—of denying it life, or of spending the rest of your own wondering where and who the child is?"

"Mother, don't you think I've thought the same things all day long?"

"Yet you don't propose to do anything about it?" Angela asked.

"I don't know what to do, I'm just mixed up . . . I . . . oh, hell." His shoulders slumped further.

"What your mother is trying to make you see is that your responsibility is to make sure the child is provided for, and that its future is made secure. She speaks for both of us. It's our grandchild. We'd like to know its life will be the best possible, under the circumstances."

"Are you saying you want me to ask that girl to marry me?"

"What we want, Clay, has been superceded by your thoughtless actions. What we want is what we've always wanted for you, an education, a career, a happy life—"

"And you think I'd have those things married to a woman I don't love?" Suddenly Clay rose and walked to a window, glanced absently at the gathering dusk outside, then turned to confront them again. "I've never said it before, not in so many words, but I want the kind of relationship you two have. I want a wife I can be proud of, someone of my own class, if it comes down to that, whose ambitions match mine, who is bright and . . . and loving, and who wants what I want out of life. Someone like Jill."

"Ah . . . Jill," Angela said with an arched eyebrow, then leaned forward intently, her petite elbow on her gracefully crossed knees. "Yes, I think it's time you considered Jill. Where was Jill when all of this happened?"

"We'd had a fight, that's all."

"Oh, you had a fight." Angela settled back again, her casualness belying the seriousness of the subject. "And so you took out Catherine to—to get even with Jill, or for whatever reason, and by doing so, wronged not one woman but two. Clay, how could you!"

"Mother, you've always liked Jill far better than any of the other girls I've gone with."

"Yes, I have; both your father and I admire her immensely. But at the moment I feel your responsibility to Catherine Anderson is far greater than that to Jill. Besides, I haven't the slightest doubt that if you'd wanted to marry Jill you'd have asked her years ago."

"We've talked about it more than once, but the timing just wasn't right. I wanted to get school behind me and pass my bar exam first."

"Speaking of which, I should like to point out a few facts you may have overlooked," Claiborne said, rising from the loveseat and taking what Clay knew was his "counsel for the plaintiff" stance: both feet flat on the floor, jaw and one shoulder jutting toward the accused. "That father of hers could make more trouble for you than you might think. You are aware that your bar examinations are less than a year off, and that the State Board of Law Examiners goes to some lengths to establish that any person making application be of good moral character. Up to this point I've never given it a second thought regarding you, but I've done nothing but consider it today. Clay, something like this could be enough for them to deny you the right to take your boards! When you apply, you'll be asked for affidavits respecting your habits and general reputation, and they are fully within their rights to demand you to furnish a character investigation report to the National Bar Examiners. Do you realize that?"

The expression on Clay's face made an answer unnecessary.

"Clay, it only takes one dyed-in-the-wool conservative who still sees abortion as immoral, regardless of its legal ramifications, or who believes that siring a bastard is cause enough to doubt your moral character, and it could be the death knell to your legal career. You have less than a year left. Do you want it all to go for nothing?" Claiborne moved to his desk, touched a pen distractedly, then sought Clay's eyes. "There is a minor concern which I cannot help but inject here. As an alumnus at the university, I'm a member of the Partnership in Excellence and the Board of Visitors. I enjoy those positions and they speak well for me. They are prestigious and would undoubtedly be an asset, if I decide to run for county attorney. I should like no slur on the Forrester name, whether it be on yours or mine. And if I do run, I am counting on you to continue my established practice during my term. Of course, we all realize what is at stake here." Claiborne dropped the pen on the desk for effect. It was implicit: he was threatening to exclude Clay from the family firm, upon which Clay had always built his plans for the future. Claiborne steepled his fingertips, looked over them at his son and finished, with further innuendo, "Your decision, Clay, will affect all of us."

At that moment Herbert Anderson was stalking back and forth across Catherine's deserted bedroom like a caged cat.

"Goddam that girl; I'll break every bone in her body if she ain't with Forrester talking money right this minute! Talk about gratitude, that's gratitude for you!" He landed a vicious kick on a drawer that gaped at him with nothing but newspaper lining its bottom. The kick left a black scuff mark beside those he'd already put there.

From the doorway Ada stammered in a quaking voice, "Wh-where do you sup-suppose she'd of gone, Herb?"

"Well, how the hell am I supposed to know!" he yelled. "She don't tell me one damn thing about her comings and goings. If she did, she wouldn't of got herself knocked up in the first place 'cause I'd of made goddam sure she'd of known something about that lover boy of hers before she went out and got herself diddled by him!"

"Maybe—maybe he took her in after all."

"He took her in all right, and she's got a belly full of his brat to prove it!" Stalking to the telephone, he elbowed Ada rudely aside, continuing his tirade as he dialed. "Damn girl ain't got the sense God gave a cluck hen if she's not with Forrester. Wouldn't know what her ship looked like if it run her down and sliced her in half! Them Forresters was my ticket, goddammit! My ticket! Damn her hide if she run off on me and . . ."

Just then Clay picked up his ringing phone, and Anderson bawled into the mouthpiece, "Where the hell is my daughter, lover boy!" The three Forresters were still in the study discussing the situation. Claiborne and Angela didn't need to hear the far end of the conversation to know what was being said.

"She's not here." There were long pauses between Clay's responses. "I don't know . . . I haven't seen her since I dropped her off at home last night . . . Now listen to me, Anderson! I told her then that if she wanted money, I'd be happy to give it to her, but she refused. I don't know what more you expect of me . . . That's harassment, Anderson, and it's punishable by law! . . . I'm willing to talk to your daughter but I have no intention of dealing with a small-time con artist like you. I'll say it one more time, Anderson, leave us alone! It will take no more than a call from your daughter, and financial aid will be in her hand before the day is out; but as for you, I wouldn't give you the directions to a soup line if you were dying of starvation! Do I make myself clear! . . . Fine! Bring them! She's nowhere in this house. If she were, I'd be happy to put her on the phone right now . . . Yes, your concern is very touching . . . I have no idea . . ." There followed a longer pause during which Clay pulled the receiver away from his ear while the muffled anger of Herb Anderson crackled through the wire. When Clay hung up, it was with equal portions of anger and worry.

"Well, it seems she's disappeared," he said, dropping down into his father's desk chair.

"So I gathered," Claiborne replied.

"The man is a lunatic."

"I agree. And he's not going to stop with one abusive phone call. Do you concur?"

"How should I know?" Clay jumped up again, paced across the room and stopped to sigh at the ceiling. "He threatened at least four various felonies during the course of the conversation."

"Have you any idea where the girl might have gone?" his father asked.

"None. All she would say was that she had plans. I had no idea she intended to disappear this fast."

"Do you know any of her friends?"

"Only her cousin Bobbi, the girl Stu's been dating."

"My suggestion is, you see if she knows where Catherine is, and the sooner the better. I have an idea we haven't heard the last from Anderson. I want him stopped before any word of this leaks out."

Meanwhile, in Omaha, Nebraska, the sister of a student in Bobbi Schumaker's Psych I class dropped a letter in a U.S. Mail depository. It was written in Catherine Anderson's clean, distinctive hand and addressed to Ada, telling her not to worry.

* * *

The following evening the Forresters were at dinner, the table set tastefully with white damask linens, bronze-colored mums and burning tapers. Inella, the maid, had just served the chicken Kiev and returned to the kitchen when the doorbell rang. With a sigh she went to answer it. She had no more than turned the handle when the door was smacked back against the wall with a violent shove, flying out of Inella's surprised fingers.

A guttural voice rasped, "Where the hell is he!"

Too shocked to attempt forestalling him, she only gaped while the man used an elbow to thrust her aside. She landed against the side of the stairs, overturning the brass pitcher of eucalyptus. Before she could right herself, the words *Warpo's Bar* were disappearing into the living room, trailed by a string of filth that made Inella's ears ring worse than the thud her head had just suffered.

"I told you I'd get you, lover boy, and I'm here to do it!" Herb Anderson shouted, surprising the trio at the dining room table.

Angela's hand was poised halfway to her mouth. Claiborne dropped his napkin and Clay began getting to his feet. But halfway there he was caught on the chin by a set of crusty knuckles whistling through the candlelit room without warning. His head snapped back and the sickening sound of the fist landing on her son's face made Angela scream and grope for her husband's help. Clay reeled backward, taking his chair with him to the floor while the red nylon jacket dove after him. Before Claiborne could reach Anderson's poised arm, it cracked downward again in a second punishing blow. From the doorway Inella screamed, then covered her mouth with her hands.

"My God, call the police!" cried Angela. "Hurry!"

Inella spun from the room.

Claiborne got Anderson's arm, avoiding the swings that continued falling seemingly in every direction at once. He managed to catch the crook of Anderson's elbow, spinning the heavy man in a circle. Anderson's backside struck the edge of the table, sending crystal wine goblets, water glasses and candleholders teetering. The tablecloth caught on fire as candle wax sprayed across it, but Angela was embroiled in attempting to subdue the madman along with her husband. Clay got to his feet, bleeding, stunned, but not too stunned to throw his weight into a fist that settled satisfyingly into Anderson's paunch. The air whoofed from Anderson, and he doubled over, clutching himself, while Angela grabbed a handful of his hair and yanked as hard as she could. She was crying, even as she held the detestable hair in a painful tug. Clay stood like a crazed man himself, the look on his face pure fury as he pinned one of Anderson's arms behind his back and leaned a knee across the words on the back of the red nylon jacket. The fire on the tabletop grew, but just then a sobbing Inella ran back into the room, tipped the bouquet of chrysanthemums over to douse the flames, then stood clutching her knuckles against her lips while tears streamed down her cheeks.

"The police are coming."

"Oh, God, make them hurry," Angela prayed.

The shock of the attack was sinking in as the three Forresters looked at each other across the subdued man. Angela saw the cut on Clay's jaw, another above his right eye.

"Clay, are you all right?"

"I'm okay. . . . Dad, how about you?"

"I'll get you rich sonsabitches!" Anderson was still vowing, his face now pressed into the yellow carpet. "Goddammit! Let go o' my hair!"

Angela only pulled harder.

Outside, sirens grew closer and Inella fled from the room to the front door, which was still yawning open. Blue uniforms sped through the house behind the maid, who was shaking uncontrollably now.

Anderson was cuffed quickly and forced to remain on the dining room floor, all the while spewing threats and oaths at the Forrester family in general. The smell of burned linens permeated the room. The officers saw the charred tablecloth, the overturned dishes and the flowers strewn across the table and onto the floor.

"Is anybody hurt?"

Everyone turned to look at Angela first, as at last she flung herself into her husband's arms, crying.

"Angie, are you hurt?" he asked concernedly, but she only shook her head, leaving it buried against his chest.

"Do you know this man?" an officer asked.

"We've only met him once, day before yesterday."

"What happened here tonight?"

"He forced his way in and accosted my son while we were having dinner."

"What's your name, Bud?" This to Anderson, who was now kneeling on the floor.

"You ask *them* what my name is, so they'll never forget it!" He jerked his head viciously in Clay's direction. "Ask lover boy there who I am. I'm the father of the girl he knocked up, that's who!"

"Do you want to press charges, sir?" an officer asked Claiborne.

"What about me?" Anderson whined. "I got some charges need pressin' here if anybody does. That son of a bitch—"

"Take him to the squad car, Larry. You'll get your chance to answer later, Anderson, after we read you your rights."

He was pulled to his feet and pushed ahead of the officer to the front door. Outside, the flashing scarlet light was still circling, the radio crackling a dispatcher's voice. Anderson was locked in the caged backseat to rain accusations on the entire Forrester family only to be ignored by the officer who calmly sat up front, writing on his clipboard.

Shortly before supper the following day, the hall phone at Horizons rang. Someone shouted through the house, "Phone call . . . Anderson!"

Running downstairs, Catherine knew it could only be Bobbi, and she was anxious for word about her mother.

"Hello?"

"Cath, have you read the paper today?"

"No, I had classes. I didn't have time."

"Well, you'd better."

Catherine had a sudden, horrible premonition that her fears had become reality, that Herb Anderson had taken it all out on his wife.

"Is Mom—"

"No, no . . . she's all right. It's Clay. Your old man busted into his house last night and laid one on him."

"What!"

"I'm not kidding, Cath. He pushed his way in there and popped him. The police came and hauled sweet old Uncle Herb off to jail."

"Oh, no." Catherine's fingertips covered her lips.

"Just thought you'd want to know."

There was a hesitation, then, "Is—is Clay hurt?"

"I don't know. The article didn't say. You can read it for yourself. It's on page eight-B of the morning *Trib*."

"Have you talked to my mother?"

"Yeah, she's okay. I talked to her last night, must have been while your dad was in Edina beating up Clay. She almost sounded happy that you were gone. I told her not to worry because you were safe and that she'd be hearing from you."

"Is she—"

"She's okay, Cat, I said she's okay. Just stay where you are and don't let this change your mind, huh? Clay can take care of himself, and a night in jail might even mellow out your old man."

Before she ended the conversation, Bobbi added a fact that she'd earlier decided not to tell Catherine, then had decided to tell after all.

"Clay called me and asked if I know where you are. I lied."

The line buzzed voicelessly for a moment, then Catherine said quietly, "Thanks, kiddo."

Catherine found the article in the *Minneapolis Tribune* and read it several times, trying to picture the scene her father had created. Although she hadn't seen the dining room of the Forrester house, she could well imagine a luxurious setting there and what it must have been like when her father burst in. Clay Forrester's face welled up before her, his gray eyes, handsome jawline, and then her old man's fist ramming into it. Guilt welled up unwanted. She heard Clay's voice as he'd asked her to accept his money, and somehow knew that if she'd accepted it he would not have been assaulted by her old man. She knew, too, that her running away had thwarted Herb Anderson's plans for getting rich quick and had been further cause for him to turn his rage on Clay. At least Herb's volatile anger had been diverted away from

Ada, but Catherine's conscience plagued her mercilessly until she
assuaged it with the thought that, after all, the elder Mr. Forrester was an attorney and could easily prosecute his son's as-
sailant, which would be no more than Herb deserved. The
thought brought a short smile to Catherine's lips.

Bobbi wasn't surprised to answer the door the next day and find
Clay Forrester there.

He said without preamble, "I've got to talk to you. Can we
take a ride?"

"Sure, but it won't do any good."

"You know where she is, don't you?"

"Maybe I do, maybe I don't. Who wants to know, her old
man?"

"I do."

"You're a day late and a dollar short, Clay."

"Listen, could we go somewhere and have a cup of coffee?"

She studied him a moment, shrugged, and answered, "Let me
get my sweater."

The Corvette was at the curb. She eyed it appreciatively and
wondered again at Catherine's foolishness in not exploiting the
situation, if only financially. Watching Clay round the front
fender, Bobbi couldn't help thinking that if she were in Catherine's shoes she herself might not mind exploiting Clay Forrester
in more ways than one.

They drove to a small restaurant called Green's where they
ordered coffee, then sat avoiding each other's eyes until it came.
Clay hunched over his cup, looking totally distraught. His jawline had been altered and a bandage rode his right eyebrow.

"That's a nice little shiner you've got there, Clay." She eyed it
and he scowled.

"This thing is getting out of hand, Bobbi."

"Her old man's always been out of hand. How do you like him?"

Clay sipped his coffee and looked at her over the rim of the cup. "Not exactly my idea of a model father-in-law," he said.

"So what do you want with Catherine?"

"Listen, there are things involved here which I don't care to get into. But, for starters, I want her to take some money from me so her old man will leave me alone. He's not going to stop until he's seen green, and I'll be damned if I'll lay it in his hand. All I want her to do is to accept money for the hospital bills or her keep or whatever. Do you know where she is?"

"What if I do?" There was an unmistakable note of challenge in her attitude. He studied her a moment, then leaned back, toying with his cup handle.

"Maybe I deserved to get knocked around a little bit, is that what you're thinking?"

"Maybe I was. I love her."

"Did she tell you I offered to pay my dues, financially?"

"She also told me you offered her money for an abortion." When he remained silent Bobbi went on. "Supposing she's off having one right now?" Bobbi studied his face carefully and found the reaction she wanted: dread. She added sardonically, "Is your conscience bothering you, Clay?"

"You're damn right it is. If you think the only reason I want to see her is to get Anderson off my back, you're wrong." He closed his eyes and squeezed the bridge of his nose briefly, then muttered, "Lord, I can't get her off my mind."

Bobbi studied him as she sipped. The black eye and bruised jaw Uncle Herb had doled out could not disguise Clay Forrester's handsomeness nor the worried expression about his eyes. Something in Bobbi softened.

"I don't know why I feel compelled to tell you, but she's okay. She's got her plans all made and she's carrying through with them. Catherine's a strong person."

"I realized that the other night when I talked to her. Most girls in her position would come at a man with palms up, but not her."

"She's had it hard. She knows how to get by without any help from anybody."

"But still you won't tell me where she is?" He turned appealing eyes to her, making it extremely difficult for Bobbi to answer as she had to.

"That's right. I gave my word."

"All right. I won't try to force you to break it, but will you do just this much for me? Will you tell Catherine that if she needs anything—anything at all—to let me know? Tell her I'd like to talk to her, that it's important, and ask her if she'd call me at home tomorrow night. That way neither one of you will have to give away her whereabouts."

"I'll give her the message, but I don't think she'll call. She's stubborn . . . almost as stubborn as her old man."

Clay looked down into his cup. "Listen, she's"—he swallowed, looked up again with an expression of worry etched upon his eyebrows—"she's not having an abortion, is she?"

"No, she's not."

His shoulders seemed to wilt with relief.

That night when Catherine answered the phone, Bobbi opened by saying, "Clay came to see me."

Catherine's hand stopped where it was upon her scalp, combing her hair back from her face. Her heart seemed to stop with it. "You didn't tell him anything, did you?"

"No, I just complimented him on his shiner. Your dad really meant business!"

It took great effort for Catherine to resist asking if Clay was really all right. She affected a businesslike tone, asking, "He didn't come to show you his battle scars, I'm sure. What did he want?"

"To know where you are. He wants to talk to you."

"About what?"

"Well, what do you suppose? Cath, he's not so bad. He didn't even complain about getting beaten up. He seems genuinely worried about your welfare and wants to make some arrangements for paying for the baby, that's all."

"Bully for him!" Catherine exclaimed, casting an anxious glance down the hall to make sure no one was within earshot.

"Okay, okay! All I am is the messenger. He wants you to call him at his house tonight."

The line grew silent. The picture of his house came back all too clearly to Catherine. His house with its comfortable luxury, its fire burning at dusk, his parents in their finery, Clay walking in whistling with his hair the color of autumn. A weakness threatened Catherine, but she resisted it.

"Cath, did you hear me?"

"I heard."

"But you're not going to call him?"

"No."

"But he said he's got something he has to talk over with you." A rather persuasive tone came into Bobbi's voice then. "Listen, Cath, he kind of threw me. I thought he'd try to wheedle your whereabouts out of me, but he didn't. He said if you'd call him, neither one of us would have to give away any secrets."

"Very upstanding," Catherine said tightly, haunted even further by the remembered look of concern on Clay's face as she got out of his car.

"This might sound disloyal, but I'm beginning to think he is."

"What, upstanding?"

"Well, is it so unbelievable? He really seems . . . well, concerned. He isn't acting at all like I thought he would. I find myself wondering what Stu would do if he found himself in Clay's situation. I think he might have left town by now. Listen, why don't you give Clay a chance?"

"I can't. I don't want his concern and I'm not going to call him. It wouldn't do any good."

"He said I should tell you if there's anything you need, just say so, and you've got the money for it."

"I know. He told me that before. I told him I don't want anything from him."

"Cath, are you sure you're doing the smart thing?"

"Bobbi . . . please."

"Well, heck, he's loaded. Why not take a little of it off his hands?"

"Now you sound like my old man!"

"Okay, Cath, it's your baby. I did what he asked; I gave you the message. Call him at his place tonight. From there on out it's up to you. So how's the place?"

"It's really not bad, you know?" Then, fighting off thoughts of Clay Forrester, Catherine added, "It has no men, so that's a plus right there."

The voice at the other end became pleading. "Hey, don't get that way, Cath. Not all men are like your father. Clay Forrester, for instance, is about as far from your father as a man could get."

"Bobbi, I get the distinct impression that you're changing sides."

"I'm not changing sides. But I'm getting a better view of both sides, caught in the middle like I am. I'm always on your side, but I can't help it if I think you should at least call the guy."

"Like hell I will! I don't want Clay Forrester or his money!"

"All right, all right! Enough! I'm not going to waste any more time arguing with you about it, because I know you when you get your mind made up."

Absorbed as she was in her conversation with Bobbi, Catherine was unaware that three girls had gone into the kitchen for a snack, and from there any telephone conversation could be easily heard. When she hung up, she headed back to her room, more rattled than she'd care to admit by what Bobbi had said. It would be so easy to give in, to accept money from Clay, or to solicit his moral support during the difficult months ahead, but should she rely on him in any way she feared he would have a hold on her, on the decisions about her future that must still be made. It would be better to stay here where life was better than what she'd left. At Horizons there was no censure, for everyone here was in the same boat.

Or so they thought.

FIVE

The tension around the Forrester home grew as Catherine's whereabouts remained unknown. Angela walked around with a drawn expression about her mouth, and often Clay found her eyes upon him with such a hurt expression that he carried its memory with him to the law school building each day. His concentration was further thwarted by the fact that Herb Anderson was released after twenty-four hours without a formal charge made against him. The necessity to let him go scot-free rankled mercilessly, not only on Clay but on his father. They knew the law, knew they could pin Anderson to the wall for what he'd done. To be unable to do so only raised the pitch of their taut nerves.

Once Anderson was free, he became more self-righteous than ever. He smiled in self-satisfaction all the way home while he thought, I got them sonsabitches where I want them and I ain't lettin' go till they come through with the greenbacks!

When Herb got home, Ada was standing in the living room with her coat still on, reading a postcard. She looked up, startled to see him coming in the door.

"Why, Herb, you're out."

"Goddam right I'm out. Them Forresters know what's good for 'em, that's why I'm out. Where's the girl?" His eyes were bloodshot, his knuckles still taped, the bandages dirty now. He already had the rank stench of gin on his breath.

"She's all right, Herb," Ada offered timorously, holding out the card. "Look, she's in Omaha with a friend who—"

"Omaha!" The word rattled the windows as Herb reeled and smacked the postcard out of his wife's hand. She cowered, watching with huge eyes as he teetered and stooped to pick up the card off the floor. He gaped at the handwriting to make sure it was Catherine's. He swiped the soiled bandage across the eyes that always wore a film of water over their ocherous whites. When his vision cleared, he studied the card again, then whispered, "Them rich sonsabitchin' whorin' no-good bastards are gonna pay for this! Nobody makes a horse's ass outa Herb

Anderson and gets away with it!" Then he shoved past Ada as if she weren't there, heading out again.

She collapsed into a chair with a shudder of relief.

At Horizons, Francie got even with a few of life's injustices by stealing a bottle of Charlie perfume from the top of Catherine Anderson's dresser.

At the University of Minnesota one of those very injustices was at that moment folding her exquisite, thoroughbred legs into Clay Forrester's Corvette.

"You're late," Jill Magnusson scolded, placing one gleaming fingernail on the door to prevent Clay from closing it, at the same time turning upon him a stunning smile that had cost her father approximately two thousand dollars in orthodontia. Jill was a beauty, and a member of the elite sorority Kappa Alpha Pheta, whose members were loosely referred to as the "Phetas," known down through the years as the rich girls' sorority at the U of M.

"Busy day," Clay answered, suddenly piqued by her method of holding them up. He was too distracted to be charmed by those supple limbs right now. He slammed the door and walked around to his side. The engine purred as they pulled away from the curb.

"I need to stop by the photo lab to check on some pictures for a research project." Jill was more than a superficial appearance; she was majoring in aviation electronics and had every intention of designing the first jet shuttle between the earth and moon. With career goals set high she wasn't the least bit in-

terested in getting married yet. She and Clay understood each other well.

But tonight he was unusually testy. "I'm late and you're the one who's going to stop at the photo lab on our way to the party!" Clay snapped, laying a thin line of rubber as the car peeled away.

"My, aren't we touchy tonight."

"Jill, I told you I wanted to stay home and study. You're the one who insisted we go to this party. You'll forgive me if I dislike playing escort service on the way."

"Fine. Forget the lab. I can pick up the photos myself tomorrow."

Gearing down at a stop sign, he screeched to a halt, throwing Jill forcefully forward.

"What in the world is the matter with you!" she exclaimed.

"I'm not in a party mood, that's all."

"Obviously," she said dryly. "Then forget the photo lab and the party, too."

"You dragged me out to this damn party, now we're going!"

"Clay Forrester, don't you speak to me in that tone of voice. If you didn't want to go with me you could have said so. You said you had a case to study this weekend. There's a vast difference between the two."

He threw the car into gear and screamed down University Avenue toward the heart of the campus, zinging in and out between other cars, intentionally laying rubber with every shift of the gears.

"You're driving like a maniac," she said coolly, her auburn hair swinging with the erratic motions of his lane changes.

"I'm feeling like one."

"Then please let me out. I'm not."

"I'll let you out at the goddam party," he said, knowing he was being despicable but unable to help it.

"Since when have you taken to insouciant cursing?"

"Since approximately six P.M. four nights ago," he said.

"Clay, for heaven's sake slow down before you get us both killed, or at the very least get yourself a walloping ticket. The campus police are thick tonight. There's a concert at Northrup."

Ahead at an intersection he could see a cop patrolling traffic, so he slowed down.

"Have you been drinking, Clay?"

"Not yet!" he snapped.

"You're going to?"

"If I'm smart, maybe."

Jill studied his profile, the firm jaw, the tight expression about his usually sensual mouth. "I don't think I know this Clay Forrester," she said softly.

"Nope, you don't." He glared straight ahead, curling his lower lip over his upper, waiting for the cop to flag the traffic through the intersection. "Neither do I."

"It sounds serious," she ventured.

Instead of replying, he hung his right wrist over the steering wheel and continued to glare at the cop, that lip still curled up with contempt at something.

"Wanna talk about it?" she asked in what she hoped was a coercive voice. She waited, dropping her head slightly forward so her hair fell like a rust curtain beyond her cheek.

He looked at her at last, thinking, God but she's beautiful. Poised, intelligent, passionate, even a little cunning. He liked that in her. Liked even more the fact that she never tried to hide it. She often teased him that she could get him to do anything she wanted, simply by using her long-limbed body. Most of the time she was right.

"What would you say if I admitted that I'm afraid to talk to you about it?"

"For starters, I'd say the admission has added some common sense to your driving habits."

He had indeed begun driving more sensibly. He reached over and rubbed the back of her hand. "Do you really want to go to the party?"

"Yes. I have this gorgeous new lamb's-wool sweater and this magnificent matching skirt and you haven't even noticed. If you won't compliment me, I'd like to find someone who will."

"All right, you got it," he said, swinging left, heading for the Alcorn Apartments, where the party was in full swing when they arrived. Inside it was a maze of voices and music, too many bodies packed into too little space. The Alcorn was a converted gingerbread house with bays, nooks and pantries, the kind of place easy to get lost in if playing hide-and-seek. The furniture throughout the first-floor apartment was positively decimated, but nobody cared because nobody seemed to own it. Jill led the way through the press of people, taking Clay's hand, tugging him to the kitchen where the bar was set up on a dilapidated porcelain-topped table, the kind that went out with World War II. A guy named Eddie was tending bar.

"Hey, Jill, Clay, how's it going? What'll you have?"

"Clay wants to get smashed tonight, Eddie. Why don't you give him a little help?"

In no time Eddie extended a drink that was supposed to be mixed; it was the color of weak coffee. Clay took one sip and knew three like this would knock him smack off his feet. If he really wanted to get smashed, it wouldn't take long. Jill accepted a much weaker drink. She was too intelligent to get drunk. He'd never seen her have more than one or two cocktails in an evening.

He teased her now. "Why don't you come down one notch and show you're at least as human as me and have a couple of strong drinks tonight? Then when we go to bed you'll be as uninhibited as I intend to be."

Jill laughed and swung her waist-length hair back behind a well-turned shoulder.

"If you want to get roaring drunk go right ahead. Don't expect me to abet it by being equally as stupid."

He raised a sardonic eyebrow to Eddie. "The lady thinks I'm stupid." Then he mumbled into his drink, "If she only knew the half."

In the crush of bodies and the assault of noise Jill didn't quite hear what Clay said, but he was troubled tonight, not acting like himself. "I don't know what's gotten into you tonight, but whatever it is, I don't like it."

"You'd like it even less if you knew."

Just then somebody came by and bumped Jill from behind, spilling a splash of her drink on her new sweater at the fullest part of her left breast.

"Oh, damn!" she exclaimed, sucking in her stomach, searching in her purse for a Kleenex. "Have you got a hanky, Clay?"

He reached for his hind pocket. "That's the second time this week that a lady has needed my hanky. Here, let me help you with that, mademoiselle." He grabbed Jill by the hand, found a vacant corner beside the refrigerator and pushed her into it. With the hanky he began dabbing at the spot where the liquor had already darkened the sweater. But an odd, troubled look overtook his face. His motions stilled, and his eyes found hers. Then he grabbed hanky, sweater, breast and all and flattened himself against her long, lithe body, kissing her with a sudden fierceness that startled her. Fondling her breast, controlling her mouth, he pressed her into the corner where the refrigerator met the wall.

She thought he'd lost his mind. This was not the Clay she knew, not at all. Something was more wrong than she'd guessed.

"Stop it, stop it! What's the matter with you!" she gasped, breaking away from his kiss, trying to push his hand from her breast.

"I need you tonight, Jill, that's all. Let's go someplace and leave this noisy bunch."

"I've never seen you like this, Clay. For God's sake let go of my breast!"

Abruptly he released her, backed up a step, put the guilty hand in his trouser pocket and stared at the floor. "Forget it," he said, "just forget it." He raised his drink and took an abusive swallow.

"You're going to get sick if you continue at this pace."

"Good!"

"All right, I'll go with you, but to make sense, not sex, agreed?"

He looked at her absently.

"Whatever it is that's bothering you, let's talk it out."

"Fine," he said, taking her glass almost viciously and depositing it and his back on the table, which was littered with dozens of others. Without another word he grabbed Jill's wrist and started pushing his way through the mob.

When they were halfway to the door someone yelled, "Hey, Clay, hold up!" Turning, he saw Stu Glass's ruddy face making its way toward him, both hands raised above the press of elbows, trying to keep from spilling a pair of drinks. Over his shoulder Stu shouted, "Follow me close, honey; I want to talk to Clay a minute."

The two couples converged in the milling crowd. "Hey, Clay, you leaving already?"

"Hey, Stu, whaddya say?"

"Haven't seen you around all week. Dad wanted to know if you and your father decided about partridge hunting next weekend yet."

The two fell to discussing hunting plans, leaving Bobbi and Jill to exchange small talk. They knew each other only slightly, through their relation with the men, but now, for the first time, Bobbi studied Jill Magnusson more assessingly than ever before. She took in Jill's expensive wine-colored sweater and skirt, that angel's face of hers, and the negligent way Clay Forrester's arm looped around her waist while he went on talking to Stu. If ever two people were made for each other it was these two, thought Bobbi. Jill, with her burnished skin, her cover-girl's features and that glorious mane of hair, and Clay with his sun-drenched good looks, flawless taste in clothing to match the girl's, and both of them blessed with self-assurance, wealthy families and preordained success.

It struck Bobbi quite suddenly that Catherine was positively out of her class with a man like Clay. He belonged with the kind of girl he was with now. How futile it was to wish she'd used better judgment last Fourth of July, yet, observing Clay and Jill together, Bobbi felt a sting of deep regret.

All the while Clay talked with Stu he was aware of Bobbi. When at last someone from the crowd bumped through and took Jill momentarily away from his side, and Stu along with her, he got his chance.

"Hi, Bobbi."

"Hi, Clay."

The two eyed each other a little warily.

"What's new with you?"

"Same old thing."

Damn her, thought Clay, she's going to make me ask it. He

threw a quick eye at Jill, who stood near enough to overhear anything being said.

"Have you heard anything from your cousin lately?"

"Yeah, just today, as a matter of fact."

"How's everything?"

"The same."

Clay's eyes shifted away and back again. "I never got that
call."

"I gave her the message."

"Could you please ask her again?"

"She's not interested."

Someone from the crowd jostled his way behind Bobbi,
pushing her forcibly closer to Clay. He used the opportunity to
insist, "There've been some serious repercussions. I've got to talk
to her!"

But just then Jill recaptured Clay, running her painted nails
up his arm in a familiar way, taking his elbow in her own. There
are people in this world who have things just a bit too good,
thought Bobbi, and others who never get a break. Just to even
the scales a little bit, some cunning gremlin inside Bobbi made
her call after the couple, "I'll tell Catherine you said hello,
Clay!"

He turned and burned her with a look that seemed to say
he'd like to throw a hex on her. But he replied civilly, "Give her
my best."

When Jill and Clay had disappeared, Stu asked, "What was
that all about?"

"Oh, nothing. We lined Clay up with my cousin Catherine
last summer one time, remember?"

"We did? Oh yeah, that's right, we did." Then, shrugging, he
took her elbow and said, "Come on, let's go freshen our drinks."

*   *   *

Clay and Jill decided to drive out to the Interlachen Country
Club, a place where both of their parents belonged and where
they'd been coming for as long as they could remember, to play
golf or eat Sunday brunch. The dining room was half empty, left
now to those members who stayed to dance on the small parquet
floor to the music of a trio that played old standards. They were
seated at a table situated in the lee of corner windows overlooking
the golf course, which was lit by single lights strewn along the
fairways. The dapples of brightness created a jeweled view from
this vantage point in the high, glass-walled room. The course
boasted fifty different species of trees. Were it high noon, they'd
be seeing every warm color of the spectrum across the expanse
below, but now, night having settled over the acres of trees and
manicured grass, it looked like something from a fairy tale, the
trees shimmering silhouettes against the strategically placed lights.

For some minutes after they were seated, Clay continued
staring out at the view below while Jill swirled her wine in its
lengthy stem glass. When she'd waited as long as she intended to
wait, Jill forced the issue.

"And who is Catherine?" Even a question such as this reflected Jill's breeding, for her voice grew neither accusing nor
harpyish. It flowed instead like the amber liquid around the sides
of her glass.

After a moment's consideration Clay answered, "Bobbi's
cousin."

Raising the stem glass to her lips, Jill hummed, "Mmm . . ."
then added, "Has she got something to do with this sour mood
of yours?"

But Clay seemed far removed again, pensive.

"What's so interesting out there in the dark?"

He turned to her with a sigh, rested his elbows on the linen tabletop and kneaded his eyes with the heels of his hands. Then, leaving his eyes covered, he grunted dejectedly, so she could scarcely hear, "Damn."

"You might as well talk about it, Clay. If it's about this . . . *Catherine*, I think I deserve to know. It is, isn't it?"

His troubled eyes appeared once again, gazing at her, but instead of answering her question, he asked one of his own. "Do you love me, Jill?"

"I don't think that's the subject of this discussion."

"Answer me anyway."

"Why?"

"Because I've been wondering lately . . . a lot. Do you?"

"Could be. I don't know for sure."

"I've been asking myself the same question about you, too. I don't know for sure if I love you either, but it's a very good possibility."

"That's a little too clinical to be romantic, Clay." She laughed softly, sending the lights shimmering off her sparkling lips.

"Yeah, I've been in a clinical mood this week—you know, dissecting things?" He gave her a brief rueful smile.

"Dissecting our relationship?"

He nodded, studied the weave of the tablecloth, then raised his eyes to study Jill's flawless face, her hair gleaming beneath the subdued lights of a massive chandelier. Her long fingers with tapered nails glistening as she absently fondled her footed glass, her grace as she relaxed back into her chair, one arm draped limply on its armrest. Jill was like a ten-karat diamond: she belonged in this setting just as surely as Catherine Anderson did not. To bring Catherine Anderson here would be like setting a rhinestone in gold filigree. But Jill . . . ah, Jill, he thought, how she dazzles.

"You're so damn beautiful it's absurd," Clay said, a curiously painful note in his voice.

"Thanks. Somehow it doesn't mean as much tonight as if you'd said it just that way, with just that tone of voice, with just that particular look in your eyes, say . . . a week ago, or, say, four days ago?"

He had no reply.

"Say, before the subject of Catherine Whoever-she-is intruded?"

Clay only chewed his lower lip in a way with which she was utterly familiar.

"I can wait all night for you to spill it out, whatever it is. I'm not the one who has studying to do this weekend."

"Neither do I," Clay admitted. "I used that as an excuse because I didn't want to see you tonight."

"So that's why you pounced on me like a parolee fresh out of prison?"

He laughed softly, admiring her cool, unruffled presence. "No, that was self-flagellation."

"For?"

"For last July fourth."

A light dawned in Jill's head. She remembered quite distinctly the fight they'd had back then.

"Who was she? Catherine?" Jill asked softly.

"Exactly."

"And?"

"And she's pregnant."

Jill's poise was commendable. She drew in a deep, swift breath, her perfect nostrils flaring into slight imperfection during the length of it. The cords in her neck became momentarily taut before relaxing once more as her eyes and Clay's locked, searching. Then she gracefully braced an elbow on the tabletop and lowered her forehead onto the back of her hand.

Into the silence, a waiter intruded.

"Miss Magnusson, Mr. Forrester, can I get you anything else?"

Clay looked up, distracted. "No, thank you, Scott. We're fine."

When Scott had drifted discreetly away, Jill raised her head and asked, "Is she the reason for the shiner, which I have so graciously avoided mentioning all night?"

He nodded. "Her father." He took a drink, gazed out at the lights below again.

"I'll forgo the obvious question," Jill said, with a hint of asperity creeping into her tone, "realizing you wouldn't have told me unless the situation were clearly defined and you're certain it is yours. Are you going to marry her?"

This time it was Clay's turn to draw a ragged breath. He sat with ankle crossed over knee, one elbow slung on the edge of the table. To look at him, at the careless pose, at the classic cut of his tailored clothes, his handsome profile, one would not have guessed the slightest thing to be amiss. But inside he was a knot of nerves.

"You haven't clearly answered whether or not you love me." Slowly Clay drew his eyes back to hers, suffering now nearly as much as he could see she was.

"No, I haven't, have I?"

"Is it"—Clay searched for the correct word—"superfluous now?"

"I think so, yes, I think so."

Each of their gazes dropped down to their drinks; each of them experienced a touching sense of loss at her words.

"I don't know if I'm going to marry her or not. I'm getting a lot of pressure."

"From her parents?"

He only laughed ruefully. "Oh, Jill, that's so incredibly funny. Too bad you'll never know how incredibly funny that is."

"Sure," Jill retorted caustically, "Ha—ha—ha . . . aren't I funny, though."

He reached for her hand on the tabletop. "Jill, it was a thing that happened. You and I had had that big fight the night before. Stu and Bobbi lined me up with this cousin of Bobbi's . . . Hell, I don't know."

"And you got her pregnant because you wanted to set up housekeeping with me and I refused to leave Pheta House. How chivalrous!" She yanked her hand free.

"I expected you to be bitter. I deserve it. The whole miserable thing is a lousy mistake. The girl's father is a raving lunatic, and believe me, neither the girl nor I want anything to do with each other. But there are, shall we say, extenuating circumstances that may force me to ask her to marry me."

"Oh, she'll be overjoyed that you *have to*! What girl wouldn't be!"

He sighed, thought in exasperation, Women! "I'm being pressured in more ways than one."

"What's the matter, has your father threatened to deny you a place in the family practice?"

"You're very astute, Jill, but then I never did take you for a dumb redhead."

"Oh, don't humor me; not at a time like this."

"It's not only my father. Mother walks around looking like she's just been whipped, and to complicate matters Catherine's old man is threatening to get vocal about it. If that happens, my admission to the bar is in jeopardy. And to complicate matters even more, Catherine has run away from home."

"Do you know where she is?"

"No, but Bobbi does."

"So you could reach her if you wanted to?"

"I think so."

"But you don't want to?"

He drew a great sighing breath and only shook his head forlornly. Then he reached for her hand again across the corner of the table. "Jill, I don't have much time to waste. All the devils of hell seem to be riding on my back right now. I'm sorry if I have to lay one of them on yours, and I'm sorry, too, if the occasion isn't what it should be at a time like this, but I want to know your feelings about me. I want to know if, at some time in our future, when all of this is straightened out, when I've completed law school and gotten my life back in working order, would you ever consider marrying me?"

Her composure slipped a notch and she cast her eyes aside as they grew too glisteny. But they were drawn back to his familiar, lovable face, of which she knew every feature so intimately. In a choked voice she answered, "Damn you, Clay Forrester. I should slap your Adonis's face."

But the softness of her words told him how very hurt she was.

"Jill, you know me. You know what I'd have planned for us if this hadn't interfered. I'd never have asked you this way, at a time like this, if I'd had the choice."

"Oh, Clay, my heart is—is . . . falling in little pieces down to the pit of my stomach. What do you expect me to say?"

"Say what you feel, Jill." He rubbed a thumb lightly across the back of her hand while she covered his face, hair and body with her eyes, letting her hand remain passively in his.

"You asked me too late, Clay."

Pained moments spun by while the piano player tinkled some old tune and a few dancers moved across the floor. At last he picked up Jill's hand, turned it over and kissed its palm. Returning his gaze to her face he whispered, "God, you're beautiful."

She swallowed. "God, you are, too. That's our trouble. We're too beautiful. People see only the facade, not the pain, the faults, the human failings that don't show."

"Jill, I'm sorry I hurt you. I do love you, you know."

"I don't think you'd better bank on me, Clay."

"Do you forgive me for asking?"

"No, don't ask me to do that."

"It mattered to me, Jill. Your answer mattered a lot."

She slowly pulled her hand free of his and picked up her purse.

"Jill, I'll let you know what comes of it."

"Yeah, you do that. And I'll let you know when my space shuttle leaves for the moon."

This time it happened so fast that Clay saw nothing. He stepped out of the Corvette in the driveway and a husky shadow slinked swiftly from behind the bulk of a pyramidal arborvitae. Clay was yanked roughly around, slammed against the fender of the car just as a meaty fist smashed into his stomach, leaving no mark, breaking no bones, only cracking the wind from him viciously as he doubled over and dropped to his knees on the ground.

Through his pain he heard a grating voice informing, "That was from Anderson. The girl's run off to Omaha." Then heavy, running footsteps disappeared into the night.

*   *   *

When Bobbi called the following evening, she sounded breathless. "I ran into him at a party last night, Cath. He asked about you again and said to tell you it's really important. He has to talk to you."

"What good would it do? I'm not marrying him and I don't need his money!"

"Oh, jeez! You're so obstinate! What harm can it do, for heaven's sake!"

But Marie passed along the hall just then and Catherine turned her face toward the wall, couching the mouthpiece furtively. But from the knowing glance Marie had flashed her way, Catherine suspected she'd heard the last remark. Quietly she said into the phone, "I want him to think I've left town."

Bobbi's voice suddenly became critical, scolding. "If you want to know what I think, I think you owe him that much. I don't think it's enough for you to insist that *you* don't need a single thing from Clay Forrester. Maybe he needs something from you. Have you considered that?"

Dead silence at Bobbi's end of the line for a long moment.

Catherine hadn't considered that before. She clasped the receiver tightly and pressed it against her ear so hard her head began to hurt. Suddenly it tired her immensely, having to think about Clay Forrester at all. Her emotions were strung out to the limit, and her own problems were more than she wanted to handle without taking on Clay Forrester's, too. She sighed and dropped her forehead against the wall.

Bobbi's voice came through again, but very calmly and quietly. "I think he's in some kind of big trouble over this, Cath. I don't know exactly what because he wouldn't say. All he said was something about serious repercussions."

"Don't!" Catherine begged, her eyelids sliding shut wearily. "J-just don't, okay? I don't want to hear it! I can't take on any of his troubles. I have all I can do to handle my own."

Again there followed a lengthy silence before Bobbi made one last observation that was to gnaw at Catherine's conscience mercilessly in the hours and days to come: "Cath . . . whether you want to admit it or not, I think they're one and the same."

SIX

The wide blue curve of the Mississippi River glinted beneath the autumn sky as it cut a swath through the campus of the University of Minnesota, dividing it into East Bank and West Bank. The more heavily wooded East Bank wore the school colors, maroon and gold. Homecoming was approaching, and it seemed almost as if the grounds had festooned themselves for the event. Stately old maples wore ruddy tones in startling contrast to the fiery elms. Constant activity churned along Union and Church streets as homecoming preparations advanced. On the lawns students soaked up summer's warm leftovers. Pedestrians dawdled, waiting for buses in the shaded circle before Jones Hall. Bicycle wheels sighed through tumbled leaves. Ornamental stone parapets adorned gracious old frat houses down along University Avenue, their retaining walls, steps and balconies draped with idlers, slung there like lazing lizards. And everywhere couples kissed, heads bare to the afternoon sun.

Passing a kissing couple now, Catherine looked quickly away. Somehow the sight of them made the books ride a little more heavily upon her hip. At times lately, leaning to lift those books, twinges caught her side in newly strange places.

Clay, too, was often disarmed by the sight of a young man and woman kissing. Striding down The Mall now, he observed an embrace in progress and his thought strayed to Catherine Anderson. Pulling his eyes to the students moving along the sidewalk ahead of him, he thought the girl with the leaf-gold hair could almost be her. He studied her back while it disappeared and reappeared around others who came between them. But it was only his preoccupation with her lately that made him look twice at every blond head in a crowd.

Still, the hair was the right color and the right length. But Clay realized he could easily be mistaken, for he'd never seen her in broad daylight before.

Dammit, Forrester, get her out of your head! That's not her and you know it!

But as he watched the tall form with its straight shoulders, its swayless hips, the books riding against one of them, a queer feeling made his stomach go weightless. He wanted to call her name but knew it couldn't be Catherine. Hadn't he gotten the message loud and clear? She'd run off to Omaha.

Deliberately Clay glanced across the street to free his eyes and mind from delusions. But it was no good. Momentarily he found himself scanning the crowd more intently, seeking out the blue sweater with blond hair trailing down its back. She was gone! Absurd, but a hot flash of panic clutched Clay, making him break into a trot. He caught sight of her once more, farther ahead, and breathed easier, but continued following. Long stride, he thought. Long legs. Could it be? Suddenly the girl crooked an arm and stroked the hair away from her neck as if she were hot. Clay skipped around a group of people, studying the long legs, the erect carriage of her shoulders, remembering her air of haughtiness and defensiveness. She came to a street and hesitated for a passing car, then glanced aside to check traffic before crossing. As she stepped from the curb, her profile was clearly defined for a fraction of a second.

Clay's heart seemed to hit his throat and he broke into a run.

"Catherine?" he called, keeping his eyes riveted on her, shouldering his way, bumping people, mechanically excusing himself, running on. "Catherine?"

She evidently did not hear, only kept on walking, the sound of traffic grown heavier as a bus pulled away from the sidewalk. He was short-winded by the time he caught up with her and swung her around by an elbow. Her books tumbled from her hip and her hair flew across her mouth and stuck to her lipstick.

"Hey, what—" she began, instinctively bending toward the books. But through the veil of hair she looked up to find Clay Forrester glowering down at her; his chest heaving, his mouth open in surprise.

Catherine's heart cracked against the walls of her chest while the sight of him made tremors dance through her stomach.

"Catherine? What are you doing here?" He reached again for her elbow and drew her up. She only stared, trying to conquer the urge to run while her heart palpitated wildly and the books lay forgotten on the sidewalk. "Do you mean you've been here all the time, right here going to school?" he asked in astonishment, still grasping her elbow as if afraid she'd vanish.

Clay could see she was stunned. Her lips parted and the look in her eyes told him she felt cornered and would surely run again. He felt the sweater slipping out of his fingers.

"Catherine, why didn't you call?" Her hair was still stuck to her lipstick. Her breath coming through billowed it out and in. Then she bent to pick up her books while he belatedly leaned to do the same. She plucked them away from his fingers and turned to escape him and the countless complications that he could mean to her.

"Catherine, wait!"

"Leave me alone," she flung over her shoulder, trying not to look as if she were running from him, running just the same.

"I've got to talk with you."

She kept half-running, half-walking away, Clay a few steps behind her.

"Why didn't you call?"

"Dammit! How did you find me?"

"Will you stop, for God's sake!"

"I'm late! Leave me alone!"

He kept up with her, stride for stride, very easily now, while Catherine's side started aching and she pressed her free hand against it.

"Didn't you get my message from Bobbi?"

But the blond hair only swung from side to side on that proud neck as she hurried on. Irritated because she refused to stop, he grabbed her arm once again, forcing her to do his bidding. "I'm getting tired of playing Keystone Kops with you! *Will you stop!*"

The books stayed on her hip this time but she tossed her head belligerently, a yearling colt defying the bridle. She stood there glaring at him while he restrained her. When at last it seemed she wouldn't bolt, he dropped his hand.

"I gave Bobbi the message to have you call me. Did she tell you?"

Instead of answering his question, she berated herself. "This is the one thing I couldn't control, chancing running into you somewhere. I thought this campus was big enough for the two of us. I'd appreciate it if you'd keep it to yourself that I'm here."

"And I'd appreciate it if you'd give me the opportunity to explain a few things and work something out with you."

"We did all the talking we needed the last time we were together. I told you, my plans are made and you don't have to worry about me."

Curious passersby eyed them, wondering what they were arguing about.

"Listen, we're making a spectacle here. Will you come with me someplace quiet so we can talk?"

"I said I'm in a hurry."

"And I'm in a fat lot of trouble! Will you just give me two minutes and stand still?" He'd never seen anyone so defiant in his life. It was more than just his parents' ultimatum driving him now. This had come down to a contest of wills as she strode away up The Mall with him just behind her shoulder again.

"Leave me alone," she demanded.

"There's nothing I'd like better, but my parents don't see it that way."

"Pity."

He grabbed the back of her sweater this time, and she nearly walked out of it before realizing why it wasn't coming along with her.

"Give me a time, an anonymous phone number, anything, so I can get in touch with you and I'll leave you alone until then."

She yanked her sweater free and spun to face him defiantly. "I've already told you, I made one mistake and it was a dilly. But my life isn't ruined as long as I don't consider it ruined. I know where I'm going, what I'm going to do when I get there, and I don't want you involved in any way whatsoever."

"Are you too proud to take anything from me?"

"You can call it pride if you want. I prefer to call it good sense. I don't want you having any kind of hold over me."

"Suppose I have the solution to our problems, and it would leave neither of us indebted to the other?"

But she only eyed him acidly. "I've solved my problems. If you still have some, it's not my fault."

People were looking at them curiously again, and Clay became incensed at her stubborn refusal to listen to reason. Before she knew what was happening, he'd clamped an arm around her waist and propelled her off the sidewalk toward an old, enormous elm. She found herself thrust against it, her ears flanked by both of his palms, which leaned against the bark.

"Something else has come up," he informed her, his face no more than two inches from hers. "Seems your father's been making trouble."

She swallowed, pressing her head back, glancing first into his eyes, then aside, afraid of the determination she saw so clearly at this close range.

"I heard about that and I'm sorry," she conceded. "I really thought he'd give up when I left."

"For Omaha?" he asked sarcastically.

Her startled eyes flew to his. "How did you learn that?" She noted the remnant of a cut above his eyebrow and wondered if her father had put it there. He glowered, holding her prisoner so that all she could see was either his face or a bronze-colored sweater smack in front of her eyes. She stared at the sweater.

"Never mind. Your father is making threats, and those threats could mean the end of my law career. Something's got to be done about it. I find the idea of paying him off as distasteful as you do. Now, can we work on a reasonable alternative?"

Catherine's eyes slid shut; she was unable to think quickly enough. "Listen, I've got to go now, honest. But I'll call you tonight. We can talk about it then."

Something told him not to trust her, but he couldn't stand there restraining her indefinitely. All he could do was let her go for the time being. He knew he could find out easily where she lived, now that he knew she was a student there. As he watched her walk away he waited to see if she'd turn around to check if he was tailing her. She didn't. She entered Jones Hall and disappeared, and guessing that her patience was probably greater than his, he turned back, heading for the car.

The following day Catherine met Mrs. Tollefson in the office with its patchwork sofa and fern. Thinking Tolly would forge ahead into the subject Catherine most dreaded, Catherine was surprised when instead the matronly woman only chatted about school and asked how Catherine was getting along now that she'd settled into Horizons. When Catherine told her she was attending college on a small study grant and supplementing it by doing typing and sewing, Mrs. Tollefson noted, "You have a lot of ambition, Catherine."

"Yes, but I'll be the first to admit it's self-serving. I want something better out of life than what I've had."

Mrs. Tollefson ruminated. "College, then, is your ticket to a better life."

"Yes, it was going to be my final escape."

"Was?" Mrs. Tollefson paused. "Why do you speak in the past tense?"

Catherine's eyes opened a little wider. "I didn't do it consciously."

"But you feel you're being forced to drop out of school?"

A brief, wry laugh escaped Catherine. "Under the circumstances, who wouldn't?"

A gentle expression complemented Tolly's soft voice. "Perhaps we need to talk about that, about where you've come from, where you are, where you're going."

Catherine sighed, dropped her head back tiredly. "I don't know where I'm going anymore. I did once, but I'm not sure if I'll get there now."

"You're speaking about this baby as an obstacle."

"Yes, one I haven't wanted to make decisions about."

"Perhaps decisions will come easier once we look at all your options." Mrs. Tollefson's voice would be well suited to the reading of poetry. "I think we need to explore where your baby fits into your plans."

Oh, God, here it comes. Catherine sank deeper into the cushions of the sofa, wishing it would take her down, down, into its depth forever.

"How far along are you, Catherine?"

"Three months."

"So you've had some time to think about it already?" The kind woman watched the cords stand out in Catherine's neck as the girl swallowed, and her eyes remained closed.

"Not enough. I—I have trouble thinking about it at all. I keep pushing it to the back of my mind, thinking someone will come along and make the decision for me."

"But you know that won't happen. You knew that when you came to Horizons. From the moment you chose not to abort, you knew a further decision was in the offing."

Childlike now, Catherine sat forward, arguing. "But I want them both, college and the baby. I don't want to give up either one!"

"Then let's discuss that angle. Do you think you're strong enough to be a full-time mother and a full-time student?"

For the first time Catherine bridled. "Well, how should I know!" She flung her hands out, then subsided with a sheepish look. "I—I'm sorry."

Mrs. Tollefson only smiled. "It's okay. It's fine and healthy to be angry. Why shouldn't you be? You just started putting your life on track when along came this major complication. Who wouldn't be angry?"

"Okay, I admit it. I'm—I'm mad!"

"At whom?"

A puzzled expression curled Catherine's blond eyebrows. "At whom?" But Mrs. Tollefson only sat patiently, waiting for Catherine to come up with the answer. "At—at me?" Catherine asked skeptically in a tiny voice.

"And?"

"And . . ." Catherine swallowed. It was extremely hard to say. "And the baby's father."

"Anybody else?"

"Who else is there?"

It grew quiet for a long moment, then the older woman suggested, "The baby?"

"The baby?" Catherine looked aghast. "It's not his fault!"

"Of course it's not. But I thought you might be angry with him just the same, maybe for making you think about giving up school, or at the very least, for slowing you down."

"I'm not that kind of person."

"Maybe not now, but if your child prevents you from completing your college education, what then?"

"You're assuming I can't do both?" Catherine was growing frustrated while Mrs. Tollefson remained calm, unflappable.

"Not at all. I'm being realistic though. I'm saying it will be tough. Eighty percent of the women who become pregnant before age seventeen never complete high school. That statistic goes up with college-age women, who must handle heavy tuition costs."

"There are day-care centers," Catherine noted defensively.

"Which don't accept a child until he is toilet-trained. Did you know that?"

"You're really laying it on heavy, aren't you?" Catherine accused.

"These are facts," continued the counselor. "And since you're not the kind to go man-hunting as a solution to your problem, shall we explore another option?"

"Say it," Catherine challenged tightly.

"Adoption."

To Catherine the word was as depressing as a funeral dirge, yet Mrs. Tollefson went on. "We should explore it as a very reasonable, very available answer to your dilemma. As hard as it may be for you to consider adoption—and I can see how it upsets you by the expression on your face—it may be the best route for you and the child in the long run." Mrs. Tollefson's voice droned on, relating the success of adopted children until Catherine jumped to her feet and turned her back.

"I don't want to hear it!" She clutched one hand with the other. "It's so—so cold-blooded! Childless couples! Adoptive parents! Those terms are—" She swung again to face Mrs. Tollefson. "Don't you understand? It would be like feeding my baby to the vultures!"

Even as she said it, Catherine knew her exclamation was unjust. But guilt and fear were strong within her. At last she turned away and said in a small voice, "I'm sorry."

"You're reacting naturally. I expected it all." The understanding woman allowed Catherine to regain composure, but it was her responsibility to delineate all choices clearly; thus, she went on.

Catherine again listened to the facts—adopted children tend to develop to their fullest potential; adopted children are as well- or better-adjusted as many children who live with their birth parents; child abuse is almost nonexistent in adoptive families; parents who adopt are generally in an above-average income bracket; the adopted child runs a better chance of graduating from college than if parented by an unwed mother.

A great vise seemed to tighten, thread by thread, at Catherine's temples. She dropped to the sofa, her head falling back as an overwhelming weariness pervaded her.

"You're telling me to give it up," she said to a shimmering reflection on the ceiling.

Mrs. Tollefson let the old guilt-laden term pass for the moment. "No . . . no, I'm not. I'm here to help you decide what is best for your welfare, and ultimately, for the child's. If I fail to make you aware of all eventualities, of all avenues open to you, and of all that may close, I am not doing my job thoroughly."

"How much time would I have to decide?" The question was a near whisper.

"Catherine, we try not to work with time limits here, which sounds ironic when each young woman is here for a limited time. But no decision should be made till the baby is born and you've regained your equilibrium."

Catherine considered this, then her concerns came tumbling out in an emotional potpourri. "Would that really happen? Would I resent the baby because he slowed me down? I only want to make a decent life for him so he won't have to live in the kind of home I had to live in. I set out to get a college education to make sure of that, only to find out, if I pursue it, I may defeat my purpose. I know what you said is true, and it would be hard. But a baby should have love, and I don't think anybody could love it as much as a real mother. Even if money is a problem, it seems like copping out to give the baby away because of the expense."

"Catherine." Mrs. Tollefson leaned forward, caring deeply, her face showing it. "You continue to use the term *give away*, as if you own the child and are rejecting him. Instead, think of adoption as perhaps a better alternative to parenting the child yourself."

Catherine's large blue eyes seemed to stare right through the woman before her. Finally she blinked and asked, "Have you ever seen anyone make it? With a baby, I mean?"

"All the way through college? Single parent? No, not that I can remember, but that's not to say you can't be the first."

"I could get . . ." She thought of Clay Forrester's offer of money. "No, I couldn't." Then she sighed. "It almost makes me look stupid for passing up an abortion, doesn't it?"

"No, not at all," the kind voice reassured.

Again Catherine sighed, blinked slowly and turned her eyes to the blue sky beyond the window. Her voice took on a rather dreamlike quality. "You know," she mused, "there's no feeling there yet. I mean, the baby hasn't moved or anything. Sometimes I find it hard to believe it's in there, like maybe somebody's just pulling this big joke on me." She paused, then almost whispered, "Freshman hazing . . ." But when she looked at Tolly again, there was true sadness in her face, and the realization that this was no hazing at all. "If I'm already feeling so protective when there's not even any evidence of life yet, what will I feel when he moves and kicks and rolls around?"

Mrs. Tollefson had no answers.

"Do you know, they say a baby has hiccups before it's born."

The room remained still again, flooded with late sunshine and emotion while Catherine dealt with possible eventualities. At last she asked, "If I decided to give him up—" A raised index finger stopped her. "Okay, if I decide on adoption as the best route, could I see him first?"

"We encourage it, Catherine. We've found that mothers who do not see their children suffer a tremendous guilt complex which affects them the rest of their lives." Then, studying Catherine's face carefully, Mrs. Tollefson posed a question it was necessary to ask. "Catherine, since he has not been mentioned so far, and since I do not see his name on the card, I must ask if the child's father should be a consideration in all of this."

The blond young woman rose abruptly and snapped, "Absolutely not!"

And had her attitude not changed so quickly, Mrs. Tollefson might have believed Catherine.

The records office of the U of M refused to give out Catherine's home address, thus it took Clay three days to spot her again, crossing the sprawling granite plaza before Northrup Auditorium. He followed at a discreet distance as she cut between buildings, following the maze of sidewalks until finally at Fifteenth Avenue she turned northward. He kept sight of her blue sweater with the blond hair swaying upon it until she turned into a street of old homes that had been stately in their younger day, but hovered now behind massive boulevard trees in a somewhat seedy reflection of the grandeur they once knew. She entered a gargantuan yellow brick three-story with an enormous wraparound porch. The house had no marking other than a number, but while Clay stood wondering, a very pregnant woman came out and stood on a chair to water a hanging fern. He might not have thought anything of it if he hadn't suddenly realized, as she turned, that she was not a woman, but was, instead, a young girl of perhaps fourteen. As she raised up on tiptoe to fetch down the plant, the sight of her swollen stomach triggered Clay's suspicion. He looked again for a sign, but there was none, nothing to indicate it was one of those homes where girls went to wait out their pregnancies. But when the girl returned inside, Clay wrote down the house number and headed back toward the campus to make some phone calls.

By the time Catherine had been at Horizons a week and a half she found herself accepted without question and knew her first taste of sorority. Because so many of the girls were in their young teens, they looked up to Catherine, who, as a college student, seemed to them much more worldly. They saw her leaving each day to pursue an outside life while they themselves had forfeited theirs for the duration of the stay, and their admiration grew. Because Catherine owned a sewing machine that was often in demand, her room came to be the gathering place. Here she heard their stories: Little Bit was thirteen and wasn't sure who was the father of her baby; plain-faced Vicky was sixteen and didn't talk about the father of hers; Marie, age seventeen, spoke amiably about her Joe, and said they still planned to get married as soon as he graduated from high school; the unkempt Grover said the father of her baby was the captain of her high-school football team and had taken her out on a bet with a bunch of his team members. There were some residents of Horizons who cautiously avoided getting too close to anyone, others who brazenly swore they'd get even with the boy responsible, but the majority of the girls seemed not only resigned to living there, but enjoyed it. Especially nights like this when, all together, a group was working on a pair of nightgowns for Little Bit to wear during her hospital stay, which wasn't far off.

By now Catherine was accustomed to the banter at times like these; it was a combination of teasing and gaunt truths.

"Someday I'm gonna find this guy and he's gonna have hair like . . ."

"Don't tell me. Let me guess—hair like Rex Smith."

"What's the matter with Rex Smith?"

"Nothing. We've just heard the story before and how he's just going to *know* you're the woman he was made for."

"Listen, kiddo, don't forget to tell him somebody else thought the same thing before him." Laughter followed.

"I want to be married like Ali McGraw in *Love Story* . . . you know, make up my own words and stuff."

"Fat chance."

"Fat chance? Did somebody say *fat* chance?"

"Hey, I'm not always going to be shaped like a pear."

"I want to go to school and learn to be one of those ladies who cleans teeth. The kind of job where you nestle the guy's head in your lap so you can move in close and throw your charms at him."

Laughter again.

"I'm never gonna get married. Men aren't worth it."

"Hey, they're not all bad."

"Naw, only ninety-nine percent of 'em!"

"Yeah, but it's that other one percent that's worth looking for."

"When I was little and my folks were still together, I used to look at this picture of them on their wedding day. It used to sit in their bedroom on the cedar chest. Her dress was silk and there were little pearls on top of her veil and it trailed way around the floor in front. If I ever get married, I'd like to wear that dress . . . 'cept I think she threw it away."

"Wanna know something funny?"

"What?"

"When Ma got married she was pregnant . . . with me."

"Yeah?"

"Yeah. But she didn't seem to remember it when I told her I wanted to get married."

And so the talk went. And somebody always suggested going down to the kitchen for fruit. Tonight it was Marie who won the honors. She waddled downstairs and was passing the hall phone when it rang.

"Phone call . . . Anderson!"

When Catherine came to pick it up, Marie was leaning a shoulder against the wall, a curious half-smile on her face.

"Hi, Bobbi," she answered, glancing at Marie.

"Guess again," came the deep voice over the line.

The blood dropped from Catherine's face. She sucked in a quick breath of surprise and remained motionless for a moment, gripping the phone, before the color seeped back up her neck again.

"Don't tell me. You followed me." Marie continued toward the kitchen then, but she'd heard all she needed to hear.

"That's right. It took me three days, but I did it."

"Why? What do you want from me?"

"Do you realize how ironic it sounds to have *you* asking *me* that question?"

"Why are you *hounding* me?"

"I have a business proposition for you."

"No, thank you."

"Don't you even want to hear it?"

"I've been propositioned—so to speak—by you once already. Once was enough."

"You really don't play fair, do you?"

"What do you want!"

"I don't want to talk about it on the phone. Are you free tomorrow night?"

"I already told you—"

"Spare me the repetition," he interrupted. "I didn't want to put it this way but you leave me no choice. I'm coming to get you tomorrow night at seven o'clock. If you won't come out and talk to me, I'll tell your father where to find you."

"How dare you!" Her face grew intense with rage.

"It's important, so don't put me to the test, Catherine. I don't want to do it, but I will if I have to. I have a feeling he might have ways to get you to listen to reason."

She felt cornered, lost, hopeless. Why was he doing this to her? Why now, when she'd at last found a place where she was happy, couldn't her life be peaceful? Bitterly, she replied, "You're not leaving me much choice, are you?"

The line was silent for a moment before his voice came again, slightly softer, slightly more understanding. "Catherine, I tried to get you to listen to me the other day. I said I didn't want to put it that—"

She hung up on him, frustrated beyond endurance. She stood a moment, trying to collect herself before going back upstairs. The phone rang again. She clamped her jaw so hard that her teeth hurt, put a hand on the receiver, felt it vibrate again, picked it up and snapped, "What do you want this time!"

"Seven o'clock," he ordered authoritatively. "Be ready or your father finds out!"

Then he hung up on her.

"Something wrong?" Marie asked from the kitchen doorway.

Catherine jumped, placing a hand on her throat. "I didn't know you were still there."

"I wasn't. Not for very long anyway. I just heard the last little bit. Was it anyone important?"

Distractedly, Catherine studied Marie, small, dark, her doll's face an image of perfection, wondering what Marie would do if Joe had just called wanting to talk to her tomorrow night at seven.

"No, nobody important."

"It was him, wasn't it?"

"Who?"

"The father of your baby."

Catherine's face turned red.

"No use denying it," Marie went on, "I can tell."

Catherine only glared at her and turned away.

"Well, you didn't see the color of your face or the look in your eyes when you picked up that phone and heard his voice."

Catherine spun around, exclaiming, "I have no look in my eyes for Clay Forrester!"

Marie crossed her arms, grinned and raised one eyebrow. "Is that his name, Clay Forrester?"

Infuriated with herself, Catherine spluttered, "It—it doesn't matter what his name is. I have no look in my eyes for him."

"But you can't help it." Marie shrugged as if it were a foregone conclusion.

"Oh, come on," Catherine said in exasperation.

"Once you've been in this place you realize that no girl who comes here is immune to the man who's the other half of the reason she's here. How could she be?"

Although Catherine wanted to deny it, she could not. It was true that when she'd heard Clay Forrester's voice something had gone all barmy in the pit of her stomach. She'd grown shivery and hot all at once, light-headed and flustered. How could I! she berated herself silently. How could I react so to the mere voice of a man who—two months after the fact!—forgot that he'd ever had sexual intercourse with me?

SEVEN

The minute she came home from classes the following afternoon, Catherine knew something was up. The atmosphere was charged, the girls giddy, giggly. Everyone turned suddenly helpful, advising her to go upstairs and get her studying done right away, not to worry about setting the table—Vicky would do it for her. Someone suggested she do her nails and Marie suggested, "Hey, Catherine, how about if I blow-dry your hair? I'm pretty good at it, you know."

"I did it this morning, thanks."

Behind her back Marie made an exasperated gesture, followed by a rash of questions about whether or not Catherine had ever worn purple eyeshadow. Apricot blush? White lip liner? By the time she went down to supper Catherine accosted the crew with a sly look on her face. "All right, you guys, I know what you're up to. Marie's been talking, hasn't she? But this is *not* a date, so don't misconstrue it as one. Yes, someone's coming for me, but I'm going exactly as I am." There stood Catherine, confronting the whole dining room full of critical faces, dressed in faded blue jeans and an outsize flannel shirt, looking like she should be slopping hogs.

"In that!" Marie fairly choked.

"There's nothing wrong with this."

"Maybe not for a game of touch football."

"Why should I primp? I told you, it's *not* a date."

"The word is out, Catherine," Grover proclaimed. "We all know it's *him*!"

Marie, without question the group leader, put a hand on her hip and sing-songed, "Not a date, huh? What'sa matter, Catherine, is he old and feeble or something? Hasn't he got any hair on his legs?"

They all started laughing, Catherine included. Someone else picked up the teasing, carrying it forward. "Maybe he's got body odor! Or halitosis. No, I know! Ringworm! Who'd want to dress up for a guy with ringworm?" By now they were circling Catherine as if she were a maypole. "I know, I bet he's married." But what had started out to be funny suddenly angered Catherine, who saw the girls as a pack of feral animals, nipping at her, closing in for the final attack.

"Nope, I know he's not married," Marie informed the group. "It's got to be something else."

"A priest then, a man of the cloth. Oh, shame, shame, Catherine."

"I thought you were my friends!" she exclaimed, confused and hurt.

"We are. All we want to do is see you dolled up for your fella."

"He's not my fella!"

"You bet he's not, and he won't be either if you don't get out of those everyday rags and paint your nails."

"I am not painting my nails for Clay Forrester. He can go to hell, and so can all of you!" Catherine broke from the circle and ran upstairs.

But she was not allowed to sulk, for momentarily Marie appeared, leaning against the door frame. "Tolly doesn't allow anybody to skip meals around here, so you'd better get back down there. The girls were just having a little fun. They're all quite a bit younger than you, you know, but you're the one who's acting childish by coming up here and sulking."

Catherine threw a derisive glance at her roommate. "I'll be back down," she said coldly, "but tell the girls to lay off! It's nobody's business how I dress."

Supper was an uncomfortable affair for Catherine, but the rest carried on as if nothing had happened. She sat stonily, her nerves as taut as fiddle strings.

"Pass the strawberry jam," Marie requested, eyeballing a silent message to Vicky, on Catherine's left, then to Grover, who was refilling milk glasses. When Grover reached Catherine, she made sure a cold splat of milk landed in the angry girl's lap. Catherine's chair screeched back, but she only glared silently at Grover.

Marie's voice was as smooth as melted butter. "Why, Grover, can't you be more careful?"

Grover set down the milk carton, grabbed some napkins and made a show of swabbing the wet leg of Catherine's jeans. Titters started around the table as Catherine viciously yanked the napkins away and said icily, "It's okay, forget it."

But as she leaned forward to pull her chair back up to the table, a hand shot out from her left, bearing a biscuit, oozing jam. The sticky strawberries caught Catherine on the left temple, smearing into her hair, ear and eyebrow.

"Oh, my, look what I've done," Vicky said innocently.

Catherine leaped up, anger bubbling uncontrollably. "What kind of conspiracy is this! What have I done to make you all so hateful?"

Just then Marie, their ringleader, arose, wearing her piquant smile, and came to put her arms around Catherine. "We only want to help." Catherine stood in the circle of Marie's unwanted hug, holding herself stiff.

"Well, you have a strange way of showing it."

But just then Marie drew back with a false gasp, and Catherine felt something warm and cloying plastering her shirt against her back where Marie's arm had been.

"Now I've really done it. I got gravy on your shirt, Catherine." Then with a sly glance at all her coconspirators, Marie suggested, "We'll just have to see what we can do about it, won't we, girls?" And standing back, hands on hips, the shorter girl surveyed Catherine critically. "Have you ever seen such a mess in your life?"

Catherine, dumbfounded, only now began to suspect the method behind their madness as smiles bloomed all around the table. One by one they passed her on their way upstairs, each offering something.

"You really should wash your hair. I have a bottle of strawberry shampoo."

"And I have some yummy Village Bath Oil you can borrow."

"I haven't done my laundry yet. If you'll leave your jeans and shirt in the hall, I'll throw them in with my stuff."

"Institution soap is the pits. I'll leave mine in the bathroom."

Marie swiped a finger across Catherine's temple, then sucked the jam from it. "Yuck! I guess we'll have to give you a fresh hairdo after all."

"For heaven's sake, get her upstairs and do something with that jam, Marie!"

Marie winked at Catherine, reached out a small hand, waiting. In the moment before she placed her own in it to be led upstairs, Catherine felt a lump lodge in her throat, a curious, new growing thing, a learning thing, a trusting thing. But before she quite decided how to deal with it, she was in their hands.

Many times during the next hour Catherine raised her eyes to Marie's in the mirror, understanding now, feeling warmed and grateful because they cared—they all cared so very much. "You're crazy, you know," she laughed, "you're all a little bit crazy. It's not even a date."

"By the time we get done, it will be," Marie deemed.

The pile of makeup that appeared would have put Cleopatra to shame. With gratitude but reservation, Catherine accepted pedicure, manicure, coiffure, jewelry, even lacy underwear, all offered with the best and most optimistic intentions. After holding her dress while she slipped it on, the stubby Marie stood on top of one of the beds to fasten a gold chain around Catherine's neck.

"Hey, when you gonna grow up, Marie?" someone quipped.

"Hadn't you noticed?" she rubbed her belly. "I'm growing daily, only in the wrong direction." Laughter followed, but subdued now, almost reverent, while Catherine stood in their midst, looking unbelievably lovely.

"Go on, have a look," Marie prompted, nudging Catherine's shoulder.

Catherine walked to the mirror, fully expecting to see a Kewpie doll looking back at her. But she was stunned at the surprisingly lovely woman reflected there. Her hair was glowing, flowing back from her face as if its golden streaks were blowing in the wind. The makeup had been done tastefully, giving her cheeks a delicate, hollow look, her blue eyes a new luminous size and glitter. The gloss on her lips reflected a bead of light, as if she'd just passed her tongue along them and left them provoca-

tively wet. Small gold hoops at her ears complemented the shadowed length of her neck and emphasized her delicate jawline,
while the loop of gold around her neck drew her eyes downward
to the open collar of the soft, blue wool shirtwaist with its long
sleeves and front closure. The collar stood up in back, flared
open in front, leaving a bit of exposed skin above the highest
button.

Without conscious thought, Catherine lifted a manicured
fingertip and touched the hollow of her right cheek, the hollow
she'd never been aware of before. Her own sober eyes stared
back at her approvingly, but with a new worry in them.

My God, she thought, what will Clay Forrester think?

Behind her the girls observed the telling movement of her
fingers upon her own cheek, the hand that rested briefly upon
her pulsing heart as if to say, "Can it be?" And while the silent
group stared, a frowsy, brown-haired fifteen-year-old with tortoiseshell glasses came forward. In the mirror, Catherine saw her
coming and fought to control emotions that bubbled up and
threatened. She did not want to be their hope. She did not want
Clay Forrester to think she'd done all this for him. But while the
hopelessly plain Francie came forward, Catherine knew that for
this one evening she was doomed to play the role these girls so
desperately needed her to play.

Francie, who had never spoken a word to Catherine before,
came forward, bearing a bottle of Charlie perfume.

"Here," she said. "I stole this from you."

Catherine turned to take the bottle, smiling into Francie's
eyes, which held no more sparkle than cold dishwater. "I have a
couple of different kinds. Why don't you keep it?" But as Francie
extended the bottle, Catherine could see the girl's hand tremble.

"But this one must be your favorite. It's the most used up."

Francie's eyes impaled her, wavering neither right nor left. Then Catherine smiled and took the bottle and sprayed herself lightly behind her ears and on her wrists. When she finished she said, "You're right, Francie, it is my favorite, but why don't you put it on your dresser and when I want it, I'll just come in and take a squirt."

"Really?" Had Catherine been a movie star who suddenly stepped off the screen to materialize before Francie in flesh and blood, the girl could not have been more awed.

This is ridiculous, thought Catherine. I'm not Cinderella. I'm not what they want me to be. But something stung her eyelids as she pushed the bottle of perfume more firmly into Francie's hands, undone by the look in the younger girl's eyes.

Marie, still standing on the bed, broke the tension by quipping, "I think this is what's called a pregnant silence."

So Catherine was saved from tears, and Francie was saved from shame, and everyone laughed and began drifting from the room until Catherine was left alone with Marie. Impulsively she gave the shorter girl a hug.

"Mutt and Jeff, aren't we?" Marie joked.

"I don't know what to say. I misjudged all of you earlier. I'm sorry."

"Hey"—Marie reached to fix a certain curl at the side of Catherine's cheek—"we laid it on a little heavy. We understand."

"So do I . . . now."

"You're going for all of us, Cath."

"I know, I know."

"Just hear him out, okay?"

"But he's not coming to ask me to marry him. We already—"

"Just hear him out, that's all. Give the girls a little something to hope for. Pretend for them that it's real. Promise? Just for one night?"

"Okay, Marie," Catherine agreed, "for all of you. But what happens to their hopes when it doesn't come to anything?"

"You don't seem to realize that this is a first for them. Just give them something to talk about when he comes to the door. Be nice. Make them dream a little bit tonight."

Marie wondered how any man could resist a woman as beautiful as Catherine. Being short herself she naturally admired Catherine's height. Being dark, she admired her blondness. Being bubbly, she admired her reserve. Being round-faced, she admired the long elegance of Catherine's face. Catherine was everything that Marie was not. Perhaps that's why they felt so strangely drawn to each other.

"Hey, Cath," Marie said, "you're a knockout."

"No, I'm not. You just want me to be."

"This guy must be something to have a girl like you."

But just then someone hollered from downstairs, "Hey, what kind of car has he got?"

Knowing before she answered that her response was certain to raise a hullabaloo, Catherine mentally grimaced, then called, "A silver Corvette."

Marie looked like she'd swallowed a live crayfish. "A what!"

"You heard right."

"And you're resisting him! No wonder you look pained."

I do not look pained! thought Catherine. I *do not.*

From downstairs issued a noisy mingling of catcalls, wolf howls, whistles, and out-and-out girlish squeals, followed by violent shushing.

"Too bad you have to miss the talk after you leave," Marie giggled, smirking. "It'll be something tonight. Come on, Cleopatra, your barge has arrived."

Standing at the top of the stairs, Catherine told herself this was not Cleopatra's barge nor high-school prom nor Cinderella's ball. But as she clutched her knotted stomach, a little ache of expectation created a quiver there. A damning rush of blood crept up the V of exposed skin behind the blue collar. She could feel it as it rose and heated her cheeks.

This is insane, she told herself. The girls put ridiculous fancies in your head with all their giddy teenage fussing. So your nails are cinnamon and your hair is terrific and you're powdered and perfumed. But none of it is your doing, none of it is because a silver Corvette is coming to pick you up with Clay Forrester behind the wheel. So close your glistening lips, Catherine Anderson, and act like you're breathing normally and don't make more of an ass of yourself than you're already going to seem when he walks in that door and sees you!

Suddenly all the commotion stopped downstairs. Then footsteps ran in every direction and the silence that followed was ridiculous! Somebody, thankfully, got to the stereo and turned it on just as the doorbell rang.

Upstairs, Catherine felt a trembling begin somewhere down low in her groin and silently cursed every girl in this place for what they were forcing her to do. Down below she heard his voice and she closed her eyes, steadying herself.

"Is Catherine Anderson here?"

Suddenly Catherine wished she were a snail and could crawl inside her shell. Vicky's voice—utterly innocent, utterly fake—came clearly. "Just a minute, I'll see."

I'll see? thought Catherine, rolling her eyes behind closed lids. Oh, Lord!

"Catherine?" Vicky called up the stairs.

Behind her Marie whispered, "A silver Corvette, huh? Git going," and gave her a nudge.

The stairs came up to meet her high heels, and the clicks

sounded like gunshots in her ears. In a last panic she thought, I should have washed off the perfume and blotted that glossy lipstick. Damn you, damn you, damn you! What am I doing?

The town idiot would not have been fooled by the obvious lack of activity downstairs. The staged poses, the casually lounging bodies, strategically placed so that each girl could see into the hall from her vantage point in the living room, the Scrabble board on the dining room table with not a wooden letter on it, and every eye in the place trained on Clay Forrester who stood by the colonnade as if framed for display and purchase.

It might not have been so bad if he hadn't dressed up, too, but he had. He was wearing a gray Continental-cut suit that made him look like an ad for some high-priced Canadian whiskey. Catherine set her eyes on the top of his wine-colored tie; it was knotted so perfectly that it stood away from his neck like a crisp new hangman's noose. She let her gaze move up to the pale blue collar that cinched him just below the Adam's apple, where the bronze tan began.

"Hello," he said as casually as possible, considering that the change in her that made him feel like her old man's goon had only now smashed him in the stomach.

Oh, Christ! thought Clay Forrester. Oh, sweet Christ!

"Hello," she returned, trying to make the word as cool as a cucumber sandwich. But it came out wilted by the scorching heat of her face.

Her eyes were different, he thought, and her hair, and she was wearing an understated dress worthy of a travel ad in *The New Yorker*. Looking at her face again he saw that she was blushing. *Blushing.*

Catherine saw Clay's Adam's apple move like it was trying to dislodge a fish bone stuck in his throat. She bravely looked him in the face, knowing full well that her own was scarlet, silently warning him not to give away any hint of either surprise or approval. *Please!* But one glance told her it was too late. He, too, was red to the collar. To his credit, he acted as refined as his grooming, all except for one quick glance down at her stomach, followed by a quicker one at the crowd of gawking faces in the living room and dining room.

"Do you have a coat?"

Oh, God, she thought, October and I leave my coat upstairs!

"I left it up—"

But of all the girls, Marie finally did the right thing. She came down at an ungainly half-gallop, bringing the coat. "Here it is." And without any sign of ill ease, thrust out a hand toward Clay. "Hi, I'm Marie. Don't keep her out too late, okay?"

"Hi. I'm Clay and I won't." He smiled for the first time, shaking her hand firmly.

Jumping Jehoshaphat! thought Marie, he looks good enough to eat! And that smile. Look at that smile!

So when Catherine reached for her coat, Marie handed it instead to Clay. Correctly trained young swain that he was, he did the proper thing, and Catherine gratefully faced the door as he slipped the coat over her shoulders.

"Have a good time," Marie said.

"Good night," Catherine wished them all.

Like a kindergarten class, they all said in unison, "Good night."

Wanting to disappear into thin air, she reached for the doorknob, but Clay's hand shot around her, forcing her to allow him to open it for her or contest his gallantry before the girls.

Catherine dropped her hand and moved out into the blessedly cool October night that touched her scorching skin in sweet relief. But still from behind them, Clay and Catherine could feel the eyes that peered out of every front window of the house.

Following her to the car, Clay caught the smell of a pleasant scent threading from her, heard the tap of high heels on the sidewalk, saw in the beam from the porch light the back of her artfully arranged hair. And although he hadn't intended to, he walked first to her side of the car and opened her door, conscious yet of all those curious eyes, his mind half on them, half on the long legs Catherine pulled into the car.

Indoors, a chorus of giddy sighs went swooning.

Within the car, the atmosphere was so tense and silent even the low rumble of the engine was welcome as Clay turned the key. Carefully, Catherine kept her eyes off him—something about a man and his car and the things he does when he gets into it, moving to start it, touching things on the dash, folding himself into the seat, the way the shoulder of a suit coat ridges high as he reaches for the mirror, disarming things that are too peculiarly masculine for comfort. She kept her eyes straight ahead.

"Where do you want to go?"

She looked at him at last. "Listen, I'm sorry about that in there. They . . . well, they . . ."

"It's all right. Where do you want to go?"

"It's not all right. I don't want you to get the wrong impression."

"I think the windows still have eyes." There was a touch of amusement in his tone as he waited, seemingly at ease now with his hands on the familiar wheel.

"Anywhere . . . I don't care. I thought we'd just go ride and sit somewhere in the car and talk like we did the other time."

The car moved away from the curb and she felt his quick assessing glance and knew he was adding up the dress, the hair, the makeup, the high heels. She wanted to die all over again. Go for a ride, indeed, she could hear him thinking.

"Do you drink?" he asked, taking his eyes back to the street.

She shot him a look, remembering last summer and that wine. "I can take it or leave it. Most of the time I leave it."

He thought of her father and thought he knew why.

"I know of a quiet place where the music doesn't start up till nine. It should be uncrowded this early and we can have a drink there while we talk, okay?"

"Fine," she agreed.

He pulled out onto Washington Avenue, heading toward downtown, across the Mississippi River. The silence grew uncomfortable so he reached, found a tape, engaged it in the deck, all without taking his eyes from the road. It was the same kind of music as before, too pulsing for her taste, too lacking in subtlety and musicality. Just a bunch of noise, she thought disparagingly. Once again she reached over and turned the volume down.

"You don't like disco?"

"No."

"Then you never tried dancing to it?"

"No. If I danced anything it would be ballet, but I never had the chance to take lessons. But people used to say I'd make a good ballet dancer." She realized she was rambling on to hide her nervousness.

He sensed it, too, and replied simply, "They were probably right." He recalled where the level of her hair had matched his eyebrows.

She considered telling him that her father's beer and whiskey had sopped up all the spare money that might have meant ballet lessons, but it was too personal a comment. She wanted to avoid delving into personalities at all costs.

"Are all those girls back there pregnant?" he asked.

"Yes."

They stopped for a red light and Clay's face took on an un-earthly tint as he looked at her. "But they're all so young."

"I'm the oldest one there."

She could sense his amazement, and suddenly she was chattering as fast as if this were a debate she wanted to win. "Listen, they won't believe this isn't a date. They *want* it to be a date. They want it so badly *they* did all of this to me. We were at sup-per and . . ." And the whole story came tumbling out, all about how they messed her up, then fixed her up as if she were a high priestess. "And I couldn't make them understand they were wrong," Catherine ended. "And it was awful . . . and wonder-ful . . . and pathetic."

So that's why, he thought. "Don't worry about it, okay? I understand."

"No! No! I don't think you do. I don't think you possibly can! They're making me their—their emissary!" She threw her palms up hopelessly, and related the tale about Francie and the perfume and how she was forced to put it on.

"So you smell terrific and you don't want to?"

"Don't be funny. You know what I'm trying to say. What could I do besides use the perfume, with a kleptomaniac looking at me with big eyes, begging me to make something in her life okay?"

"You did the right thing."

"I did what I had to do. But I wanted you to know it was out of my hands. When you arrived I wanted to die because I thought you'd think I—I had designs on you."

By now they'd pulled into a parking lot where a neon sign identified the place as The Mullion. Clay killed the motor, turned to her and said, "All right, I admit it was pretty uncomfortable there for a minute, but just so their efforts won't have been for nothing, you can tell them I said you look fantastic."

"That's not what I was fishing for, don't you understand!"

"Yes, I do. But if you make anything more of it by being so insistent, I'll think you really do have designs on me." Already Clay knew the signs warning of her approaching anger. So he got out quickly, slammed the door and came to open hers.

And though she simmered from his last comment, she couldn't help wondering, as they crossed the parking lot, why he'd worn that expensive suit.

EIGHT

The Mullion took its name from the series of leaded bay windows facing east across the river. Clay touched Catherine's elbow, leading her to a table placed within a deep-set bay that afforded semi-privacy, surrounded on three sides as it was by leaded glass and the night beyond. He reached for her coat, but she held it on like armor, sitting down before he could pull her chair out for her.

He sat down opposite, asking, "What will you have to drink?" He noticed how she now removed her coat by herself and let it fall back over the chair.

"Something soft."

"Wine?" he suggested. "White?" It was disconcerting that he remembered she preferred white to red. But then, in the early part of the evening on their one and only date, they'd been quite sober, sober enough for him to remember such a thing.

"No, softer. Orange juice—unadulterated."

He let his gaze drift to her stomach momentarily before looking back up to find her expression unreadable.

"They encourage the drinking of fruit juice there," she said, enlightening him.

Their eyes met, his rather sheepish, she thought, and she quickly looked away at the lights of automobiles threading their way across the Washington Avenue bridge, creating bleeding, golden shimmers in the water's reflection. Clay surprised Catherine by ordering two unadulterated orange juices. She braved a glance at him, but quickly shifted her eyes away. She couldn't help wondering if the baby would look like him.

"I want to know your plans," he began, then added pointedly, "first."

"First?" She met his eyes. "First before what?"

"Before I tell you why I brought you here."

"My plans should be obvious. I'm living in a home for unwed mothers."

"Don't be obtuse, Catherine. Don't make me eke every answer out of you again. You know what I'm asking. I want to know what you're planning to do with the baby after it's born."

Her face hardened. "Oh, no, not you, too."

"What do you mean, not me, too?"

"Just that every time I turn around lately somebody wants to know what I plan to do with the baby."

"Who else?"

She considered telling him it was none of his business, but knew it was. "Mrs. Tollefson, the director of Horizons. She says her job is not to find babies for the babyless, but any way you slice it, that's what she does."

"Are you planning to give it away, then?"

"I don't consider that anyone's business but my own."

"Meaning, you're having trouble coming to a decision?"

"Meaning, I don't want you to be part of that decision."

"Why?"

"Because you're not."

"I'm the father."

"You're the sire," she said, impaling him with a stabbing look that matched her words. "There is a big difference."

"Funny," he said in some strangely colorless voice, "but it doesn't seem to make any difference when I think of it."

"Are you saying you're suffering a fit of conscience?"

"That baby's mine. I can't just wipe it off the slate, even if I want to."

"I knew this would happen if I saw you. That's why I didn't want to. I don't want any pressure from you to either keep the baby or give it away. The responsibility is mine. Anyway, what happened to the man who offered me money for an abortion?"

"You may recall that I was under a bit of duress at the time. It was a quick reaction. Whether or not I'd have wanted you to go through with it, I don't know. Maybe I just wanted to know what kind of person you are."

"Well, I'm afraid I can't enlighten you, because I don't know what I'm going to do yet."

"Good," he said, surprising her.

The waitress arrived just then with two tall, skinny glasses of orange juice on the rocks.

Clay reached into an interior breast pocket, and Catherine automatically reached for her purse. But before she could retrieve her wallet Clay had laid a five-dollar bill on the tray.

"I want to pay for my own."

"You're too late."

The sight of his money being taken away unnerved her.

"I don't want . . ." But it was hard for her to explain what she didn't want.

"You don't want me buying orange juice for my baby?"

She stared at him, unblinking, trying to figure out her motives. "Something like that."

"The cost of a glass of orange juice doesn't constitute a lifelong debt."

"Skip it, okay? I feel you're infringing on me and I don't like it, that's all. Taking me out, buying me drinks. Just don't think it changes anything."

"All right, I won't. But I'll reiterate something that does. Your father."

"Have you told him—" she began accusingly.

"No, I haven't. He doesn't have any idea you're here. He thinks you're out in Omaha someplace. But he's been making a nuisance of himself in more ways than one, only he's sly enough to stop just short of getting pinned for anything. Now he's taken to sending his—shall we call them—emissaries around to the house occasionally to remind us that he's still waiting for a payoff."

"I thought he came himself."

"That was only the first time. There've been others."

"Oh, Cl—" She stopped herself from uttering his name, began again. "I—I'm sorry. What can we do about it?"

He was very much his lawyer-father's son as he leaned toward her, outlining the situation, his eyes intense, his expression grave. "I am a third-year law student, Catherine. I've worked very hard to get where I am, and I intend to graduate and be admitted to the bar this summer. Unfortunately, I also have to prove I'm morally upstanding. If your father continues his vendetta and it gets to the Board of Examiners that I've fathered a bastard, it could have serious repercussions. That's why we haven't pressed charges against your father so far. And while it has not been stated explicitly, it has been implied that even should I pass and be accepted to the bar, my father may deny me a place in the family practice if I've shirked my responsibility to you. Meanwhile, my mother walks around the house looking like I've just kicked her in a broken leg. Your father wants money. You want your whereabouts to remain unknown. People are pressuring you to give up the baby. A bunch of pregnant teenage girls see you as their hope for the future. What do you think we can do about it?"

The glass stopped halfway to her open, gleaming lips. "Now just a min—"

"Before you get angry, hear me out."

"Not if you say what I think you're going to say."

"It's a business proposition."

"I don't want to hear it."

Her face became highly colored and her hand shook. She turned her cheek sharply away, not quite hiding it behind a hand.

"Drink your orange juice, Catherine. Maybe it will cool you down and make you listen to reason. I propose that you marry me and we'll—"

"You're crazy!" she snapped, dumbfounded.

"Maybe," he said coolly, "maybe not."

She tried to push her chair back but he deftly hooked one foot around its leg, guessing she was preparing to bolt.

"You're really one for running out on unpleasantness, aren't you?"

"You're mad! Sitting there suggesting that we get married! Get your foot off my chair."

"Sit down," he ordered. "You're making a spectacle again."

A quick perusal told her he was right.

"Are you adult enough to sit here and discuss this level-headedly, Catherine? There are at least a dozen sensible reasons for us to get married. If you'll give me a chance, I'll delineate them, starting with your father . . ."

That, above all, made her ease back into her chair.

"Are you saying he's caused you to get beaten up more than once?"

"Never mind. The point is, I'm beginning to understand why you vowed never to see him benefit from this situation. He's not exactly what I'd call ideal father-in-law material, but I'd take him as a temporary one rather than give him what he wants. If you and I marry, he'll be forced to give up his harassment. And even if the Board of Examiners somehow learns that a baby is due, it won't throw a shadow on my reputation if you and I are already married. I know now that what you said is true—your father is not really interested in your welfare as much as he is in his own. But my parents are.

"I feel like a juvenile delinquent every time my mother throws those censuring looks at me. And for some ungodly reason, my father is right in there with her. They're feeling . . ." He glanced up briefly, then down at his glass ". . . they're feeling like grandparents, reacting as such. They want to keep the baby in the family. They've taken a stand they won't back down from. And as for me, I won't bore you with my emotional state. Suffice it to say that it bothers me immeasurably to think of the baby being given up for adoption."

"I didn't say I was going to."

"No, you didn't. But what will you do if you keep it? Live on welfare in some roach-infested apartment house someplace? Give up school?" Again he leaned both forearms on the table, accosting her with his too-handsome, Nordic features set in an expression of worry. "I'm not asking you to consider marrying me without getting something out of it. When I saw you crossing the campus the other day, I couldn't believe my eyes. I didn't know you were a student there. What are you using for money?"

She didn't answer; she didn't need him to know finances were tight for her.

"It's going to take you some time to get through, isn't it? Even without the baby?"

Again, no answer.

"Suppose . . . just suppose we marry, agreeing in advance that it will be only until I finish school and take my bar exams. Your father will leave both of us alone; you'll be able to keep the baby; I'll be able to get my *juris doctor*; I'll be taken into my father's practice. When that happens you'll have your turn, and I'll pay for your schooling and for the child's support. That's my proposition. From now until July, that's all. And six months after that we'll have our divorce. I can easily handle it, and it is far less damaging to a career than a bastard child."

"And who keeps the baby?"

"You do," he answered without hesitation. "But at least I won't lose track of him and I'll see to it that neither he nor you ever has any financial worries. You can keep the baby and finish school, too. What could be more sensible?"

"And what can be more dishonest?"

A look of exasperation crossed his face, but she knew that rankled, for he sat back in his chair and studied the lights across the river in a distracted fashion. She went on.

"You told me once that your father is the most exasperatingly honest person you know. What will he and your mother think when they learn their son has deceived them?"

"Why do they have to learn? If we do it, you'll have to agree never to tell them."

"Oh," she tossed out casually, knowing her remark was barbed, "so you don't want them to know you're a liar."

"I'm not a liar, Catherine. For God's sake, be reasonable." But he ran his fingers through his perfect hair and came forward on his chair again. "I'd like to finish law school and become part of my father's business. Is that so awful? That's the way we've always planned it, only now he seems to have lost reason."

She mused awhile, then toyed with her glass. "You never had to worry about your ship coming in, did you?"

"And you resent that?"

"Yes, I suppose in a way I do."

"Enough to reject my offer?"

"I don't think I could do it."

"Why?" He leaned forward entreatingly.

"It would require acting talent that I don't possess."

"Not for long. About a year."

"At the risk of sounding hypocritical, I have to say it: your parents seem like decent and honest people and it would not settle well with me to hoodwink them just to make things easier for myself."

"All right, I admit it. It's not honest, and that bothers me, too. I'm not in the habit of lying to them, no matter what you might think. But I don't think they're being totally honest, either, by taking the stand they've taken. They're forcing me to own up to my responsibilities, and I am. But, like you, I have a certain kind of life mapped out for myself, and I don't want to give it up because of this."

"There simply is no way I would marry someone I don't love. I've had a bellyful of living in a house where two people hated each other."

"I'm not asking you to love me. All I want is for you to think sensibly about the benefits we'd both derive from the arrangement. Let's backtrack a minute and consider one question which still needs answering. Do you want to give the baby up for adoption?"

He was leaning toward her now quite beseechingly. She studied the glass within his long, lean fingers, unwilling to look into his eyes for fear he might convince her of something she did not want.

"That's not fair and you know it." She spoke in a strained voice. "Not after what I told you about the girls and my conversation with Mrs. Tollefson."

He sensed her weakening and pressed on. "None of this is, is it? I'm no different than you, Catherine, no matter what you might think. I don't want that baby living with strangers, wondering for the rest of my life where he is, what he is, who he is. I'd like to at least know that he's with you, and that he's got everything he needs. Is that such a bad bargain?"

Like a recording she repeated what Mrs. Tollefson had said, hoping to shore up her defenses. "It's a well-known fact that adopted children are exceptionally bright, happy and successful."

"Who told you that, your social worker?"

Her eyes flashed to his. How easily he can read me, she thought. The waitress approached, and without asking Catherine, Clay signaled to order two more orange juices, more to get rid of the interference than because he was thirsty. He watched the top of Catherine's hair as she toyed with her glass. "Could you really give it up?" he asked softly.

"I don't know," she admitted raggedly.

"My mother was decimated when she found out you were gone. I never saw her cry in my life, but then I did. She didn't have to mention the word *abortion* more than once for me to know it was on her mind night and day. I guess I learned some things about my parents and myself since this thing happened."

"It's so dishonest," she said lamely. Then after long silence, she asked, "When are the bar exams?" She could not quite believe what she was asking.

"I don't know the exact date yet, but sometime in July."

She rested her forehead against her hand, as if unutterably tired of everything.

Suddenly he felt obliged to reassure her so he reached for her arm, which lay disconsolately on the tabletop. She didn't even try to resist the small squeeze he gave it.

"Think it over," he said quietly.

"I don't want to marry you, Clay," she said, raising her sad, beautiful eyes to him, a pinched expression about their corners.

"I know. I'm not expecting it to be a regular marriage, with all the obligations. Only as a means to what we both want."

"And you'd start divorce proceedings immediately after the exams and you wouldn't use some clever tricks to get the baby away from me?"

"I would treat you fairly, Catherine. I give you my word."

"Would we live together?" Her eyelids flickered; she looked aside.

"In the same place, but not together. It would be necessary for my family to think we were married in more than name only."

"I feel utterly exhausted," she admitted.

Some musicians filed in, turned on some dim stage lights and began tuning up their guitars.

"There's not much more to be said tonight"—Clay fiddled with the table edge a moment—"only that I'd keep out of your way if you marry me. I know you don't like me, so I won't push anything like that."

"I don't dislike you, Clay. I hardly know you."

"I've given you plenty of good reason though, haven't I? I've gotten you pregnant, offered you abortion money, and now I'm suggesting a scheme to get us out of it."

"And am I so lily-white?" she asked. "I'm actually thinking it over."

"You'll consider it then?"

"You don't have to ask. Against my better judgment, I already am."

They drove back to Horizons in silence. As he pulled the car to a stop at the curb, Clay said, "I could come and pick you up at the same time tomorrow night."

"Why don't you just call?"

"There are too many inquisitive ears around here."

She knew he was right, and though it was difficult for her to be with Clay, neither did she want to give him her answer with an audience around the corner. "Okay, I'll be ready."

He let the engine run, got out and came around to open her door, but by the time he got there she was already stepping out of the car. He politely closed the door for her.

"You don't have to do all these things, you know, like opening doors and pulling out chairs. I don't expect it."

"If I didn't, would it make you feel better?" They walked toward the porch steps.

"I mean, you don't have to pretend it's *that* real."

"Force of habit," he said.

Under the garish light of the porch she at last dared to look directly into his face.

"Clay." She tested the word fully on her tongue. "I know you've gone with a girl named Jill Magnusson for a long time."

Catherine struggled to find a way to say what was on her mind, but found she couldn't say it.

He stood still as a statue, his expression void, unreadable. Then he reached for the screen door, opened it and said, "You'd better go in now."

He turned on a heel, took the steps in one leap and ran to the car. As she watched the taillights disappear up the street she felt, for the first time in her pregnancy, like throwing up.

NINE

The following day was one of those flawless Indian summer days in Minnesota that are like an assault on the senses. The warmth returned, dormant flies reawakened, the sky was deep azure, and the campus crimson and gold was vivid as autumn color peaked. It was October; new match-ups had been made, and to Catherine it seemed the entire population of the university moved in pairs. She found herself captivated by the sight of a male and a female hand with their fingers entwined, swinging between two pairs of hips. Without her consent her mind formed a picture of Clay Forrester's clean, lean hands on the wheel, and she wiped her damp palm on her thigh. She passed a couple kissing in the entrance to Tate Lab. The boy had his hand inside the girl's jacket just above her back waistline. Unable to tear her eyes away, Catherine watched his hand emerge from under the garment, then pass along the girl's ribs as the two parted, went their separate ways. She remembered Clay's words, *not a regular marriage with all the obligations*, and though that's what she, too, insisted it must be, there were goose bumps on her flesh. In the late afternoon, on her way home, she spotted a couple sitting on the grass Indian style, face-to-face, studying. Without taking his eyes from his book, the boy absently ran his hand up inside the girl's pantleg to her knee. And something female prickled down low inside of Catherine.

But I'm pregnant, she thought, and Clay Forrester doesn't love me. Still, that didn't make the prickly longing disappear.

Back at Horizons Catherine carefully changed clothes, though casually enough so as not to appear seductive. But when her makeup was complete, she looked closely in the mirror. Why had she reconstructed last night's careful shadings and highlights? Subtle mauve shadow above her eyes, a faint hint of peach below them, sandy brown mascara, apricot cheeks, glistening cinnamon lips to match her nails. She told herself it had nothing to do with Clay Forrester's proposal.

Turning from the dresser, Catherine found Francie waiting hesitantly in the doorway, wearing the first suggestion of a smile Catherine had seen on her face. In silence, Francie extended the bottle of Charlie.

Catherine forced a bright smile of her own. "Why, thank you, I was just coming to get it." The perfume followed the makeup, and a moment later Marie came in to say Clay had arrived.

When Catherine came downstairs, there was a first awkward moment while they each scanned the other's clothes and faces, that too-meaningful assessment making her heart thud heavily.

He was wearing navy blue trousers this time, stylishly pleated, and a V-necked sweater of pale blue lamb's wool. Beneath was an open collar, short tips clearly stating it was this season's style. He wore a simple gold chain around his neck, and it seemed to accent the golden hue of his skin. Admitting how utterly in vogue Clay always dressed, and how it pleased her,

Catherine wondered for the hundredth time that day if she was doing the right thing.

There was a feeling of unreality about walking out before him, passing through the door he held open, feeling him behind her shoulder as they took the porch steps and walked toward the car. She battled to submerge the feelings of familiarity that were already cropping up: the way he leaned sideways from the hip when he opened her car door, the hug of the bucket seat as she slid in, the sound of his footsteps coming around the car, his own peculiar movements as he settled into his seat. Then once again the smell of his shaving lotion in the confined space, and all of those thrice-noticed motions of a man and his car: already she knew in just which order he would do them, wrist over wheel as he started the engine, the unnecessary touch on the rearview mirror, the single shrug and forward jut of his head as he made himself comfortable, the way he left his hand on the stick of the floor shift as the Corvette pulled away from the curb. He was driving sensibly tonight. Instead of the tape deck, the radio was on this time, softly, voices proclaiming musically that they were tuned to KS-ninety-five. Then, without warning, The Lettermen began singing, "Well, I think I'm going out of my head . . ." And Clay just drove. And Catherine just sat. Each of them wanting to reach over and turn the song off. Neither of them daring. Lights coming, going, flashing, waning while the car moved through the mellow Indian-summer night, its engine cooing along on a note as rich as any coming from The Lettermen, whose song finally reached its medley stage and wove its way into words that were even worse: "You're just too good to be true . . . can't take my eyes off of you . . ."

Catherine thought she would do anything for some wildly pulsating disco! But she found she could not give credence to the meaningful words coming from the radio, so she braved it out until the song ended. When it did, Clay asked her a single question.

"Did the girls do all that to you tonight?"

But with the end of the suggestive song, she'd regained control of her senses. There was no reason to lie. "No."

He gave her a sidelong look, then tended to his driving again.

She somehow guessed where they would go. She needn't know the exact route to be sure of the destination. He drove as if it were predetermined, out onto the interstate, under the tunnel and west on Wayzata Boulevard to Highway 100, then south toward Edina. Again the unwanted feeling of familiarity crept over her. She had a sudden desperate hope that she might be wrong, that he'd choose to drive to some other place, thus avoiding the establishment of further familiarities. But he did not.

The wooded trail wound up into the park, taking them to the same secluded spot as that first night. He stopped at the top of the gravel road and switched off the engine but left the radio playing softly. Outside it was full dark, but the vague light from the dash illuminated his profile as he entwined his fingers behind the steering wheel and distractedly tapped a thumb upon it in time to the music.

Panic clawed its way up her throat.

At last he turned, propping his left elbow on top of the wheel. "Have you . . . have you thought about it any more or decided anything?"

"Yes." The lone syllable sounded strained.

"Yes, you've thought about it, or yes, you'll marry me?"

"Yes, I'll marry you," she clarified, with no hint of joy in her voice. She answered instead with a throb of regret tumbling her stomach. She wished he would not study her so and wondered if he was feeling as hollow as she was at that moment. She wanted to get out of the car and run down the gravel hill again. But where would she run? To what?

"Then we might as well work out a few details as soon as possible."

His businesslike tone thrust her back to reality.

"I suppose you don't want to waste any time?"

"Considering you're three months pregnant already, no I don't. I don't suppose you do either?"

"N-no," she lied, dropping her eyes to her lap.

A short, nervous laugh escaped him. "What do you know about weddings?"

"Nothing." She gazed at him helplessly.

"Neither do I. Are you willing to go and talk to my parents?"

"Now?" She hadn't expected it so soon.

"I thought we might."

"I'd rather not." In the dim light she looked panic-stricken.

"Well, what do you want to do then, elope?"

"I hadn't given it much thought."

"I'd like to go talk to them. Do you mind?"

What else could she do? "We'll have to face them sooner or later, I guess."

"Listen, Catherine, they're not ogres. I'm sure they'll help us."

"I have no illusions about what they must think of me and of my family. They can't be martyrs enough to be willing to forget all that my father has done. Can you blame me for being less than anxious to face them?"

"No."

They sat there thinking about it for a while. But neither of them knew the first thing about planning a wedding of any kind.

"My mother will know what to do."

"Yeah, like throw me out."

"You don't know her, Catherine. She's going to be happy."

"Sure," she replied sullenly.

"Well, relieved then."

But still they sat, aware of the sharp contrast between what *was* happening and what *should be* happening at a time like this.

Finally Catherine sighed. "Well, let's get it over with then."

Clay started the car abruptly. He took them back down the twisting streets, through the rolling neighborhoods of elegant lawns whose breadth spoke of estates rather than lots. She heard the unfamiliar sound of tires on cobblestone as they swept up the curve and stopped before that massive pair of front doors she had once studied so critically from inside. They cowed her now, but she made up her mind not to let it show.

Following Catherine to the house, Clay found himself think-ing of Jill Magnusson, and how it should be her going with him to speak to his parents.

The foyer assaulted Catherine with memories of the last time she'd been there: the way Clay had come breezing in and the scene that had followed. She found herself before the mirror, glanced quickly away from his regarding eyes and stopped her hand from touching a wisp of hair that was out of place. Dis-armingly, he read her thoughts.

"You look fine . . . Come on." And he took her elbow.

Angela looked up as they approached the study door. The sight of them stirred her warmest blood, made it race crazily at their unexpected arrival. They were like a pair of sun children, both of them blond, tall and strikingly beautiful. Nobody had to tell Angela Forrester how beautiful a child of theirs would be.

"Are we interrupting anything?" Clay asked. His father

glanced up from something he'd been working on at his desk. Everything in the room marked time for that interminable moment while they all allowed the surprise to run its course. Then Angela unwound her ankles in slow motion and removed a pair of reading glasses. Claiborne rose, halfway at first, as if stunned. He and Angela stared at Catherine, and she felt the blood whipping up her neck and fought the urge to duck behind Clay.

At last he spoke. "I think it's time you all met properly. Mother, Father, this is Catherine Anderson. Catherine, my parents."

And yet, for a painful moment more, the room remained a Still Life With Parents and Children.

Then Angela moved. "Hello, Catherine," she said, reaching out a flawless, jeweled hand.

Immediately Catherine sensed that Angela Forrester, like the girls at Horizons, was an ally. This woman wants me to marry her son, she thought, amazed.

But when Claiborne Forrester emerged from around his desk, it was with a less-welcoming mien, although he extended his hand and greeted Catherine, also. But where Angela's touch had been a warm peace offering, there exuded from her husband a coolness much the same as the other time Catherine had been in this room.

"So you found her, Clay," the older man noted unnecessarily.

"Yes, several days ago."

Angela and Claiborne looked at each other, then quickly away.

"Several days ago. Well . . ." But the word dangled there, leaving everything awkward again. "We're glad you've changed your mind and come back to talk things over a little more sensibly. Our first meeting was, well, shall we say, less than ideal."

"Father, could we forgo the obvious recrim—"

"No, it's all right," Catherine interrupted.

"I think we'd all better sit down." Angela motioned toward the love seat where she'd been sitting. "Catherine, please." Clay followed and sat down beside her. His parents took the chairs beside the fireplace.

Although her stomach was twitching, Catherine spoke calmly. "We thought it best to come and talk to you immediately."

The eagle's frown was there on Mr. Forrester's face, just as Catherine remembered it.

"Under the circumstances, I should certainly think so," the man said.

Clay edged forward as if to respond, but Catherine hurried to speak first. "Mr. Forrester, I understand that my father has been here more than just once. I want to apologize for his behavior, both the night I was with him and any other times when I wasn't. I know how irrational he can be."

Claiborne grudgingly found himself admiring the girl's directness. "I assume Clay has told you we have refrained from pressing charges."

"Yes, he has. I'm sorry that's what you decided. I can only say I had nothing to do with his actions and hope you'll believe me."

Again Claiborne felt an unwanted twitch of admiration at the girl's straightforward manner. "We, of course, know that Clay offered you money, and that you refused his offer. Have you changed your mind?"

"I haven't come here asking for money. Clay told me you haven't paid my father anything he demanded, but I'm not here pleading his case, if that's what you think. I never intended for any of it to happen. That night I came here I had already made plans to run away from home and make it look like I was headed across the country where he couldn't catch up with me. I thought when I was gone he'd leave you alone. If any of it could have been avoided by my staying, I'm sorry."

"I make no pretense of liking your father or of excusing him, but I must admit I'm relieved Clay found you so this mess can get straightened out once and for all. I'm afraid we've all been rather anxious and have been upset with Clay's behavior."

"Yes, he told me."

Claiborne quirked an eyebrow at his son. "Seems you and Clay have been doing a lot of talking lately."

"Yes, we have."

Whatever Clay had expected, it wasn't Catherine's cool control. He was pleasantly surprised by the way she was handling his father. If there was one thing Claiborne Forrester admired it was spunk, and she was displaying an inordinate amount of it.

"Have you come to any conclusions?" Claiborne pressed on.

"I think that's for Clay to answer."

"He didn't bother to tell us that he found you, you know."

"I made him promise he wouldn't. I'm living in a home for unwed mothers and didn't care to have my whereabouts known."

"Because of your father?"

"Yes, among other reasons."

"Such as?"

"Such as your son's money, Mr. Forrester, and the pressure it could exert on me."

"Pressure? He offered you money, which you refused to accept. Is that what you call pressure?"

"Yes. Isn't it?"

"Are you upbraiding me, Miss Anderson?"

"Are *you* upbraiding *me*, Mr. Forrester?"

The room crackled almost electrically for a moment before Claiborne admitted in a less accusing voice, "You surprise me. I hadn't expected your . . . detachment."

"I'm not at all detached. I've been through two very hellish weeks. I've been making decisions that haven't been easy."

"So have my wife and I, and—I dare say—Clay."

"Yes, he told me about your—I dare say—ultimatum."

"Call it what you will. I don't doubt that Clay represented it to you in anything but its true light. We were grossly disappointed in the lack of good judgment he showed and took steps to see that he not only own up to his responsibilities, but that he not ruin his chances for the future."

Angela Forrester sat forward then on the edge of her chair, legs crossed, leaning a delicate elbow on one knee. "Catherine," she said, her voice the first emotional one in the room, "please understand that I—we—have all been utterly distraught about your welfare and that of the child. I was so afraid you'd gone off to have an abortion anyway, in spite of what you told Clay."

Catherine could not help angling a quick glance at Clay, surprised that he'd told them he'd suggested abortion.

"They know everything that we talked about that night," he confirmed.

"You're surprised, Catherine?" Angela asked. "That Clay told us the truth or that we . . . rather . . . forced the issue?"

"At both, I guess."

"Catherine, we knew you were here against your wishes the first time. Believe me, Clay's father and I have asked ourselves countless times what is the right thing to do. We coerced Clay into bringing you back here, so are we any less guilty of force than your father?"

"My father is a man who doesn't know how to reason, or rather, who won't. Please don't think that I'm anything like him.

I . . ." Catherine looked down at her lap, her first outward show of inner turmoil. "I intensely dislike my father." Then she confronted Claiborne's eyes again, continuing. "You may as well know that part of the reason I am here now is to see that he doesn't bleed you for a single red cent, and that my reasons have little to do with altruism."

Claiborne rose, crossed back to his desk and seated himself behind it. He picked up a letter opener and began toying with it. "You're a very direct young woman."

Angela could tell this pleased her husband. While the girl's directness put her off somewhat, she was moved to sympathy by a daughter harboring such strong negative emotions for a father. The girl, it was obvious, was defensive about it, too, which meant she was hurt by it. All of this touched the mother in Angela.

"Does that bother you?" Catherine was asking.

"No, no, not at all," Claiborne blustered, ruffled that someone else controlled the conversational reins, which he was accustomed to controlling.

Again Catherine dropped her eyes to her lap. "Well, anyway, I don't have to live in the same house with him anymore."

Again Angela experienced a twinge of pity; her eyes met her husband's and went to Clay, who was studying Catherine's profile.

Clay dropped his hand from the back of the love seat onto the back of Catherine's neck, to the spot where he'd once detected the evidence of her father's abuse. Startled, she met his eyes, burned by the heat of his hand through her hair. Then the heat disappeared and Clay looked toward his father. "Catherine left home and arranged for her father to think she was running across the country so that she could continue school without being hassled by him."

Surprised, Claiborne asked, "You're a student?"

"Yes, at the university."

Again Clay spoke. "It goes without saying that she'd have a tough time of it with the baby. I managed to convince her that it was sensible to let me help with finances." He allowed a moment to pass silently before capturing Catherine's hand, pressing it onto his knee in a way she found embarrassingly familiar. "Catherine and I have talked everything over. Tonight I asked her to marry me and she accepted."

Angela carefully kept the pain from showing in her face, but her throat worked convulsively. The letter opener slipped from Claiborne's fingers and clattered onto the desktop. He then rested one elbow on each side of it and covered his face with both hands.

"We've agreed that it's best this way," Clay said quietly, and his father's eyes emerged from behind his fingertips just in time to see Catherine slip her hand cautiously off Clay's knee.

What have I done? thought Claiborne.

Angela murmured, "I'm so relieved," and wondered if she really was.

Claiborne could not help asking, "Are you sure?"

Catherine felt Clay's eyes pulling her own to his face. He gave her a secretive look that could easily be misinterpreted by his parents. Then he rested an elbow on the back of the sofa and laid a hand on her shoulder nearest his chest. "Catherine's friends and I have managed to convince her," he said, with just enough implied intimacy to give them the fully wrong impression.

Catherine felt her face redden.

Angela and Claiborne witnessed their son's eyes caressing the young woman's face, and their own startled eyes met. How could

this possibly have happened so quickly? Yet they each remembered that the two had been intimate once; apparently there was
some basis for attraction. Everything about Clay's attitude suggested it, and the girl's blush confirmed it. But sensing that
Catherine was displeased with the way Clay allowed his appetites
to show, Angela moved toward them, offering congratulations.
Claiborne rose and came to clasp their hands. When he held his
son's hand firmly within both of his, he said honestly, "We're
proud of your decision, Clay."

But there was an undeniably painful mixture of eagerness
and disappointment permeating the room. Feeling it, Catherine
thought this must be how a thief feels while casing victims who
are also friends.

It was some time later that the issue of the wedding came up
as Angela asked, unassumingly, "Do you want your father and I
in on the arrangements?"

"Of course," Clay answered without hesitation. "Catherine
and I don't know the first thing about planning a wedding."

"Why not have the wedding here?" Angela asked most unexpectedly.

It was immediately apparent Catherine had not thought that
far ahead. Angela placed a hand on her arm apologetically. "Oh,
forgive me, have I been too assuming? From the things you've
said about your father I thought perhaps . . ." But her words
trailed away, leaving an uncomfortable void. She realized she'd
put her foot in her mouth, something Angela Forrester rarely did.

Catherine attempted to ease the tension by affecting a wan
laugh. "No, no, it's all right. You're probably right. My father
wouldn't be inclined to lay out money when it was his intention
all along to realize a profit from this situation."

"But I've embarrassed you, Catherine, and that was not my

intention. I don't mean to usurp your parents' place, but I want you to understand that Clay's father and I would be more than happy to give both of you whatever you want in the way of a wedding. I simply don't want you to think we would stint you on anything. Clay is our only son—please understand, Catherine. This will happen only once. As his parents, we'd love to indulge in our dreams of a perfect wedding celebration. If you'd . . . well, if you'd both agree to have the service here at the house, we'd be utterly happy, wouldn't we, darling?"

Claiborne, looking rather lost and beleaguered, could only concur. But, goddammit, he thought. It should have been Jill. *It should have been Jill!* "What Angela says is true. We certainly are not strapped, and we'd be happy to foot the bill."

"I don't know yet," Catherine said, floundering in this new possibility that she hadn't considered.

"Mother, we haven't had a chance to talk about it yet," Clay explained.

Angela chose her words carefully, hoping that Clay would understand there were social obligations that people of their position must fulfill.

"I see no reason for either of you to feel you must sneak off like two chastised children. A marriage should be treated as a celebration. I . . . Catherine, I can see that I *have* embarrassed you, but please take our offer in the light it is intended. We can very easily afford to pay for a small affair here. Call it selfish, if you want to. Clay is our only son, you must understand."

"Mother, Catherine and I will talk it over and let you know."

To Clay, she said, "There are so many people who would be disappointed if you eloped—not the least of whom are your father and me. I'd like the family and a few close friends anyway.

You know how your grandparents would be hurt if they were not included. And I'm sure Catherine will want her family."

But neither Clay nor Catherine knew what the other's feelings were on the subject.

"Well"—Angela straightened her shoulders—"enough said. I've been rather premature, I realize, but whatever you decide, I know we can implement your plans."

"Thank you, Mrs. Forrester. We'll have to talk it over."

Again an awkward silence fell, and as if suddenly inspired, Claiborne clapped his hands with mock joviality, suggesting a glass of wine to honor the occasion.

Clay immediately seconded the motion, going to find an untapped bottle while Claiborne fetched four crystal goblets.

A glass of white wine of excellent vintage was placed in Catherine's hands. Momentarily the goblet blotted out Clay's face before its rim touched her lips, and above it she telegraphed Clay a message that he, thankfully, understood. The toast done, he took Catherine's glass from her hand and set it, along with his own, on the table.

"Catherine and I will see you . . . when, Catherine?" He looked to her. "Tomorrow night?"

So fast! she thought, things are moving so fast! But she found herself agreeing to tomorrow night.

Preparing to leave, Catherine tried to thank Angela, but Angela's eyes were unmistakably dewy as she said, "Things will work out." The diamonds upon her hands flashed as she made a gesture of command with the wineglass. "Go now," she finished, "and we'll see you tomorrow."

As she left the room where Claiborne and Angela stood with their arms around each other's waists, Catherine found herself comparing them to her own parents and admitted that the Forresters did not deserve to be deceived. They were the "rich sons-abitches" her father despised, whom she'd nearly caught herself despising. But she saw them now only as a mother and father who wanted nothing but the best for their son. Leaving their house Catherine thought, I'm no better than my father.

TEN

Outside, it had turned colder, and a spiritless rain had begun. The heater, not yet warmed up, breathed clammy air onto Catherine's legs as she girded her knees with both hands to keep from shivering.

Headed back to Horizons, Clay asked peremptorily, "Well, what do you think?"

"I have a feeling this thing is going to get out of hand right before our very eyes. I never thought your mother would come up with such a suggestion."

"I didn't either, but I guess I didn't have time to think. Still, it's better than the whole church thing with a thousand guests, isn't it?"

"I don't know what I expected, but it wasn't grandpas and grandmas." Somehow Clay Forrester seemed too chic to have grandparents hidden somewhere in the woodwork.

"I didn't evolve from a splitting cell, you know," he said, attempting to inject a little humor into the otherwise humorless situation.

"Right now I almost wish you had. Me too."

"Don't you have any grandparents?"

"No, they're all dead. But if I did, I think I'd burn an effigy on their front lawn to protest their having an offspring like my dad. Clay, I will not have that man at our wedding, no matter what."

"Well, it wouldn't hurt my feelings not to invite him, but how can you leave him out and still have your mother? Is that what you're suggesting?"

"I don't know what I'm suggesting. This whole idea of a—a real *ceremony* is . . . well, it's preposterous! My old man would get pickled and become obnoxious as usual and the whole scene would be worse than any so far. Either that, or he'd go around telling all the guests how his ship just came in!"

"Well, I don't see how we can avoid him."

"*Clay!*" she said in an I-don't-believe-this tone of voice.

"What? What does that mean—*Clay?*" He repeated her exact tone of disbelief.

"You really want to go along with this whole shindig, don't you? I mean, you think we should let your mother go through with all the preparations and the expense of a real wedding, and let them believe it's for keeps?"

"If she wants to do it, let her do it. She's in her glory when she's organizing what she calls her 'little social events,' so let her organize one. Who's it going to hurt?"

"Me! I feel like a felon already, planning what we're planning. I don't want to haze your parents any more than necessary."

"Catherine, I think you have to put things into perspective. The whole occasion will probably cost less than one of the rings on my mother's hands. So why not let her have her fun?"

"Because it's dishonest," she said stubbornly.

He grew a little irritated. "That fact is already established, so what's the difference how we go about it as long as we're going to go about it anyway?"

"Can't we just go off to some justice of the peace or something?"

"We can if that's what you really want. But I think it would only hurt my parents more. I don't know about yours—your mother anyway—but I doubt that she'd be too disappointed to see you getting married with a show of my parents' support. That's really what it boils down to, you know. My parents have chosen to accept our marriage and want it known that they do. Isn't that what weddings are all about?"

"No. Most weddings are about a lifelong commitment between a man and a woman."

But Clay sensed something more behind Catherine's refusal. "You wouldn't like any *vile ostentation* on your account, is that it? Especially if the bill was picked up by the despicable rich you've been cultured to hate so much?"

At the beginning that had been part of it, but no longer. "Okay, I'll admit it, I've been prejudiced by my father's prejudices against the rich. And yes, I had preformed notions about what your family would be like, but your parents are not bearing them out."

Clay worked the edges of his teeth together, noting that she did not include him in her summary of findings. "You mean you like them?"

But Catherine had decided that liking them was a pitfall she would do well to guard against.

"I respect them," she answered truthfully, "and that in itself is something new for me."

"Well then, couldn't you respect their wishes and go along with my mother?"

Catherine sighed heavily. "Lord, I don't know. I'm not very good at any of this. I don't think I ever should have agreed to it."

"Catherine, whatever you might think, my mother is not a manipulator. She does try to do things in the accepted fashion, and I haven't mentioned it before, but I know that part of the reason for a reception of some kind is political. It may not have been mentioned, but business etiquette requires invitations to occasions such as these for certain long-established associates who have become more than just business connections down through the years. Some of them are close personal friends of my parents by now. I'm sorry if that lays an extra burden on you, but that's the way it is."

"Why didn't you tell me this when you first suggested the scheme?"

"Frankly, I didn't think of it then."

She groaned softly. "Oh, this gets worse all the time."

"If you ask Mother to scale it down, I'm sure she will. But I guarantee that whatever she has a hand in will be handled with taste and efficiency. Would that be so hard to accept?"

"I . . . it scares me, that's all. I don't know anything about . . . society weddings."

"She does. Let her guide you. I have a feeling the two of you could work well together, once you get to know each other."

Again Catherine felt cornered, this time by Clay's obvious wish to please his parents, even if it meant a wedding that was larger than prudent. And again as she remembered his light touches, the looks of implied intimacy, she decided to take up the subject now so that he clearly understood her stand on the matter.

"That was quite a performance you put on back there, and totally unnecessary. I'm sure your parents aren't that gullible."

"You may have thought it unnecessary; I didn't."

"Well, spare me in the future, please. It's bad enough as it is."

"I wanted as few questions as possible, that's all. And I think it worked."

"You have no conscience whatsoever, do you?"

"We've been over this once before, so let's not go over it again. I don't like it any more than you do, but I'm going through with it, okay? If I have to touch you now and then to make it convincing, I'm sorry."

"Well, that wasn't part of our agreement."

"Are you that insecure that a touch on the shoulder threatens you?"

She would not grace him with an answer to such nonsense. But when she sat silently stewing for some time, he added, "Just forget it. It didn't mean anything; it was only an act."

Only an act, Catherine thought. Only an act.

It was warm in the car as Catherine sighed, leaned back in the comfortable seat and let the whisper of rain beneath the tires hypnotize her. The purring syllable of the engine, the faint vibration of the road, the gentle sway now and then as they rounded a curve or changed lanes—she let it engulf her in a place halfway between sleep and wakefulness, halfway between worry and security. The swoop of the windshield wipers mesmerized her and she drifted away, playing the game of pretend, as she and Bobbi had done so often in childhood. What happened to the girl who romanticized stories in her diary all her growing years? What happened to those dreams that had been an escape hatch then? What would it be like if this wedding were not some trumped-up scheme? What if it were real, and she and Clay both wanted it?

There was a bouquet of sweet-scented flowers in her hands as she drifted through a crowd of people with radiant smiles. She wore a stunning white gown with a skirt so voluminous it filled the width of the stairway from banister to wall. The diaphanous veil on her head tumbled around her, following like an aureole as she passed a table spread with lace and laid with silver, and another that bore an eruption of gifts that scarcely took her notice as she searched the throng for the eyes she knew so well. Bobbi was there, kissing her cheek, crying a little bit from happiness. But again the search for gray eyes and she found them and they smiled. He waited for her to reach him, and when she had she knew peace and fulfillment. Rice flew, and the bouquet flew, straight into Bobbi's upraised hands, and Bobbi tossed her a kiss that said, "See? It happened just like we pretended, you first, then me." And Mother's face was in the crowd, eased of worry, because Cathy had picked the right man. Then she and the very right, very gray-eyed man were sailing through the door toward a honeymoon, a honey-life, and it was real . . . real . . . real . . .

Catherine's head leaned at a fallen angle upon the seat of the car. Clay leaned near her, shaking her elbow gently. "Hey, Catherine, wake up." The dash lights picked out a series of golden needle-points from the tips of her eyelashes, which formed a dim fan of shadows across her cheek and nose. Her hair was messed up on one side, caught against the car seat and billowed out in disarray around her ear. He noticed for the first time that the ear was pierced. She wore a tiny silver stud in it. Her lips had relaxed, all of their earlier gloss now gone. The very tip of her tongue showed between her teeth. The tendons of her neck were high-lighted, creating intimate shadows behind them. The faint, inviting scent of her perfume still clung there.

How defenseless she looks, Clay thought, all wilted sideways, with her usual air of aloofness erased. She was a beautiful girl this way, but when she awoke he knew her stern facade would quickly return, and with it the cold overtones that Clay already disliked so intensely. He wondered if he might not learn to love her if her personality were as warm and sweet as the look of her right now. His eyes moved down to her lap. One hand was still lightly closed around a clutch purse, the other lay against her lower abdomen. Behind that hand his child thrived. He let the thought carry him. He considered what he wanted out of life and wondered what she wanted out of hers. The hand in her lap twitched and he studied it, thinking how easily she could have had an abortion. Momentarily he wished she had, then again, was relieved she hadn't. He wondered what the baby would look like. He wondered if it would be a boy or a girl. He wondered if it was a mistake, this wedding idea. He felt a momentary tenderness toward her because of the life she carried, and decided no, it was no mistake; his child deserved a better start in life than he, Clay, had given it so far. He wished, oh, how he wished, that things were different, that this girl was different, so he could love her. He realized he still held her arm, just above the elbow. He could feel her pliant flesh, her body heat through her coat sleeve.

"Catherine, wake up," he repeated softly.

Her eyelashes lifted and her tongue glanced across her lips. Her head rolled upright, and her eyelids shut once more.

"You fell asleep," he said, close to her, that hand still resting on her forearm.

"Mmmm . . ." Catherine murmured, resisting wakefulness a little longer. She stretched without stretching, using only her shoulders. She was aware of his touch, and she pretended for a minute longer, knowing now that he was very near, even though her eyes were still closed.

"You were supposed to be thinking things over instead of sleeping." But his voice was devoid of criticism, holding instead a note of warmth. She opened her eyes to find him a hovering shadow before her, his features eclipsed, for he'd slung one elbow over the wheel and half-turned her way.

"Sorry. I seem to do that so easily lately. The doctor said it was natural though."

Her words created an intimacy that lightly lifted Clay's stomach, coming as they did on the heels of his thoughts about the baby. He had never considered the personal changes going on inside her body before, nor the way they affected her day-to-day routine. It struck him that he was responsible for many changes she was undergoing, of which he was totally unaware.

"It's okay. I really don't mind."

It was the first time they ever had spoken unguardedly to each other. Her defenses were down, drowsy as she was.

"I was pretending," she confided.

"Pretending what?"

"Not really pretending, but remembering how Bobbi and I used to sit for hours and plan our weddings and make gowns out of dishtowels and safety pins, and veils from old curtains. Then we'd write it all in our diaries, all our glorious fantasies."

"And what did you write?"

"Oh, all the usual things. Girlish dreams."

"*Lohengrin* and trailing veils?"

She laughed softly in her throat and shrugged.

"You never said that before. If you wanted all those things, why did you argue earlier?"

"Because the traditional things will only be empty and depressing if all they do is create a front for what's missing."

"Hearts and flowers?"

She had never seen him this mellow before. Again she wondered what it would be like with him if this were real. "Don't mistake my meaning if I say yes."

He moved away slightly, squaring himself in the seat. "I won't. Do you assume that men don't want the same things?"

"I never thought about what men want."

"Would it surprise you to learn that I've recently done some wishing of my own?"

Yes, she thought, yes, it would. Have I robbed you of your dreams? She stole a glance at his profile. It was a very appealing profile, one she had looked at directly very few times. It wore an amenable expression now.

"Did you?" she asked at last, unable to stop the question.

"A little, yes. Mostly hindsight, you know."

She tried for an understanding note as she observed, "You really don't like being a disappointment to your parents in any way, do you?"

"No."

She didn't want to seem prying, yet she had to know—it had been bothering her for so long. She took a careful breath, held it, and finally asked softly, looking down at her lap, "This other girl you've been going with. . . . Jill . . . she's the one they hoped you'd marry, isn't she?"

He turned, saw the way she idled her fingers back and forth across her purse, staring down. She looked up and their eyes met.

"Maybe. I don't know." But he squared his shoulders and studied the lights on the dashboard again. A muscle in Catherine's stomach set up a light twitching. A little trail of guilt went weaseling its way upward.

"Maybe they'll get their wish when this is all over," she said.

"No, it'll never happen now."

They'd talked about it, then, Clay and Jill. Maybe this wedding would be his only chance to be feted in the recognized style. He seemed to be admitting that it bothered him. But just as Catherine came to that conclusion he spoke.

"You make the choice about the wedding, and whatever you want, it'll be okay with me. Mother will just have to accept it, that's all. But she'll be making plans in her head, so I'd like to tell her your decision as soon as possible."

"It's your wedding, too, Clay," she said quietly, undone by what she'd guessed about his feelings.

"Weddings are mostly women's doings. You make the arrangements."

"I . . . th-thank you."

"You know, it seems like every time I drop you off here, it's to give you a limited time to come to some monumental decision."

"But I've got plenty of helpers inside to help me with this one."

He chuckled. "A whole houseful of pregnant, unmarried teenagers. I can imagine how unbiased their advice will be. They're probably still pinning curtains on their heads for veils."

Catherine thought of how utterly close to the truth he was. The rain pattered on the roof, the windows had steamed up. It was warm and insular in the car, and for a minute, Catherine did not want to get out, back to reality again.

"Whatever you decide is okay, huh?" he said. "And don't let those kids talk you into anything."

He reached for his door handle, but she quickly insisted that he stay in the car. She could make it to the house just fine. When she reached to open her door, he stopped her by saying, "Catherine?"

She turned.

"It's been . . . well, I was going to say fun, but maybe I should just say better. It's been better, talking without arguing. I think we needed this."

"I think we did, too."

But, getting out of his car, running to the house, Catherine knew she'd lied. She didn't need this at all, not at all. Oh, God, she was beginning to like Clay Forrester.

Marie was still awake, waiting, when Catherine came inside, and though she hadn't intended to, Catherine found herself admitting, "I'm going to marry Clay Forrester."

Pandemonium broke loose! Marie leaped up, hit the light switch, bounded to the center of her bed and bugled, *"Wake up, everybody! Catherine's getting married!"* In no time at all the place was a madhouse—everybody whooping, rejoicing, jumping and hugging.

Mrs. Tollefson called from the bottom of the stairs, "What's going on up there?" and joined the fracas to congratulate Catherine, then offered to make cocoa for everyone.

It took an hour for things to settle down, but during that time some of the girls' undaunted enthusiasm crept into Catherine. Maybe it began while they hugged her and—for the first time—she found herself unreservedly hugging back. They seemed to have given her some indefinable gift, and even now, lying in bed, wide awake, she was not sure what it was.

Marie's voice came quietly from across the way. "Hey, you asleep?"

"No."

"Give me your hand, huh?"

Catherine reached and in the dark her fingers were grasped by Marie's. There was silence then, but Catherine knew Marie, the always gay, always cheery Marie, was crying.

ELEVEN

The following afternoon Clay called before Catherine got home and left a message saying his mother had invited her out to the house for dinner, so would Catherine please not eat at Horizons? He'd be there to pick her up around six-thirty.

Speculation ran rampant among the Horizons residents, who swarmed all over Catherine as she came in the door. When she admitted she was going there to make wedding plans, wide eyes gaped at her from every angle. "You mean they want a *real* wedding . . . *the real McCoy!*"

The real McCoy, it seemed, was exactly what Angela Forrester had in mind. From the moment Catherine put herself into Angela's hands, she sensed that what Angela had called an "intimate affair" was destined to be an extravaganza.

Yet it was hard to resist the charming Angela, with her laugh like the song inside a Swiss music box and her constant striving to put Catherine at ease and her unaffected touches, especially for Claiborne. From the first Catherine noted how the two touched, lovingly, without conscious thought, as her parents never had, and how Angela always called him *darling* and he called her *dear.* "Isn't it wonderful, darling, we'll have a wedding here after all," Angela fairly sang.

Though the details made Catherine's head swim, she drifted along with Angela's irresistible tide of plans for caterer, florist, photographer, even engraved invitations.

There were times during the following days when Claiborne thought his wife guilty of bulldozing. But Catherine gave Angie full sway. Sometimes he met the girl's eyes and read in them a hint of helplessness. Maybe it was this, and the fact that she understood what the wedding meant to Angie, that began to make Claiborne look at the girl differently.

The subject of the guest list was the first at which Catherine assertively gainsaid Angela by refusing to have Herb Anderson included.

"But, Catherine, he's your father."

"I won't have him here," Catherine stated vehemently, and stuck to it. The Forresters were surprised when Catherine said she wanted her brother Steve to give her away. They hadn't known she had a brother stationed at Nellis Air Force Base in Las Vegas.

In her turn, Catherine was surprised at Angela's lack of compunction in inviting the residents of Horizons.

Catherine stammered, "B-but they're all pregnant."

Angela only laughed and inquired charmingly, "Are they too big to fit in my house?" That issue settled, Angela suggested Catherine call her brother immediately, using the phone in the study.

Catherine sat in the deep leather desk chair. Dialing, waiting for the phone to ring, she felt the empty longing that always overtook her at thoughts of Steve. She thought of the photographs he'd sent over the last six years, of how, during that time, he'd grown from a lean boy into a full-grown man, and she'd missed it all.

A crisp voice answered her ring. "Staff Sergeant Steven Anderson here."

"S-Steve?" she asked, a little breathlessly.

"Yes?" A brief hesitation, then, "Who's—Cathy? Babe, is that you?"

"Yes, it's me. But nobody's called me *babe* for a long time."

"Cathy, where are you?" he inquired with undisguised eagerness.

She glanced around the shadowed, private study, knowing Steve wouldn't believe it if she described her whereabouts fully. "I'm in Minnesota."

"Is anything wrong?"

"No, nothing. I just wanted to call instead of writing." Phone calls were costly and rare; Catherine reminded herself to thank Mr. and Mrs. Forrester.

"It's so good to hear your voice. How are you?"

"Me?" She was close to tears. "Oh, I'm . . . why, I'm in clover."

"Hey, you sound a little shaky. Are you sure nothing's wrong?"

"No, no. I just have some news that couldn't wait."

"Yeah? Well, out with it."

"I'm getting married." As she said the words Catherine smiled.

"What! A skinny, flat-chested sack of bones like you?"

She laughed shakily. "I'm not anymore. You haven't seen me for a long time."

"I got your graduation picture so I know you're telling the truth. Hey, congratulations. And you're in college now, too. Lots of changes, huh?"

"Yeah . . . lots." Her eyes dropped to the rich leather of the desktop.

"So when's the big day?"

"Soon. November fifteenth, in fact."

"But that's only a couple weeks away!"

"Three. Can you make it home?" Catherine held her breath, waiting.

The line hummed momentarily before he repeated skeptically, "Home?"

She said pleadingly, "You wouldn't have to stay at the house, Steve." When he didn't reply, she asked, "Is there any chance of you getting here?"

"What about the old man?" A coldness had crept into Steve's voice.

"He won't be there, I promise you. Only Mom and Aunt Ella and Uncle Frank and Bobbi, of course."

"Listen, I'll try like hell. How are they all? How's Mom?"

"The same. Nothing much has changed."

"She's still living with him, huh?"

"Yes, still." She rested her forehead on her knuckles a moment, then picked up the letter opener from Claiborne's desk and began toying with it. "I gave up trying to convince her to leave him, Steve. He's the same as he ever was, but she's too scared of him to make a move. You know how he is."

"Cathy, maybe if I come back there the two of us together can get her to see some sense."

"Maybe . . . I don't know. Nothing's any different, Steve. You might as well know that. I don't think she'll ever admit how she hates him."

Steve injected a false brightness into his voice. "Listen, Cathy, don't worry about it, okay? I mean, this is your time to be happy, okay? So, tell me about your husband-to-be. What's his name, what's he like?"

The question disconcerted Catherine, who had never tried to put Clay into a nutshell. Her first instinct was to answer, "He's rich." But she was startled to learn there was much that mattered more. "Well . . ." She leaned back in the tilting desk chair and considered. "His name is Clay Forrester. He's twenty-five and in his last year of law school at the U of M. Then he plans to go into practice with his father. He's . . . well . . . smart, polite, well dressed, and not too hard on the eyes." She smiled a little at this admission. "And he has a very proper family, no brothers and sisters, but his father and mother, who want to have the wedding at their house. I'm at their house now."

"Where do they live, in the old neighborhood?"

"No." Catherine tapped the letter opener against the tip of her nose, leaning back and looking at the ceiling. "In Edina."

There was an expressive pause, then, "Well, well . . . what do y'know about that? My kid sister marrying into Old Establishment. How did you manage that, babe?"

"I-I'm afraid I managed that by becoming slightly pregnant."

"Preg— Oh, well, it . . . it was none of my business. I didn't mean to—"

"No need to sound so embarrassed, Steve. You'd find out sooner or later anyway."

"I'll bet the old man had plenty to say about that, huh?"

"Don't mention it."

"Have they met him yet, the Forresters?"

Catherine recalled the small scar that still showed above Clay's eyebrow. "I'm afraid so."

"I suppose the old man thinks his ship came in this time, huh?"

"Your memory is right on target. It's been hell around here. I moved out of the house to get away from him."

"I can just imagine what he was like."

"Hey, listen, he's *not* coming to the wedding, understand? I won't have him there. I don't owe him a thing! This is one time in my life that the choice is mine, and I intend to exercise it!"

"What about Mom?"

"I haven't told her yet, but she's next. I don't know if she'll budge without him. You know how she is."

"Tell her I'll do my best to be there and take her, maybe that way she'll go."

"When will you know for sure if you can get leave?"

"In a few days. I'll put in for it right away."

"Steve?"

"Yeah?"

Catherine came forward on her chair, blinking dangerously fast, her lips compressed with emotion until at last she stammered, "I—I want you here . . . s-so bad." She dropped the letter opener, spanned her forehead with her hand, fighting tears.

"Hey, babe, are you crying? What's the matter? Cathy?"

"N-no, I'm not crying. I n-never cry. We agreed to give that up long ago, remember? It's just so damn good to hear your voice and I miss you. After six years I st-still miss you. You were the only good thing around that place."

After a long, intense silence Steve said shakily, "Listen, babe, I'll make it. One way or another, I'll make it. That's a promise."

"Hey, listen, I've got to go. I mean, I don't want to run up the phone bill here any more than I have to." She gave him the number at Horizons.

Just before they hung up, he said, "God, I'm happy for you. And tell Mom hi, and tell Clay Forrester thanks, huh?"

Catherine wilted back against the high leather chair; her eyes slipped closed and she rode the swells of memory. She and Steve, childhood allies, sharing promises of never-ending support. Steve, a freckle-nosed boy of thirteen, standing up to Herb for her, regardless of his fear of the man. Steve and Cathy, children, huddling together, waiting to see who the old man's wrath would be turned on this time; Cathy's tears when it was Steve's turn to take a licking; Steve's tears when it was Cathy's; their trembling, tearless terror when it was their mother's turn; their mute agony of helplessness. But as long as they had each other they could bear it. But then came the day Steve left, the day he was old enough. She relived again her dread sense of desertion when he was so quickly gone for good. She felt again the desolation of being the one left behind in that house where there was only hatred and fear.

"Catherine?"

Her eyes flew open at Clay's soft question. She sprang forward as if he'd caught her rifling the desk drawers. He stood in the doorway, one hand in the pocket of his trousers as if he'd been studying her for some time. He came into the dim room, and she spun to face the shuttered window as two tears scraped down to her lashes and she covertly wiped them away.

"Couldn't you reach him?"

"Y-yes, I reached him."

"Then what's wrong?"

"Nothing. He's going to put in for leave immediately."

"Then why are you upset?"

"I'm not." But she could barely get the two words out. She was uneasy knowing Clay studied her silently. His tone, when at last he spoke, was concerned and gentle.

"Do you want to talk about it, Catherine?"

"No," she answered stiffly, wanting nothing so much as to turn to him and spill out all the hurtful memories of the past, to exorcize them at last. But she found she could not, especially not to Clay Forrester, when he was only passing through her life.

Clay studied her back, recognizing the defensive stance, squared shoulders and proud set of head. How unapproachable she could make herself when she wanted to. Still, he wondered, if he crossed the short distance of the room and touched her shoulders, what would she do? For a moment he was tempted to try it, sensing her utter aloneness in whatever it was she was suffering. But before he could move, she spoke.

"Clay, I'd like to make my own dress for the wedding. I'd like to provide at least that much."

"Have I given you the impression I'll object to anything?" He couldn't help but wonder what had brought on this abrupt defensiveness again. She turned to face him.

"No, you haven't, you've been more than compromising. I only want to make sure I don't shame you before your guests in a homemade dress."

She saw questions flit through his eyes, knew he was puzzled, but how could she explain to him her need to lash out sometimes, when she didn't fully understand it herself? What was she challenging? His place in society? His safe, secure, loved upbringing? Or the fact that he'd caught her with her defenses down a moment ago?

"You don't need my permission," he said quietly, and she suddenly felt sheepish. "Do you need any money to buy things for it?"

She felt the red creep up her neck. "No. I have some saved for next quarter's tuition I won't be needing."

Now it was his turn to feel slightly uncomfortable.

Although the days before the wedding were interrupted by these emotional point counterpoints, on the whole, Clay and Catherine grew increasingly comfortable with each other. There were even times when their moods were undeniably gay, like the following night when they called Bobbi and Stu to ask them to be attendants at the wedding. Clay had settled comfortably on the love seat in the Forrester study, to eavesdrop, he admitted. Dialing the phone, Catherine grinned, glanced up and couldn't resist revealing, "Bobbi considers you quite a catch, you know." He only smirked, stretched out with both hands locked behind his head and settled down to listen to one side of the conversation.

"Hi, this is Catherine . . . No, everything's just fine . . . No, I'm not . . . as a matter of fact, I'm out at Clay's house . . . Yes, Clay Forrester." The corners of Clay's mouth tipped up amusedly. "Well, he brought me out to have supper with his parents." Catherine's eyes met his. "What do you think I'm doing? . . . Yes, a few times . . . He ran into me on campus and followed me there . . . You might call it that . . . No, he's been very polite, nothing like that." Catherine wanted to wipe the smirk off Clay's face. "Bobbi, prepare yourself, you're in for a shock. Clay and I have decided to get married and I want you to be my maid of honor." Catherine covered the mouthpiece, made silly eyes at Clay and let Bobbi rave on a moment. "Well, I am, I mean, I called as soon as we decided . . . Stu . . . Yes, he just talked to him . . . Steve is going to try to make it home, too . . . In three weeks, on the fifteenth . . . I know, I know, we'll have to find a dress for you . . . Listen, I'll talk to you tomorrow. I just wanted to let you know right away."

When Catherine hung up, her eyes met Clay's, and they both burst out laughing.

"That must have been quite a jolt to old Bobbi, huh?" He sat as before, amusement painted all over his face.

"Well, you heard her, didn't you?" Catherine's expression was perhaps a little bedeviling.

"And after all her efforts to keep your whereabouts a secret," he mocked.

"Did you have to sit there smirking all through my conversation?"

"Well, you sat there smirking through mine." He noted she was still doing so.

"Yes, but guys react differently than girls."

He rose lazily, sauntered toward Catherine and pressed his palms to the desktop, leaning forward as he teased, "Just getting to know my . . . bride, is all. See how she works under pressure." His gray eyes sparkled into hers.

He had never called her *his bride* before. It conjured up intimacy and made secret shivers tiptoe down Catherine's spine. She turned the chair aside, slid to her feet and pressed her blouse against her still-flat stomach, looking down at it. "Give me six months or so and you'll see precisely how I work under pressure."

Then she gave him one of her first genuine smiles. He thought if she'd be this way more often, the coming months could be enjoyable for both of them.

Catherine's adamant refusal to have her father at the wedding left Angela in a quandary. There was only one way she could think of to see that Herb Anderson was tidily out of the way the day of the wedding. When she tactfully brought it up to Claiborne, he reluctantly admitted the idea had been on his mind, too. There was no guarantee it would work. Three weeks was a very short time; there was no assurance the case could be fitted on the docket that soon; there was no guarantee Anderson would be found guilty or be given a sentence.

But just to tip the scales, Claiborne hired the finest criminal lawyer in the Twin Cities. If Leon Harkness couldn't do the trick, no lawyer could.

TWELVE

Ada Anderson worked the day shift at the Munsingwear plant on Lyndale Avenue on the north side of Minneapolis. She had worked there so long the place and its surrounding area no longer affected her. Its utilitarian setting in a dismal commercial zone, its clattery workrooms and changelessness were what she'd come to expect. But Catherine, getting off the city bus, looking up at the building, was hit by a wave of desolation at the thought of how long her mother had labored there, sewing pockets onto T-shirts and waistbands onto briefs. The factory had always depressed Catherine, but it was the only place she could talk to her mother and be sure she wouldn't run the risk of bumping into the old man.

Ada came scuffing out of the noisy, lint-strewn room with a look of fear on her simple face, put there by the fact that her supervisor had called her away from her machine to see a visitor—something highly unusual in this place. The moment Ada saw Catherine the fear disappeared, to be replaced by a smile with more seams than Ada Anderson had stitched in her sixteen years in this place.

"Why, Catherine," Ada said in that tired, surprised way.

"Hello, Mom."

"Why, I thought you was gone someplace out west."

"No, Mom, I've been in the city all the time. I just didn't want Daddy to know I was here."

"He's been awful mad about you running off."

Catherine would have welcomed a hug, but there was

none, only her mother's tired acceptance of the way things were.

"Did he . . . has he taken it out on you, Mom?"

"No. Just on the bottle. Hasn't been sober a day since you left."

"Mom, is there somewhere we can sit down?"

"I don't know, honey, I don't get a break yet for another thirty minutes or so."

"How about the lunchroom?"

"Well, there's always the girls in there, and they got big ears, if y'know what I mean."

"Could we at least get away from the noise? Out on the stairway maybe?"

"Just a minute, I'll ask."

Something cracked in Catherine, some fissure of irritation at her mother's spinelessness. Not even here, after sixteen years, not even given the situation, which should mean so much to her, could she simply take command and step away for a while.

"For heaven's sake, Mother. You mean you have to ask for five minutes away from your machine?"

Ada touched her chin in a feeble, troubled way, making Catherine instantly sorry for attacking her for something Ada was perhaps helpless to change in herself. Quickly Catherine touched her mother's arm. "Ask then, go ahead. I'll wait."

When they were out on the steps and the noise became a muffled clatter behind them, it somehow seemed an appropriate background for this worn woman who looked fifteen years older than she was. Catherine suddenly thought of it as a song of lament for the defeated. A surge of tenderness overtook her.

"Come on, Mom, let's just sit down here, okay? What'd you do to your finger?" There was a bandage on Ada's right index finger.

"Wasn't nothing much. I ran it under the machine last week. You'd think I'd've had more sense after all this time. They said I had to have a tetanus shot, though, and that was worse than this."

Catherine wondered if her running away, then, had distracted her mother that much. "I didn't mean to make you worry, Mom. I just didn't know how to keep Daddy off my back. I thought he'd track me down at college and start making trouble for me again and for the Forresters. I thought that if he thought I was gone where he couldn't find me, he'd let it go. But he didn't."

"I tried to tell him he'd best let up, Catherine. I tried to tell him. 'Herb,' I says, 'you can't go badgerin' people like them Forresters. They ain't gonna put up with it.' But he went there and he beat up that young man and spent the night in jail. He started drinkin' worse than ever after that, and now he walks around whisperin' to himself about how he's gonna get them to pay up. It scares me. You know how he is. I says to him, 'Herb, you're gonna make yourself sick if you keep this up.' "

"Mom, he is sick. Don't you understand that by now?"

"Don't say that, honey . . . don't say things like that." The fear was back in Ada's eyes. She glanced skittishly away. "He's bound to slack off pretty soon."

"Pretty soon? Mom, you've been saying that for as long as I can remember. Why do you put up with it?"

"There's nothing else I can do."

"You could leave," Catherine said softly.

Again Ada's eyes did what Catherine expected. They grew fearful and twitchy. "Why, where would I go, honey? He wouldn't let me go nowheres."

"I'll help you any way I can. I told you I'd find out what

needs to be done to get help for him. There are places, Mom, right here in the city, that could help him."

"No, no," Ada insisted in her pathetically fierce way, "that wouldn't do any good. He'd just come out and be worse than ever. I know Herb."

Catherine thought of the Johnson Institute right at their fingertips, where help could be had for a phone call. But she gave up the argument that was, by now, as shopworn as Ada herself, defeated once again by her mother's self-inflicted blindness.

"Listen, Mom, I have some good news."

"Some good news?" Even when her eyes registered hope they looked sad.

"I'm not exactly sure how it happened, but I'm going to marry Clay Forrester."

Catherine held both of her mother's hands, rubbing her thumbs across the shiny surfaces where the skin seemed so thin the veins looked exposed. The expression on Ada's face visibly brightened.

"You're going to marry him, honey?"

Catherine nodded her head. Her mother at last squeezed her hands.

"Marry that handsome young man who said he didn't know you? How can that be?"

"I've been seeing him, Mom, and I've been back to his house several times and have talked with his parents and they're really quite nice. They've been very understanding and helpful. Can you believe it, Mom? I'm going to have a real wedding in that beautiful house of theirs."

"A real wedding?" Ada touched Catherine's cheek while her own eyes turned glossy. "Why, honey . . ." Again she squeezed Catherine's hand. "So that's where you run off to, to that young man of yours. Well, isn't that something."

"No, Mom, I've been living near the campus, and I've made lots of new friends, and I've seen Bobbi, and she's been letting me know how you've been all along."

"You don't have to worry about me, honey. You know I always end up on my feet. But you, look at you, ain't you something. A real wedding." Ada reached into her pocket and found a tissue and dabbed at her rheumy eyes. "Listen, honey, I got a little money saved, not much, but—"

"Shh, Mom. You don't have to worry about paying for anything. It's all taken care of."

"But you're my baby, my own little girl. It should be me that—"

"Mother, the Forresters want to take care of it, honest. I could have eloped if I'd wanted to, but Mrs. Forrester . . . Well, she's really on our side, Mom. I've never met anyone like her."

"Oh, she's a fine lady all right."

"Mom, I want you there at the wedding."

Startled eyes were raised to meet Catherine's. "Oh, no, honey. Why, I would never fit in that place. I couldn't."

"Listen, Mom. Steve's coming."

Surprise held Ada's tongue a moment before she repeated disbelievingly, "Steve?" Her eyes turned alight with that inextinguishable flicker of mother-love. "You talked to Steve?"

"Yes, and he's going to try to come home."

"Come home?"

Together they counted back six years.

"Yes, Mom. And he said to tell you he'll take you to the wedding with him. That's what I came to tell you."

"Steve . . . coming home?" But at the thought Ada raised those tentative fingers to her lips again. "Oh, but there'll be trouble. Herb and Steve . . ." Her eyes dropped down to her lap.

"Daddy's never going to know. Steve and you are coming to

the wedding, but not Daddy." Determinedly Catherine squeezed her mother's hands.

"But I don't see how."

"Please, Mom, please listen. You can tell him you're going to play Saturday bingo like you do sometimes. I want you at my wedding, but you can see that if he came, too, it would only mean trouble, can't you?"

"But he'll know, honey, he'll guess. You know how he is."

"He won't know if you don't tell him, not if you just walk out like you're meeting Mrs. Murphy for bingo like you've done a hundred Saturdays before."

"But he's got that sixth sense. He's always had it."

"Mama, Steve's not coming to the house, you know that, don't you? He swore when he left that he'd never set foot in it again, and he hasn't changed his mind. If you want to see Steve, you'll have to see him at my wedding."

"Is he all right?"

"He's just fine. He sounded really happy and asked how you are and said to give you his love."

"Steve's twenty-two now." Ada's mind seemed to drift away into the racket of the machines from the workroom. The rhythmic clack and thump accompanied her lost thoughts while she hovered on the steps with her knees almost touching her daughter's. The lines of fatigue on her face could not be smoothed, but as she reached back in time, thoughts of her son placed some new determination in the network of wrinkles around her lips. When she raised her eyes to Catherine again, she said, "Twyla's got a bolt of blue knit in the remnant room'd make me a pretty nice dress. I get it at employee's discount, you know."

"Oh, do you mean it, Mom?" Catherine smiled.

"I want to see Steve, and I want to see my little girl's wedding. Why, stitching up a dress ain't nothing to me after all the years I put in here."

"Thank you." Impulsively Catherine leaned forward to hug her mother briefly around the thin shoulders.

"I'd best get back now, or my daily quota will be low."

Catherine nodded.

"I won't say a word to Herb this time, you'll see."

"Good. And I'll let you know if Steve calls again."

Ada braced hands to knees as she creaked to her feet. "I'm glad you come, honey. I didn't like to think of you off acrosst the country someplace like Steve." She climbed two stairs, then turned around, looking down at Catherine.

"Is it gonna be the kind with flowers and cake and a white dress for you?"

"Yes, Mom, it is."

"Well, feature that," Ada said thoughtfully. Then she stopped to do so, with the expression of wonder growing grander by the minute upon her time-worn features. "Just feature that," she repeated, as if to herself.

And for the first time, Catherine was fully, totally, one hundred percent happy that she'd gone along with all of Angela Forrester's wishes.

The invitations were ice blue, embossed with rich, ivory letters of finest English Roundhand that pirouetted across the marbled parchment like the steps of a dancer. As she lifted a card from the box, it crackled like dancer's crinoline beneath Catherine's fingers. She touched a raised character, ran her fingertips lightly along a line, as the blind read braille. The ascenders and descenders formed graceful swirls that rose to meet her searching touch.

You can feel these words, Catherine thought, you can feel them.

Awe-filled, she studied the invitation, not quite accustomed yet to everything that was happening so fast. The words read in that formal lexicon peculiar to occasions that mark the stepping-stones of life:

Catherine Marie Anderson
and
Clay Elgin Forrester
invite you to share in their joy
as they celebrate
the solemnization of their marriage vows
at seven p.m. on November fifteenth
at the home of Claiborne and Angela Forrester
Number Seventy-nine
Highview Place
Edina, Minnesota

Again, Catherine grazed the words with her fingertips. But with a woeful sense of yearning she thought, Yes, the words can be felt, but it is not enough to feel only with the fingertips.

THIRTEEN

By now Catherine and Clay could meet in the front hall of Horizons and display a friendly familiarity that lacked the edginess of those first couple of meetings. Catherine invariably found herself scanning his clothing, invariably, too, found herself pleased by what greeted her. Likewise, Clay found himself approving of her appearance. Her clothes were neat, if unostentatious, and she wore them well. He watched for a first sign of roundness on her, but so far none was showing.

"Hi," he said now, while his eyes performed that first perusal that she'd come to expect. "How are you holding up?"

She struck a pose. "How does it look like I'm holding up?"

He glanced once again over the plum wool dress, loose-belted, trimmed with top-stitched pockets at hip and chest.

"Looks like you're doing fine. Nice dress."

She dropped her pose, wondering if she'd done that on purpose to wrest a compliment from him. She found his approval pleasing. But since that night she'd fallen asleep on the way home, they had each made a conscious effort to be nice to each other.

"Thank you."

"You're going to meet my grandparents tonight."

By now she could manage to be less alarmed at such announcements. Still, this one made her slightly apprehensive.

"Do I have to?"

"They come with the package, I'm afraid."

Her eyes moved down his length. "The package, as usual, is wrapped to perfection." And so it was, in bone-colored pleated trousers and a complementary Harris Tweed sport coat with suede elbow patches.

It was the first compliment she'd ever paid him. He smiled, suddenly warm inside.

"Thanks, glad you approve. Now let's hope my grandparents do."

"The way you put that sounds forbidding."

"No, not really. But then, I've known them all my life. My Grandmother Forrester is a crusty old gal though. You'll see what I mean."

Just then Little Bit came downstairs, stopped and hung over the banister halfway down. "Hi, Clay!"

"Hi, Little Bit. Is it okay if I take her for a while?" he asked teasingly.

"Why don't you take me instead tonight?" Little Bit swooned farther over the railing. The girls had given up trying to hide their fascination with Clay.

But at that minute Marie came down the steps. "Who's taking you where? Oh, hi, Clay."

"Do something with that child, will you, before she drops on her head and gives birth to a dimwit?"

Marie laughed and slapped Little Bit lightly on the rump as she passed behind her. They both came the rest of the way downstairs.

"Where you off to tonight?" Marie asked, eyeing them appreciatively.

"To my house."

"Yeah? What's the occasion this time?"

"Another one of the seven tortures. Grandparents, I'm afraid."

Marie raised an eyebrow, took Little Bit's hand to tug her off toward the kitchen while giving Catherine one last conspiratorial glance over the shoulder. "Lucky thing you decided to wear your newest creation, huh, Cath?"

Clay looked the dress over a second time, with greater interest.

"We do have nimble fingers, don't we?" he asked, and without winking, gave the impression he had.

"Yes, we do. Of necessity." And Catherine laid a hand lightly on her stomach. Smiling with Clay, she felt a little happy, a little venturesome.

Something had changed between them. The lurking sense of anger and entrapment had begun to wane. They treated each other civilly, and occasional spurts of repartee such as this were becoming more frequent.

By the time Clay turned into his parents' driveway full dark had fallen. The headlights picked out the herringbone design of cobblestones while upon them the tires hummed the note that by now Catherine unconsciously listened for.

The yard was dressed for winter. Leaves were but memories, while tree trunks were swathed in white leggings. The shrubs had hunched their shoulders and pulled mulch quilts up beneath their chins. An occasional pyramidal bush was laced into winter bindings like an Indian papoose.

The house was lit from within and without. Catherine glanced at the twin carriage lanterns on either side of the front door, then down at the tips of her high heels as she approached the house. Her pocketed hands hugged her coat close as she tried to keep her growing apprehension from getting the best of her. Without warning, from behind, Clay's fingers circled her neck, closing lightly in a warm grip.

"Hey, wait, I have to talk to you before we go in."

At his touch, she instantly turned, surprised. He left both hands on her shoulders with his thumbs pressing her coat collar against each side of her windpipe. Catherine needn't have said it for him to be reminded that she'd rather not be touched this way.

"Sorry," he said, immediately raising his palms.

"What is it?"

"Just a technicality." Gingerly he inserted a single index finger into her coat sleeve, tugging until the hand came out of her coat pocket. "There's no ring on this." Her bare hand dangled out of the sleeve. While he looked at it, the fingers suddenly clenched protectively, shutting the thumb inside.

"Grandmothers tend to become suspicious when they don't see what they expect to see," he noted wryly.

"And what do they expect to see?"

"This."

Still holding her coat sleeve, he lifted his other hand to reveal a jeweled ring riding the first knuckle of his little finger. In the meager light from the carriage lanterns it wasn't at first evident exactly what it looked like. Clay wiggled the finger a little and the gems glittered. Catherine's eyes were drawn to it as if he were a hypnotist using it to mesmerize her. Her mouth went dry.

It's so big! she thought, horrified. "Do I have to?"

He commandeered her hand, sliding the ring onto the proper finger. "I'm afraid so. It's family tradition. You'll be the fourth generation to wear it."

With the ring not quite on, she gripped his fingers, stopping them, feeling the ring cut into her.

"This game is going too far," she whispered.

"The significance of a ring is in the mind of its wearer, Catherine, not in the fact that it's on a hand."

"But how can I wear this with three generations behind it?"

"Just pretend you got it in a box of Cracker Jacks," he said unconcernedly, completing the adornment of her third finger, pushing the ring all the way on. Then he dropped her cold fingers.

"Clay, this ring is worth thousands of dollars. You know it and I know it, and it is not right that I'm wearing it."

"But you'll have to anyway. If it helps to relieve your mind, remember that the Forrester side of the family made a business of gems before my father broke the tradition and went into law.

Grandmother Forrester still owns a thriving business, which she refused to relinquish when Grandfather died. There are hundreds more where this came from."

"But not with this one's significance."

"So, humor an old lady." Clay smiled and shrugged.

She had no choice. Neither did she have a choice when, in the entry after he'd taken her coat, Clay returned and laced his hand half around her neck in that careless way of his. That was how they entered the living room, with him affectionately herding her along and Catherine doing her best to keep resilient under his touch.

They approached first a withered little pair of people who were dressed formally and sat side by side on a velveteen sofa. The man wore a black suit and looked like an aged orchestra conductor. The woman, in mauve lace, wore a little twinkling smile that looked as if she'd donned it seventy years ago and hadn't taken it off since. Approaching the pair, Catherine felt Clay's hand slide down her back, linger at her waist, then depart as he bent to take the woman's cheeks in both hands and plop a direct, noisy kiss on her mouth.

"Hi, sweetheart," he said irreverently. Catherine could have sworn the old girl actually blushed as she looked up at Clay. Then she twinkled as she shook a crooked, arthritic finger at him—her only greeting.

"Hello, sonny," the grandfather greeted him. "You get your grandma more excited with that word than I can anymore." Clay's hearty laugh swept the two.

"So, Granddad, are you jealous?" He put an arm around the shoulders of the bald man who might have been stepping up to a podium with his aging slump. To Catherine's surprise, the two embraced unabashedly, chuckling together.

"I want you both to meet Catherine." Clay turned back, reached out a palm and drew her forward. "Catherine, this is Grandma and Grandpa Elgin, better known around here as Sophie and Granddad."

"Hello," Catherine said, smiling easily, squeezing each parchment hand in turn. Sophie's and Granddad's smiles were so alike it was like seeing double.

Then Clay captured her elbow, turning her toward a woman who sat with a matriarchal air in a high-backed chair that need not be a throne to bespeak the woman's regal mien. The feeling was there. It permeated the very air about her. It was evident in her bearing, her facial expression, the faultless blue-white waves that crested her head, the shrewd eyes, the glitter flashing from her fingers and the glacial assessment she gave Catherine.

Before Clay could speak, the woman pierced him with an arch, amused look.

"Don't try those flirtatious tactics with me, young man. I'm not the blushing fool your Grandmother Sophie might be."

"Never, Grandmother," assured Clay, wearing a devilish grin as he lifted one of her bejeweled hands and bent over it quite correctly. He made as if to kiss its blue-veined back, but at the last minute, turned it over and kissed the base of her thumb.

Catherine found herself amused at these cat-and-mouse goings-on. The old lady's mouth pursed to keep from smiling outright.

"I've brought Catherine to meet you," Clay said, dropping the hand, but not the half-smile. Again he urged Catherine near with a slight touch on her elbow. "Catherine, this is my Grandmother Forrester. I never call her by her first name for some reason."

"Mrs. Forrester," Catherine repeated, while her hand disappeared within all those flashing gems.

"My grandson is a precocious young upstart. You'd do well to watch your *p*'s and *q*'s around him, young lady."

"I intend to, ma'am," Catherine rejoined, wondering what the old lady would think if she knew the extent to which *p*'s and *q*'s would need to be watched in the months ahead.

Mrs. Forrester raised an ivory-headed cane and tapped Catherine's shoulder lightly, perusing her with gray irises from beneath one straight eyebrow and one that was cocked in an aristocratic arc.

"I like that. I might have answered in just that way myself." She rested the cane on the floor again, crossed her hands upon the ivory elephant with its sapphire eyes, and angled a bemused expression again at her grandson, asking, "Where did you find this perceptive young lady?"

Clay moved a hand lingeringly up and down the inside of Catherine's elbow while he searched her face and answered his grandmother. "I didn't. She found me." Then his hand trailed down, enclosing hers. Elizabeth Forrester's eyes followed it and registered the way the girl's fingers failed to clasp Clay's. The pair turned toward Claiborne and Angela, who were pouring port and making room on a marble-topped table for the silver tray of canapés that Inella carried in at that moment.

Clay had a greeting for Inella, too. He dropped a hand on her shoulder as she leaned to set down the tray. "And what kind of epicurean delights have you dreamed up tonight, Inella? Don't you know Father's been concerned about his waistline?"

Everyone laughed.

"Epicurean delights," scoffed the pleased maid. "Where do you dream up such stuff?" She left, smiling. There followed a full-fledged hug between Clay and his mother and a clasp of hands with his father.

Catherine had never seen so much touching in her life. Nor

had she seen Clay in this element before, warm, humorous, obviously loved and loving everyone in the place. The scene gripped her with something akin to envy, yet deep in some part of her, Catherine was slightly intimidated. But she could not pull away as the next warm touch fell her way and Angela's cheek pressed against her own while Claiborne—thankfully—only smiled on and gave her a friendly verbal greeting.

"Young woman, sit here," ordered Elizabeth Forrester imperiously.

Catherine could do nothing but perch on a love seat at a right angle to Elizabeth Forrester's chair. She was actually grateful when Clay sat down beside her. His presence somehow made her feel fortified. Elizabeth Forrester's shrewd eagle eyes assessed Catherine, probing like a laser while she made what appeared on the surface to be inconsequential conversation.

"Catherine . . ." she mused, "what a quaint and lovely name. Not clever and will-o-the-wisp like so many of today's insubstantial titles. I dare say there are many I'd be thoroughly ashamed to be plagued with. You and I, however, have each been preceded in name by an English queen, you know. My given name is Elizabeth."

Catherine wondered if she were being given permission to use the name or being tested to see if she were so presumptuous. Assuming the latter, Catherine consciously used the more formal mode of address.

"I believe, Mrs. Forrester, that the name Elizabeth means 'consecrated to God.' "

The regal eyebrow raised a notch. The girl is astute, thought Elizabeth Forrester. "Ah, so it does, so it does. Catherine . . . is that with a *C* or a *K*?"

"With a *C*."

"From the Greek, then, meaning 'pure.' "

Catherine's stomach did somersaults. Does she *know* or does she *want* to know? Catherine wondered, making a great effort to appear unruffled.

The matriarch observed, "So, you are the one who will carry the Forrester name forward."

Catherine's stomach tightened further. But Clay, whom she didn't know whether to damn or to thank, nestled closely beside her with his thigh against the length of her own, meeting his grandmother's probe directly.

"Yes, she is. But not without some persuasion. I think Catherine was a little put off by me at first. Something to do with our having different stations in life, which I had trouble convincing her didn't matter one damn bit."

My God, thought Catherine, he's actually challenging the old girl!

Understanding that challenge very clearly, Elizabeth Forrester only chided. "In my day, your grandfather didn't pronounce vulgarities in my ear."

Clay only grinned, sparring expertly. "Oh, Grandmother, you're sterling, pure sterling. But this is not your day, and a man can get by with a little more." But then, feeling the muscle of Catherine's leg grow rigid, he dulcified his remark by adding, "*Damn* is hardly considered a vulgarity anymore, not even a crudity."

She merely cocked the eyebrow again.

"Father," Clay said, "bring your mother a glass of port. She's being testy tonight and you know how port always mellows her. Catherine, do you like port?"

"I don't know."

Elizabeth Forrester missed not a word.

"White wine, then?" her grandson suggested. The girl's reaction was curious. She attempted to move her thigh away from his. Unconcerned, he rose without waiting for an answer and went to get the wine.

"How long have you known Clay?" his Grandma Sophie asked then, leaning forward with birdlike tentativeness.

"We met this summer."

"Angela says you are sewing your own dress for the wedding."

"Yes, but I have lots of help," Catherine answered, realizing too late that she'd left herself open for further questioning.

"Why, how nice. I never could sew a stitch, could I, Angela? Is your mother helping you?" Sophie's manner of speech was exactly the opposite of her counterpart's. Where Elizabeth Forrester was audacious and quizzing, this woman was shy and unassuming. Still, her innocent line of questioning made Catherine again feel boxed into a corner.

"No, some friends of mine are helping me with the dress. I do some sewing to help out with college expenses."

"My, Clay didn't tell us you're in college."

He came to her rescue then, returning with a stem glass of imported German liebfraumilch. As Catherine reached for it, the gems in her ring glittered like the lead crystal glass that held the wine. Before she sipped, she changed hands, resting her left, knuckles down, on her lap.

"Yes, she is. She's a clever girl, too. She made the dress she's wearing tonight, Grandma. She's very good with her hands, isn't she?"

Catherine almost choked. Quickly she added, "I also type theses and manuscripts."

"You do? My, my," Grandma Sophie remarked inanely.

"You see, Grandma, now I won't have to pay to have my papers typed this year. That's really why I'm marrying her." He grinned mischievously and laid his hand along the back of the love seat as he said it, making Sophie's eyes soften in approval.

"Mother," Angela put in, "Clay is up to his usual teasing again. Don't pay any attention to him."

The talk moved on, interspersed with the nibbling of crab-stuffed *petits choux* and marinated mushroom caps. Clay relaxed beside Catherine, his knees lolling wide so there was the ever-present intrusion of his thigh against hers. He kept up the small talk, asked once, close to Catherine's ear, if she didn't like the crab, confirmed that's what it was she was eating, murmured just loud enough that the elder Mrs. Forrester overheard him tell his fiancée there were lots of things he'd teach her to like. He bantered with Elizabeth, teased Sophie, agreed to play racquetball with his father one evening soon, and, through it all, managed to act as if he doted on Catherine.

By the time they went to dinner, she was nearly undone. She wasn't used to sitting so close to him, nor being wooed in so obvious a manner for the benefit of others. At the table it went on, for Clay was seated directly beside her, and now and then during the meal he rested his elbow on the back of her chair and spoke trumped-up confidences into her ear in a highly convincing way. He could laugh just softly enough, glance at her just beguilingly enough to make his grandmothers smile at each other over their salmon steaks à la Inella. But long before the meal ended either the steaks or Clay or both had caused Catherine's stomach to begin to churn. Add to that the fact that Elizabeth Forrester brought up the ring, and Catherine wondered if she'd make it through the meal.

"I see Angela has given you the radiant. How wonderful, Angela, to see it on Catherine's hand. What does your family think of it, dear?"

Catherine forced herself to continue cutting a cheese-encrusted Irish potato.

"They haven't seen it yet," she answered truthfully, learning the game quickly, determined not to give the hawk-eyed woman an edge.

"It looks beautiful on such long, slim fingers, don't you think so, Clay?"

Clay picked up Catherine's hand, took the fork from it, kissed it, replaced the fork and said, "Beautiful."

"Would you like to prick my grandson with that fork, Catherine, just to let a little of that self-satisfied hot air out of him? Your fondling seems to distract Catherine from her eating, Clay."

But it was as much the ring as everything else that was distracting Catherine.

Clay only laughed and delved into his food again. "Grandmother, I think I detect a note of testiness again. Nobody told you you had to pass the ring on to Mother. Would you like it back?"

"Don't be cheeky, Clay. As your bride, Catherine should and will wear the ring. Your grandfather would be thrilled to distraction if he could see it on a girl as beautiful as she."

"I give up. For once you've left me speechless because you're right."

Elizabeth Forrester was left to wonder if her suspicion was correct. The boy seemed incapable of stopping himself from fawning over the girl. Well, time would tell, soon enough.

In the car on the way home Catherine laid her head back against the seat, struggling with each passing mile to control her roiling insides. But halfway there Catherine ordered, "Stop the car!"

Clay turned to find her eyes closed, one hand convulsively gripping the console.

"What is it?"

"Stop the car . . . *please*."

But they were on the freeway where controlled accesses made it difficult to stop.

"Hey, are you all right?"

"I have to throw up."

An exit ramp beckoned and he pulled over, careened halfway up, drove the car completely over the curb and onto the shoulderless area of grass, then slammed on the brakes. Immediately Catherine rolled out her side of the car. He heard her retching, then she gasped and spit.

Sweat broke out under Clay's armpits. Across his chest the skin grew tight and hot, and saliva pooled beneath his own tongue as if he were the nauseated one. He got out, unsure of what to do, saw her huddled over, her hair hanging down over her cheeks.

"Catherine, are you all right?"

"Do you have a tissue?" she asked shakily.

He came up behind her, reached in his hip pocket and extracted his handkerchief. He handed it to her and took her elbow to lead her a few steps aside.

"This . . . is your . . . han . . . hanky. I can't use . . . your hanky." Her ordeal had left her fighting for breath.

"Christ, use it . . . anything. Are you okay now?"

"I don't know." She gulped air like a person coming up for the second time. "Don't you have any tissues?"

"Catherine, this is no time to be polite. Use the damn hanky."

In spite of her wretchedness, it suddenly dawned on Catherine that Clay Forrester swore when he was scared. She swabbed the inside of her mouth with his clean-tasting handkerchief.

"Does this happen often?" His voice was shaky, concerned, and he left a solicitous hand on her arm.

She shook her head, waiting yet, unsure if there was more.

"I thought it only happened in the mornings."

"I think it was the fish and the grandmothers." She tried to laugh a little, but didn't quite succeed, so instead sucked in the starlight.

"Cat, I'm sorry. I didn't know it would be that hard on you or I wouldn't have added to it."

She heard mostly the word *Cat*. God, no, she thought, don't let him call me that. Not that!

"Do you want to go back to the car?" he asked, at a loss, feeling protective toward her, yet utterly useless.

"I think I'll stay here in the air awhile longer. I still feel funny." She refolded the hanky and wiped her forehead with it. He reached to push aside a strand of hair that had caught on her cheek.

"Are you going to keep this up when we're married?" There was a smile in his question, an attempt to make her feel better.

"If I do, I'll wash the hankies for you. I don't know, it's never happened before. I'm sorry if I embarrassed you."

"You didn't embarrass me. I just got scared, that's all. I don't know much about handling retching girls."

"Well, live and learn, huh?"

He smiled, waiting for her to gain her equilibrium again. She ran a shaky hand over her forehead and down one temple. Her stomach was calming down, but Clay's continued touch as he held her arm was unsettling. Wisely, she extricated herself from it.

"Clay, your grandmother Forrester knows." Catherine's voice shook.

"So what?"

"How can you say that when she's so . . . so . . ."

"So what? Dictatorial? She's really not, you know. She loved you, couldn't you tell that?"

"Loved me? . . . *Me?*"

"She's a shrewd old devil, and there's not much she misses. I had no notion of trying to deceive her tonight. Yes, she knows, but she's given you her stamp of approval anyway."

"She chose an odd way to show it."

"People have their ways, Catherine. Hers are . . . well, different from those of Mother's parents, but believe me, if she hadn't approved, she would never have said what she did about the ring."

"So the ring was a test—that's why you made me wear it tonight?"

"I guess in a way it was. But it's tradition, too. They all know that there's no way I'd be taking a bride without putting it on her finger. That was understood before I was ever born."

"Clay, I was . . . well, scared. It was more than just the ring and the way your grandmother quizzed me. I have to be told when I'm eating crabmeat that it's crab and I don't know port wine from a fishing port and I don't know that pink diamonds are called radiants and—"

His unconcerned laughter interrupted her. "A radiant is a cut, not a color, but what does it matter? You foiled the old girl, Catherine, don't you know that? You foiled her by letting her guess the truth and having her approve of you anyway. Why feel scared about that?"

"Because around your family I'm out of my league. I'm like a . . . like a rhinestone among diamonds. Can't you see that?"

"You have a surprising lack of confidence lurking behind that composed exterior you usually display. Why do you insist on putting yourself down?"

"I know my place, that's all, and it isn't in the Forrester family."

"It is as long as I say it is, and nobody's going to contest it."

"Clay, we're making a mistake."

"The only mistake made tonight was when you ate Inella's salmon." He touched her shoulder. "Do you think you've finished with your revenge on her?"

She couldn't help smiling. "What *is* it with you that you can be so casual about all this?"

"Catherine, it's only temporary. I made up my mind to enjoy what I can of it, and not to let the rest bother me, that's all. And I'm even learning in the process, so there."

"Learning?"

"Like you said . . . how to handle a pregnant lady." He turned her toward the car. "Come on, I think you're okay now. Get in and I'll drive like a good boy."

Farther down the road, Clay began talking about Sophie and Granddad, reminiscing about them, and the stories he told made Catherine understand where Angela got all her loving ways. Riding with Clay, listening to stories about his youth, she found herself enjoying his company fully.

She laughed once, saying, "I had all I could do to keep from bursting out laughing when Granddad called you 'sonny.' " She turned a skeptical grin toward Clay and repeated, "*Sonny?*"

Clay himself laughed. "Well, I guess that's how he'll always think of me. You know, I really love that old dude. When I was little, he used to take me to see the ore boats on Lake Superior. Just him and me. Once he took me up on the train, because he said trains would soon be gone and I shouldn't miss the chance to ride on one while I could. Saturday afternoons he'd take me to see Disney movies, to museums, all kinds of places. And I'd go to the ballet with both Granddad and Sophie."

"The ballet?" She was genuinely surprised.

"Uh-huh."

"How lucky."

"You've never been to one?"

"No, only dreamed about it."

"I assumed you had, from what you said once about being a ballerina."

"No, you assumed wrong," and for the first time Catherine opened up a portion of her secret regret to him. Not much, but a little—an important little. Like wiping off a tiny peek-through from a dirt-filmed window, she gave him a first glimpse of what was inside. "My dad drank a lot, so there was never any money for the ballet."

Suddenly afraid she should not have said it, she waited for Clay's reaction. She did not want him to think she was eliciting his sympathy. She could feel his gaze on her for a moment before his words made her heart dance against her rib cage.

"There is now," was all he said.

FOURTEEN

The short trio of weeks before the wedding, coupled with the countless necessary arrangements, saw Catherine and Clay together almost as much as they were apart. The thing Catherine feared most began to happen: she grew familiar with Clay. She began expecting things before they happened—to have her car door opened, her coat held, her fast food paid for. Personal things about Clay intruded, too—the way he always took time to kid the girls at Horizons before snatching Catherine away again;

the continuing sense of closeness he displayed with his family; the endless touching about which none of them felt inhibited; his laugh. He laughed easily, she discovered, and seemed to accept what was happening far more readily than Catherine herself was able to.

She grew familiar with the incidental things: the way his eyes were drawn to the vapor trails of jets; the way he removed the pickles from his hamburgers but added extra ketchup; the fact that most of his clothes were brown, that he was slightly color-blind between browns and greens and sometimes mistakenly chose socks of the wrong color. She came to know his wardrobe and the scent of him that lingered in his car, until one evening when it changed it came as a shock that she'd even detected the change. She learned which of his tapes were favorites, then the particular songs on those tapes that were even more favored.

Then one day he offered her the use of his car to complete all her errands. Her wide blue eyes flew from the keys, dangling off his index finger, to his grinning eyes.

She was speechless.

"What the hell, it's only a car," he said offhandedly.

But it wasn't! Not to Clay. He took care of it the way a trainer takes care of a Kentucky Derby winner and with equally as much pride. His trusting her to drive it was another stitch in the seam of familiarity binding Clay and Catherine ever closer. She saw all this clearly as she stared at the keys. To accept them was to break down another of the barriers between them, this barrier so much more significant than any that had fallen before, for it had delineated their separate rights. Accepting the keys would only meld the two, which was something Catherine sought to avoid.

Yet she took the keys anyway, tempted by the luxury they represented, the freedom, the thrill, telling herself, "One

time . . . just this once . . . because there's so much running to
do, and it'll be so much easier by car than by bus."

Driving the Corvette, she felt she had usurped Clay's world,
the car was so much a part of him. There was a sense of willful
intrusion that made her heart race when she placed her hands on
the wheel in the precise spot where his usually rested. The feel of
her flesh on *his* spot was decidedly intimate, so she quickly re-
verted to the more cavalier pose with one wrist draped indolently
over the wheel, put the machine in motion and turned on the
radio, experiencing a heady jolt of freedom when the music
poured from the speakers. She even used the horn once, unnecessarily, and laughed aloud at her precociousness. She adjusted the
rearview mirror, amazed at how suddenly exotic Minneapolis,
Minnesota, looked when viewed in reverse from a white leather
bucket seat inside a sleek, silver bullet.

She watched men's heads snap around and women's faces affect expressions of disdain, and allowed herself to feel temporarily superior. She smiled at other drivers while sitting at stop
signs. The Corvette was superficial, ostentatious, and somebody
else's. But she didn't care. She smiled anyway.

And she took first Marie, then Bobbi, out shopping in it.

And for one day—one magic day—Catherine allowed herself
to pretend it was all real. And somehow, for that one day, it was.
For that single day Catherine had a taste of the full flush of joy
wedding preparations can bring.

The making of Catherine's wedding dress became a "family
project" with almost every girl at Horizons sharing the work in
some way. Then one day before the gown was finished Little Bit
had her baby. It was a girl, but they all knew Little Bit had long
ago made the decision for adoption, so nobody spoke much
about the baby. When they visited Little Bit in the hospital they
spoke of the wedding, the gown, even the Corvette ride. But on

the shelf by her bed there was only an ice blue wedding invitation where there should have been baby cards, too.

After that Catherine sensed a new wistfulness when the girls
touched her wedding gown. They vied for the right to zip it up
the back when Catherine tried it on, touching it with a reverence
she found heartbreaking. It was a lovely creation of ivory velvet,
with wrist-length sleeves, an Empire waist and a miniature train.
The front bodice was gathered at the shoulder and on up the
high, tight neck, and draped in soft swags from shoulder to
shoulder. Studying her reflection, Catherine could not help wondering what the months ahead would bring.

The plans for Catherine and Clay's immediate future came
down to more personal things. They had to think about a place
to live and furnishings for it. Once again the fairy-tale aura pervaded as Clay announced his father owned various properties
around the Twin Cities and there were at least three different
ones unoccupied. Would Catherine like to look at them?

He took her to a complex of town houses in the suburb of
Golden Valley. Catherine stood back, watching Clay fit the key
into the lock with an odd thrill of expectation. The door swung
open and she stepped inside, hearing the door close behind her.
She stood in the foyer of a split-level house. It was disconcert-
ingly silent. Before her, chocolate-carpeted stairs led up one level
and down one. Clay touched her arm and she jumped. They
walked up the steps, unspeaking, to be greeted by a great open
expanse of space that ended in sliding glass doors on the far side
of the living room. To her left was a kitchen, to her right steps
leading to the sleeping level. She hadn't expected such luxury,
such newness.

"Oh, Clay," was all Catherine said, sweeping the living room
with her eyes.

"I know what you're thinking."

"But I'm right. It's too much."

"Don't you like it? We can look at others."

She swung to face him in the middle of the bright, vast room. "I can't live in this with you. It would be like cheating on my income tax."

"Okay, let's go. Where else do you have in mind?"

"Wait a minute." She reached out to detain him, for he'd turned impatiently toward the foyer. "I'm not the only one who has a say."

He paused, but she could tell his teeth were clenched.

"Clay, what are we going to fill all this up with?"

"Furniture, but it won't be *filled*. We'll just get what we need."

"Just . . . *get*?"

"Well, we'll go out and buy it, dammit! We have to have furniture, and that's the usual way of getting it." It was unlike him to speak in such a brittle manner. She could tell that he was disappointed and not a little angry.

"You want it, don't you?"

"I've always liked this place, but it doesn't matter. There are others."

"Yes, so you said before." She paused, met his displeased eyes and said quietly, "Show me the rest of it."

She followed him up the short flight of stairs. He switched on a light and a spacious bathroom was revealed. It had a long vanity, topped with gold-veined black marble, sporting two sinks and a mirror the size of a bedsheet. The fixtures were almond-colored, and the walls papered in a bold geometric of beige and brown with touches of silver foil adding a richness for which she was not prepared. She quickly glanced from the vanity stool to the shower stall—separate from the tub—with its opaque glass walls.

"Any of the paper can be changed," he said.

"That won't be necessary. I can see why you like it as it is—all these browns."

He switched off the light and she followed him to a small bedroom on the opposite side of the hall. Here again was a room papered in brown and tan geometric, very masculine, evidently decorated as a den or study.

Silently they moved on to the other bedroom. It was massive and could easily have been divided into two rooms. It, too, was papered in shades of brown, but this time a cool, restful dusty blue had been added. Clay walked over and opened a door, revealing a generous walk-in closet with built-in drawers, shoe shelves and luggage racks up above.

"Clay, how much is this going to cost anyway?"

"What difference does it make?"

"I . . . we . . . it just does, that's all."

"I can afford it."

"That's not the point and you know it."

"What is the point then, Catherine?"

But for answer, her eyes slid to the spot where the bed so obviously belonged. His eyes did the same, then they quickly looked away from each other. She turned from the room and abruptly went back downstairs to check the kitchen.

It was compact, efficient, had a dishwasher, disposal, side-by-side refrigerator-freezer, glossy flooring of rich vinyl, almond-colored appliances—everything. She thought of the kitchen at home, of her father slinging coffee grounds in the sink without bothering to wash them down, of the dirty dishes that were forever piled in the sink unless she herself washed them.

Catherine thought about what it would be like working in this clean kitchen with its gleaming appliances, its wood-grained

Formica countertops. She turned to eye the peninsula and imagined a pair of stools on the other side of it—a cozy, informal eating spot. She pictured Clay sitting there in the morning, drinking coffee while she fried eggs. But she'd never been with him early in the morning and didn't know if he liked coffee, or fried eggs. And furthermore, she had no business imagining such things in such a wishful way.

"Catherine?"

She jumped and whirled to find him leaning in the doorway, one elbow braced high against it. He was dressed in a rust-colored corduroy jacket with a matching vest beneath. The way he stood, the jacket flared away from his body creating inviting shadows around his torso. It struck her again how flawless his appearance was, how his trousers never seemed to wrinkle, his hair never to be out of place. She felt her mouth go dry and wondered what she was letting herself in for.

"There's only a week left," he said sensibly.

"I know." She turned toward the stove, walked over and switched on the light above it because it gave her a reason to turn her back to him and because she'd been wondering if he drank coffee in the morning and because she'd been thinking of the shadows within his corduroy jacket.

"If it's what you want, Clay, we'll take it. I know the colors suit you."

"Do you want to look at something else?" He was no longer angry, not at all. Instead his voice was mellow.

"I love this, Clay. I just don't think that we . . . that I . . ."

"Deserve it?" he finished as she faltered.

"Something like that."

"Would it make things more fair if we lived in a hovel someplace, is that what you think?"

"Yes!" She spun to face him. "No . . . Oh, God, I don't know. This is more than I ever imagined I'd live in, that's all. I'm trying very hard not to be overcome."

He smiled, raised his other hand so both were now braced against the door frame above his head, then he shook his head at the vinyl floor.

"You know, sometimes I don't believe you."

"Well, sometimes I don't believe you either." She threw her hands wide, indicating the whole place in one gesture. "Now furniture, too!"

"I said we'd only get the necessities."

"But I'm fast learning what you consider *necessities*."

"Well, I'll do my damnedest to hunt up some stick furniture if it'll make you happy. And I'll string some thongs from the bedroom wall and haul in a fresh load of straw for on top of them. How's that?"

His face wore the most engaging grin; it was irresistible.

He was teasing her. Standing there leaning against their future kitchen doorway looking good enough to serve for dinner, Clay Forrester was teasing. His laughter started as a soft bubble of mirth deep in his throat, but when it erupted into full, uninhibited sound, all she could do was laugh back.

He chose an enormously long davenport because, he said, his mother drove him nuts with all her love seats that a man couldn't even stretch out on. And two armchairs of tweed, and a pecan coffee table and end tables, and a lamp that cost as much as one of the chairs, although Catherine could not convince him this was utterly spendthrift and silly. He said he liked it, expensive or not, and that was that. They chose two stools for the kitchen peninsula, but Catherine adamantly refused to furnish the formal dining room. They really wouldn't need it, she said. She won on that point, but the bedroom set she said was "good enough" wasn't good enough for Clay. He picked out one that cost nearly double that of her choice, and a triple dresser *and* a chest of drawers, which she said were unnecessary because the closet had built-in drawers.

They were standing in the aisle arguing about nightstands and lamps when their salesman returned to them.

"But why do we need more lamps? There are ceiling fixtures; that's good enough."

"Because I like to read in bed!" Clay exclaimed.

The salesman began to clear his throat, thought better of it and withdrew discreetly to let them argue it out. But Catherine knew he'd overheard Clay's last comment and was left beet-faced, feeling like a complete fool, standing there in the aisle of a furniture store arguing with a fiancé who exclaimed he liked to *read* in bed!

Things started happening so fast.

Steve called to say he'd be arriving on Thursday, the thirteenth.

Ada called to say she'd finished making her dress.

The store called to make arrangement for delivery of the furniture.

Bobbi called to say the Magnussons would definitely be at the wedding.

The doctor's office called to say Catherine's blood count was low.

Angela called and apologetically explained that Claiborne

had pressed charges against Herb Anderson and successfully managed to have him convicted to ninety days in the workhouse for assault and battery.

And then one evening Catherine walked into Horizons to find a surprise bridal shower awaiting her, and not only were all the girls there, but seated side by side on the sofa were her mother and Angela. And Catherine, giving in to what is each bride's right, covered her face with both hands and burst into tears for the first time since this whole charade began.

FIFTEEN

When Clay came to pick up Catherine and take her to meet Steve's plane, she was totally unprepared for the sight that greeted her. She stopped stupidly, dead in her tracks!

Clay was dressed in faded denims and a faded blue flannel shirt beneath a disreputable-looking old letter jacket that would have been shaped like Clay even had his body not been inside it. It was the kind of possession taken for granted. The jacket hung open haphazardly, limp from age, its pocket edges worn bare, its zipper long since grown useless. The rough clothes gave Clay a rugged look, flattering in its unexpectedness, disarming because it brought back memories of the first time Catherine had ever seen him. Oh, he was neater that night, but he'd been dressed in faded Levi's jeans and a tennis shirt.

Catherine stood transfixed while Clay, oblivious to her reaction, only greeted her with, "Hi, I brought the Bronco. I thought we'd be more comfortable in it." He'd already turned toward the door before realizing she wasn't following, so turned back to her.

"What's the matter? Oh, should I have dressed up more? I was waxing the Corvette in the garage and forgot about the time. Sorry."

"No—no, it's okay . . . you look . . ." But she didn't finish, just gaped at him.

"What?"

"I don't know—different."

"You've seen me in jeans before."

Yes, she certainly had, but she didn't think he remembered.

She moved, at last, out the door with him.

At the curb was the vehicle she remembered from last July, some kind of man's toy with high bench seats and plenty of windows all around, and room for hunting equipment in the rear. She stopped walking as if she'd run up against a barbed wire fence.

"I thought we'd be a little crowded in the Corvette with your brother's gear and the three of us." Clay caught her elbow, propelling her forward. She began shivering; it was bitter for November—easy to blame her shakes on the weather. Clay moved ahead to open the door of the Bronco, but looked back again impatiently to find her eyeing him in a curious manner.

Catherine stood there, swallowing, fighting the overwhelming surge of familiarity—those jeans, and the old jacket, his hair that—for once—wasn't quite tidy. His collar was turned up, and as he stood waiting, his breath formed a white cloud. His nose was a little bit red, and he shivered, then hunched his shoulders.

"Hurry up," he said with a small smile. "Get in or you'll be scolding me for being late."

"Is this your father's?"

"Yeah."

He took his hand off the icy handle and buried it in his other pocket. Without thinking, she dropped her eyes to the zipper of

his jeans, staring at the way the old, faded spots undulated between patches of deeper blue. Her eyes darted to his face, discovering that he'd been watching her. And suddenly the color of
his cheeks matched his nose.

Appalled at herself, she climbed hurriedly into the seat and
let him slam the door shut.

Neither of them said a word all the way out to the Air Force
Reserve Base in Bloomington. Catherine stared out the side window, damning herself for letting memory play upon her this way.
Clay drove, seeing over and over again the way her eyes had
dropped to his zipper, recalling now the reason why. Women, he
realized, placed greater importance on memories than men do.
Until that happened back there he hadn't given a thought to the
Bronco or his blue jeans, or the fact that he'd used them both
last Fourth of July.

Clay did not touch her as they walked to the correct building.
The stab of self-consciousness was again too concentrated.

A tall, strapping blond man, dressed in civvies, turned from
his conversation with a uniformed desk clerk at the sound of
their approach. He glanced up and hesitated. Then his mouth
fell open, he smiled, and he started running toward the tall blond
girl who, also, had broken into a run. They met like thwarted
lovers and it came as something of a surprise to Clay, seeing for
the first time a genuine display of affection from Catherine.
There was a near greediness in the way her fingers dug into the
back of her brother's jacket, a hungry desperation as their eyes
closed while they clasped each other tightly and swallowed tears.
Clay stood back uneasily, not wanting to watch them, unable not
to. Steve swung Catherine off her feet, whirled her around, re-

peating an endearment that struck Clay as ill-suited, yet touched him all the same.

"Babe . . . oh, God, babe, is it really you?"

Her lips quivered and she clung. She could say little more than his name, backing away, spanning his tan cheeks with her palms, looking into his changed face, then at the breadth of his shoulders, then lunging into his arms again, burying herself, unable to restrain her tears now that she'd seen his.

To Clay it was a revelation. He watched Catherine's face, recalling this same expression on it that night after the long-distance call.

Finally Steve pulled back and said, "If that's Clay over there, I think we're making him uncomfortable." He tucked Catherine securely beneath his armpit, and she circled his torso with both arms while the two men shook hands.

Catherine's smile was unreserved. Her hold upon Steve was possessive. For Clay, it created an odd momentary twinge of jealousy, soon lost in the inanities of introductions, the first assessment of man to man.

"So you're the one she told me about." Steve's grip was solid, winning.

"So you're the one she told *me* about."

Clay reached for the duffel bag, and the three walked down the corridor and across the parking lot, Catherine and Steve catching up with bits of news about each other and the family. He squeezed her extra hard once and laughed. "Will you look at my baby-sister. What happened to your cowlicks and pimples?" There followed another impulsive hug, then they clambered into the Bronco.

"Where to?"

"I made reservations downtown."

"But, Steve, we won't even get a chance to talk!" wailed Catherine.

"Listen, you two, why don't I drive out past the house and you can drop me off and Steve can take the Bronco?"

"Oh, Clay, really?" Catherine's blue eyes radiated appreciation.

"We've got more cars at home than we need."

Steve leaned around Catherine. "That's damn nice of you, man."

"Think nothing of it. I can't leave my future brother-in-law stranded in a downtown hotel, can I?"

Steve smiled.

"Then it's settled."

Catherine and Steve talked all the way out to the Forresters. When they arrived, Steve took in the sprawling house, cobbled drive, extensive lawns, and said, "Well, well."

Catherine couldn't help the tiny thrill of pride, realizing how the house must appear to Steve for the first time. "This is where the wedding's going to be."

"Babe, I'm happy for you."

Clay pulled up, shifted into neutral, but he'd only dropped one leg out when Catherine laid a hand on his arm.

"Clay?"

He looked back over his shoulder at the touch on his sleeve.

"I don't know what to say."

Neither did he just then. He only looked at her, at the pleasant, warm expression she had willingly displayed toward him. She was so different today; he'd never seen her like this before. This, he thought, is how I've always wondered if she could be.

"Thank you," she said sincerely.

"It's okay. Like I said, we've got more cars around here than we know what to do with."

"Just the same—thanks." She moved impulsively toward him and brushed her cheek briefly against his, not quite kissing it, not quite missing, while he hung half in the seat, half out.

"You two have a good talk. But make sure you get some sleep, huh?"

"Promise."

"I'll see you tomorrow night then."

She nodded.

He lowered his voice and pleased her immeasurably by saying, "I think I like him."

Her only answer was the same genuine smile that he was already enjoying. Then Clay swung out, found Steve standing there waiting, and said, "Time enough for you to meet my folks tomorrow. I know you and Catherine are anxious to be alone."

"Listen, man . . ." Steve extended a hand. There followed a prolonged grip, then, "Thanks a lot." Steve then glanced up at the house and back once again at Clay. His tone changed, then he added quietly, "For both of us."

There was an instantaneous sense of rapport between Clay and Steve, the inexplicable thing that happens only rarely when strangers meet. It had nothing to do with Catherine or her relationship to either of them. Neither had it anything to do with gratitude. It was simply there: some compelling invitation coursing between the clasped hands. "Here," it seemed to say, "is a man I feel good with."

Odd, thought Clay, but of all Catherine's family, this is the first person I've felt drawn to, and that includes Catherine herself.

He'd been expecting someone like Catherine's father, some harsh, forbidding younger version of Herb Anderson. Instead, he found a genuine smile, intelligent eyes and a face much like Catherine's, only warmer. He thought perhaps the years away from home had given Steve Anderson the ability to smile at life again, which Catherine could not yet readily do. In her brother's face, Clay found the possibility of what Catherine could be, should she ever stop carrying that chip on her shoulder and that shield of armor over her emotions. Perhaps, after all, Clay liked Steve because he alone seemed able to move Catherine, to make her feel, and make it show.

When the noon break came and Ada Anderson left her machine, there was a sparkle of life in her eyes that had been missing for years. The skin around them was as corrugated as ever, but the eyes themselves were alive with expectancy. Her usual lifeless shuffle was replaced by a brisk step. Ada had even put a touch of lipstick on.

"Ada?"

She turned at the sound of her supervisor's voice, impatient to be out the door.

"I'm kind of in a hurry, Gladys. My boy is home, you know."

"Yes, I know. I checked on your output and the week's been good. The whole line had a good week, as a matter of fact. Why don't you just take the rest of the afternoon off, Ada?"

Ada stopped fussing with her coat collar. "Why, Gladys, do you mean it?"

"Of course I do. It's not every day a boy comes home from the Air Force."

Ada smiled, slid the handle of her vinyl purse onto her arm, casting one eye at the door, then back at Gladys Merkins.

"That's awful nice of you, and if you ever get in a bind when the girls get behind on their quotas, I'll put in extra."

"Get going, Ada. The quotas we'll worry about some other time."

"Thanks a lot, Gladys."

Gladys Merkins watched Ada hurry out the door, wondering how a person becomes so downtrodden, so stolid and unassuming that she doesn't even ask for a day off when she hasn't seen her son in six years. If word hadn't been passed around the shop, Gladys herself wouldn't have known. It did her heart good to see the pitiful woman with a smile on her face for once.

Outside, Ada scanned the street, clutching her coat at her throat where her heart beat in wild expectancy. The wind caught at the hem of the garment, lifting it, tugging at Ada's gray-streaked hair. She scanned the ugly street uncertainly. It sported only cold brick structures of commerce, and noisy truck traffic that never seemed to cease. Chain-link fences were decorated with weathered paper scraps. There was the ever-present smell of exhaust fumes. Huddled against the wind, Ada looked like a deserted scrap of refuse herself.

But then a vehicle careened past and swerved to an abrupt halt beside the curb. A young man burst from it, forgetting to shut the door, waving, smiling, running, calling, "Mom! . . . Mom!" And the little scrap of refuse was transformed into vibrant life. Ada ran, her arms outstretched, her face tear-streaked. As her arms clung at last to her son's neck she wondered how it could possibly be him, so big, so broad, so real at last.

"Oh, Mom . . . Jesus . . . Mom."

"Steve, Steve, let me go so I can look at you."

He did, but then he saw her better, too.

She appeared infinitely older, sadder. He could only hug her again, guilty because he knew some of that age, some of that sadness had been caused by his leaving. She was crying, but he saw past the tears to a much more profound sorrow, hopeful that somehow he could help erase it before he had to leave her once more.

"Come on, Mom. Cathy's in the car and we're all going out for lunch."

SIXTEEN

It was Catherine's wedding day, the last day she would share with the girls at Horizons. So she allowed their suffocating attentions, feeling at times like she was smothering in their over-caring midst. The expressions on their faces—those doe-eyed looks—were etched on her conscience; she thought they would be her penance forever, long after she gave up her place as Mrs. Clay Forrester. The saga she had brought to Horizons would remain legend within its walls, rivaling any Hans Christian Andersen tale. But its ending, which none of them yet knew, would be her own private hair shirt.

She swallowed the knowledge of it while the girls played "wedding day" with her, dressing her up as they had their dolls as children, humming from *Lohengrin* as they had for their dolls, pretending that the doll was themselves.

For Catherine it was an ordeal. Keeping the smile on her lips, the lilt in her voice, the eagerness in her pose became a task of sheer love. She realized it as the last hour neared—that she loved, genuinely loved, so many of these girls.

She sat before a mirror, her face flushed and framed by an appealing aureole of soft blond curls, slung high and held by a winter gardenia set in baby's breath, trailing a thin white ribbon down her back. They had bought her a garter and were putting it on her calf, laughing, making silly jokes. Catherine was dressed in the sexiest undergarments she'd ever owned. Her mother had bought them from the employees' store at Munsingwear, surprising everyone at the shower. The bra was an incidental thing, plunging low in front, molding Catherine's lower breasts in lotus-shaped satin fingers that curved up to the crests of her nipples, barely covering them. Exquisite satin briefs, trimmed in peekaboo lace, left a strip of skin nearly exposed up each hip. The slip was beautiful enough to be an evening gown. It followed closely the low décolletage of the bra, flowing and clinging to her thighs and the perceptible bulge of her tummy. She placed her hands on it now, looking at the garter, at all the faces around her. Her eyes filled. She took a deep breath, fluttered a fingertip beneath her lashes, knowing the girls' eyes followed the twinkle of the diamond.

"Come on, you guys, don't!" she said, laughing shakily, quite close to breaking down completely. "Don't look so happy for me. It should be every single one of you, not me!" She widened her eyes to make room for the tears.

"Don't you dare cry, Catherine Anderson!" Marie scolded. "Not after all the work that's gone into that makeup. If you get one single tear on it, we're all going to disown you."

Another fragile, borderline laugh, and Catherine sputtered, "Oh, no, you won't. You can't disown me any more than I can disown you. Not anymore. We're all in this together."

But Catherine compressed her lips. A tear had its own way, hovered, then splashed over the edge of her lashes, and she laughed shakily, flapped her hands and demanded a tissue.

Somebody quipped, "Hey, Anderson, dry up, or else!"

It relieved the tension. The makeup passed inspection, and somebody brought the plain dress Catherine would wear in the car, her gown, carefully sheathed in plastic, her purse and the small bag she'd packed.

"Have you got your perfume in there?"

"Yes, thank you for reminding me, Francie."

"How about your Dramamine pills?"

"Dramamine pills?"

"You'll need them for flying high."

"Clay's the one that'll need them when he gets a load of that underwear!"

"Be careful of the gardenia when you get in the car now."

"Your brother is here, he just pulled up!"

They thronged downstairs. Steve was at the door. He carried Catherine's things outside, came back for a second load and for her.

Then there was nothing left to do but go. It was so hard to do, suddenly, to turn away from all the warmth and love. Mrs. Tollefson was there, hovering near the colonnade, then coming forward to be the voice of the entire group.

"Catherine, we're all so happy for you. I think you've made every girl here into something more than she used to be. Right, girls?" Catherine was hugged against Mrs. Tollefson quite roughly. She pinched her eyes shut.

"Listen . . . I—I love you all." As she said it, she experienced an explosive force of emotion. Those words, so unfamiliar to her tongue, created an expansiveness like she'd never felt before. She knew it twenty-five-fold, for at that moment it was true. She loved each woman crowded around her and suddenly wanted more than anything to stay among them, to let their hands pull her back into the security of their fold.

But that phase of her life was over. She was swept out into the November afternoon where a fine snow was falling, glittering onto her hair like stardust. The skies were pale, with smudges of gray clouds lying low, shedding their enchanting burden into Catherine's wedding day. With eyes now dry, Catherine watched their progress through the city, in a sort of enhanced state of clarity. Bare trees stood out in crisp distinction, blacker than black when wet by the snow. The snow had a pristine smell of newness, as each first snow does. It tantalized her, falling like petals strewn before the bride, touching everything with white. She stared out the window, sighed, closed her eyes, told her heart to beat right. But it beat all the more erratically as she envisioned the Forrester house, the guests who would soon be arriving, and Bobbi and Stu on their way, and somewhere, waiting . . . Clay.

Clay.

Oh, Clay, she thought, what have we done? How can all of this be happening? Me riding toward you with a velvet gown on the seat behind me and this diamond on my finger? And all those starry-eyed looks burning into my soul from the house I've just left? And your father and mother and grandparents all waiting to welcome me into your family? And guests coming, bringing gifts, and—

"Stop the car!"

"What?" Steve exclaimed, surprised.

"Stop the car. I can't go through with this."

He pulled over, watching his sister drop her face into her hands. He slid across the seat and gathered her into his arms.

"What is it, babe?"

"Oh, Steve, what should I do?"

"Shh, come on now. Don't start crying, not today. It's just the last-minute jitters. But, really, babe, I don't think you should have the slightest qualms." He lifted her chin, making her look at him. "Cathy, if I could handpick a brother-in-law, I'd probably pick Clay Forrester, from what I've seen so far. And if I could handpick a family to trust you to, it would probably be his. You're going to be loved and taken care of for the rest of your life, and I couldn't be happier with who's going to be doing it."

"That's just it. It's not for the rest of my life."

"But—"

"Clay and I are being married under duress. We've agreed to divorce as soon as the baby has a name and he's passed his bar exams and entered his father's business."

Steve sat back, absorbing this news. His brows gathered into a scowl.

"Don't look at me that way! And don't ask me how this mess got started because right now I don't think I could even explain it to myself. I only know I feel like the biggest fraud on the face of the earth, and I don't think I can go through with it. I thought I could but I can't."

Steve slid back behind the wheel and stared at the wipers that slapped disconsolately across the windshield. His eyes seemed focused on nothing. "You mean none of them know?"

"Oh, Steve, I shouldn't have told you, but I had to get it off my chest."

"Well, now that you have, you're going to listen to what I have to say. You *should* feel like a swindler. It's a damn rotten trick you're playing on some damn fine people; at least I think they are. And since you obviously do, also, you haven't got any choice but to go through with it. If you back out now, you're going to embarrass them even further than our illustrious father already has. They've been more than fair to you, Catherine. They've been supportive and decent and, in case you've forgotten, quite lavish with their money. Frankly, the things I've learned about the Forrester family have boggled my mind. I find myself wondering how I'd have accepted the situation if I were in their position and faced with the bizarre set of circumstances they've been faced with. It takes some pretty big people to be as accepting as they've been. I think you owe it to them not only to go through with this marriage, but to make a helluva stab at making it work afterward.

"Furthermore, if I were faced with the opportunity, like you are, I think I'd do my damnedest not to let a man like Clay slip out of my fingers as easily as you intend to."

"But, Steve, you don't understand. We don't love each other."

"You're carrying something that says you'd better, by God, try to!"

She'd never seen Steve so upset with her before. She, too, raised her voice. "I don't want to have to *try* to love my husband. I just *want* to!"

"Listen, you're talking to old Steve here." He tapped his chest. "I know how stubborn you can be, and if you set your mind to something you'll stick with it, come hell or high water. And what you're telling me is that you aren't going to try to make this marriage work, right?"

"You make it sound like it's all my idea. It's not. We agreed to start the divorce in July."

"Yeah, and you wait and see how far your agreement goes when he gets a load of his own kid in some hospital nursery."

Catherine's heart flew to her throat. "He promised the baby will be mine. He won't fight for it."

"Yeah, sure." His hands hung on the wheel. He stared unseeingly. "The baby goes with you, you go your way, he goes his. What the hell kind of agreement is that to make?" He looked down at his thumbs.

"You're angry with me."

"Yes, I am."

"I don't blame you, I guess."

He felt robbed, robbed of all the elation he'd held for her, angry that she'd stolen it from him. Frustrated, he slammed the butts of both hands against the steering wheel.

"I like him, goddammit!" he blustered. "I felt so damn happy for you, ending up with a guy like him." Then he stared a long time out his side window.

"Steve." She slid over and touched his shoulder. "Oh, Steve, I'm sorry. I've hurt so many people already, and hardly any of them know yet that they've been hurt. You're the only one, and look how you feel. And when Mom finds out, and his folks, well, you can see why I don't think we should go through with it."

"You back out now and you'll break Mom's heart. She thinks you're set for life, and she'll never have to worry about you living like she's done, with that—that . . ."

"I know."

"Well, Christ! She's waiting at home right now in her home-made dress, probably all nervous about it, and—hell, you know how she gets. She's actually, honest-to-God happy, or as close to happy as I've ever seen her, with the old man gone and your future set. Don't do it to her, Cathy."

"But what about me?"

"You started it, all those people heading for your wedding, all the preparations made, and you ask 'What about me?' I think you'd better think it over and consider what happens if you back out now. Count the number of people involved."

"I have! Every day I have! Facing all those pregnant teenagers at Horizons while they treated me like I was Snow White and they were dwarves, stitching on my wedding dress all starry-eyed. Do you think that's been easy?"

He sat stiff and silent. She slid back to her own side. The snow fell in flat plops while she stared at it unseeingly. Finally she quoted, as if to herself, "Oh, what a tangled web we weave, when first we practice to deceive."

The silence was broken only by the sweep of the windshield wipers, which were still slapping away. Catherine spoke to the snow. "I had no idea at the beginning how many lives would be touched by this wedding. It seemed like a decision that would mainly affect Clay and me and the baby. But things got out of hand somehow. Angela said he's their only son and wanted to have at least a few of the family—an intimate little affair she called it. And then all the girls at Horizons got into it, helping me make the dress. Then Mom sees me heading for what she thinks is the good life. Clay's grandparents even gave me their approval, to say nothing of the family jewels." She turned to Steve at last. "And you, my God, it even brought you home. Do you know what it means to me to have you here, and how I hated telling you the truth? I'm getting in deeper than I wanted though. Steve, please understand."

"I understand what it would do to a lot of people if you say no at the eleventh hour."

"And even after what I told you, you think I should go through with it?"

"I don't know. . . . What a mess." But then he turned to her with a look of appeal on his face. "Cathy, couldn't you try to give it a chance?"

"You mean, me and Clay?"

"Yes, you and Clay. What are your feelings for him?"

That was a tough one; she thought for a minute before answering. "I honestly don't know. He's . . . well, he's able to accept all of this far more easily than I can. And the funny thing is, once he got over the first shock, he never blamed me in any way. I mean, most men would be throwing it up to a woman all the time how their plans were ruined. But he's not that way. He says he's going to make the best of it, takes me out and introduces me to his family just as if I'm his real choice, gives me this huge old ring that's been in the family forever, and treats me like a lady. Yet, at the same time, I know it's all a hoax. He does very well at keeping his family from suspecting it though. They've accepted me surprisingly well. The trouble is, Steve, I think I'm accepting them, too. Oh, Steve . . . it's awful . . . I . . . don't you think I realize all those things you felt about them? They're genuinely good and loving people, and I'm drawn to them; I like them. But it's dangerous for me, don't you see? I'm to be a part of them, yet I'm not. Giving them up in a few months will be tougher than leaving Horizons was today."

"All this time you've talked about his family, but you still haven't answered my question about Clay."

"How can I? The truth is I don't know him as well as you think I do."

"Well, it's obvious you were attracted to him once."

"But it's not . . ." She paused, looked away. "I met him on a blind date. He was going with another girl at the time, and they'd had a fight or something."

"So what?"

"So it was a one-night stand, that's what."

"Are you saying he loves someone else?"

"He never mentions her."

"Hey"—Steve's voice was as gentle as his touch upon her arm—"babe, I don't know what to say, except, maybe—just maybe—Clay is worth fighting for."

"Steve, you above all people should understand that I don't want a marriage like Mom and Dad's. If there's one thing I learned in that house it's that I will not merely *survive* a marriage; I want to *live*."

"Hey, give it a chance. Have you considered that you kind of fell into the pot here and could come out smelling like a rose?"

She couldn't help smiling. "If it'll put your mind at ease, the baby will be taken care of for the rest of his life. That's part of the arrangement. After Clay graduates, he'll help me with tuition so I can go back to school."

"So the deal is made, huh? I guess we both know you can't back out of it now, don't we?"

She sighed. "You're right. I can't, and I knew it all the time, even when I told you to stop the car."

He studied her a moment before saying, "You know, little sister, I'll give you odds you won't come out of this feeling quite as platonic about him as you claim to be now. How much you wanna bet?"

"That's wishful thinking and you know it. And I'm going to be late for my own wedding if you don't get this thing into gear."

"Okay." He shifted into drive and they pulled back into traffic.

After a few minutes she touched his arm and smiled at Steve. "Thanks for letting me unload on you. I feel better now."

He winked at her. "You really are a babe, in lots of ways," he said, covering her hand with his own, hoping Clay Forrester recognized that fact.

SEVENTEEN

The windows of the Forrester home were all ablaze, throwing oblique patches of gold across the snow of early evening. Each of the front columns was festooned with an enormous arrangement of Indian corn, scarlet leaves and bearded wheat with nutmeg-colored ribbons trailing streamers that drifted in a meek breeze. Snow settled softly on the scene and Catherine gave a soft exclamation of surprise at the liveried attendant who was sweeping the cobbled walk.

She could see that Angela's expert hand had done its work and wondered what other surprises awaited her inside. Catherine fought against the overwhelming sensation of coming home. She fought, too, against the both terrible and wonderful sense of expectation. Surely this incredible day was not happening. Yet the scent of gardenia was real. And the diamond on her hand was so large she couldn't draw her glove over it. Summoning common sense did little good. The flutter of excitement persisted, disquieting, reducing Catherine to nervous jitters.

Then the attendant was smiling, opening the door, while Catherine fought the crazy sensation that she was debarking from a coach-and-four.

The foyer door opened upon yet another dreamlike setting: bronze and yellow flowerbursts threaded with ribbons, cascading from the spooled stair rail at evenly spaced intervals. Angela appeared with Ada in tow, sweeping Catherine into a hurried hug, whispering conspiratorially, "Hurry on up. We don't want you to be seen here."

"But, Steve—" Catherine strained to glance over her shoulder, dismayed at being whisked through the tantalizing foyer without being allowed to dote on it. Angela's laughter tinkled into the softly glowing space as if she understood Catherine's reluctance to be swept through so hastily.

"Don't worry about Steve. He knows what to do."

The floral impressions had to be left behind momentarily. Yet a last look behind her gave Catherine the sight of two white-capped maids peeking over the banister for one forbidden glimpse of the bride.

Insanity continued as Catherine was ushered into a stunningly appropriate bedroom, trimmed in pink flounced ruffles and floor-length priscillas. It was carpeted, too, in palest pink, and furnished with a glorious brass bed and free-standing cheval mirror, ruffled pillows and a girlish look that seemed the counterpart to Angela's giddiness.

When the door closed behind them, Angela immediately captured both of Catherine's hands. "Forgive an old-fashioned mother her whims, my dear, but I didn't want to run the risk of your meeting Clay somewhere in the hall." Angela squeezed the damp palms. "You look lovely, Catherine, so lovely. Are you excited?"

"I . . . yes . . . it . . ." She glanced at the door. "All those flowers down there . . . and a doorman!"

"Isn't it exciting? I can't think of another affair I've had more fun arranging. I believe I'm a little breathless, as well. Can I tell you a secret?" She smiled conspiratorially again, then turned to include Ada in the secret. "So is Clay."

The idea seemed preposterous, yet Catherine asked, "He is?"

"Ah! He's been driving us crazy all day, worrying if there was enough champagne and if the flowers would arrive on time and if we'd forgotten Aunt Gertie's family on the guest list. He's been the typical bridegroom, which pleases me immensely." Then Angela breezily commandeered Ada. "Now we'll leave you alone for a minute. I want to show your mother the cake and gifts. You'll find everything you need in the bath there, and if you don't find it, let one of the maids know. Come on, Ada. I think we deserve a little glass of sherry to calm our mothers' nerves."

But before they could leave, a maid opened the door and ushered in a breathless Bobbi, with a plastic clothing carrier over her arm. There followed a flurry of kisses and greetings and hanging up of gowns, and exclamations over all the subdued activity going on downstairs.

"We'll see you later, Catherine." Angela waved two fingers and took Ada away, but not before warning, "Now remember, you're not to leave this room until I come for you."

"Don't worry," Bobbi promised. "I'll see that she doesn't."

Left alone, Catherine and Bobbi had only to look at each other to burst into matching grins and hug each other again, before Bobbi exclaimed, "Have you seen what's going on down there!"

Catherine, panicked afresh, placed a hand on her hammering heart and pleaded, "Don't tell me. I'm giddy enough as it is. This is all so unbelievable!"

Whatever Catherine had expected the evening to be, she had not in her wildest dreams believed it would turn out like the make-believe weddings she and Bobbi had conjured up during childhood. Yet it seemed to be. Each of the girls realized it as they stood in the feminine bedroom, exchanging inanities, occasionally giggling. A maid knocked to ask if their dresses needed any last-minute pressing. They sent her away and went into the bathroom to check each other's hair, giving a last swish of hair spray, then laughing into each other's eyes in the huge mirror. Another knock sounded and produced a maid with two large boxes containing their bouquets.

They laid them on the bed and looked at the unopened, white containers.

"You first," Catherine said, clasping her hands beneath her chin.

"Oh, no, not this time. We're not eight-year-olds pretending anymore. You first!"

"Let's open them together then."

They did. Bobbi's held a quaint basket of bronze mums and apricot roses, with streamers of pale ribbon falling from its handle. Catherine stood back, quite unable to reach for the stunning spray of white gardenia, baby's breath and apricot roses nestled in their transparent bag with dewy beads of moisture clinging inside. Bobbi watched her press her hands to her cheeks, then close her eyes momentarily, open them once again to remain stock-still, staring at the blossoms. So Bobbi leaned down, removed the pearl-headed pin and lifted the huge spray from its wrapper, releasing the heady fragrance of gardenia and roses into the room. She pinned one of the gardenias into Catherine's hair. Still, Catherine seemed unable to move.

"Oh, Cath, they're beautiful."

Bobbi lifted the bouquet and at last Catherine moved, wordlessly plunging her face into the nosegay. Looking up again across the flowers, she stammered, "I—I don't deserve all this."

Bobbi's voice was soft with emotion. "Of course you do. It's exactly what we dreamed about, Cath. One of us has made it, and everything turned out even better than make-believe."

"Don't say that."

"Don't dissect it, Cath, just enjoy every precious minute of it."

"But you don't know—"

"I know. Believe me, I do. I know that you have doubts about the way you and Clay got started, but don't think about them tonight. Think of the good side, okay?"

"You wanted me to marry Clay all along, didn't you, Bobbi?"

"I wanted something good for you, and if it's Clay Forrester, then, yes, I wanted it."

"I think you've always been a little soft on him yourself."

"Maybe I have. Maybe not, I don't know. I only know if it

were me standing there holding that bouquet, I'd be ecstatic instead of depressed."

"I'm not depressed, really I'm not. It's just more than I bargained for, and it's all so sudden."

"And so you doubt and question? Catherine, for once—just for once—in your godforsaken life, will you accept a little manna from heaven? You're so used to living in hell that a little heaven scares you. Come on, now, smile! And tell yourself that he asked you to marry him because he wanted to. It's going to work. Clay is one of the nicest men I know, but if you tell Stu I said so, I'll kill you."

At last Catherine smiled, but she was affected more than she cared to admit by Bobbi's opinion of Clay.

"Now, come on, let's get your dress on."

They stripped off its protective plastic, looked at each other meaningfully once again, recalling all those childhood games, all that make-believe. But the luxurious velvet was real. Bobbi lifted it high while Catherine raised her arms. When she was halfway into it a sound—suspiciously like a harp—came from below.

"What's that?" Bobbi cocked an ear.

"I can't hear in here," came the muffled voice from inside the dress.

"Oh, here, get your ears out of there!"

When Catherine emerged, they posed like robins listening for worms. They looked at each other in disbelief.

"It sounds like a harp!"

"A harp?"

"Well, doesn't it?"

They both listened again.

"My God, it does!"

"Could there really be a harp in this house?"

"Apparently so."

"Leave it to Angela."

Then they both burst into laughter and finished drawing the dress over Catherine's arms. By now she was shaking visibly. Her palms were damp but she dared not wipe them on the velvet.

"Bobbi, I'm scared stiff."

"Why? You're the main attraction and you look it. Be proud!"

Bobbi zipped and buttoned busily, then walked around behind Catherine and extended the miniature train onto the pink carpet. Catherine caught a glimpse of herself in the mirror, pressed her hands to her tummy and asked, "Do I show a lot?"

Bobbi slapped her cousin's hands down, scolding, "Oh, for heaven's sake, will you *please!*" Then she had an inspiration; she handed over the bouquet. "If you must worry about it, hide behind this."

Catherine struck a prim pose that made them both laugh again, but now the sounds from downstairs were definitely steadier, the hum of voices intermingling with the mellow tones of the music.

The door opened and this time it was Inella who stood there with a tiny, foil-wrapped box.

"Why, don't you look lovely, Miss Catherine," the maid said with a wide smile. "Your groom gave me the honor of delivering this." She extended the box. Catherine only gaped, then reached out a tentative hand, withdrew it, then finally took the gift.

"What is it?"

"Why, I'm sure I don't know, miss. Why don't you open it and see?"

Catherine turned wide eyes to Bobbi.

"Inella's right, open it! I'm dying to see!"

"But what if it's something—" She stopped just short of saying "expensive." The box was too small to be anything but jewelry. It lay in her hand accusingly while she wondered with a sinking feeling why Clay had done this to her. Again her eyes sought Bobbi's, then Inella's. Quickly she stripped away the foil and found a small, velveteen ring box. Her heart was hammering, her throat went suddenly dry. She lifted the lid. Inside no jewels glittered, no rings twinkled. Instead, couched in the velvet slot was a brass key. No message, no clues. Catherine breathed again.

"What's it for?"

"Why, I'm afraid I couldn't guess, Miss Catherine."

"But—"

A knock sounded and Angela came in. As the door opened, the gentle swell of voices told that the crowd was growing below.

"It's nearly time," announced Angela.

"Look." Catherine held up the key. "It's from Clay. Do you know what it's for?"

"I'm afraid I haven't any idea. You'll have to wait until after the ceremony and ask him."

Catherine tucked the key away in her garter, where it seemed to burn warmly against her leg.

"Is Mother okay?"

"Yes, dear, don't worry. She's already in her place."

Inella ventured a tidy kiss on Catherine's cheek, then said, "You do look radiant, Miss Catherine." Then she was gone to attend to her duties below.

Again Bobbi picked up Catherine's bouquet, handed it to her and gave a last caress on the cheek, and stood awaiting her signal. The door swung open and Catherine watched Angela meet Claiborne in the upstairs hall. There was a brief smile from him, a last hovering look from her before they left Catherine's range of vision. Next came Stu, in a lush tuxedo of rich spice brown, with an abundance of starched, apricot-colored ruffles springing from his chest below a high, stiff collar and bow tie. Stu grinned in at Catherine, and she attempted a quavering smile in return before Bobbi moved out into the hall and headed for the stairs.

And then came Steve. Her beloved Steve, looking so handsome in a tuxedo of his own, holding out both hands to her as if inviting her to a minuet. He wore a smile that melted her heart, that washed away their earlier disagreement. Catherine knew she must move forward, but her feet refused. Steve, sensing her thoughts, stepped gallantly to the bedroom doorway, bowed from the waist and extended an elbow. Suddenly she realized that people below were awaiting them and were more than likely gazing up the steps.

She felt the tug of the train on the carpet, Steve's firm arm beneath her hand and the pressure of her heart thudding high against her rib cage. From below came a collective "Oooh . . ." as she stepped to the head of the stairs. A sudden intimidation gripped her as the raised sea of faces swam into view. But Steve, sensing her hesitation, closed his free hand over hers, urging her down the first step. She was dimly aware of candles washing everything with a mellow glow. They were everywhere: in wall sconces, on shelves and tables, gleaming and twinkling from the floral sprays attached to the railing and from within the study where an overflow of guests watched. A path emerged as she and Steve rounded the newel post and glided toward the living room. Catherine had a fleeting memory of the first time she'd been in that foyer, sitting on the velvet bench now hidden behind the multitude of guests. How apprehensive she'd been then, yet this was not really so different. Her stomach was in knots. She moved in hypnotic fashion toward the living room doorway, toward Clay. From somewhere an electronic keyboard had joined the harp in a simple Chopin prelude. And everywhere, everywhere, there was the aura of candleglow, all gold and amber and warm and serene. The smell of flowers mingled with the waxen scent of candle smoke while Catherine drifted through the throng of guests, quite unaware of their great number, of their admiring gazes, or of how, for many of them, the sight of her brought back quicksilver memories of their own breathless walk down the aisle. The living room doorway captured her every thought; the idea of Clay waiting on the other side of it sent her heart flitting and her stomach shaking.

She had a dim impression of her mother waiting in a semicircle of countenances that faced her from the bay window, of space emerging as people rustled back to clear the way. But then all others were forgotten as Catherine's eyes fell upon Clay. He stood in the classic groom's pose, hands clasped before him, feet spraddled, face unsmiling and a bit tense. She had thought to avoid his eyes, but hers had a will of their own. As if he had materialized at the whim of some talented spinner of fairy tales, both he and the setting were too perfect.

Lord help me, thought Catherine, as their eyes met. Lord help me.

He waited, his hair like ripe wheat with the sun setting over it. A tall sconce of countless candles turned his skin to amber, reflecting from the deep apricot ruffles that only added to his masculinity. He wore a vested tuxedo of rich cinnamon, a sternly tied bow tie that suddenly bobbed up, then settled back in place at his first sight of her. His eyes—in that flawless face—widened, and she caught the nearly imperceptible movement as he began locking and unlocking his left knee. Then, just before she lost his glance, his hands dropped to his sides and he wet his lips. Blessedly, he then became only an impression at her side. But she knew he turned to gaze once more at her flushed cheek while the organ and harp faded into only a murmurous background.

"Dearly beloved . . ."

The charade began. Things became surreal to Catherine. She was a child again, playing wedding with Bobbi, walking across a lawn dressed in dishtowels and curtains, carrying a bouquet of dandelions. Pretending she was back there took away the sting of guilt at what she was doing.

"Who gives this woman?"

"I do, her brother."

Reality returned and with it Clay's arm, taking the place of Steve's. It was solid, but surprising, for minute tremors scuttled there, felt but not seen.

This time I wanna be the bride.

But you're always the bride!

No, I ain't! You were the bride last time!

Aw, come on, don't cry. Okay, but next time I get to wear the curtain on my head!

From her left, Bobbi smiled, while sweet, naive memories came whirling back. The minister spoke; he had a mellifluous voice and could manage to sound as if what he said were being spoken solely to her and Clay. Catherine trained her eyes on the minister's lips, concentrating hard on the words as he reminded those about to be joined of the importance of patience, love and faithfulness. Some muscle tensed into a knot beneath Catherine's hand, was forcibly relaxed, then twitched again. She realized that the minister had asked all the married couples present to join their hands and renew their wedding vows silently along with the bride and groom. Silently Catherine pleaded, No! No! What you're witnessing is a sham! Don't base your reaffirmation of love on something that is meaningless!

She escaped once again into the play days of yesteryear.

When you get married, what kinda man are you gonna marry?
Rich.
Oh, Bobbi, honestly, is that all you think about?
Well, what kind you gonna marry?
One who likes to be with me so much he comes straight home
instead of stopping at bars. And he's always gonna be nice to me.

The minister asked them to turn and face each other and hold hands. The profusion of gardenias and roses was given into Bobbi's hands. During the exchange their childhood fantasies were reflected within a glance the two exchanged.

Then Catherine's hands were clasped firmly in Clay's brown, strong fingers, and she felt dampness on his palms and on her own. The minister's voice droned on, far away, and Catherine was suddenly afraid to look Clay full in the face.

I'm gonna marry a man who looks just like Rock Hudson.
Not me. I like blond hair and stormy eyes.

My God, thought Catherine now, did I really say that?

She raised her eyes to blond hair, to gray, sober eyes that wore an expression of sincerity as they probed hers for the benefit of their guests. His face was limned by flickering candlelight that accented the straight nose, long cheeks and sensitive lips that were parted slightly, but somber. An errant pulse beat showed just above his high, tight, apricot-colored collar and the stern bow tie. His manner was faultless, convincing. It created havoc within Catherine.

A man who is nice to me. Blond hair and stormy eyes. One who
is rich.

Phrases from the past resounded through the chambers of Catherine's heart, filling it with remorse unlike any she'd suffered before. But those who looked on couldn't guess the turmoil within her, for she paralleled Clay's superb act, searching his eyes as he searched hers, while the pressure on her knuckles grew to sweet agony.

What are we doing? she wanted to cry. Do you know what you do to me with those eyes of yours? What do I do to myself by clenching your too-strong fingers this way, by pretending to idolize your too-perfect face? Don't you recognize the pain of a girl whose youthful dreams painted this very illusion, time and time again, who escaped into scenes such as this when reality threatened? Don't you understand that I honestly believed those dreams would come true one day? If you do, release my hands, release my eyes, but above all keep my heart free of you. You are too flawless and this is too close to the real thing and I have suffered long enough for the lack of love. Please, Clay, turn away before it's too late. You are a temporary illusion, and I must not, must not get lost in it.

But she was trapped in a farce of her own making, for Clay did not turn away, nor release her eyes or her hands. Her palms felt seared, her heart blistered. And for a moment she knew the cruel bite of wishfulness.

At last she dragged her eyes downward. Then Stu stepped forward, drawing a ring from his pocket. She extended her trembling fingers and Clay slid a diamond-studded band halfway on and held it hovering there.

"I, Clay, take thee, Catherine . . ."

While his deep voice spoke the words, Catherine's cheated heart wanted suddenly for this to mean something. But this was only a fantasy. Her thoughts tumbled on while Clay completed the ring's journey to its nesting place beside the heirloom already there.

She was startled then to find a ring placed in her palm— Angela had thought of everything—and her eyes fled once more to Clay's. Another prop for the play? hers asked. But perhaps he had chosen it himself, not Angela. Obediently she dropped her gaze and adorned his finger with the wide, gold unstudded florentine band.

"I, Catherine, take thee, Clay . . ." Her unsteady voice was threatened by shredded nerves, lost dreams and the awful need to cry.

But still there was more to be endured as they turned once again full-face to the blurred minister's garb. Hazily Catherine heard him pronounce them man and wife. Then the cleric smiled benevolently and sealed Catherine's and Clay's joined hands with both of his own.

"May your lives together be long and happy," he wished simply, never suspecting what the words did to Catherine's already strained emotions. She stared at the wavering sight of all their hands together, quite numb now. Then the minister's hands disappeared and his voice poured out softly for the last time. "And now you may seal your vows with your first kiss as Mr. and Mrs. Clay Forrester."

Shattered already, Catherine didn't know what to do. She felt as if she aged years in the mere moment while Clay took the lead, turning toward her with every misty eye in the house upon them. She lifted her face; the breath caught in her throat. She expected no more than a faint brush of lips, but instead his face loomed near, those gray eyes were lost in closeness, and she found herself enfolded in Clay's arms, gently forced against the starched ruffles of his elegant shirtfront, besieged by soft, slightly opened lips that were far, far too compelling. Haunting memories came flooding back.

No, Clay, don't! she longed to cry. But he did. He kissed her fully. And in that moment of first contact she sensed his apology, but found herself unable to forgive him for the convincing job he was doing.

He released her then, to the accompaniment of a collective murmur, and his breath touched her nose as he stepped back and looked into her startled eyes. There followed the kind of smile she'd been waiting for since childhood, sweeping Clay's face as if the moment were genuine, and she was forced to return one equally as bright. Then Clay tucked her hand possessively within his arm and turned her to face their guests.

She wore the pasted-on smile until it held its own. She was beleaguered by hugs, kisses and congratulations, starting with Stu, who unabashedly kissed her hard on the mouth. Next came Steve, holding her a little too long, a little too protectively, rocking a little while he squeezed her and whispered, "Chin up" in her ear.

"Oh, Steve," she allowed herself to say, knowing that he alone understood.

"Shh, babe, you're both doing fine. I wish you could see how you look together."

Clay's father appeared, held her by the upper arms and welcomed her to the family with a generous hug and a direct kiss—the first kiss from him ever. Over his shoulder she saw Clay with his arms wrapped around Ada. Grandma and Grandpa Elgin gave her elfin pats and smiles, and Elizabeth Forrester bestowed upon her a regal kiss for each cheek and a tap of her cane on the right shoulder, as if she were being knighted.

"You are a beautiful young woman. I shall expect beautiful children from you," the old eagle stated sagaciously before turning away as if the matter were settled. Then Catherine was passed around like a dish of divinity, tasted by many mouths until she was actually quite grateful to be returned at last to

Clay—until he pleased every guest there by voluntarily giving them what they waited for!

He swooped down, smiling boldly, and grasped Catherine firmly around her ribs, then picked her cleanly up off the floor until she hung suspended like a marionette. Indeed, she had no more choice than a marionette whose strings are controlled by the puppeteer. She could only submit to Clay's lips while the gardenias were wrapped so far around his neck that her nose was buried in them. She closed her eyes, spinning like a leaf in a whirlwind, intoxicated by the overpowering fragrance of the waxy flowers, by the awful sense that this was real, pretending momentarily that it was. The instant he touched her lips, Catherine felt the almost automatic reach of Clay's tongue toward her own, then her own surprised tongue arching in hesitation, not quite knowing what to do with itself. Then Clay's withdrawing politely again. She was faintly aware that the crowd had burst into applause but allowed herself to become mesmerized by the sensation that the world was twirling crazily. With her eyes closed and her arms around her husband's neck she endured an endless kiss while he slowly turned them both in a circle. But the kiss had grown long—difficult to find a place for a tongue in the midst of such a kiss if it does not take its natural course—until at its end, his tongue again touched hers, then, elusive as quicksilver, was gone.

But the crowd saw nothing more than a groom turning his bride in a slow circle in the middle of a candlelit room, kissing, rejoicing in the accepted fashion. They knew nothing of the elusive tongue-dance that accompanied the embrace.

Catherine came out from behind her gardenias with scarlet cheeks, which added to everyone's delight except her own. But then she was grateful to Clay for the convincing ploy, for when she turned from his arms it was to find a string of familiar faces with sparkling eyes that had just witnessed the entire scenario with awestruck rapture. For the first time Catherine didn't need to act. Her elation was genuine as she flew to greet Marie, then Francie, and Grover and Vicky, too!

Having them there made it nearly perfect. Catherine was touched by the sight of the usually unkempt Grover with her hair all shining and curled like Catherine had never seen it before. And Vicky, who had miraculously managed to let her nails grow beyond the tips of her finger and had polished them the most horrendous shade of bloodred. And Francie, smelling of Charlie perfume. Marie, tiny and petite in spite of how close she was to her due date. Marie, the sprite, the matchmaker, who had first taught Catherine to accept the contact of a caring hand. How many times had they touched hands since?

Clay arrived at Catherine's side again, encircling her waist loosely, then pulling her against his hip with a smiling expression she knew was for the girls.

"Isn't she something?" Francie demanded. And obligingly Clay tightened his grip, spread his hand on Catherine's ribs and dropped a loving kiss on the corner of her eye.

"Yes, she's something, my bride." Catherine refused to look up at Clay. His fingers rode perilously close to her breast.

"What do you think of our dress?" Marie asked.

Again he moved the hand, caressing the velvet appreciatively, answering, "Gorgeous," then continuing to play their game by asking, "Who's going to wear it next?"

"Well, that depends on which one of us can snag a guy like you. Hey, why don'tcha let go of her and let us have our turns?"

Deftly Marie divided Clay from his bride while he gave Catherine the required Help! What can I do? look, then threw his all into a tremendous kiss for the tiny Marie. Now it was Clay's turn to be passed around like a sweet. Catherine could only look on, smiling in spite of herself. He kissed them all, giving them a taste of what they wished was theirs. He returned to his bride only when they'd tasted their fill, some of them for a little too long, some with too-rapt expressions as their kiss ended.

But for his understanding, Catherine was again grateful to Clay.

They moved through the crowd again, Catherine at last realizing it was far, far larger than Angela had hinted it would be. Not only the girls from Horizons, but business associates, family friends and numerous relatives had been impetuously added to the invitation list. Angela's "intimate little affair" had blossomed into a full-blown social event of the season.

EIGHTEEN

She and Clay were ensconced in the study to sign the marriage certificate under the gaze of the minister. They gave away no more than shaky fingers, then the photographer was there popping his bulbs at their hands posed upon the document, then upon Catherine's bouquet, then herding them back into the living room to pose in the bay window with the other members of the wedding party. Throughout all this Catherine succeeded in being spontaneous and gay, as brides are expected to be. Bright repartee fell from her lips and from Clay's while they touched again and again until it became automatic, this reaching for each other's waists. And somehow Catherine found herself beginning to enjoy it.

Upon the dining room table a fountain of champagne cascaded. Clay and Catherine were buffeted there to catch their glasses full and sip around each other's love-knotted arms while the cameras again recorded the moment for posterity. The gentlemen guests posed around Catherine's gartered leg. She caught Clay's eye—was it twinkling?—above the glass of champagne he sipped. Next she posed on the stairway, where she tossed her bouquet over the banister. It was caught by a young girl Catherine didn't recognize.

Small tables appeared, set up with smooth efficiency by a host of hired waiters. Angela managed to oversee the dinner arrangements with silent skill while giving the impression that she'd never left her guests' sides nor swayed her attentions away from them.

Angela's know-how brought off a masterpiece of coordination. By the time Catherine was seated beside Clay at the head table, her admiration for his mother had grown immensely. It took more than money, Catherine realized, to achieve what Angela had here tonight.

The guests were served elegant plates of chicken breast stuffed with Minnesota's rare and delectable wild rice, garnished by crisp broccoli and spiced peach halves. The plates were as delightful to look at as they were to dip into. But what was most appreciated was the almost slick transition from reception rooms to dining hall. The entire festivity was proving to be a stunning success. Gratified, Catherine leaned around Clay to tell Angela so. But she only waved a nonchalant hand and assured Catherine the joy had been hers, she'd have felt cheated to do less and every minute had been worth it. Then she squeezed Catherine's hand.

It was in the middle of the meal that Catherine remembered the key. "Clay, I got your gift. Inella brought it upstairs before the ceremony, but I don't know what it's for."

"Guess."

She was afraid to. The whole evening was already over-whelming.

"The town house?" she ventured, but there was too much noise. Clay leaned down, his ear directly in front of her lips.

"What?"

"The town house, I said."

He straightened, smiled teasingly and only shook his head. She saw his lips move, but there was such a tinkling clangor going on that she couldn't hear him either. Now she lowered her ear to his lips, but while she was thus posed, straining to hear his reply, she became aware that all voices in the room had stopped and only the demanding sound of spoons striking wineglasses filled the air.

Startled, she looked up to find every eye waiting. Then she realized Clay's hand rested on the back of her neck. It slid away and he smilingly began getting to his feet. Realization dawned, but still she hesitated, linen napkin forgotten in one hand, fork in the other, unprepared for yet another assault on her senses.

Clay stepped behind her chair, leaned near her ear. "Apparently they're not going to let us off with a couple of quick kisses that half of them didn't see."

Quick kiss, she thought, was that last what he calls a *quick kiss?*

It was an old custom, one on which Catherine hadn't reckoned. The first kiss had been part of the ceremony. The second had taken her by surprise. But this one—this one was something altogether different. This was the one where plenty of schmaltz was expected.

From behind her came the innocent invitation, "Mrs. Forrester?" But Catherine suspected that could she see his face she'd find one eyebrow cocked up saucily, along with the corners of his mouth. She had no choice, so she gave the expected nervous laugh and got to her feet. There was no evading the issue this time as Clay gave her a regular Valentino job. Oh, he laid it on with aplomb! He pinned both of her arms at her sides, bent his head sideways and her slightly backward until she thought they'd both land on the floor. Her hands spread wide, finding nothing to hold onto but the taut fabric across his back. And while his tongue plundered the inside of her mouth in no uncertain terms, everyone in the room whistled and hooted and tapped their glasses all the more noisily until Catherine thought she would die of agony or ecstasy or a combination of the two. She died of neither. Instead, she found some welcome reserve of humor. He released her, straightened and laughed into her eyes for the benefit of their guests, holding her loosely now about the waist with his hips resting against her own.

"Ah, Valentino, I'm sure," she said with a smile.

"They love it," he rejoined above the burst of applause. If anyone cared to read lips, Catherine was sure it would appear that Clay had said, "I love it." He held her a moment longer in that relaxed and familiar slackness. From the far reaches of the room it appeared they were the typically starstruck nuptial pair. He even rocked her sideways once, then plunged forward again to whisper in her ear, "Sorry."

Catherine's stomach felt at that moment like she'd eaten too much of Inella's salmon again. But before she could dwell on it, the photographer was there, demanding that they pose, feeding each other from filled forks. It was disconcerting, watching Clay's mouth open to receive food, holding the pose like a statuette, watching the glistening tip of his tongue, which had only a moment ago unabashedly invaded her own.

The meal progressed, but Catherine couldn't eat another bite. Clay poured more champagne into her glass and she dove

into it like a sailor from a burning ship. It made her head light
and fuzzy and she warned herself to be careful. It was confusing
stuff.

But before the bubbles cleared from her eyes, the glasses were
ringing out again and Clay was standing up, taking her by the
upper arm. This time it was easier, better, the wine having gone
to her head somewhat, and her inhibitions sagged shamelessly
while Clay gave her a kiss the likes of which turned her spine to
aspic.

What the heck, the bride thought, give them what they want
and forget it. And so she threw a little more of her heart into it—
to say nothing of her tongue, which found a readily receptive
mate within Clay's mouth. She even emoted a little, plopping her
hand on top of her head as if holding it on, quite tickled by her
own ingenuity.

The kiss ended. Clay laughed into her eyes. "Good job, Mrs.
Forrester."

"Not bad yourself, Mr. Forrester." But she was all too aware
of the way his hips again nudged her own through the velvet
gown and the way her slightly bubbled tummy intruded upon
the spot where his crisp tuxedo jacket hung open. "But I think
you'd better stop filling my glass."

"Now why would I want to do a thing like that?" He smirked
cutely, raising an eyebrow suggestively. His hands skimmed
lightly downward to rest on her hips. She wondered if it was her
imagination or had he pressed himself momentarily closer? But
then she decided it was her imagination. After all, he was per-
forming—just as she was—for the benefit of all the tinkling
glass-tappers out there.

The cake was wheeled in on a glass cart. It was a towering
creation of fluted columns and doves with ribbons threaded
through their confectionary beaks, and it raised a chorus of aah's

that gratified Angela. Clay's and Catherine's hands were trained upon the knife handle with its voluminous white satin bow. Flashbulbs exploded, the knife sliced through the cake, and the bride was instructed to feed her groom, this time from her fingertips. But he not only took the cake, he lipped the frosting from her knuckle while, above it, his gray eyes crinkled at the corners. Naughty sensations tingled their way down to Catherine's toes and her eyes swerved swiftly aside.

"Mmm . . . sweet stuff," he said this time.

"Bad for your teeth." She smiled up at him. "And rumored to cause hyperactivity."

He reared back and laughed wholeheartedly, and once again they sat down.

"Let's have one of the groom feeding the bride," the photographer suggested, zooming in on his quarry.

"How many more must we take?" Catherine asked, flustered now, but not entirely disliking the game.

"I'll be neat," Clay promised in an aside. But that same devilish crinkle tugged at the corners of his mouth and eyes. He lifted a morsel of cake and she took it, tasted sugar, swallowed, then found him still standing there with an index finger frosted and waiting.

With a smile as sweet as any confection she said, "This is getting bawdy." But all she could do was suck the end of his finger, finding it slightly salty, too.

"Our guests find it amusing."

"You, Mr. Forrester, are unforgivably salty." But at that moment she caught Elizabeth Forrester's bright, knowing gaze snapping down the table at them, and she wondered what the old girl suspected.

The moment turned serious when Claiborne rose to give Catherine his official welcome. He came around the table and gave her a hug and a kiss and his approval for all to see. She sensed sobriety returning to Clay as he leaned an elbow on the table's edge and absently brushed an index finger across his lip, watching. Then he rose and shook hands with his father. Applause followed as Clay sat back down. The whole thing had been appallingly earnest on Claiborne's part, and as their eyes met, both Catherine and Clay realized it.

"On second thought, you'd better pour me another glass," she said, "and smile. Your grandmother Forrester is watching every move we make."

"Then this is for her, and for Mother and Father," Clay said, and reached a finger to tip her chin up and placed the lightest kiss upon her lips. Then he reached for the champagne bottle. But his smile and gay mood did not return.

The meal ended and dancing began. Catherine met more of Clay's relatives and spent the appropriate amount of time with each. Then she found time to move off by herself and seek out her mother, and Uncle Frank and Aunt Ella. The evening was moving inexorably toward its close, and with each passing minute Catherine's apprehension grew.

Standing with Bobbi in the living room, Catherine caught sight of Clay out in the foyer. He stood with a remarkably beautiful girl whose auburn hair trailed down to the middle of her back. She cradled a champagne glass as if she were born with it in her hand. She smiled up at Clay, gyrated her head as if to toss her hair back. But it fell alluringly across her cheek. Then the girl circled Clay's neck with the arm bearing the stem glass, raising her lips to his and kissing him differently than any of the starry-eyed girls from Horizons had. Catherine observed the somber look on Clay's face as he spoke to the girl, dropping his eyes to the floor, then raising them to her face again with a look of apology etching his every feature. Catherine would have been lying to herself had she not admitted that the touch he gave the girl's upper arm was a caress. He spoke into her eyes, rubbed that arm, then gave it a lingering squeeze before he bent to drop an unhurried kiss on the crest of one flawless, high-boned cheek.

Quickly Catherine turned her back. But the picture rankled until something pinched at her throat and made it hard to swallow the champagne she lifted to her lips.

"Who is that girl out there with Clay?"

Bobbi glanced toward the foyer and her smile immediately faded.

"It's her, isn't it?" Catherine questioned. "It's Jill Magnusson."

Bobbi turned her back on the couple too quickly. "Yes, it is. So what?"

"Nothing."

But try as she might, Catherine could not resist looking their way again to find Clay now relaxed, one hand in his trouser pocket while Jill threaded her arm through his and rested her breast leisurely against his biceps. She was the kind of girl who could get by with a touch like that. Her sophistication made it look chic instead of shabby. An older man had joined them now and Jill Magnusson laughed, leaned sideways without relinquishing her claim on Clay and gave the older man a swift kiss on the side of his mouth.

"And who's he?" Catherine asked, carefully keeping the ice from her tone.

"That's Jill's father."

There was a sick and empty feeling settling in the pit of Catherine's stomach. She wished she hadn't witnessed Jill leaning casually against Clay in the presence of her own father, nor her obvious lack of unease at kissing Clay with an arm looped around his neck. But Catherine was in for a further surprise, for even as she looked on, Elizabeth Forrester approached the group and it was immediately apparent that Jill Magnusson was as comfortable with the old eagle as she was with the champagne glass and Catherine's new husband. The unapproachable old woman didn't daunt Jill one bit. The brunette actually linked her remaining arm through Elizabeth's, laughing gracefully at whatever Clay's grandmother said. Then—unbelievably—the old eagle laughed, too.

And Catherine finally turned away.

At that moment Clay's eyes drifted up, found Bobbi observing the quartet, and immediately he withdrew his hand from his pocket, excused himself and crossed toward her and Catherine.

"Jill and her parents were just leaving," he explained. It became apparent as soon as the words left his mouth that explanations should not have been necessary. They had not been for the other guests who'd already departed.

"Somehow it seems that Catherine was not introduced to the Magnussons."

"Oh . . . I'm sorry, Catherine. I should have seen to it." He glanced uncertainly from Catherine to the front door. But it was opening. Angela and Mrs. Magnusson were touching cheeks fondly while the two men shook hands, and Jill gave a long, last look across the expanse that separated her from Clay. Then they were gone.

"Catherine . . ." Clay began, but realizing Bobbi was still there, said, "Excuse us, will you, Bobbi?" He took Catherine's elbow and moved her beyond earshot. "I think it's time we left."

Certainly, now that Jill Magnusson is gone, thought Catherine. "But shouldn't we thank your parents first?"

"I've done that already. Now we're expected to simply slip away unnoticed."

"But what about the gifts?" She was grasping at straws and she knew it.

"They'll be left here. We're not expected to thank anyone for them tonight. We're only supposed to disappear while they're busy."

"Mom will be wondering . . ." she began lamely, looking around.

"Will she?" Clay could see how nervous Catherine had suddenly become. "Steve is with her. He'll see that she gets home okay."

Catherine saw Ada in happy conversation with Bobbi's parents and Steve. Catherine raised her glass to her lips, but found it empty. Then Clay removed it from her lifeless fingers, saying, "Slip upstairs and get your coat and I'll meet you by the side door. And don't forget the key."

Once more in the pink bedroom, Catherine at last allowed her shoulders to sag. She plopped down on the edge of the gay little bed, then leaned back and let her eyelids close wearily. She wished this was her own room, that she could snuggle in and awaken in the morning to find that no wedding had taken place after all. Absently she picked up a small pillow, toyed with the ruffled edge, staring until the design on it seemed to wriggle. She blinked, tossed the pillow aside and went to stand before the cheval mirror. She pressed her dress against her lower abdomen, visually measuring. She raised her eyes and stared at the reflected face, wondering how it could be so pink when she felt so bloodless. From the depths of the silvered glass, blue eyes watched her fingertips touch one cheek, then flutter down uncertainly to her lips. Her brows wore a troubled look as she assessed her own reflection and found countless imperfections in it.

"Jill Magnusson," she whispered. Then she turned and flung her coat loosely around her shoulders.

Outside the world wore that semi-dark glow of the first snow of the season, glittering almost as if from within. The night sky looked as though someone had spilled milk across it, obscuring the moon behind a film of white. But as if a droplet slipped off now and then, an occasional snowflake drifted down. The lights from the windows twinkled playfully on the white frosting, and the leafless limbs of the trees looked warm now beneath their blankets. The air was brittle, though, brittle enough to freeze the tender petals of the gardenia forgotten in Catherine's hair.

Catherine clutched her coat beneath her chin, raised her face and sucked in the taste of the cold. Revitalized, she hurried through the shadows to the end of the house near the garages. It was quiet. Not even the hum of distant traffic intruded, and she savored it, trying to make it calm her.

"Sorry it took so long."

She jumped at the sound of Clay's voice and clutched her coat tighter. He materialized out of the darkness, a tall shadow with its coat collar turned up. "I got caught by a few well-wishers and couldn't get away."

"It's okay." But she drew her mouth down within the protective folds of her coat.

"Here, you're freezing." He touched her back, steered her toward a strange, dark car that waited there. Even in the blackness she could see that it had streamers trailing from it. He opened the driver's-side door.

"Have you got the key?" he asked.

"The key?" she asked dumbly.

"Yes, the key." He smiled with only one side of his mouth. "I'll drive tonight, but after this, it's yours."

"M-mine?" she stammered, uncertain of which to look to for verification, the car or his face.

"Happy wedding day, Catherine," he said simply.

"The key was for this?"

"I thought you'd like a wagon, for groceries and things like that."

"But, Clay . . ." She was shivering worse now, the tremors quite pronounced in spite of the way she hugged herself into the coat.

"Have you got the key?"

"Clay, this isn't fair," she pleaded.

"All's fair in love and war."

"But this is not love or war. How can I just . . . just say, 'Thank you, Mr. Forrester,' and drive off in a brand-new car as if I have every right to it?"

"Don't you?"

"No! It's too much and you know it."

"The Corvette isn't exactly a family car," he reasoned. "We'd have trouble getting even the wedding gifts to the town house in it."

"Well, fine, then, trade it in or—or borrow the Bronco again, but don't hand me the world on a platter that I feel guilty to eat from."

His hand dropped from the car door; his voice sounded slightly piqued. "It's a gift. Why do you have to make so much of it? I can afford it, and it will make our lives infinitely easier to have two cars. Besides, Tom Magnusson owns an auto dealership and we get great deals from him on all the cars we buy."

Common sense returned with a cold swipe. "Well, in that case, thank you."

Catherine got in and slid across to the passenger side. He got behind the wheel to find her leg angled across the transmission hump, her skirt pulled up. She produced the key from within her garter and handed it to him.

It was warm in his palm.

He seemed a little ill at ease as he started the engine, but let it idle. He adjusted the heater, cleared his throat. "Catherine, I don't know how to say this, but it seems we each got a key tonight. I got one, too."

"From whom?"

"From Mother and Father."

She waited, trembling inside.

"It's for the honeymoon suite at the Regency."

She made a sound like air going out of a balloon, then moaned, "Oh, God."

"Yes, oh, God," he agreed, then laughed nervously.

"What are we going to do?" she asked.

"What do you want to do?"

"I want to go to the town house."

"And let the Regency phone tomorrow and ask why the bride and groom didn't show up?"

She sat silent, shaking.

"Catherine?"

"Well, couldn't we . . . couldn't we just"—she swallowed—"check in and leave again and go to the town house, maybe leave the key for them to find in the morning?"

"Do you want me to go back into the house and pick up a load of gifts and hope we find some sheets and blankets when we open them?"

He was right; they were trapped.

"Catherine, this is adolescent. We've just gotten married and we've agreed to spend the next several months living together. You realize that we're going to bump into each other now and then during that time, don't you?"

"Yes, but not in any honeymoon suite at the Regency." Still she knew that before the night was out they'd have put the lie to her words.

"Catherine, what the hell did you expect me to do, stuff the key back into my father's hand and say, 'Use it yourselves'?"

There was no point in arguing. They sat there thinking until finally Clay put the car in reverse and backed away from the shadow of the garage.

"Clay, I don't have my suitcase!" she gulped.

"It's in the back with mine," he said, while the doorman grew small behind them, his arms folded and his collar turned up.

They drove along in silence, Catherine still gripping her coat although the car had long since grown warm. The smell of new, hot oil mingled with that of new vinyl. With each mile Catherine grew tighter.

Finally she said, "Why does it seem like everything important that happens between us happens in one of your cars?"

"It's one of the few places we've ever been alone."

"Well, your parents sure took care of that, didn't they?"

With an abrupt swerve he pulled to the side of the road, skidded to a halt and craned to look back over his shoulder.

She perked alert. "Now what?"

He was already turning around. "You want to go to the town house, okay, we'll go to the town house," he snapped.

She clutched his arm. "Don't," she pleaded. "Don't, not tonight."

He brooded silently, tense now, too.

"I was wrong, okay?" she conceded. "Just don't drive crazy—

not tonight. I know they meant well to get the room for us, and you're right. What difference does it make where we sleep?" She dropped her hand from his arm. "Please try to understand, though. It's been a nerve-racking night. I'm not used to lavishness."

"Maybe you better get used to it, because they never do anything halfway."

He drove on more sensibly now.

"How much do you imagine it cost them to arrange all that?"

"Don't let it bother you. Mother loved it all. I've told you before, she's in her element planning things like that. Couldn't you tell how she was enjoying her success?"

"Is that supposed to ease my conscience?" she asked.

"Catherine, are we going to go through this every time we get something from them? Why do you constantly berate yourself? Has it occured to you that maybe you're not the only one benefiting from our arrangement? It may surprise you to learn that I'm actually quite happy to be moving away from home. I should have done it years ago, but it was easier to stay where I was. It's not exactly a hardship being coddled and taken care of. But I'm tired of living with them. I'm glad to be getting out. I wonder if they aren't equally relieved to have me leave at last.

"And as for my parents—don't think they didn't get something out of that production number. Did you see my father's face when he was brandishing his champagne glass? Did you see Mother when she was directing waiters around, watching while everything slipped into place like greased gears? They get high off social success, so just think of it as another autumn gala thrown by the Forresters. They throw one quite like it several times a year anyway.

"What I'm trying to say is that it's their style. Giving us the night at the Regency is what their friends expect them to do, plus—"

"Plus what?" She shot him a look.

"Plus, giving us the right start gives them a false sense of security. It helps them believe everything will turn out right between us."

"And you don't feel guilty accepting any of it?"

"Yes, dammit!" he burst out. "But I'm not going to go out and buy a hair shirt over it, all right?"

His belligerence surprised her, for he'd been mellow for days. They arrived at the Regency in strained silence. Catherine made a move toward her door handle and Clay ordered, "Wait here until I get the suitcases out."

He walked around the car, yanking the crepe paper streamers off. His breath formed a pale pink cloud, refracting the glow from the colorful hotel sign and the lights at the entry. He opened the tailgate, and she heard the muffled swish as he tossed the streamers in.

When he opened her door and she'd stepped out, he reached for her arm. "Catherine, I'm sorry I yelled. I'm nervous, too."

She studied his odd-colored visage in the neon night, but she could find nothing to reply.

NINETEEN

The porter flourished his hand toward the room and Catherine followed it with her eyes. It felt as though she were couched in a Wedgwood teacup. The room was elegant and tasteful, decorated exclusively in oyster white and Wedgwood blue. The cool blue walls were trimmed with pearly moldings done in beadwork, arranged in rectangles with a carved acanthus centered in each. The design was repeated on two sets of double doors that led to closet and bath. Elegant white silk draperies were crowned by an ornate swagged valance while alabaster French Provincial furniture contrasted soothingly with the room's plush blue carpeting. Besides the enormous bed there was a pleasant grouping of furniture: a pair of chairs and a coffee table of Louis XVI persuasion, with graceful cabriole legs and oval, marble tops. On the table sat a profuse bouquet of white roses whose scent was thick in the air.

When the door closed, leaving them alone, Catherine approached the flowers, found the tiny green envelope and turned questioningly to Clay.

"I don't know, open it," he said.

The card read simply, "All our love, Mother and Dad."

"It's from your parents." She extended the card, then sidled a safe distance away while he read it.

"Nice," he murmured, and stuck the card back into the roses. He pushed back his jacket and scanned the room with hands akimbo. "Nice," he repeated.

"More than nice," she seconded, "more like smashing."

Upon the triple dresser was a basket of fruit and a silver loving cup bearing a green glass bottle. Clay walked over, lifted the bottle, read the label, set it back down, then turned, tugging the knot from his bow tie and unfastening a single button of his shirt. Her eyes flew off in another direction. She walked over and gave a careful peek into the depths of the darkened bathroom.

"Can I hang up your coat for you?" he asked.

She looked surprised to find it still crumpled between her wrist and hip. "Oh—oh, sure."

He came to reach for her garment and again she retreated a step.

"Don't be skittish," he said laconically, "I'm only going to hang up your coat."

"I'm not skittish. I just don't know what to do with myself, that's all."

He opened the closet doors, spoke at the tinging hangers inside.

"I'd call that skittish. Maybe a glass of champagne would help. Do you want one?" He hung up his tux jacket, too.

"I don't think so." But she wandered back to the dresser anyway and looked over the bottle and the basket. "Who is the fruit from?"

"The management. You want some? How about a last pear of the season?" A tan hand reached around her and hefted one.

"No, no pears either. I'm not hungry."

As she drifted away he tossed the fruit in the air once, twice, then forgot it in his hand, studying her.

"No champagne, no fruit, so what would you like to do to pass the time away?"

She looked up blankly, standing there in the middle of the room as if afraid to come into contact with any article in it. He sighed, dropped the pear back into the basket and moved to carry their suitcases across to the bed.

"Well, we're here, so we might as well make the best of it."

He stalked to the bathroom door, flicked on the light, then turned, gesturing toward it.

"Would you like to be first?"

And the next thing Catherine knew, she was laughing! It started as a silent flutter in her throat and before she could control it, it erupted and she had both hands over her mouth before she flung them wide and continued laughing to the ceiling. At last she looked across to find Clay—the corners of his eyes crinkled now—still waiting just outside the bathroom doorway.

"Come on, hey, wife, I'm trying to be gallant and it's getting tougher by the minute."

And suddenly the tension was relieved.

"Oh, Clay, if your father could see us, I think he'd demand his money back. Are we really in the honeymoon suite of the Regency?"

"I think so." Gamely, he looked around, checking.

"And did you just sign our names in the register as Mr. and Mrs. Clay Forrester?"

"I think so."

She looked up as if appealing to the heavens. "Help, I'm floundering."

"You should do that more often, you know?" He smiled her way.

"Do what, flounder?" She chuckled and made a hapless motion.

"No, laugh. Or even smile. I was beginning to think you were going to wear your stiff face all night long."

"Do I have a stiff face?" It looked mobile and amazed as she asked.

"*Stiff* might not be the right word. Deadpan is probably more accurate. Yes, deadpan. You put it on like armor at times."

"I do?"

"Mostly when we're alone."

"So you'd like it if I smiled more?"

He shrugged. "Yeah, I guess I would. I like smilers. I guess I'm used to being around them."

"I'll try to remember." She glanced toward the window, then back at him. "Clay, what you said down there in the car, well, I'm sorry, too." Her face had turned suddenly serious, contrite.

"No, it was me who got short with you. My timing really stunk."

"No, listen, it was partly my fault, too. I don't want us to fight all the time we're married. I've been around it all my life and now I simply want . . . well, *peace* between us. I know this sounds silly, but it feels better already, just admitting that we're nervous, instead of the way we were acting on the way over here. I want you to know that I'll try to do my part to maintain some kind of status quo."

"Good. Me too. We're stuck with each other for better or for worse, so let's make the better of it instead of the worse."

She smiled a little. "Agreed. So . . . me first, huh?"

They both looked at the bathroom door.

"Yup."

What the heck, she thought, it's only a regular old bathroom, right? And I'm choking in this dress, right? And dying to get comfortable, right?

But once inside the bathroom she was too aware of his presence just outside. She turned on the faucet to cover any personal sounds. She kept glancing furtively at the doors. She confronted herself in the mirror, moving close to analyze her reflection until her breath beaded on the glass.

"Mrs. Clay Forrester, huh?" she asked her reflection. "Well, don't go getting ideas. He told you once you don't play around without paying for it, and he was right. So put on your nightie and go out there and clamber into bed with him, and if you're uncomfortable doing it, you've got nobody to blame but yourself."

Her fingers trembled as she undressed. She stared herself down with too-wide eyes as she removed her velvet wedding gown, then the slip and that ridiculously minuscule bra. Her breasts were weightier now, the nipples broad and florid. At their sudden release, dull twinges of ache flowed through them—not pain exactly, but something akin to it—and she closed her eyes and cupped one in each hand, squeezing and lifting in that way that lately could abate those unexpected throes. Once the pangs were gone came the relief of being unbound. She watched herself scratch the red marks where her bra had bitten too tightly at the top of her ribs, then her stomach, which felt like the head of a drum and itched mercilessly now as the skin began stretching.

Unbidden the thought came that the man who waited on the other side of the door had created these changes in her body.

She shook off the thought, brushed her teeth, ran warm water and soaped a cloth. But just as she was about to scrub off her makeup, it struck her that her face had many shortcomings that would be emphasized without the makeup, so she left it on.

She threw up her arms and a yellow nightgown drifted down like a parachute in the wind, followed by a matching peignoir. Her hands slowed, tying the cover-up at her throat. It was so obviously new. Would he mistake her reason for wearing such frillery? Should she march out there and announce that Ada had bought it at the company store at an employee's discount and had given it to her for a shower gift?

Through the peignoir her new girth was disguised, and she soothed the front, thoughts skittering from one to another. She was putting off opening the door and she knew it. She closed her eyes and swallowed . . . and swallowed again . . . and felt a hidden tremor deep within her stomach.

Suddenly the memory of Jill Magnusson was there in full color behind her eyelids and Catherine knew beyond a doubt that had it been Jill here getting ready to join Clay, there would be no schoolgirl shyness.

She supposed Clay was wishing right now she *was* Jill Magnusson. A hint of self-pity threatened, but she barred it. She remembered that last, long look of regret on Jill's face as she looked back across the room at Clay before walking out the door.

At last Catherine admitted, I carry his child. But it should be her, not me.

The door was soundless. Clay stood with his back to her, gazing down into her open suitcase, his tie forgotten in one hand, toothbrush in the other.

"Your turn," she said quietly, expecting him to jump guiltily. Instead he looked over his shoulder and smiled. His eyes made one quick trip down and up the yellow peignoir.

"Feel better?"

He had pulled his shirttails out of his trousers. Her eyes went down to them like metal shavings to a magnet, to the network of wrinkles pressed into the fabric by his skin. Then farther down, to his stocking feet.

"Much."

They exchanged places and Clay moved into the bathroom, leaving the door open while he only brushed his teeth. In the suitcase, Catherine found a corner of her diary showing beneath the neatly folded clothing there. She tucked it away and closed the suitcase with a snap.

"Are you tired?" he asked, coming back from the bathroom.

"Not a bit."

"Do you mind if I break into that champagne then?"

"No, go ahead. It might help after all."

When his back was turned, she tugged at the top of her neckline; it was far from seductive, but not quite demure. His shoulders flexed and twisted as he worked away at the cork, and the wrinkles on the rear tails of his shirt did incredible things to her stomach, hanging free that way, shifting against his buttocks with each movement. The cork exploded and he swung the bottle over the loving cup.

"Here," he said, coming back with bottle in one hand, glasses in the other. She held the glasses while he poured. But his shirt was unbuttoned all the way now, exposing a thin band of skin a slightly deeper shade than the fabric itself. She dragged her eyes back to the champagne glasses, to the tan, long-fingered hand that reached out to reclaim one.

"To your happiness," he said simply, in his Clay-like, polite, usual way, while she wondered just what would make her happy right now.

"And to yours."

They drank, standing there in the middle of the room. There was a lump in her throat, she realized, as she swallowed the golden liquid. She looked down into her glass.

"Clay, I don't want either of us to pretend this is something it isn't." Rattled now, she put a palm to her forehead and swung away. "Oh, God."

"Come on, Catherine, let's sit down."

He led the way, set the bottle on the table beside the roses and strung himself out on a chair, lying low against its back, legs outstretched, ankles crossed, while she curled up opposite. He had a glimpse of her bare feet before she tucked them up beneath her in the corner of her chair. Together they raised their glasses, eyeing each other as they drank.

"I suppose maybe we're setting out to get drunk," she mused.

"Maybe we are."

"That doesn't make much sense, does it?"

"Not a lick."

"It won't change a thing."

"Nuh-uh."

"Then why are we doing it?"

"Because it'll make crawling into bed easier."

"Let's talk about something else."

"Whatever you say."

She fiddled with her glass, then sat back, drawing circles with it upon her turned knee. Finally she asked, "You know what was the hardest?" Across the table, he was looking very relaxed.

"Hmm-mmm." His eyes were closed.

"Your father's official welcome at the dinner table. I was very touched by it."

Clay's eyes drifted open, studied her a moment before he observed, "You know, I think my father likes you."

With a fingertip she toyed with the bubbles on the surface of her drink. "He still scares me in so many ways."

"I suppose to a stranger he seems formidable. Both he and Grandmother Forrester have an air about them that seems rather officious and puts people on their guard at first. But when you get to know them, you realize they're not that way at all."

"I don't intend to get to know them."

"Why?"

She raised expressionless eyes to his, then dropped them as she answered, "In the long run that'd be best."

"Why?"

His head lolled sideways, yet she suspected his catlike pose was not all real. She considered evading the issue, then decided against it. She leaned to take one rose from the bouquet and held it before her upper lip.

"Because I might learn to like them after all."

He seemed to be mulling that over, but he only tipped his glass again, then shut his eyes.

"Do you know what your Grandmother Forrester said to me tonight?"

"What?"

"She said, 'You are a beautiful bride. I shall expect beautiful children from you,' as if it was an official edict and she'd brook no ugly grandchildren spawned with her name."

Clay laughed appreciatively, his eyes again scrutinizing

Catherine from behind half-closed lids. "Grandmother's usually right—and you were, you know."

"Was?" she asked, puzzled.

"A beautiful bride."

Immediately Catherine hid behind the rose again, became engrossed in studying the depths between its petals.

"I didn't know if I should say it or not, but—dammit, why not?—you were a knockout tonight."

"I wasn't fishing for a compliment."

"You make a habit of that, you know?"

"Of what?"

"Of withdrawing from any show of approval I make toward you. I knew before I said that that you'd turn defensive and reject it."

"I didn't reject it, did I?"

"You didn't accept it either. All I said was that you were a beautiful bride. Does that threaten you?"

"I—I don't know what you mean."

"Forget it then."

"No, you brought it up, let's finish it. Why should I feel threatened?"

"You're the one who's supposed to answer that question."

"But I'm not *threatened* in the least." She swished her rose through the air offhandedly. "You were a terrific-looking groom. There, see? Does that sound like I feel threatened by you?"

But her very tone was defensive. It reminded him of a child who, taking up a dare, says, "See? I'm not either afraid to walk up and ring Crazy Gertie's doorbell," then rings it and runs to beat hell.

"Hey, what do you think," he said in a bantering tone, "are we supposed to thank each other or what?"

That at last drew a smile from her. She relaxed a little as if maybe the wine was now making her sleepy.

"Do you know what your mother said to me?" Clay asked.

"What?"

He mused silently, as if deciding whether or not to tell her. Abruptly he leaned forward and occupied himself with refilling his glass. "She said, 'Catherine used to play wedding when she and Bobbi were little girls. That's all those two would play, always arguing about who'd be the bride.'" Then he lounged back again, propped an elbow on the arm of the chair, rested his temple against two fingers and asked lazily, "Did you?"

"What does it matter?"

"I was only wondering, that's all."

"Well, don't wonder. It doesn't matter."

"Doesn't it?"

But abruptly she changed the subject. "One of your uncles mentioned that you usually go hunting at this time of year but that you haven't had much chance this year because of the wedding interruptions."

"It must've been Uncle Arnold."

"Don't change the subject."

"Did I change the subject?"

"You can go, you know, anytime you want."

"Thank you, I will."

"I mean, we're not *bound* to each other, and nothing has to change. We can still go our separate ways, keep our friends, just like before."

"Great. Agreed, Stu and I will hunt all we want."

"I wasn't really thinking about Stu."

"Oh?" He quirked an eyebrow.

"I was talking about her."

"Her? Who?"

"Jill."

Clay's eyes turned to gray iron, then he jumped up, stalked to the dresser and clapped his glass down hard. "What has Jill got to do with it?"

"I saw you standing in the foyer together. I saw the two of you kissing. I include her when I say you're not bound to me in any way."

He swung around, scowling. "Listen, our families have been friends for years. We've been—" He stopped himself before he could say "lovers." "I've known her since we were kids. And furthermore, her father was right there in front of us, and so was Grandmother Forrester, for God's sake."

"Clay"—Catherine's voice was like eiderdown—"I said it's all right."

He glared at her silently, then swung toward his suitcase, shrugging his shirt off as he went, flinging it carelessly across the foot of the bed before disappearing behind the bathroom door.

When Clay returned, Catherine was sitting on the far edge of the bed with her back to him. The wilted gardenia lay discarded on the bedside table while she brushed her hair. His eyes traveled across the white satin sheets to the robe lying on the foot of the bed, to the back of her pale yellow nightgown, to the brush moving rhythmically. Without a word, he doubled his pillow over and lay down with both hands behind his head. The brush stilled. He heard her thumbnail flicking across its bristles, followed by a clack as she laid the thing down. She reached for the lamp and the room went black. The mattress shifted; the covers over his chest were pulled slightly in her direction. He had no doubt that if he reached out, he'd find her back curled against him.

Their breathing seemed amplified. Sightlessness created such intimacy. Clay lay so rigid that his shoulders began to hurt. Catherine huddled like a snail, involute, acutely aware of him behind her. She thought she could hear her eyelids scraping on her dry eyeballs with each blink. She shivered and pinioned the satin sheet tightly between her jaw and shoulder.

A rustle, barely audible, and she sensed his eyes boring into her back—invisible though it was.

"Catherine," came his voice, "you really have a low opinion of me, don't you?"

"Don't sound so wounded. There's no reason to be. Just to keep the record straight—it should have been her who was the bride today. Do you think I don't know that? Do you think I couldn't tell how she *belongs*? I felt like a square peg in a round hole. And seeing you and her together brought me back to reality. I was becoming rather swept off my feet by all the lavish trappings around me. I'll answer your question now. Yes, I did used to play wedding with Bobbi when we were kids. I'm an old pro at weddings, so this time I found myself really getting into the act. But I'm not pretending anymore. I see things for what they really are, okay?"

Goddammit, thought Clay, I should thank her for giving me permission, but instead it makes me angry. Goddammit, I shouldn't feel like I have to be faithful to a wife, but I do.

Catherine felt the bed bounce as he tossed onto his side and punched his pillow.

Somewhere outside a jet went over, its faraway whine and whistle ebbing off into oblivion. The bed was very large; neither of them had much sensation of sharing it physically, except for the sound of their breathing, far away from each other and in opposite directions. But the animosity between them was a much more palpable presence. It seemed like hours had gone by and Catherine thought Clay had gone to sleep. But then he flung himself onto his back again so abruptly she was sure he'd been wide awake all this time. She was stiff and cramped from staying in her tight curl for so long, but she refused to budge. Her shoulder got a cramp and she had to relax it. The sheet slipped off, and at last giving up, she eased onto her back.

"Are we going to get in each other's hair this way every time bedtime arrives?" he asked coldly.

"I didn't mean to get into your hair."

"Like hell you didn't. Let's at least be honest about it. You meant to bring a third party into bed with us and you succeeded very well. But just remember, if she's here it's at your request, not mine."

"Then why do you sound so angry?"

"Because it's playing havoc with my sleep. If I have to go through this for the next year, I'll be a burned-out wreck."

"So what do you think I'll be?"

Against his will, as he lay brooding, Clay had been resurrecting pictures of Catherine at the ceremony. The way she looked when she'd come around the living room doorway, when they spoke their vows, when she'd discovered all the girls from Horizons there, when he'd kissed her. He remembered the feel of her slightly rounded stomach against his. This was the damnedest thing he'd ever been through, going to bed with a woman and not touching her. All the more absurd because for the first time it'd be legal, and here he lay on his own side of the bed. Dammit, he thought, I should've watched the champagne. Champagne made him horny.

He finally concluded that they were being quite childish about all this. They were husband and wife, they'd been through some decidedly sexual teasing during the course of the evening and were now trying to deny what it was that was keeping them both awake.

What the hell, he thought, things couldn't be worse. "Catherine, do you want to try it again, with no strings attached? Maybe then we can get some sleep."

The muscles in her lower abdomen cinched up tight and set to quivering. She shrank to her side of the bed, turning her back on him again.

"The wine has gone to your head" was all she said.

"Well, what the hell, you can't blame a guy for trying."

She felt like her chest bones might burst and fly into a thousand pieces. Angry with herself for wishing the night to be more than it was, angry with him for his suggestion, she wondered what exquisite torture it would be to turn to him and take him up on his invitation.

But she remained as she was, curled into herself. In the long hours before sleep she wondered over and over again if he had any pajamas on.

TWENTY

Catherine was awakened by the sound of draperies opening. She sat up as if a hundred-and-twenty-piece band had struck up a Sousa march beside her bed. Clay stood in the flood of sunlight, laughing.

"Do you always wake up like that?"

She squinted and blinked, then flopped backward like an old rag doll, covering her eyes with a forearm.

"Oh God, so you *did* have pajamas on."

He laughed again, free and easy, and turned toward the view of the awakening city washed in pink and gold below them.

"Does that mean 'good morning'?"

"That means I wasted a perfectly good night worrying about a dumb thing like whether or not you were wearing pajamas."

"Next time just ask."

Suddenly she was pulling herself off the bed and running for the bathroom door, which thwacked shut behind her.

"Don't listen!" she ordered.

Clay leaned an elbow against the window frame, chuckling to himself, thinking of the unexpected charms of married life.

She came out looking sheepish and went immediately for her cover-up.

"I'm sorry if I was a little abrupt about that, but this little feller in here has made some sudden changes and that's one of them. I'm still not used to it."

"Does this confidence mean you're not mad at me anymore?"

"Was I mad at you? I don't seem to remember." She busied herself doing up the front of the garment.

"Yeah," he said, moving away from the window. "I made some underhanded suggestion and you got huffy."

"Forget it. Let's be friends. I don't like fighting much, even with you."

He confronted her now, bare-chested, giving her hair the once-over so that she started combing it with her fingers.

"Listen," she explained, "I'm not at my best in the morning."

"Who is?" he returned, rubbing his jaw. Then he turned toward a suitcase and rummaged inside it, beginning to whistle softly through his teeth. Mornings she was used to her mother scuffling around the house with an air of martyrdom and tiredness as if the day were ending rather than beginning. And the old man, with his belching and scratching, drinking coffee royals and muttering imprecations under his breath.

But this was something new: a man who whistled before breakfast.

He stopped on his way to the bathroom, holding a leather case of toilet articles.

"What do you say we get dressed and find some breakfast, then go out to the house and pick up the gifts."

"I'm starved. I never did finish my dinner last night."

"And you're not the only one who's hungry?" He dropped his gaze briefly to her stomach. She was contouring it with both hands.

"No, I'm not."

"Then let me buy you both breakfast."

She colored and turned away, realizing she liked the morning Clay.

When the shower was splattering away she dropped down onto the bed again, fell back supine in the sun, thinking of how different Clay seemed this morning. She even enjoyed his teasing. She heard the bar of soap drop, then a muffled exclamation, then light whistling again. She remembered him turning from that window with those coolie-like pajamas hanging so tentatively low on his hips, and the thin line of red-gold hair sparkling its way down the center of his stomach. She groaned and rolled over and cradled her face in the L of an arm and the sun crept over her in warm fingers of gold and she fell asleep, waiting there that way, as pregnant women are prone to do.

He came into the bedroom wearing pajama bottoms and a towel slung around his neck. He smiled at the sight that greeted him. She lay there sprawled luxuriously and he studied the way the yellow fabric followed the contours of her shoulders, back, buttocks, the one knee drawn up, the other with its bare foot dangling over the edge of the bed.

In daylight, he decided, she was much more amiable. He'd enjoyed their little repartee upon waking.

He looked around, spied the roses, nabbed one and began tickling the sole of her foot with it. The toes curled tight, then the foot rotated on the ankle irritably. Then it kicked him in the knee and she laughed into the bedclothes.

"Cut it out," she scolded, "I told you I'm not at my best in the morning. I have an ugly disposition until almost noon."

"And here I was thinking how nice you were before."

"I'm a bear."

"What are you doing here? You're supposed to be getting ready for breakfast."

She looked at him with one cheek and an eye lost in the blankets.

"I was just catching a catnap."

"A catnap—when you just got up?"

"Well, it's your fault."

"Oh, yeah? What'd I do now?"

"Dunce. Pregnant ladies tend to sleep a lot; I told you that before." She reached backward and waggled her fingers. "Gimme."

He put the rose in her hand, and she sniffed it—one deep, long exaggerated pull—then rolled over and said to the ceiling, "Morning has broken." And without another word went to bathe and dress.

Catherine could see that her greatest adversary was normalcy. Clay, being well adjusted, intended to forge ahead as if their marriage were ordinary. But she herself was constantly on guard against the compelling gravity of the commonplace. That first day gave her glimpses of what life with Clay could be like if things were different.

They arrived at the Forresters' through the high sun of the November afternoon, which had melted away all but a few hints of last night's snows. The doorman was gone now—it was just an ordinary house again. Squirrels, much the color of the lawns, chittered and chased, still on the search for winter stores. A nuthatch darted from one of the festoons beside the door where it had been dining on bearded wheat.

And as it always could, the home welcomed.

They caught Claiborne and Angela nestled together on the love seat like a pair of mated mallards while the Minnesota Vikings radiated from the screen. There were the inevitable touches of greeting, in which Catherine was now included. They opened most of the gifts together—the four of them—with time out for instant replays, and for teasing Catherine about her ignorance of the game. Sitting on fat pillows on the floor, Catherine and Clay laughed over a grotesque cookie jar that looked like it belonged in a Swahili kitchen instead of an American town house. And she learned that Clay's favorite cookies were chocolate chip. They opened a waffle iron and she learned that he preferred pancakes. Halftime highlights came on and she learned he disliked the Chicago Bears. Angela made sandwiches and Claiborne said, "Here, open this one next," with a surprising giddiness, now that the game was over.

And amid a mound of used wrappings Catherine felt herself being sucked into the security of this family.

In the late afternoon they piled their loot into the cars and drove to the place they'd now call home. She met Clay at the door and watched as he set down his load and bent to put the key in the lock. Her arms were full of gift boxes overflowing with excelsior, and she peered around, watching him pocket the key.

The door swung open and before she knew what was happening he had turned and deftly scooped up the whole works—wife, excelsior, boxes and all.

"*Clay!*"

"I know, I know. Put me down, right?"

But she only laughed while he floundered, acting like his legs had turned to rubber, and collapsed onto the steps with her in his lap.

"In the movies somehow the wife never has a paunch," he teased, leaning his elbows back on the steps behind them.

She scowled, called him a very nasty name, then felt herself being pushed from his lap. "Get off me, paunchy."

The apartment lay steeped in late afternoon dusk, silent, waiting. As they stood surveying the living room, it seemed to beckon with the intimacy of a lover about to shed her clothes: new furniture, still wearing tags and dust wrappers, waited—stacked, leaning, unassembled. Lamps with their bases encased in padding lay upon the davenport while their shades waited on the floor in plastic sleeves. Barstools and tables stood about. Pieces of bed frame lay beside the mattress, and the box spring leaned against the wall. Boxes and suitcases that they'd brought earlier were stacked on the counter, strewn around the room.

The moment held a poignance that took away their laughter and made them wistful for a moment. It all seemed so ironically like the real thing. The reflection of sunset slipped its lavender fingers through the broad expanse of glass, lending an unearthly glow to the place. Catherine felt Clay's hands on her shoulders. She turned to find him startlingly close behind her, his jaw almost colliding with her temple as she swung around.

"Your coat?" he said. She thought there was a tortured expression about his mouth, wondered if he were thinking of Jill Magnusson. But—just that quick—he removed it and in its place was a grin.

They changed into blue jeans and sweatshirts and set to work—she in the kitchen, he in the living room. Again the air of normalcy returned. For Catherine it was like playing house, working away in this place that seemed too good to be true, packing away wedding gifts in the cupboards, listening to the sounds of Clay shoving furniture around. As they worked, evening spun in, and at times she allowed the line between reality and fantasy to blur.

"Come and tell me where you want the davenport," Clay called. She got up from her knees and went to ponder with him, and they arranged the room together.

And once she went laughing, asking, "What in the world do you suppose this thing is?" displaying some odd piece of steel that might have been either sculpture or a meat grinder. They laughingly agreed that it must be a sculpture of a meat grinder and relegated it to a hidden spot behind the tissue box on top of the refrigerator.

And dusk was deep when he appeared in the kitchen, asking, "Are there any lightbulbs anywhere?"

"Shove that box over here; I think it's stuff from the shower."

They found bulbs. A few moments later, still on her knees, she saw lamplight appear over the peninsula of cabinets from the direction of the living room, and smiled when she heard him say, "There, that's more like it."

She'd finished most of the kitchen unpacking and was lining the linen closet shelves as he passed through the hall, carrying pieces of clanging bed rail.

"Watch the wall!" she warned . . . too late. The bed rail dug into the door frame. He shrugged and disappeared with his burden. Next he came through with the headboard, then with a toolbox from his trunk. She began unpacking linens, listening to the sounds coming from the bedroom. She was hanging up new towels in the bathroom when he called, "Catherine, can you come here a minute?"

He was on his knees, trying to hold the headboard and bed rails at right angles while he tightened nuts and bolts—and having one hell of a time.

"Hold that up, will you?"

His hair was messed and curling across his forehead while he concentrated on his work. Holding the metal rails, she felt the vibrations wriggle their way to her palms as he plied the screwdriver.

He finished, and the thing was a square. He put the cross-slats in and stood up, saying, "I'll need a little help getting the mattress up the stairs."

"Sure," she said, uncomfortable now.

On their way up the steps with their ungainly cargo, Clay warned, "Now, just guide it, don't lift it."

She wanted to say, Don't be solicitous, but bit her tongue.

And then the bed was a bed, and the room grew quiet. They looked across the short expanse—his hair all ascatter and hers slipping free of the combs with which she'd carelessly slung it behind her ears. He had sweat rings beneath his arms and she had a dust smudge on the end of her right breast. His eyes dropped down to it fleetingly.

"There," he announced, "you can take over from here, okay?"

The new, bare mattress made them both uneasy.

"Sure," she said with affected brightness, "what color sheets would you like? We've got pink with big white daisies or beige with brown stripes or—"

"It doesn't matter," he interrupted, leaning to pick up a screwdriver and drop it in the toolbox. "Make it up to suit yourself. I'll be sleeping out on the davenport."

Catherine was brushing her palms off against each other, and they suddenly fell still. Then he swung from the room. She stood a moment, staring at nothing, then she kicked their brand-new box spring and left a black shoe mark on it. She stared at the mark, hands in her jeans pockets. She apologized to the box spring, then took back the apology, then spun and dropped down onto the edge of the unmade bed, suddenly feeling like crying. From the living room came the sound of some bluesy music with soft piano and a husky female voice as he started up the stereo. Finally she quit her moping and made up the bed with crisp, fresh sheets, then decided to put her clothing into the new dresser drawers. She stopped with her hands full of sweaters and called, "Clay?"

But apparently he couldn't hear her above the music.

She padded silently down the carpeted hall, down the few steps to the living room and found him standing, cowboylike, feet astraddle, thumbs hooked up in his rear pockets, staring out the sliding glass doors.

"Clay?"

He started and looked around. "What?"

"Is it okay if I take the dresser and you take the chest of drawers?"

"Sure," he said tonelessly, "whatever you want." Then he turned back to the window.

The inside of the dresser drawers smelled of new, spicy wood. Everything in the place was so spanking, so untouched, so different from what Catherine was used to. She was struck again with a sense of unreality, simply because of the inanity of what she was doing. But when Catherine considered where she was and what lay around her, she felt as if she were usurping someone else's rightful place, and again the image of Jill popped up.

The sound of a drawer opening brought her from her reverie, and she glanced over her shoulder to find Clay also putting his things away. They moved about the bedroom, doing their separate chores, silent except for an occasional *excuse me* when their proximities warranted. She snapped on the closet light to find he'd brought his hanging clothes over sometime during the week. All his sport coats hung neatly spaced, shirts squarely centered on their hangers, pantlegs meticulously flush and creased. She'd somehow imagined that Inella took care of his clothing, kept it flawless and groomed, and was surprised to find such neat precision all his doing.

The scent he wore lingered in the enclosure, much as it did in his car. She snapped out the light again and turned with her handful of hangers.

"I guess I'll take the closet in the other bedroom if it's okay with you."

"I can push my stuff closer together."

"No, no, it's okay. The other closet's empty anyway."

When she disappeared into the room across the hall, he stared into the drawer he'd been filling in the bureau—contemplating.

A short time later their paths crossed in the living room. Clay was occupied putting away his tapes.

"Listen, are you hungry?" Catherine asked. "We didn't have supper or anything." It was nearly ten P.M.

"Yeah, a little." He continued his sorting, never glancing up.

"Oh, well . . . gee," she stammered, "there's nothing here. We could—"

"Just forget it then. I'm really not very hungry."

"No, we could go out and get a hamburger or something."

He looked up at her stomach. "Oh, you're probably hungry."

"I'm okay."

He sighed, dropped a tape back into the cardboard box where it clacked before the room fell silent. He stared at it, kneeling there with the heels of his hands on his thighs, then shook his head in slow motion. "Aren't we even going to eat together?"

"You're the one who said first you were hungry, then you weren't."

He looked up at her squarely. "Do you want a hamburger?"

She rubbed her stomach with a timorous smile. "Yes, I'm starved."

"Then what do you say we stop playing cat and mouse and go out and get one."

"Okay."

"Let's leave the rest of this stuff for tomorrow night."

"Gladly, and tomorrow I'll get some groceries in the house."

And with that everything seemed better.

The illusion lasted till bedtime. Then, again, they walked on eggshells.

Coming in after their late supper she hurried to remove her

coat before he could help her, afraid lest he should inadvertently touch her. He followed her to the living room.

"Feel better?" he asked.

"Yes, I didn't know how hungry I was. We did a lot of work today."

Then they couldn't think of anything else to say. Clay began an exaggerated stretch, twisting at the waist with his elbows in the air.

Panic hit her and made her stomach twitch. Should she simply exit or offer to make up his bed or what?

They both spoke at once.

"Well, we have to get up—"

"Should I get your—"

She flapped her hands nervously, gestured for him to speak, but he gestured for her to speak at the same time.

"I'll get your bedding," she got out.

"Just show me where it is and I'll do it myself."

She avoided his eyes, led the way up the steps to the linen closet. When she started to reach up high he hurriedly offered, "Here, I'll get them down."

He moved too quickly and bumped into her back before she could move aside. He nearly pulled the comforter down on her head. She plucked a package of sheets and another of pillowcases from the shelves and put them on top of the comforter in his arms.

"I saved the brown and beige ones for you."

Their eyes met briefly above the bedding.

"Thanks."

"I'll get your pillow." She fled to do so.

But they had only two pillows, which were both on the king-size bed, already encased in pink-flowered pillow slips.

There was some sticky hesitancy as she returned with one, saying she guessed he wouldn't need that other pillowcase she'd given him. And then everything went wrong at once because he reached to take her pillow and the comforter tipped sideways and the plastic-wrapped packages slipped off the top and she lunged to try to catch them and somehow their fingers touched and the whole pile of bedding ended up on the floor at their feet.

He knelt down quickly and began gathering it up while she scuttled back to the security of the bedroom, shut the door and was about to begin changing into her nightgown when he came back for his pajamas. He knocked politely, and she let him pass before her to go in and get them, then shut the door again as he left.

By the time she donned her nightgown her stomach was in knots.

She sat down on the end of the bed, waiting for him to go in and use the bathroom first. But apparently he was sitting downstairs waiting for her to do the same thing. Naturally, they both decided to make the move at once. She was halfway down the hall and he was halfway up the steps when they spied each other headed in the same direction. Catherine's feet turned to stone, but Clay had the presence of mind to simply turn around and retreat. Afterward she closed herself into the bedroom again, climbed into the vast bed and lay there listening to the sounds that the walls couldn't quite hide, picturing Clay in those pajama bottoms as he'd been that morning. The toilet flushed, the water ran, she heard him spit after brushing his teeth.

In the bathroom, Clay studied her wet washcloth hanging on the towel rack, then opened the medicine chest to find her wet toothbrush inside. He laid his next to it, then picked up a bottle of prenatal vitamins, studied its label thoughtfully and returned it to the shelf.

She heard the bathroom light snap off, then he knocked gently on her door.

"Catherine?"

Heart clamoring, she answered, "What?"

"What time do you usually get up?"

"Six-thirty."

"Did you set an alarm?"

"No, I haven't got one."

"I'll wake you at six-thirty, then."

"Thank you."

She stared at the hole in the dark where the door would be if she could see it.

"Good night then," he said at last.

"Good night."

He put on a tape and the sound of the music filtered through the dark, through her closed door while she tried to erase all thought from her mind and find sleep.

She was still wide awake when the tape finally stopped.

And a long time later when she heard Clay get up in the dark and get a drink of water in the kitchen.

TWENTY-ONE

The way they did things the first time usually set the precedent for their routine. Clay used the bathroom first in the mornings; she used it first in the evenings. He got dressed in their bedroom while she was showering, then she got dressed while he put his bedding away. He left the house first, so he opened the garage door; she left second and closed it.

Before leaving that Monday morning he asked, "What time will you get home?"

"Around two-thirty."

"I'll be later by an hour or so, but if you wait I'll go grocery shopping with you."

She couldn't conceal her surprise—it was the last thing she'd expect him to want them to do together. Crisp and combed, he stood in the foyer looking up the steps at her. He put a hand on the doorknob, smiled briefly, raised his free hand and said, "Well, have a good day."

"You too."

When he was gone, she studied the door, remembering his smile, the little wave of good-bye. Juxtaposed against it came the memory of her father, scratching his belly, roaring, "Where the goddam hell is Ada? Does a man hafta make his own coffee around this dump?"

Catherine couldn't forget it all the way to school in her own car, which she kept expecting to turn back into a pumpkin.

It was an odd place to begin falling in love—in the middle of the supermarket—but that's precisely where it began for Catherine. She was still boggled by the fact that he'd come along. Again she tried to picture her father doing the same, but it was too ludicrous to ponder. She was even further dumbfounded by the silliness that sprang up between her and Clay. It had started out with the two of them learning each other's tastes, but had ended on a note of hilarity that would undoubtedly have seemed humorless to anybody else.

"Do you like fruit?" Clay asked.

"Oranges, I crave oranges lately."

"Then we shall have oranges!" he proclaimed dramatically, holding a bag aloft.

"Hey, check how much they cost first."

"It doesn't matter. These look good."

"Of course they look good," she scolded, looking at the price, "you've chosen the most expensive ones in the place."

But when she would have replaced them with cheaper ones, he waggled a finger at her and clucked, "Tut-tut!" Price was no object, he said, when he bought food. And she dropped the oranges back in the cart.

At the dairy case she reached for margarine.

"What are you going to use that for?"

"What do you think, not for a hot oil treatment for my hair."

"And not to feed to me," he said, grinning, and took the margarine from her hands. "I like real butter."

"But it's three times as much!" she exclaimed. Then she reclaimed her margarine and put his butter back in the case.

He immediately switched the two around again.

"Butter is three times as fattening, too," she informed him, "and I *do* have an imminent weight problem to consider." He made an affected sideward bow, then put her margarine in the cart next to his butter as they moved on.

She spied a two-gallon jar of ketchup up ahead, and when Clay's back was turned she picked up the ungainly thing and came waddling over with it clutched against her outthrust stomach.

"Here," she puffed, "this should hold you till next week."

He turned around and burst out laughing, then quickly relieved her of the enormous container.

"Hey, what're you trying to do, squash my kid?"

"I know how you like ketchup on your hamburgers," she said innocently. By now they were both laughing.

They wandered along behind their mountain of food, and at the frozen foods she chose orange juice and he, pineapple juice. They took turns laying them in the cart like poker players revealing their next cards.

She played a frozen pumpkin pie.

He played apple.

She drew corn.

He drew spinach.

"What's that?" she asked disgustedly.

"Spinach."

"Spinach! Yuck!"

"What's the matter with spinach? I love it!"

"I hate it. I'd as soon eat scabs!"

He perused the bags and boxes in the display case with a searching attitude. "Mmm, sorry, no scabs for sale here."

By the time they reached the meat counter they were no longer laughing, they were giggling, and people were beginning to stare.

"Do you like Swiss steak?" she asked.

"I love it. Do you like meat loaf?"

"I love it!"

"Well, I hate it. Don't you dare subject me to meat loaf!"

Warming to the game, she just had to trail her fingers threateningly over the packages of hamburger. He eyed her warningly out of the corner of his eye—a buccaneer daring her to challenge his orders.

She picked up the hamburger, weighing it on her palm a time or two, plotting the insidious deed.

"Oh, yeah, lady?" He made his voice silky. "Just try it." He grinned evilly, raking her with his pirate's eyes until she stealthily slipped it back where it had come from.

Next he turned on her, ordering autocratically, "You'd better like pork chops!" He took up a challenging stance, at a right angle to the meat counter, feet apart, one hand on a package of chops, the other on the nonexistent scabbard at his belt. The tile of the floor might very well have been the deck of his windjammer.

"Or else what?" she fairly growled, trying to keep a straight face.

He grew cocky, raised one eyebrow. "Or else"—a quick glance to the side, a hint of a smile before he snatched up a different package and brandished it at her—"we eat liver."

She hooked both thumbs up in her waist, ambled nearer, looked directly into his swashbuckler's handsome, brown face and rasped, "Suits me fine, bucko, I eats my liver rawww!"

He tilted a sardonic brow at the liver.

"More'n likely doesn't know how to cook it."

"The plague take you, I do!"

A twitch pulled at the corners of his lips. He tried to get the words out without snickering, but couldn't quite make it.

"Lucky for you, woman, be . . . cause . . . I . . . don't."

And then the two of them were dissolved in giggles again.

Where Catherine's comic instinct had come from she couldn't guess. She'd never suspected she harbored it. But she warmed to it, found herself lifted in a new, spontaneous way by their levity. Somehow Clay—who she had to admit was charming as a swashbuckler—had given her a glimpse of him that she liked. And a glimpse of herself that she liked, as well. Such bouts of good humor sprang up between them more often after that. She was surprised to find Clay not only humorous, but complaisant and even-tempered. It was the first time in her life that she lived free of the threat of erupting tempers. It was an eye-opener to Catherine to learn it was possible to live in such harmony with a male of the species.

The town house, too, wove its charm about Catherine. At times she would come up short in the middle of some mundane chore and would mentally pinch herself as a reminder not to get too used to it. She would load the dishwasher—or worse yet, watch Clay load it—and remember that in a few short months this would all be snatched away from her. He shared the house-work with a singular lack of compunction that surprised Catherine. Maybe it started the night he hooked up the washer and dryer. Together they read the new manuals and figured out the machine settings and loaded the washer with their first bundle of dirty clothes and from then on a load was thrown in by whoever happened to have the time.

She returned home one time to find him vacuuming the living room—the new blankets were linty. She stopped in amazement, a smile on her face. He caught sight of her and turned off the machine.

"Hi. What's the smile for?"

"I was just trying to feature my old man doing that like you do."

"Is this supposed to threaten my masculinity or something?"

Her smile was very genuine now.

"Quite the opposite."

Then she turned and left him and the vacuum wheezed on again while he wondered what she meant.

It was inevitable that they be bound closer by inconsequential things. A telephone was installed and their number was listed under the name Forrester, Clay. A grocery list was established on a corner of the cabinet, and on it mingled their needs and their likes. She bought herself a tape by The Lettermen and played it on his stereo, knowing full well it would not always be available for her to use. Mail began arriving, addressed to Mr. and Mrs. Clay Forrester. He ran out of shampoo and borrowed hers, and from then on they ended up buying her brand because he liked it better. Sometimes they even used the same washcloth.

But every night, out came the spare blankets, and he made up his bed on the davenport, put on a tape, and they lay in their separate darks listening to his favorite one night, hers the next.

But by now she had grown to expect that last tape of the day, and left her bedroom door open, the better to hear it.

Thanksgiving came and it was disturbingly wonderful for Catherine. Angela had included both Steve and Ada in her invitation, plus all of Clay's grandparents and a few assorted aunts, uncles and cousins. It was the first time in six years that Catherine, Ada and Steve had celebrated a holiday together, and Catherine found herself awash in gratitude to the Forresters for this opportunity. It was a day steeped in tradition. There were warm cheeks meeting cold, cozy fires, laughter drifting up through the house from the game room below, a table veritably sagging beneath its burden of holiday foods, and of course Angela's magical touch was everywhere. There were bronze football mums laced with bittersweet in the center of the table, flanked by crystal candelabra upon imported Belgian linen. Seated at dinner, Catherine swallowed back the sickening sense of future loss and strove to enjoy the day. Her mother was truly coming out of her shell, smiling and visiting. And it was crazy the way Steve and Clay took to each other. They spent much of the meal badgering each other about a rematch at pool as soon as the meal was over, but with the best of spirits.

How the Forresters take this for granted, thought Catherine, gazing around the circle of faces, listening to the happy chatter, soothed and sated as much by their goodwill as by their food. What happened to my notions about the wicked rich? she wondered. But just then her eyes met Claiborne's. She found a disturbing gentleness there, as if he read her thoughts, and she quickly looked away lest she be drawn to him further.

In the afternoon Catherine received her first lesson in how to shoot pool. Was it accidental or intentional, the way Clay crowded his body close behind her as he leaned to show her how to extend her left hand on the green velvet, crossing her hip with his right arm, his hard brown hand gripping hers on the cue?

"Let it slide through your hand," he instructed into her ear, sawing back and forth while his sleeve brushed across her hip. He smelled good and he was warm. There was something decidedly provocative about it all. But then he backed away and it was men against women in a round robin that pitted Clay and Steve against Catherine and a teenage cousin named Marcy. But in no time it was obvious the sides were uneven, so Catherine played with Steve as her partner, and they whipped the other two in short order. Steve, it seemed, had been dubbed "Minnesota Skinny" during the hundreds of hours spent at pool tables during basic training and the years since. Eventually pool was preempted by football, and Catherine found herself snuggled into a comfortable cushion between Clay and Steve. During replays Catherine received her second lesson on the sport, explained succinctly by Clay, who slouched comfortably and rolled his head toward her during his comments.

At the door Claiborne and Angela bade them good-bye, and while Claiborne held her coat, Angela asked, "How are you feeling?"

She raised her eyes to twin expressions of concern, surprised to be asked in so point-blank a way about her pregnancy. This was the first time since before the wedding that anybody had brought it up.

"Pudgy," she answered with a half-smile.

"Well, you're looking wonderful," Claiborne assured her.

"Yes, and don't let female vanity get you down," added Angela. "It's only temporary, you know."

On the drive home Catherine recalled their solicitous attitudes, the concern behind their simple comments, threatened by that concern more than she cared to admit.

"You're quiet tonight," Clay noted.

"I was thinking."

"About what?"

She was silent a moment, then sighed. "The whole day— what it was like. How all of your family seems to take it for granted . . . I mean, I've never had a Thanksgiving like this before."

"Like what? It was just an ordinary Thanksgiving."

"Oh, Clay, you really don't see, do you?"

"See what?"

No, he didn't see, and she doubted that he ever would, but she made a stab at comparison. "Where I come from, holidays were only excuses for the old man to get a little drunker than usual. By mealtime he'd be crocked, whether we were at home or going to Uncle Frank's. I don't ever remember a holiday that wasn't spoiled by his drinking. There was always so much tension, everybody trying to make things merry in spite of him. I used to wish . . ." But her voice trailed away. She found she could not say what it was she'd wished for, because it would seem guileful to say that she wished for a day like she'd had today.

"I'm sorry," he said softly. Then he reached over and squeezed her neck gently. "Don't let bad memories ruin your day, okay?"

"Your father was very nice to me today."

"Your mother was very nice to me."

"Clay, I . . ." But once again she stopped, uncertain of how to voice her growing trepidation. Catherine didn't think he'd understand that Thanksgiving had been just too, too nice.

"What?"

"Nothing."

But that *nothing* was a great big lump of something, something good and alive and growing that would—she was sure—be bittersweet in the end.

It was shortly after that when Clay came home one evening with a four-pound bag of popcorn.

"Four pounds!" she exclaimed.

"Well, I'm awfully fond of the stuff."

"You must be," she laughed, and flung the bag at him, nearly doubling him over.

That night they were sitting on the davenport studying with a bowl between them when Catherine suddenly dropped a handful of popcorn back into the bowl. Her eyes grew startled and the book fell from her fingers.

"Clay!" she whispered.

He sat forward, alarmed. "What's the matter?"

"Oh, God . . ." she whispered, clutching her stomach.

"What's the matter, Catherine?" He eased nearer, concern etched across his eyebrows.

She closed her eyes. "Ohhh . . ." she breathed while he wondered if she had written the doctor's number down where he could find it fast.

"For God's sake, what is it?"

"Something . . . something . . ." Her eyes remained closed while sweat suddenly broke out across his chest. Her eyes opened and a tremulous smile played at the corners of her mouth. "Something moved in there."

His eyes shot down to her stomach. Catherine held it like she was getting ready to try a two-hand set shot with it. Now he held his breath.

"There it goes again," she reported, her eyes closing as if in ecstasy. "Once more . . . once more . . . please," she whispered invocatively.

"Is it still moving?" he whispered.

"Yes . . . no! . . . wait!"

"Can I feel?"

"I don't know. Wait, there it is again—no, it's gone."

His hand advanced and retreated several times through all this.

"There it is again."

She made room for one of his hands on the gentle mound beside her own. They sat there mesmerized for a long, long time. Nothing happened. Her eyes drifted up to his. The warmth of his hand seeped through to her flesh, but the flutter within remained stilled.

"I can't feel anything." He felt cheated.

"It's all done, I think."

"There, what was that?"

"No, that wasn't it, that was probably only my own heart-beat."

"Oh." But he didn't take his hand away. It lay there warmly next to hers while he asked, "What did it feel like?"

"I don't know. Like—like when you're holding a kitten and you can feel it purr through its fur, only it lasted just a moment each time."

Clay's face felt hot. His scalp prickled. He still cupped her stomach with a hand that stubbornly wasn't going to move away without feeling *some*thing!

It's good to touch her, he thought.

"Clay, nothing's going to happen anymore, I don't think."

"Oh." Disappointed, he slid his hand from her. But where it had been, there were five buttery smudges on her green cotton blouse.

"You've marked me," she joked, stretching out the shirt by its hem, suddenly too aware of how good his hand had felt.

He caught a glimpse of a zipper that wasn't completely zipped, a snap that wasn't snapped.

"Yes, for life," he said on a light note, but he had the sudden urge to kiss her, she looked so expectant and crestfallen at the brevity of the sensation. "Promise me you'll let me feel it next time it happens?"

But she didn't promise. Instead, she moved a safe distance away, then muttered something about getting the butter out before it set permanently and headed in the direction of the laundry.

When she returned, she was wearing a pink duster and fuzzy booties, and he had great trouble concentrating on his studying after she resumed her place on the other side of the popcorn bowl.

*   *   *

By now Catherine well knew how Clay enjoyed his morning coffee at the counter. He was there at his usual place, reading the
morning paper a few days later when she appeared from upstairs.
He blew on his coffee, took a sip, looked up over his paper, and
his lips fell from the rim of the cup, which hovered, forgotten, in
midair.

"Well, well, well . . . lookit here," he crooned.

She pinkened, got suddenly very busy plopping a piece of
bread in the toaster with her back to him.

"Turn around so I can see."

"It's just a maternity top," she said to the toaster, looking at
her reflection in it.

"Then why so shy?"

"I'm not shy, for heaven's sake!" She swung around. "I just
feel conspicuous, that's all."

"Why? You look cute in it."

"Cute," she muttered disparagingly, "like Dumbo the elephant."

"Well, it's got to be more comfortable than going around
with your zippers open and your snaps flapping." Again she colored. "Well, I couldn't help but notice the other night when I
was feeling your tummy."

"I kept thinking of facing your grandmother in maternity
clothes and putting it off as long as possible."

He put down his paper and came around the peninsula to
pour another cup of coffee. "Nature will have its way, and not
even Elizabeth Forrester can stop it. Don't frown so, Catherine."

She turned to butter her toast. "I don't want to think about
facing her for the first time wearing these."

On an impulse he moved close behind her and touched his

lips to the back of her hair, his cup still in his hand. "That probably won't be until Christmas, so stop worrying."

Facing the cabinets, she was unsure of what it was she'd felt
on the back of her head, and then, without warning, he slipped
an arm around her middle and spread his fingers wide on her
stomach.

"Is there any more activity going on in there?" he asked.

From behind, he saw her jaw stop moving. She swallowed a
mouthful of toast as though it were having some difficulty going
down.

"Don't touch me, Clay," she warned, low, intense, fierce, not
moving a muscle. His hand stiffened, the room seemed to crackle.

"Why? You're my w—"

"I can't stand it!" she snapped, slapping the toast down on
the counter. "I can't stand it!"

He felt the blood surge to his head, stung by her unexpected
outburst.

"Well, I beg your goddam puritanical pardon!"

He clapped his cup down vehemently and stormed out of the
room, out of the house, without so much as a good-bye.

When the door slammed, Catherine leaned over, braced her
elbows on the countertop and buried her face in both hands. She
wanted to call, Come back, come back! Don't believe me, Clay. I
need touching so badly. Come back and make me let you touch
me, even if I argue. Smile at me and wish me your sweet-
tempered good-bye like always. I need you so badly, Clay. Coddle me, comfort me, touch me, touch me, touch me. Only, make
it all mean something, Clay.

She had a miserable day that day.

She made supper and waited. And waited. And waited. But he

didn't come. She finally ate alone, staring at his empty stool beside her, the food like cardboard in her mouth. She ate very little.

She put on one of his favorite tapes, just for some racket in the place, but that was worse. She felt more miserable than ever, for it only brought back the memory of his slamming out the door as he had. She put on one of her favorites, but naturally, it soon rolled around to the same old song that always reminded her of him: "You're Just Too Good to Be True." That made her more miserable than ever, so she chose to wait in silence. At eleven o'clock she gave up and went to bed.

She woke up at two A.M. and crept down the dark hall and checked the living room. In the blackness it was hard to see. She felt her way to the davenport with her feet, reached out a careful hand only to find that there was no bedding there, no Clay.

Finally, at five, she fell asleep, only to be awakened an hour and a half later by the alarm. Catherine knew before she went downstairs that he wouldn't be there.

TWENTY-TWO

School was an exercise in futility that day. Catherine sat through her classes like a zombie, seeing little, hearing less. All she saw was Clay's hand on her stomach the night when they'd been eating popcorn. All she heard was his voice, "Can I feel?" She remembered his eyes, those eyes she'd grown to know so well, with a brand-new look, wide-gray, excited. "I can't feel anything, Catherine. What did it feel like?"

Her insides trembled at the thought of his staying away all

night. She'd have to call his parents if he wasn't home when she got there. Sick at the thought that he might not come home tonight either, she delayed going there herself. She stopped at Horizons after classes for a visit with the girls. Only, she learned that Marie had gone into labor around ten o'clock that morning and they were all waiting for news from the hospital. Without a second thought, Catherine drove to Metro Medical Center and obtained permission to wait in the father's waiting room. By the time news came, it was nine o'clock. She was not allowed to see Marie, for they had taken her directly to the recovery room, so Catherine finally headed for home.

When she got there, the living room light was on. At the sight of it she felt her heartbeat go wild and racy. Catherine opened the door to silence. Slowly she hung up her coat, and even more slowly ascended the stairs. Just inside the living room Clay was standing like an outraged samurai. His shirt hung open and wrinkled, his beard was a smudge across his cheeks, his hair was unkempt and his face bore the ravages of a sleepless night.

"Where the hell were you!" he roared.

"At the hospital."

His anger swooshed away, leaving him with that gut-hollow feeling as after an elevator drops too fast. He looked at her stomach.

"Is something wrong?"

"Marie just had a six-and-a-half-pound baby girl." She turned on her heel, heading upstairs, but found herself swung around roughly by an elbow.

Madder than ever at having been duped into thinking something was wrong with Catherine, he barked, "Well, you could have called, you know!"

"Me!" she yelled back. "I could have called! What about you!"

"I'm the one that got thrown out, remember?"

"I did not throw you out!"

"Well, you sure as hell didn't make me feel anxious to come back."

"The choice was yours, Mr. Forrester, and I'm sure you didn't suffer out in the cold."

"No, I sure as hell didn't."

"Did she let you paw her nice flat stomach all night long?"

"What's it to you? You gave me permission to paw anything I want of hers, didn't you?"

"That's right," she hissed, "anything you want!"

"Catherine, let's not get into it, okay? I'm beat and I—"

"Oh, you're beat! Poor baby. I didn't get two hours' sleep last night worrying that you drove it out of your system until you cracked up the Corvette someplace and all the while you were with her and now you come home crying that you're tired? Spare me."

"I never said I was with her. You assumed that."

"I don't give a tinker's damn if you were with her or not. If it'll keep you off my back, fine! Spend all the time you want with Jill Magnusson. Only do me the courtesy of reminding me not to cook supper for you on your nights out, all right?"

"And who do you think cooked supper for you tonight?"

Her eyes slid to the kitchen. Sure enough, there was evidence of a neglected meal all over the place. Catherine didn't know what to say.

He raged on. "Just what do you suppose I thought when you didn't show up to eat it?"

"I know what you didn't think—that I was out someplace with an old boyfriend!"

He ran a hand through his hair, as if searching for control, then turned away.

"You'd better call your mother; she's worried sick."

"My mother? How did she get into this?"

"I couldn't think of anyplace else you'd be, so I called her place."

"Oh, fine, just fine! I didn't call *your* mother to check up on you!"

"Well, maybe you should have 'cause I was there."

He stomped across the living room and plunked down on the davenport. "Lord," he said to the windows, "I don't know what got into you yesterday morning. All I did was touch you, Cat. That's all I did. Was that so bad? I mean, what do you think it makes a man feel like to be treated that way?" He got to his feet and started pacing back and forth. "I mean, I've been living like a goddam monk! Don't look! Don't touch! Watch what you say! Sleeping on this davenport like some eunuch! This setup just isn't natural!"

"Whose idea was it in the first place?"

"All right, granted, it was mine, but be reasonable, huh?"

Her voice grew taunting. "What am I to you, Clay? Another conquest? Is that what you're after? Another notch on your"— she glanced insolently at his crotch—"whatever it is you notch? I should think you could do better than one banged-up, big-bellied loser like me. Listen, I plan to come out of this marriage with fewer scars than I had going in, and to do that I need to keep you away from me, do you understand? Just stay away!"

Suddenly Clay stormed across the room, grabbed one of her wrists and, in his fury, flung his other hand wide, exclaiming, "Dammit, Catherine, I'm your husband!"

Instinctively she yanked free of him, covering her head with both hands, hunkering down, waiting for the blow to fall.

At the sight of her, dropped low in that crouch, the anger fell from him, to be replaced by pity, which hurt—hurt worse than the thought that she could not stand being touched by him.

He dropped to one knee beside her.

"Cat," he said hoarsely. "God, Cat, I wasn't going to hit you."

But still she cowered on her knees, sunken in some fear too big for him to fully comprehend. He reached out a hand to soothe her hair. "Hey, come on, honey, it's Clay. I'd never hit you, don't you know that?" He thought she was crying, for her body quivered terribly. She needs to cry, he thought, she needed it weeks ago. He watched her knotted fists dig into the nape of her neck. He touched her arms. "Come on, Cat." He gentled, saying, "It's only a silly fight, and it's over, huh?" He brushed back a strand of hair that fell like a golden waterfall covering her face. He leaned down to try to see around it, but she clutched her head and bounced on her haunches as if demented. Fear tore through his gut. His heart felt swollen to twice its size.

"Cat, I'm sorry. Come on, don't. . . . Nobody's going to hurt you, Cat. Please, honey, I'm sorry . . ." Sobs collected in his throat. "Let me help you to bed, okay?" Something switched her back to reality. She raised her head at last, just enough to see him with one eye around that veil of gold. With infinite tenderness he promised, "I won't touch you. I just want to help you to bed; come on." The tears he expected to see were not there. She unfolded herself finally, tossed back her hair and eyed him suspiciously. Her face wore a protective mask of expressionlessness.

"I can do it." Her voice was too controlled. "I don't need your help."

With measured movements, she rose and left the room, left him kneeling there in the middle of it with a knot of emptiness inside him.

After that Catherine spent her evenings in the spare room. She either sewed maternity clothes or did typing jobs on a card table she'd set up in there. When she had studying to do, it, too, was done in the spare bedroom. Like a hermit crab, she crawled off into her shell.

After several nights of her incessant typing, Clay came to the bedroom doorway, stood there studying her back, wondering how to approach her.

"You're doing a lot of typing lately. Your professors laying on a heavy load or something?"

She didn't even turn around. "I got a couple of jobs typing term papers."

"If you needed money, why didn't you say so?" he asked impatiently.

"I want my typing to stay good."

"But you've got enough to do keeping up with your classes and things around the house without taking on more."

At last she looked over her shoulder. "I thought we agreed not to interfere with each other's private lives."

His mouth drew into a straight, hard line, then she turned back to her work.

The following evening when she was again seated at the typewriter, she heard the door slam. Her fingers fell still, hovering over the keys while she listened. Finally she got up and checked the living room and kitchen to find him gone. She sighed and returned to the spare room.

But there was undeniably a lonely feeling about the place, knowing he wasn't out there.

He got home around ten, offering no explanation of where he'd been, getting no questions from Catherine. After that, he would leave occasionally that way, preferring not to face her indifference, or the isolation of the living room with the sound of the clattering typewriter or sewing machine coming from upstairs.

One evening he surprised her by returning home earlier than

usual, coming into her hideout with his jacket still on. He dropped a checkbook on the card table and she glanced up questioningly. He leaned from one hip a little, hands in his jacket pockets, only his eyes and hair picking up a faint reflection from the gooseneck lamp pointed down at the table.

"What's that?" she asked.

He eyed her from the shadows. "I ran out of blank checks and had to have some new ones printed."

She looked down at the black plastic folder, opened it and found her name imprinted beside his on the top check.

"We had a deal," said Clay. "I'd support you."

She stared at the paired names on the blue rectangle, reminded of their wedding invitations, for some reason. She looked up but his features were inscrutable above her.

"But not forever," she said. "I'll need money next summer and recommendations from satisfied customers. I want to take these jobs."

He shifted feet, leaned on the opposite hip. His voice was slightly hard. "And I want you back out in that living room in the evenings."

"I've got work to do, Clay." And she turned back to her typewriter, making the keys fly. He left the checkbook where it was and strode angrily from the room.

After he was gone, she leaned her elbows on the machine and rested her face in her palms, confused by him, afraid—so afraid—of allowing her feelings for him to sway her. She thought of the coming summer, the separation that was inevitable, and sternly began typing again.

The spare bedroom soon became cluttered with her things: piles of blank paper and manuscripts lying in heaps on the floor beside patterns and fabric scraps. Textbooks, a tote bag, her schoolwork.

Christmas break arrived and she spent most of it holed up, typing, while he spent most of his time in the law library at the university, which was open seven days a week, twenty-four hours a day.

He arrived home one evening just before supper, tired of the austere law library and its dry books and rigid silence. He hung up his coat while cocking an ear toward the spare room. But everything was silent; the clack of the typewriter was disturbingly absent. He wandered upstairs, glanced into the cluttered room only to find it dark. He hurried downstairs again, to find a note.

"Bad news this time. Grover's baby born early. Going to Horizons. Back late." It was signed simply "C."

The house seemed like a tomb, silent and lifeless without her. He made himself a sandwich and wandered to the sliding glass doors to stand looking out at the snow while eating. He wished they'd have a Christmas tree, but she expressed no desire to buy one. She said they had no ornaments anyway. He thought about her cold withdrawal from him, wondered how a person could insulate herself from feeling as she did, and why. He was used to living in an environment where people conversed at the end of the day, sat and shared some talk with their dinner, sometimes watched television or read books in the same room, companionable even in silence. He missed his mother and father's house very much, picturing the enormous Christmas tree that was an annual fixture, the fires, the aunts and uncles dropping in, the gifts, the decorations that his mother lavished upon the house. For the first time ever, he wished Christmas would hurry up and get past.

He took his sandwich and wandered idly upstairs to change into a jogging suit to lounge around in. He stopped at the doorway of the dark workroom, took another bite of the sandwich, wandered in and snapped on the gooseneck lamp. He touched the keys of the typewriter, read a few words from the paper she'd

left in the platen and glanced over the papers that covered the
top of the crowded table.

Suddenly he stopped chewing, arrested by the dark corner of
a book that was peeking from beneath a stack of papers. He
licked off his fingers, slid the book out to reveal a half-filled page
of Catherine's handwriting.

"Clay went out again tonight . . ." it began. He pushed the
book back and hid it as it had been, took another healthy bite of
tuna salad and stared at the corner of the book. It lured him,
peeking out that way. Slowly he set his plate down, licked some
mayonnaise from a finger again, drawn by that volume. Finally
he gave in and laid the diary across the typewriter platen.

"Clay went out again tonight but didn't stay out quite as late
as last time. I try not to wonder where he goes, but somehow I
do. It always seems lonesome here without him but it's best not
to get used to having him around. Today he mentioned buying a
Christmas tree, but no matter how bad I want one, too, what's
the use? It's just another tradition to break next year. He wore
his brown corduroy jacket today, the one he wore the time—"

There she had stopped.

He dropped down into her chair, still staring at the words,
feeling great guilt at having read them, but rereading them just
the same. He pictured her sitting there, holed up in that room
away from him, writing her secret feelings instead of talking
about them with him. Again and again he read the words, "He
wore his brown corduroy jacket today, the one he wore the
time—" and wondered what she'd have written had she completed the thought. She never mentioned anything about his
clothes. He'd never thought before that she even was aware of
what he wore. Yet this . . .

He closed his eyes, remembering how she had said she
couldn't stand to have him touch her. He opened them again

and read, "He wore his brown corduroy jacket today, the one he wore the time—" Was it a pleasant memory she attached to the brown jacket? He remembered the fight they'd had over Jill. He reread, "It always seems so lonesome here without him."

Before he could do something foolish he rose, buried the book the way he'd found it, snapped off her light and went down and turned on the television. All this very abruptly. He sat through three commercials and one act of a show he didn't recognize before going back upstairs and pulling the diary out again. He told himself that this was different, that *he* was different, that he wasn't out to use anything he read against her.

She had used up so many pages last Fourth of July that he didn't waste time counting them.

"Today was a day of discovery.

"For once we were going to be all together and have a family picnic out at Lake Independence. As usual, Daddy got blind drunk and ruined everything. Mom and I had the picnic all packed when she changed her mind and called Uncle Frank to say we wouldn't be coming. One thing led to another, and Daddy accused Mom of making him the family scapegoat when all he'd had was a couple shots. Ha! He started in on her and I stepped in, so he aimed his attack at me, calling me the usual only it was worse this time because I was wearing my bathing suit, all ready to take off for the lake. I took it as long as I could, but finally retreated to my room to contemplate Life's Injustices.

"Bobbi called in the late afternoon and said she and Stu were going to Powderhorn to watch fireworks and how would I like to come along with a friend of Stu's. If it hadn't been such a miserable day, I might not have gone. But it was, and I did, and now I'm not sure if I should have.

"His name was Clay Forrester, and when I first met him I'm afraid I made an absolute fool of myself by staring. What a face! What hair! What everything! His eyes were gray and he seemed a little brooding at first, but as the night went on, he smiled more. His eyebrows are not exactly the same. The left one quirks up a little more and gives him a teasing look at times. His chin has the suggestion of a dimple. His hair was the color of autumn leaves— not the reds, not the yellows, but the ones in between, like some maples, maybe.

"When Stu introduced us, Clay was just standing there with his thumbs hooked in his jeans pockets and all he said was Hi and smiled and just like that my heart hit my throat. I wondered if he could tell.

"What happened was insane. I'm not sure if I believe it yet. We walked around Powderhorn with this huge jug of wine, taking turns sipping, and waiting for full dark. I remember that we laughed a lot. Bobbi and Stu were ahead of us, holding hands, and sometimes Clay's shoulder bumped mine and shivers went up my arm. By the time the fireworks started, we were all nearly as high as they were!

"It turned out there were blankets in the truck and pretty soon Bobbi and Stu disappeared with one of them. I remember just the way Clay stood there with the bottle of wine in one hand and the handle of the truck door in the other. He asked if I wanted to sit in the truck and watch the fireworks or use the other blanket. I still can't believe I really answered, 'Let's use the blanket,' but I did.

"We sat down under a huge tree with lacy black branches, and Clay pulled the cork out of the wine bottle with his teeth and spit it high in the air and we both laughed. I remember thinking how different it felt, getting drunk, when you were the one doing it instead of watching somebody else.

"He was leaning on one elbow, stretched-out-like on the blanket, resting the bottle on the ground between us when he leaned over and put an arm around my neck and pulled me over to kiss me the first time, and somehow my breast came up against his hand and the neck of that bottle. 'Fireworks,' he whispered in my ear afterward. He put his hand under my hair and held me there, moving the back of his hand and the top of the bottle against me. I guess I said 'Yeah' or something, just to see what'd happen. What happened was that he said 'Come here' and put his other arm around me, wine and all, and pulled me over there beside him and stretched out. I went willingly, remembering the names that Daddy had called me that morning, thinking to myself that maybe I'd prove him right.

"Clay took his time. He was some kind of a kisser. I've kissed boys before but this was different. And I've been pulled tight against guys before, but somehow they always were panting and clumsy and overeager and I was repelled. I waited for that to happen again, but it didn't. Instead, when I stretched out beside Clay, he gave me all the time I needed to make up my mind. I had it made up long before he pressed himself against me. I could feel the wine bottle bump against my back, cold through my shirt compared to his tongue, warm in my mouth. Lazy, it was at first, lazy and slow. I remember the feeling of his teeth against my own tongue, and the taste of wine in both of our mouths together. I remember him using his lips to urge me to open my mouth wider, then the feel of his tongue exploring me made me go all barmy and warmy. Funny thing was, while he did it, he loosened his hold on me and I found myself lying there drifting into submission more from his lack of force than the presence of it. At last he nudged himself away and collapsed onto his back with a wrist over his eyes. He was still holding onto the wine bottle with the heel of it against the ground, rocking it back and forth.

"He said something like 'Whew, you're good at that.' Did I say 'So are you' or not? I don't remember. I only know I felt all loose and woozy, and by then my heart was pounding between my legs and both of us were breathing so hard you could hear it above the boom of the fireworks.

"I think it was me who said I needed more wine, and I think it was him who said he needed less. Anyway, we both laughed then and when the wine bottle was corked up again and not hindering him, he pulled me over half on top of him and this time the kisses were harder and hotter and wetter and both of our bodies were doing a lot of talking. He rolled me onto my back, lying half across me, and I remember thinking how secure it felt to have somebody hold me that way. It seemed to take away the hurt of the awful things Daddy was always yelling at me. It was like coming home ought to feel, or like Christmas, or like all the best scenes from all the best movies all rolled into one. He flattened me with the length of his body and began moving, moving, moving against my hips, kissing me all over my face. Once he broke away and groaned, 'Oh, God,' but I wouldn't let him go. I pulled him back on top of me and made him not stop. Maybe if I hadn't done that, things would have eased up a little. But by that time I didn't want them to ease up.

" 'Hey, listen, I think we're both a little drunk,' he finally said, and rolled off of me. But I found the wine bottle and said, 'Not yet.' Then I took a mouthful of wine and leaned over and kissed him and when his mouth opened, I let the wine drizzle into it. He took the bottle and sat up and filled his mouth, pushed me onto my back again and did what I'd just done to him. The wine was warm from the inside of his mouth. When I swallowed it, he bathed my lips with his tongue, running it over them like a mother cat washes her kitten. And before I knew what was happening, he ran his tongue down my jaw and laced his fingers through my hair and forced my head back. Then I felt the neck of the bottle against my own neck and the cool trickle of the wine as he poured it in the hollow of my arched throat.

"Crazy! I thought. We're crazy! But I felt like my pores were alive for the first time ever while he lapped the wine from my neck, then he moved up to continue kissing me under my jaw, intentionally touching me nowhere else, I think.

"I remember the pulsing happening in my body in places where I wished he'd pour the wine and cool me off. But I knew pouring the wine wouldn't really cool me off, and anyway, I didn't want to be cooled. When his tongue left me again, my hand groped for the wine bottle and he played along, letting me take my turn at drinking from him. I made him lie on his side and we were both giggling terribly while I tried to pour wine into his ear and he said, 'What are you doing?' and I said, 'Deafening you,' and he said, 'What?' and I said, 'Deafening you!' and he said, 'What?' again, louder and louder and we were laughing and I was taking wine from his ear with the tip of my tongue. Only most of it had gone running down behind it and into the soft hair at the back of his neck and I followed it and we laughed and laughed.

"When it was his turn again, he teased me by pretending to consider for a long, long time, and finally he rolled me onto my stomach and said, 'Pick your hips up off the blanket a little.' I did and felt him pull my shirttails out of my jeans. Next I felt the wine run into the hollow of my spine before he slipped his arm under me and held me up a little while taking the wine off my back. And always we were laughing, laughing, even when he lay down on top of me and started kissing the back of my neck, using his hips from behind to tease me, while I pleaded breathlessness with his weight on top of me that way.

"My turn next, and there was only one place I could think of—if you could call it thinking by that time, my mind was so fuzzy. We were kissing when I pushed him onto his back again. Then I sat up and boldly unbuttoned his shirt and—like he'd done to me—pulled it out of his jeans. I poured my turn into the shallow valley between his ribs, and tried to lap it up before it ran down to his stomach, but of course I couldn't and we started giggling foolishly, getting hotter all the time, avoiding the final confrontation with this silliness we'd somehow cooked up together. I've read about different kinds of foreplay before, but this one beat anything I've ever read about.

"Next it was his turn, and suddenly the giggling stopped. He unbuttoned my blouse in the flashes from the fireworks and without uttering a word, poured wine in my navel, and ever so slowly pushed the cork into the bottle and threw it far away onto the grass someplace. He leaned over and no sooner had I felt his tongue on my stomach than he got both arms around my hips some way, and we rolled back and forth with his face against my stomach, and one of his hands swept up and down from the small of my back to the back of my thighs and I knew what would happen if I didn't stop him, so I reached down to pull at his shoulders, but he rolled over and pinned the bottom half of me down, kissing his way around the waist of my jeans. Then he tried to open the snap with his teeth. Finally I managed to make him come up and join me, stretched out again. But my blouse was open and he had my bra off before his lips got to mine. Again we were flattened against each other and his skin felt so good against mine. He ground himself against me and I ground right back. He raised his knee and pressed it high between my legs and I clung to him, to the very, very good and right feeling of being close that way to another human being.

"He had a way of moving his hands over my breasts that made me forget all the names Daddy had ever called me, that made me feel utterly right to lie there beneath his touch, letting his knee ride hard and high between my thighs, letting him pull one of my legs over his hip until we were as close to joined as it's possible to be when you're both still wearing jeans.

"Once he whispered, 'Hey, listen, are you sure you want to do this?' and something about him not usually doing this with strangers and I think I stopped his words with my mouth and then his hand plunged down into the back of my jeans and I gave him every permission with the movement of my body. Names Daddy had called me came teasing, but somehow they didn't apply. I wanted that closeness, needed it like nothing I had ever needed in my life. And when Clay zipped down my zipper and tucked the backs of his fingers against my bare skin, I sucked in my stomach to make it easier for him. His hand moved down and I closed my eyes and lay there pretending that at last somebody loved me. Who was I at that minute? Was I some heroine from a forgotten childhood film or was I myself, the me that had gone without affection all her life? I think maybe I was a little of each, for I knew a treasured feeling that could only happen in the movies. At least, I'd always believed it only happened in the movies, yet here it was, happening to me. I felt like all nineteen years of my life had been pointed to this moment, to this man who was showing me that there was more than hate in this world, there was love, too. He called me Cat then. 'Ah, Cat,' he said, 'you feel good,' and I was sure that he could feel me throbbing, touching the inside of me that way, and I wanted to say to him that I'd never felt that way before, not ever, not even close. But I didn't. I only closed my eyes and let everything in me swim toward his touch until my body thrust against his hand of its own accord, and I knew my mouth hung slack but could not seem to close it. I seemed to forget how to kiss even, but lay there beneath his kiss nearly unaware of it, for its adequacy seemed to pale compared to the sensations that wanted completion in the lower half of my body. And the wine led my hands to search his hard hips, feeling them pull away, giving me consent, freedom, space.

"The heat of him was a surprise and I felt awkward and graceful, both at once, knowing this was what I was expected to do, yet unsure of how to go about it. At my touch he grunted, pressed closer against my hand, moved sinuously, 'Go ahead, Cat,' he said in my ear, and his breath on my neck was equally as hot as the beating of his blood through denim.

"I did it, in slow motion, I think, fearing with every opening tooth of his zipper that somehow my father would know what I was doing. Then I put him from my mind. No, that's not true. I didn't have to put him from it, because thoughts of him and everything else fled when I touched Clay Forrester for the first time. Whatever I had expected, I had not expected such heat. Neither had I expected the silkiness. But he was both hot and silky and I had enough sanity about me to marvel at the fluid way he could move, his thrust and ebb making me feel the experienced one holding his flesh in my hands, when I feared being naive and inexpert.

"When I used to imagine making love, I always thought it must be awkward and clumsy. First times are bound to be, I thought. But it wasn't. Instead, it was easy and as graceful as any dance. When he came into me, he called me Cat again, plunging deep while little of the discomfort I'd been led to expect happened. I learned that my body had had some hidden knowledge all along that my mind had not, for it undulated and surprised me and pleased Clay (I think) and it really was like the ballet, each movement so in tune with the other. It was effortless and natural and rhythmic, and would be beautiful to watch, I thought later. But when we were soaring everything came clear, and I suddenly knew why I was doing it. I was doing it to get even with Daddy, and maybe even Mom.

"In the middle of it all, my muscles suddenly lost motion and I only clung to Clay and let him finish without me. I wanted to cry out loud, 'Why didn't you love me? Why didn't you hug me? Why did you make me do this? You see, it's not so hard to touch, to be tender. Look, a total stranger can show me all this, why couldn't you? I didn't want much, just a smile, a hug, a kiss sometime to know you approved of me.' I wanted to cry then but stopped myself. And maybe I hung onto Clay too tight, but that's all. I'll show them! I'll show them all!"

The room was a circle of dark around the light blot shining over the cluttered tabletop. The words on the page became hazy and Clay's hand shook as he replaced the diary where he'd found it. He propped his elbows on the typewriter and pressed his lips against his folded hands. His eyes closed. He tried to gulp down the lump in his throat but it stubbornly remained. He dropped his face into his palms, picturing a father reading that from his daughter. Further, he tried to conceive of a father so devoid of emotion as to fail to respond to such a cry for love. His mind wandered back to the evening he'd first learned that Catherine was expecting his child. Vividly he recalled her stubborn refusal to ask anything of him, and for the first time he thought he understood. He thought he understood, too, why she had done such a convincing job during the wedding and reception. *I'll show them! I'll show them all!* He felt a new and oppressive weight of responsibility that he'd not known until now. He recalled her aversion to being touched, her defensiveness, and realized why it was so necessary for her to build such a barrier around herself.

He pictured her face the few times he'd seen it genuinely happy, knowing now the reasons for her quicksilver changes and why she had been striving so hard to remain independent of him.

His elbows hurt. He realized he'd been sitting for a long time with them digging into the sharp edges of the typewriter. He opened his eyes and the light hurt them. Listlessly he rose and turned off the lamp, wandered into the bedroom and fell on the bed. He lay there with his mind reeling and groping, waiting for her return.

Clay heard her come in, sat up, wondering how to treat her, an odd sensation, for now his concern was with her, not with himself. When he came downstairs, she was sitting with her coat still on, her head laid back against the davenport, eyelids closed but quivering.

"Hi," he said, stopping across the room from her.

"Hi," she said, without opening her eyes.

"Something wrong?" The lamplight shone on her windstrewn hair. She hugged her coat very tightly around herself and turned the collar up around her jaw.

"The baby died."

Without another word he crossed the room, sat down on the arm of the davenport and put a hand on top of her hair. She allowed it but said nothing, showed no signs of the heartbreak and fear that bubbled inside her. He moved his hand, rubbing in warm circles upon her hair, then smoothing it down in wordless communion with her. She swallowed convulsively. He wanted desperately to kneel down before her and bury his head in her lap and press his face to her stomach. Instead, he only whispered, "I'm sorry."

"They said its l-lungs were underdeveloped, that wh-when a baby comes early there's always a ch-chance of . . ." But her sentence went unfinished. Her eyes opened wider than normal, focused on the ceiling, and he waited for only a single sob, but it never came. He tightened his fingers gently on the back of her neck—an invitation to avail herself of him in whatever way she needed. He could tell how she needed to be held and comforted but she overcame it and sprang up, away from his touch, jerking her coat off almost angrily.

He stopped the coat while it drooped yet over her shoulder blades, grasping her upper arms from behind, expecting her to yank free of his touch. But she didn't. Her head sagged forward as if her neck had suddenly gone limp.

"It doesn't mean ours is in danger," he assured her. "Don't let it upset you, Catherine."

Now she yanked free and spun. "Don't let it upset me! What do you think I am? How can I not let it upset me when I've just seen Grover crying for a baby she never wanted! Do you know how she got pregnant? Well, let me tell you. She was suckered into a date with a high school jock who did it on a dare because she was such a troll! That's how! And she thought she hated the thing growing inside her and now it's dead and she cried like she wished she had died, too. And you say, 'Don't let it upset you'? I don't understand h-how this w-world got s-so . . . screwed up . . ."

He moved suddenly before he could change his mind, before she could run from him again or hide her need behind more of her anger. He wrapped both arms around her and gripped her fiercely. He cradled the back of her head and forced it into the hollow of his neck and made her stay that way, their muscles quivering, straining until at last she gave in and he felt her arms cling to his back. More like combatants than lovers, they clung.

Her nails dug into his sweater as she gripped it. Then he felt her fists thumping against the small of his back in desperation, although she wasn't trying to escape him anymore. Just those pitiful thumps, growing weaker and weaker while he waited.

"Catherine," he whispered, "you don't have to be so strong all the time."

"Oh, God, Clay, it was a boy. I saw him in the incubator. He was so beautiful and fragile."

"I know, I know."

"Her mom and dad wouldn't come. Clay, they wouldn't come!" A fist hit his back again.

Let her cry, he thought. If only she'd cry at last. "But your mom's going to come and so is mine."

"What are you trying to do to me?" She suddenly started pushing, palms against his chest, almost thrashing.

"Catherine, trust me."

"No, no! Let me go! This is hard enough without you mixing me all up even worse."

Then she ran up the stairs, taking with her all her years of bottled-up hurt. But now he knew that gentleness would work. It would take time, but eventually, it would work.

TWENTY-THREE

It began snowing shortly after noon on Christmas Eve day. It came down like diamond dust, in light, puffy feather flakes. By evening the earth looked clean-white. The sky bore a soft luminescence, lit from below by the lights of the city reflecting off the snow.

Catherine wore a new homemade jumper of mellow rust wool, with a tie that cinched it loosely beneath her breasts. She had decided to meet Elizabeth Forrester head-on this time. Yet as she approached the front door, some of Catherine's aplomb quavered at the thought of the grande dame eyeing her popping stomach for the first time.

"Do you think she's here yet?" she asked Clay timorously, while he paused with his hand on the door latch.

"I'm sure she is. Just do like I said, face her squarely. She admires that."

The smile she managed nearly faded as they entered, for Elizabeth Forrester was advancing upon them from the height of the open stairway. Her cane led the way, but it had a surprising tuft of Christmas greenery tied about its handle with a red ribbon.

"Well, it's about time, children!" she scolded imperiously.

"Merry Christmas, Grandmother," Clay greeted, taking her arm as she approached the lowest step.

"Yes, I'm given to understand that it certainly is. I can help myself down the steps, if you please. If you want to pamper someone, I understand that your wife is in the way of a woman who needs pampering. Is that so, my dear?" She turned her hawk eyes on Catherine.

"Hardly. I'm as healthy as a horse," replied the girl, removing her coat into Clay's hands, revealing the maternity dress.

About Elizabeth Forrester's lips a thin smile threatened, and the eyes that pointedly refrained from dropping to Catherine's abdomen glittered like the jewels upon her fingers. Then she cocked a brow at her grandson.

"You know, I like this young woman's style. Not unlike my own, I might add." The ivory-headed cane pecked twice at Catherine's stomach while the matriarch passed on her decree. "As I've said once before, I shall most assuredly expect him to be

beautiful, not to mention bright. Merry Christmas, my dear."
She bestowed a cheek to Catherine's, miming a kiss that did not
quite land, then exited to the living room in her usual grand style
to leave Catherine gaping at Clay.

"That's all?" she whispered, wide-eyed.

"All?" he smiled. "Beautiful *and* bright? That's a pretty big
order."

A smile began about the corners of Catherine's eyes. "But
what if *she* is only *cute* and of *average intelligence?*"

Clay looked shocked. "You wouldn't dare!"

"No, I don't suppose I would, would I?"

Their smiles lingered for a long moment, the encounter with
Elizabeth Forrester somehow already forgotten. Gazing up at
Clay, at the smile on his firm cheeks, his charmingly handsome
mouth, and that brow that curled provocatively over his left eye,
Catherine found her self-restraint slipping. She realized she'd
been standing there with her eyes in his for some time and
thought, It's this house. What is it that happens to me when I'm
in this house with him? Breaking the spell, Catherine swept her
glance around the magnificent foyer, searching for something
to say.

"I think this place deserves to have its gentlemen arrive in
capes tonight, and its ladies with fur muffs, with sleighs outside
and nickering horses."

"Yes, Mother's been having fun, as usual."

Then they turned to join the others.

If the house exuded cordiality at other times of the year, it
had a special spell at Christmas. Pine swags looped their way up
the banister, their pungent aroma a heady greeting to all, while
red candles sprang from freshly cut holly branches on tables
everywhere. The pine scent mingled with that of smoke from the

blazing fireplaces and cooking aromas from the kitchen. Within the study, hurricane lanterns couched blazing candles on the mantel, while a childish rendition of "Deck the Halls" came from the piano in the living room. There, within the bay window, stood a tree of enormous size, a proud old balsam with traditional multicolored lights that cast their rainbows across the walls and faces there and were redoubled in gilded swags of tinsel garland that threaded the balsam's limbs. It bore so many dazzling ornaments that its green arms fairly drooped. A mountain of gifts—foiled, beribboned, sprigged with greens—cascaded around the foot of the tree. Upon the longest living room wall was an outsized wreath of nuts, garnished with a red velvet bow whose streamers were caught within the beaks of gilded partridges that hung on either side of the wreath. Everywhere there was the buzz and babble of happy voices, and above them came the laugh of Angela, who'd been ladling eggnog in the dining room, looking like some delicate little Christmas ornament herself in a pale lavender lounging outfit of soft velour, her tiny silver slippers matching the thin belt at her waist and the fine chains around her neck.

"Catherine, darling," she greeted, immediately leaving her task and crossing to them, "and Clay!" Her melodious voice carried its usual note of welcome, but Clay affected an injured expression.

"You know, it used to be 'Clay, darling,' first and then 'Catherine, darling,' but I seem to have been upstaged."

Angela gave him a scolding pout, but nevertheless kissed Catherine first, then him, flush on the mouth.

"There. Is that what you were waiting for, standing there so innocently?"

She quirked an eyebrow at the archway above his head,

which held a kissing ball of mistletoe. "As if you didn't know," teased Angela, "it's there every year."

Clay quickly ducked aside, playing the beleaguered male while Angela only laughed and bore Catherine away toward the eggnog where Claiborne now turned with a warm greeting.

The doorbell kept ringing until the laughter and voices were doubled. Left momentarily alone, Catherine scanned the ceiling to find the place peppered with mistletoe. Someone approached to congratulate her on her pregnancy, and she tried to forget about mistletoe. But everybody else was using it to great advantage, and it made for a gay mood. Catherine assiduously avoided it.

The food was served buffet-style, crowned by real English plum pudding that arrived steaming from the kitchen. That was when Granddad Elgin caught Inella under the mistletoe in the kitchen doorway as she fussily gave orders not to touch the pudding until she returned with the warmed dessert plates. Catherine laughed to herself, standing nearby with a cup of coffee in her hand. It was delightful and so unexpected to see little bird-like Granddad Elgin kissing the maid in the kitchen doorway. Catherine felt someone behind her and glanced over her shoulder to find Clay there. He raised his eyebrows, then his eyes, to a spot over her head.

"Better watch out. Granddad Elgin will get you next," he said.

She quickly scuttled from beneath the mistletoe. "I wouldn't have suspected it of your granddad," she said smilingly.

"Things get a little crazy around here at Christmastime. It's always this way."

"They certainly do," Clay's father said, approaching just then. "Do you mind, Young Mr. Forrester, if Old Mr. Forrester kisses your wife while she's standing in that advantageous spot?"

Catherine wasn't under the greens anymore; still, she looked up and backed up a step. "I wasn't—"

"Not at all, Mr. Forrester."

Claiborne captured her for a hearty kiss, then stepped back, squeezing her biceps, looking into her face.

"You're lovelier than usual tonight, my dear." He put one arm around her shoulders, his other around Clay's. He looked first into one face, then into the other. "I don't think I remember a happier Christmas."

"I think a little of the glow might be from you spiking the eggnog," Clay teased his father.

"A little, not all though."

Catherine and Clay found a corner to sit in and eat their plum pudding, but she only dabbled at hers. It seemed they had little to say to each other, although time and again she felt Clay's eyes on her.

Soon Angela rounded everyone up and took her place at the piano to accompany the younger children, who piped carols off-key until the entire group ended with "Silent Night." Claiborne stood behind Angela as she played, with his hands on her shoulders, singing robustly. When the last note finished, she kissed one of his hands.

"You weren't singing," Clay said behind Catherine.

"I'm a little inhibited, I guess."

He was close enough to smell her hair. He thought of what he'd read in her diary. He'd been wanting her ever since. "People will be leaving now. I'll help them find their coats."

"And I'll start picking up glasses. I'm sure Inella is tired."

It was after midnight. Clay and Catherine had ushered the last straggler out the door, for somehow Angela and Claiborne had disappeared. The entry was dim, pine-scented and private. With slow steps, Catherine radiated toward the living room and the soft glow of tree lights. Clay was just behind her, where it seemed he'd hovered more and more as the night moved on. His hands were in his pockets. She ran her fingers through her hair, brushing it behind an ear as they ambled thoughtlessly toward the archway.

But there Catherine stopped, warned by a movement in the shadows at the far end of the dining room. Claiborne and Angela stood there, wrapped in each other's arms, kissing in an impassioned way in which Catherine did not think people of their age kissed. Claiborne had a dishtowel slung over his shoulder and Angela was shoeless. His hand moved over Angela's back, then stroked her side and moved to her breast. Quickly Catherine turned away, feeling like an intruder, for the two were certainly unaware of her presence across the wide, dimly lit rooms. But as she turned discreetly to withdraw, she bumped into Clay, who, instead of retreating, only placed a single finger over his lips, then raised it to point at the mistletoe above their heads. His hair and face and shirt were illuminated in the muted hues of Christmas, all red, blue, green and yellow, and he looked as inviting as the gifts beneath the tree. His eyes, too, reflected the glow of the tree lights as with a single finger he traced the line of Catherine's jaw, burning its path to the hollow beneath her lower lip. Her startled eyes widened and the breath clawed its way into her throat. She laid a hand against his light-dappled shirt, meaning to hold him off, but he captured it, along with her other, and carried them around his neck.

"My turn," he whispered.

Then he lowered his lips to hers, caught them open in surprise, expecting the struggle to begin. But it didn't. He knew he did not play fair, catching her while his parents were right there doing the same thing. But it had been on his mind all night, and playing fair was the furthest thing from his mind as he delved into the silken depths of her mouth. Their warm tongues touched. He plied her with singular lack of insistence, remembering what she had written about such things, inviting rather than plundering, with a luxuriant slowness. He felt fingers curve around the back of his collar and stilled his tongue—waiting, waiting, with his hold still merely a suggestion upon her body. Then a single fingertip found the skin of his neck and gently he tightened the arm around her waist.

Her body had grown since their wedding. It had blossomed into a captivating fullness that now held their hips apart. But he ran a hand possessively up and down her back, wishing that now the baby would kick—just once—so he could know the feel of it against his loins.

Reluctantly he ended the kiss.

"Merry Christmas," he whispered, near her face.

"Merry Christmas," she whispered back, her lips so close he felt the whisper of breath from her words. The room was utterly still. A needle dropped from the Christmas tree, making an audible ping as they gazed into each other's eyes. Then their lips were willing and warm and seeking again and her stomach was pressed lightly against him. She wished this could go on forever, but the very wish reminded her that it couldn't, wouldn't, and she withdrew. But when she would have been turned loose he instead entwined his fingers loosely behind her back, leaning away, swiveling lazily back and forth with her, smiling down at her hair, her lips and her breasts, which were undeniably growing.

She knew she should insist on being turned loose, but he was tempting, tender this way, handsome with his face limned by the low lights, his hair colored like fire. They turned their faces to look at the Christmas tree. Contented for the moment, she let him pull her lightly near him until her temple rested on his jaw. And from the shadows the pale faces of Angela and Claiborne—in a like embrace—watched the younger couple, and Claiborne wordlessly tightened his embrace.

"I have a marvelous idea," Angela said softly.

Catherine started slightly, but when she would have pulled away, Clay prevented it.

"Why don't the two of you spend the night and that way we'll be able to creep down in the wee hours in our nighties and robes just like we've always done."

Clay felt Catherine stiffen.

"Fine by me," he said, rocking her as before, the picture of a satisfied spouse.

"But I don't have my nightie," she said, alarmed.

"I'm sure I can find one for you, and we must have a spare toothbrush around here someplace. You could stay in the pink room."

Catherine groped for excuses, came up with one. "But we have to pick up Mother on our way over tomorrow morning anyway."

"Oh, that's right."

Clay's heart fell.

"Well," Angela mused, "it was a good idea anyway. But you two make sure you get here bright and early."

At home, Clay took his sweet old time about dragging out his own bedding and using the bathroom. He hovered around the upstairs hall, leaning against her doorway, watching while she slipped off her earrings and shoes. "Want a glass of soda or something?" he asked.

"No, I'm stuffed."

"I'm not very tired, are you?"

"I'm beat."

He unbuttoned his shirt. "I guess that's to be expected, huh?"

"Yes, the heavier I get the less zip I have."

"How much longer are you planning to stay in school? Shouldn't you be quitting pretty soon?" He finally decided to come into the bedroom, passing close behind her to stand beside the chest of drawers and empty his pockets.

"I can go as long as I want."

"How long is that?"

"A while yet, maybe till the end of second semester."

He watched her moving around the room, knew she was making motions at inconsequential things to look like she was busy. He wandered to the closet door, idle himself, leaning against the door frame and watching while she opened a dresser drawer. Her fair hair swayed forward over her shoulder as she leaned to retrieve something from inside. The skin across his chest felt as tight as a piano string. His heart beat upon it like a velvet hammer. His voice, when he spoke, was a deep, resonant note, softly struck.

"How long can a pregnant woman safely have intercourse?"

Catherine's hands fell still. Her head jerked up and she met his eyes in the mirror. The muscles of her groin involuntarily tightened, as did her hands upon the garments she'd been needlessly straightening in that drawer. Clay didn't move a muscle, just lounged there against that door frame with a hand strung negligently in his trouser pocket and a thin strip of golden-haired skin showing behind his open shirt. His expression was unreadable as she struggled to think of a reply.

"I want to, you know," he said, in that same hushed tone that raised every hair along the base of her spine. "And since you're already pregnant, what else could happen? I mean, if it's safe for you, of course." But she only stared at him. "I've been wanting to for weeks, and I've told you in every possible way except in words. Tonight when we were kissing under that mistletoe I decided I'd tell you. You're a very desirable wife, did you know that, Catherine?"

At last she found her voice, trembling though it was. "I'm a very pregnant wife."

"Ah, but that doesn't detract from your desirability in the least. Particularly since it's my baby you're carrying."

"Don't say any more, Clay," she warned.

"Don't be afraid of me, Catherine. I'm not going to force the issue. It's entirely up to you."

"I'm not afraid of you, and the answer is no." Suddenly she found what she was looking for in that drawer and slammed it shut.

"Why?"

She kept her back to him, looking down at something on the dresser top, but in the mirror he could see how she pressed herself against the edge of it, clutching some blue filmy thing in her hand.

"Why are you doing this tonight when it's been such a perfect day?"

"I told you, I'd like to go to bed with you. Would it be dangerous?"

"The subject never came up at the doctor's."

"Well, why don't you bring it up next time you're there?"

"There's no point in it."

"Isn't there?"

The silence that followed was as pregnant as the woman leaning against the dresser. Then Clay's voice became convincing.

"I'm tired of sleeping out there on that davenport when there's a luxurious king-size bed in here and a perfectly good, warm woman to snuggle up to. And I think she'd enjoy it, too, if she'd let herself. What do you say, Catherine, it's Christmas."

"Don't, Clay. You promised."

"I'm breaking my promise," he said, bringing his shoulder away from that doorframe in slow motion.

"Clay," she said warningly, turning to face him.

"How can you kiss that way and not get turned on, will you tell me that?"

"Stay away from me."

"I've been staying away. All it does is make me need it all the more." He advanced halfway across the room.

"I am not going to bed with you, so you can just forget it!"

"Convince me," he said low, still advancing.

"Do you know what your problem is? It's your ego. You simply can't believe I can live with you and not give in to your deadly charms, can you?"

In a voice like velvet he accused, "Cat, you're a goddam liar. You're forgetting I'm the one that was kissing you earlier. What's the harm in it? After all, it's legal, if it comes down to that—all signed, sealed and documented by the preacher. What are you afraid of?"

He was no more than an arm's length in front of her now, his gray eyes warmer than she'd ever seen them. Unconsciously she covered her widening girth with both hands.

"Why do you do that? Why do you try to hide from me? Always keeping me at a distance, avoiding even being in the same room with me. Why can't you be like you were earlier tonight more often? Why don't you talk to me, tell me how you're feeling, even complain about something? I need some human contact, Cat. I'm not used to living this insular life."

"Don't call me Cat!"

"Why? Tell me why."

"No." She would have turned away, but his arm stopped her.

"Don't turn away from me. Talk to me."

"Oh, Clay, please. It's been the most wonderful night. Please don't ruin it now. I'm tired, and happier than I've been for the longest time; at least I was until you started this. Can't we pretend the kiss never happened and be friends?"

He wanted to put voice to the root of her problem, to say to her that making love with him would not make her the slut her father told her she was. But she wasn't ready for it yet, and furthermore, it was a truth she must discover for herself. He knew if he forced her before she recognized that truth, the damage would be irreparable.

"If you mean it, and you're genuinely going to be friendly toward me from now on, that's a start. But don't expect me to forget that kiss ever happened, and don't expect me to believe that you'll forget it either."

"It's that house. Something about that house. I feel different when I go there, and somehow I do crazy things."

"Like letting your husband kiss you under the mistletoe?"

She was struggling with emotions she could not control, wanting him, afraid of the heartbreak he could cause her in the end. He reached out one brown hand, capturing the back of her neck, pulling her a little nearer, though she stiffly resisted.

"You are afraid of me, Catherine. But you don't have to be. When and if . . . the decision will be yours."

Then he kissed her lightly on the mouth, still holding her with that single hand on her tight neck muscles.

"Good night, Cat," he whispered, and was gone.

Her determination to resist Clay was further weakened when on Christmas morning she opened up a small package from him and found two tickets to *Swan Lake*, coming up at Northrup Auditorium in late January. She read the words on the tickets and raised her eyes, but he was tearing into a gift from his mother, so Catherine leaned over and touched his arm softly. He looked up.

"You remembered," she said, with the warmth expanding in her chest. "I . . . well, thank you, Clay. I'm sorry I have no gift for you."

"I haven't been to a ballet in a long time," he said.

The moment grew complicated by the looks in their eyes, then she broke the tension by teasing, "Who says you're invited?"

But next Catherine bestowed one of her rare smiles.

TWENTY-FOUR

During the following week, Clay invited Catherine to go shopping with him. He needed something to wear on New Year's Eve, which they'd agreed to spend with Claiborne and Angela at the country club. But Catherine declined, believing it best to avoid such little domestic sallies.

Clay came home one night with a pair of plastic-sheathed garment bags and tossed one casually across the back of a living room chair. "Here, I thought we both ought to have something new."

"You bought something for *me?*" she asked from the kitchen.

"Sure. You were stubborn so I had to. It's quite formal at the club—kind of a tradition."

Then he bounded up the stairs with his hanger. She wiped her hands on a dishcloth and walked around the peninsula with her eyes riveted on the dress bag.

When Clay came back, she was standing with the dress aloft, holding the black crepe skirt like an open fan.

"Clay, you shouldn't have."

"Do you like it?"

"Well, yes, but it's so impractical. I'll probably only wear it once."

"I want you looking just as classy as every other woman there."

"But I'm not. I've never owned a dress like this in my life. I'll feel funny." She looked momentarily crestfallen, but he could tell how much she liked it.

"Listen, Catherine, you're my wife, and you have as much right to be at the club as anyone else. Understand?"

"Yes, but—"

"*Yes, but* nothing. All I'm worried about is if the thing will fit. It's a first for me, you know—buying a maternity dress."

She couldn't help chuckling. "What did you do, go in the store and say, 'Gimme a dress that's, say, four ax handles around?"

He rubbed his chin, measuring her visually. "No, I figured more like five."

She scarcely looked at him as she laughed; she had eyes for nothing but the dress.

"I'll look like a circus tent, but I love it . . . really."

"You're awfully touchy about losing your shape. Isn't it time you accept it? I have."

"It's easy for a man to say when he doesn't have to face getting blown up like some dirigible and having to lose the extra pounds afterward. If I'm not careful, no man will look twice at me next summer."

As soon as Catherine said it she felt him bristle. His good humor fled as Clay remarked, "Oh, so you plan to go husband-hunting then?"

"I didn't mean it that way. But I certainly don't intend this marriage to mean the end of my love life."

For Clay the pleasure of giving her the dress suddenly dissolved, leaving him feeling angry, his ego stung. It irritated him that she could make a comment like that while she wouldn't even let him lay a hand on her. He'd given her the best home she'd ever had, all the things he could think of to make her life easy. He'd taken on his share of the housework, given her the freedom to come and go and to do her abominable typing—which irked him no end and made him want to drop the damn typewriter off the balcony. And he'd been more than patient with her, even when he wanted more attention than she gave. And how did she repay him? By being cold and standoffish, then bemoaning the fact that no man would look twice at her if she didn't preserve her shape? What the hell was she trying to do to him anyway?

While they were getting ready to go out on New Year's Eve, Clay was as stony as he'd been during the three days since he brought the dress home. Catherine had learned how lonely it felt to be the one on the receiving end of such treatment.

She put the finishing touches on her hair. Just then Clay came in the bedroom to rummage through his jewelry box for a tie pin. From behind, he was tantalizingly thin and tapered in the new smoky blue suit with its trim cut and double vents at the rear.

Clay swung around to find her studying him.

"I'm almost ready. Excuse me," he said, edging around her briskly.

"I see that. Is that your new suit?"

He didn't answer, just moved to the mirror to insert the needle of the pin through a new striped tie.

"You always manage to look like an ad in *The New Yorker*," she tried.

"Thank you," he replied icily.

"And the dress fits, see?"

"Good."

She was stung by his indifference. "Clay, you've hardly talked to me at all this week. What's wrong now?"

"If you don't understand it, I'm not going to waste my breath explaining."

She knew very well what was wrong, but it was hard for her to apologize.

He dropped the back clasp of the tie pin and muttered, "Damn."

"Clay, I know I act ungrateful sometimes, but I'm not. And you and I had an agreement before we got married."

"Oh, sure! So why are you in here offering me compliments? Why do I suddenly merit applause for how I dress?"

"Because it's true, that's all."

"Catherine, don't, okay? I don't know how to handle you anymore. You've walked around me like I was some cigar-store Indian for weeks now. And when you finally decide to start talking to me, it's to tell me you're worried you might gain too much weight so it'll be tough when you go on the make again. How do you think that makes me feel when you practically start shopping for chastity belts every time I try anything with you?"

"Oh, for heaven's sake, what's the matter with you, anyway!"

"You want to know what's the matter with me?" he barked, whirling on her, accosting her face-to-face. "What's the matter with me is the same damn thing that was the matter with me last week and the week before that and the week before that. I'm horny! That's what's the matter with me! You want the truth, lady? There it is in a nutshell! So don't come sashaying in here after all this time and suddenly start fawning over my looks, which are the same as when you married me! You know what you are?"

She had never seen Clay this angry. His face was suffused with color; the veins above his collar stood out boldly.

"You, Mrs. Forrester, are a—" But even as angry as he was he couldn't say it.

"What!" she yelled. "Finish it! Say it!"

But he got control of himself and turned away, tugging at his lapels and adjusting the knot of his tie.

"My mother raised me to speak with respect around females, so I'll refrain from using the four-letter prefix to the word *teaser*."

"How dare you, you bastard!"

He gave her an insolent look in the mirror. "Take a look at what happens to you after a few days of being ignored. You come in here with your cute little compliments, just enough to keep me swimming after the bait, huh? Do you know how many times you've warmed up to me just enough to keep me interested? I won't bother to recount them because you'd deny it anyway. But it's the truth. You've accused me of being the one exploiting you to boost my ego, but I believe the shoe's on the other foot."

"That's not true! I've never led you on!"

"Catherine, at least I've been honest about it, starting with our wedding night. I've come right out and said that I wanted to make love to you. But do you know what you do? You skirt the issue, you skitter away, then allow me close enough only when it suits you. Your problem is you want to forget you're a woman but you can't. You like being pursued, but on the other hand, you're afraid if you break down and allow yourself to be made love to, you'll be what your father always accused you of being. What you don't realize is, that makes you as sick as your old man!"

"You bastard," she growled, low in her throat.

"Go ahead, call me names so you don't have to face yourself."

"You said, 'no sex,' when you asked me to marry you."

"You got it. I've decided not to harass you anymore. You want to sleep in your big bed alone, fine. But let's end this sweet little charade we play in between bedtimes, okay? I won't press you for attention, and you won't give me cute little compliments you don't mean, huh? Let's just keep out of each other's way until July, like we agreed."

There was nothing in the world she wanted to do less than go to the club that night. Things became even less tolerable when, shortly after they arrived, so did Jill Magnusson, along with her date and her family.

Clay put on a devoted-husband act, timing his repeated returns to Catherine's side very assiduously all night long, making sure she had whatever drink she wanted, making sure introductions were made where necessary, making sure she was never left at the table alone when every other woman was dancing. Around his parents Clay was the epitome of husbandly courtesies, but Catherine lost track of how many times he danced with Jill. At two minutes before midnight Clay was dancing with his wife, but when the band broke into "Auld Lang Syne" and he kissed her, it was the most impersonal, tongueless kiss she'd ever had. Furthermore, he had artfully maneuvered them near enough to Jill and her partner that it appeared quite natural when they were the first couple to exchange partners. Catherine found herself pressed into the arms of a stocky, black-haired man who solicitously refrained from embracing the pregnant lady too tightly. But while she and the dark man kissed, her eyes were open, watching Clay and Jill sending a silent message into each other's eyes—long and tenuous—before enfolding each other in a painfully familiar fashion. Clay's hands caressed Jill's bare back, his fingers spread seductively so that his little finger hooked beneath a red spaghetti strap, traveled up Jill's shoulder blade and disappeared beneath her cascading hair. Catherine dropped her eyes only to see Clay's hips pressed provocatively against Jill's. The couple broke apart momentarily, then Jill laughed and half-turned to Clay as she captured him again. Now Catherine could see Jill's long fingernails glittering through Clay's hair. Unable to drag her eyes away, Catherine watched as their mouths opened wide upon each other and could see a movement at Clay's cheek as his tongue danced into Jill's mouth.

Then, thankfully, Stu was there to claim a kiss from Catherine. But he could see the way she fought the intimidating rush of tears and whispered, "Don't think anything of it, kiddo, okay? We've all been kissing each other Happy New Year since we were too young to know what it meant."

Then Stu smoothly parted Clay and Jill and moved in for a kiss. But Catherine noticed when Stu kissed Jill there was none of that open-mouthed business, nor did she run her glistening nails through *his* hair.

Before one o'clock arrived, Jill and Clay were both mysteriously missing. Nobody seemed to notice except Catherine, who checked the clock at least twenty times during the twenty minutes they were gone. When they returned, they entered carefully from opposite doors. But Clay's tie had been loosened and she could tell he'd freshly run a comb through his hair.

*   *   *

Dreary January settled in, bringing snow and cold and little to cheer anyone. Clay began leaving the house in the evenings again, although he never stayed out overnight. He and Catherine withdrew into their polite roles of roommates, and nothing more. The spirited teasing they'd once shared seemed gone forever, and the consideration Clay had once shown Catherine disappeared with New Year's Eve. When they were at home at the same time, they rarely ate together, avoided even passing each other in the hall. With Herb still in the workhouse, Catherine visited her mother more often, raising no objection in Clay when she'd return home later than he. The night before the ballet she reminded him of it, but without looking up from his book he suggested she take Bobbi or her mother because he wouldn't be free to go with her. Catherine took Bobbi, but somehow the ballet had lost its appeal.

Clay spent the night of the ballet at home. Occasionally his thoughts meandered to Catherine, remembering her pleasure at receiving the tickets. He'd thought back then that it would be fun to take her to see her first performance. Most of the time when he was alone he tried not to think of her at all, but tonight it was hard, knowing where she was. There had been times during the past month when, if she would have offered even the slightest warming toward him, he might have reneged and dropped the uncaring front behind which he'd been posing. But he'd been hurt by her rebuffs too many times to approach her again. A man could stand being turned away only to a point before withdrawing a safe distance, or—better yet—going where he knew he'd find a positive response.

When Catherine came home, Clay was drowsing in the living room with a book on his lap. He yawned, sat up and ran a hand through his hair. It had been a long time since they'd said anything civil to each other. He thought, maybe . . .

"How was it?" he inquired.

She glanced over his tousled hair, wondering why he bothered to make it appear as if he'd been home all night when she hadn't the slightest doubt whom he'd been with. She kept her voice intentionally expressionless as she replied, "I didn't like the way you could hear the dancers' feet echoing on the floor every time they landed."

Clay withdrew further into his protective shield.

February came, bringing gray days that thwarted even the most blithe spirits. Catherine decided to stay in school until the semester ended in mid-March, but the chore became harder and harder as she grew heavier and more listless.

And in the town house in Golden Valley not even the briefest word was spoken between husband and wife.

TWENTY-FIVE

The day they released Herb Anderson from the Hennepin County Workhouse, the chinook winds were blowing elsewhere in the country, but in Minnesota the cold, leaden skies matched Anderson's temperament. Gusty winds lapped at his ankles, whipping their icy tongues along the frozen slush beside the road as he walked. It was hard going without overshoes. Time and again his slick soles skittered on the uneven wayside and he swore under his breath. He hitchhiked his way into Minneapolis, finding the city as dismal as the highway had been, malcontent under the dirty blanket of late-winter ice that bore the remnants of the road crews' seasonal efforts at sanding and salting.

It was late afternoon, everybody scurrying with their chins pulled low into coat collars, scarcely looking up. Herb was forced to take a city bus to the old neighborhood, and even on it, the cold seeped in. He rode with arms crossed tight, staring out the window with unsmiling eyes.

Jesus, a drink sounds good. Kept me dry all these months, thinking they finally got old Herb. Hah, just who in the hell do they think they are, taking away a man's free will? I can dry out any damn time I want to. Didn't I always say I could! Well, I did it, by God, just like I said I could. But what gave them sonsabitches the right to force it on me? When I get to Haley's I'll show them sonsabitches that Herb Anderson quits drinkin' when Herb Anderson's good and ready, and not one day sooner!

At Haley's Bar the usual old crowd was there, picking up glasses instead of their kids.

"Well, look who's here! Been keepin' a stool warm for ya, Herb."

All of his cronies moved aside to make room, slapping him on the shoulder, settin' 'em up.

"First one's on me, huh? Hey Georgie, bring Herb here a taste of what he's been missin'!"

Ah, this is what a man needs, thought Herb. Friends who talk your language.

The feel of the varnished bar was like balm beneath his elbows. The smoky, neon haze around the jukebox burned his unaccustomed eyes wonderfully. The blaring medley of good ole country songs about wronged loves and foiled hearts made the wounds bleed like ulcers, self-opened. Herb raised another shot and downed it, then squeezed the shot glass and reveled in being the center of attention.

And all the while the alcohol did its dirty work; all the outrage that life had handed Herb Anderson came doubling back.

Ada tensed, placed trembling fingers to her lips at the sound of someone fumbling at the door. It was locked, but there came the click of a key. Then the door was flung wide and Herb wavered before her.

"Well, well, well, if it isn't Ada, keeping the home fires burning," he observed thickly.

"Why, Herb," she exclaimed in her timid way, "you're out."

"Goddam right I am, no thanks to you."

"Why, Herb, you should've told me you were coming home."

"So you coulda had lover boy here to keep me out?"

"Shut the door, Herb, it's cold."

He eyed the door sullenly. "You think it's cold in here, you oughta try prison awhile." He swung wide and slapped hard at the door, which cracked against the frame and bounced back open. Ada edged around him and shut it again. He watched her suspiciously, weaving slightly, hanging onto the front edges of his jacket with both hands.

"H-how are you, Herb?"

He continued to glower at her with sallow eyes. "What the hell do you care, Ada? Where was your concern in November? Man expects his wife to stand behind him at a time like that."

"They told me I didn't need to come, Herb, and Steve was home."

"So I heard. Bet the bunch of you got together and saw to it I wouldn't even see my own kid, didn't you!"

"He was just here for a little while."

"Ada, he's my only goddam kid, and I got rights!"

She dropped her eyes and fidgeted with a button on her duster.

"You know what a man thinks about in prison, Ada?"

"It wasn't prison, it was just the workh—"

"It was the same as a prison and you know it!" he roared.

Ada began to turn away, but he caught one thin arm and swung her around to face him. "Why the hell'd you do it to me? Why!" The blast of his breath made Ada turn her face sharply away but he caught a fistful of her duster and lifted her to her toes, an inch from his mouth. "Who was he? I deserve to know after all these years."

"Please, Herb." She plucked at his knotted fist but he only clenched the cotton all the tighter.

"Who! I sat in that stinkin' hole and made up my mind I'd get it out of you once and for all."

"It don't matter. I stayed with you, didn't I?"

"You stayed because I'd've found you and your lover boy and killed you both, and you knew it!" He suddenly thrust her away and she fell sprawling on the sofa behind her. "Just like I'd like to kill that slut of a daughter you spawned while I was off fighting the goddam Vietcong! How could you do a thing like that? How! Everybody looks at you and me together and I can read their minds. Poor little Ada, living with that no-'count bum, Herb! You had 'em all fooled, all these years with your little mouse-in-the-corner act. But not me, not me! I never forgot, not for one minute, what you done to me while I was good enough to go out and fight your war for you. Every time I look at that blond hair and that bastard face of hers I remember, and I swore long ago I'd get even with the pair of you one day. And finally I get my chance when the little slut gets herself knocked up by

that rich son of a bitch, and I figger for once in his life Old Herb
is gonna get paid back for what he put up with all those years.
And do you know how sweet it was to think it was comin'
straight from the hand of one who owed it to me—that whorin'
no-good who's just like her mother?" Herb was weaving, his eyes
bright with rage. "You owed it to me, Ada! You both owed it to
me! But what did you do? You saw to it that I ended up empty-
handed again, didn't you!"

"I never—"

"Shut up!" he barked, pointing a finger straight at her nose.
"Shut up!" He towered over her, leaning dangerously near. "You
had this comin' for nineteen years, Ada. Nineteen years I looked
at your bastard and seen my own flesh and blood turned against
me by the two of you till he finally run away from home. Then
when he comes back the first time, you side with them and let
them railroad me into prison. And just to twist the knife in the
wound, you marry her off to my meal ticket. Goddammit, Ada,
I had to read about the wedding in a *newspaper*. You kept me
away on purpose, and I never even got to see Steve!"

"I didn't have nothing to do with—"

But Ada's cowering body was jerked to its feet.

"Don't lie to me, slut! I took nineteen years of your lies, and
what does it get me but prison!"

He reeled back and swung the first blow to the side of Ada's
head, sending it twirling while she fought to cover her face.

"You was on their side all the time, always siding against me!"

The next blow fell on her jaw and dropped Ada to the floor.

"That was my ship comin' in and you knew it!"

A savage kick raised Ada and dropped her back onto the floor.

Incensed now beyond reason, Herb Anderson's injustices
fed upon themselves. The hate that had been too shallowly
submerged for so long erupted in a wild red rage that found

vent upon the hapless Ada. The alcohol lent its beastly hand in raising the man's temper and fists until the deed he'd begun lay senseless and broken on the floor before him. He stared at the huddled heap, wiped a trickle of sputum from the side of his mouth, then tasted her blood on his knuckles and ran from the house, then from the neighborhood, and the next day from the town, then the state.

Catherine was typing when the phone rang downstairs. A moment later she heard Clay's footsteps pelting up the stairs, then his voice behind her.

"Catherine?"

He watched as she raised an elbow and kneaded the back of her neck.

"Cat?" he said gently.

The word—that above all others—made her suddenly swing around to find apprehension written on Clay's face.

"What is it?"

"That was Mrs. Sullivan, your mother's neighbor."

"Mother?" She half-rose from her chair. "What's wrong?"

Clay saw the lines of fright that suddenly pinched up her face. Instinctively he moved to her and laid a hand on her shoulder. "Your mother is in the hospital. They want us to come right away."

"But what's wrong?"

"Come on, we'll talk about it on the way."

"Clay, tell me!"

"Catherine, don't panic, okay?" He took her hand and led her hurriedly through the house. "It's not good for you in your condition. Here, put your coat on and I'll back the car out."

She nearly tore his jacket sleeve off stopping him. "Don't coddle me, Clay. Tell me what's wrong."

He covered her hand, squeezed it so hard that he curled it up. "Cat, your father is out of the workhouse. He got drunk and went home that way."

"Oh, no," she wailed from behind her fingertips.

Fear trickled through Clay, but not for her mother, for her.

"Come on, we'd better hurry, Cat," he said gently.

For the first time ever Catherine was grateful for Clay's penchant for speed. He drove the Corvette with the grim determination of an Indy-500 racer, taking curves and lane changes in robotlike fashion, taking his sight from the road only long enough to assure himself Catherine was still all right. She sat huddled and shivering, reaching out to clasp the dashboard occasionally, eyes riveted straight ahead. Once they arrived at the hospital, she was out of the car like a shot, and Clay had to jog to catch up with her. When they reached the emergency ward, Catherine broke away from Clay, surging toward the broad-beamed woman who immediately rose from a chair and came forward with outstretched hands.

"Cathy, I'm so sorry."

"How is she, Mrs. Sullivan?"

The woman's eyes immediately sought Clay's. He nodded.

"The doctors are still with her. I don't know yet. Oh, girl, what that man done to her . . ." And Mrs. Sullivan dissolved into tears. Clay's first thought was for Catherine, and he urged her into a chair while Mrs. Sullivan whimpered into a limp handkerchief. He stood before the pair, clutching Catherine's icy hand in his.

"She—she made it to the phone to call me," choked Mrs. Sullivan. "I don't know how, though."

Clay felt utterly helpless. He could do nothing but take the chair next to Catherine's and hold her hand while she stared with glazed eyes at the other pieces of cold, uncomfortable furniture across the room. Finally a nurse approached, saying the doctor would talk to them now. Clay restrained Catherine, pulling on her hand.

"Maybe I should go."

"No!" she insisted, yanking her hand out of his. "She's my mother. I'll go."

"Not alone then."

The doctor introduced himself, shook their hands and glanced at Catherine's roundness.

"Mrs. Forrester, your mother is in no danger of dying, do you understand?"

"Yes." But Catherine's eyes were locked on the door behind which her mother lay.

"She has been badly beaten and has a very bruised face. She's been sedated so there's really no point in your seeing her. Perhaps tomorrow would be just as well."

"She insists," Clay said.

The doctor took a deep breath and sighed.

"Very well, but before you go in I must warn you that she is not a pretty sight. I want you to be prepared for that. In your condition, shock won't help you at all. Don't be frightened by the amount of equipment—it looks far more complicated than it is. Your mother has suffered a fractured nasal septum, which is why her nose appears to be pushed to one side. She also has two fractured ribs. They compromised the breathing so a tracheotomy had to be performed, and she has a tube projecting from her throat. The respirator machine looks alarming, but is only helping her breathe temporarily. She'll soon be doing it on her own again. She has a nasal-gastric tube, a prophylaxis, to empty the stomach and prevent vomiting, and of course we are giving her some IVs, a little plasma.

"Now, do you still think you want to go inside?" He found himself wishing the girl would spare herself the sight. But she nodded, so the doctor was given one of the unpalatable tasks that sometimes made him ask himself why he'd chosen this profession.

The woman on the bed did not even remotely resemble Ada. Her nose was flattened. Her forehead was grotesque with bulging, strawberrylike welts. The cracked lips were puffed beyond recognition and showed telltale marks of blood. Tubes seemed to be stitched into her everywhere, leading to inverted bottles above the bed, a plastic sack hanging beside the mattress, and the respirator, which created the only sound in the room with its bellowslike mechanism breathing steadily. A blood-pressure cuff circled her arm, its cords connected to a computer that gave a constant digital printout of vital signs. In contrast to her puffed face, the rest of Ada looked shrunken and dissipated. Her hands lay limp and blue; the little finger of the left was in a splint.

Clay found himself swallowing repeatedly at the pitiful sight before him. He clutched Catherine's hand and felt the tremor there. She gave no other sign of the struggle within, but he was smitten with pity for her, knowing how she held her emotions in check. He thought of his own feelings, should this be Angela, and rubbed the inside of Catherine's elbow and pulled her arm hard against him. After only a brief moment, the doctor ushered them silently out. Catherine walked like a zombie all the way to the car.

When Clay opened the car door, he had to gently urge Catherine to bend, to sit, to turn her legs inside. He wished the doctor could have prescribed a tranquilizer for her, but it would be dangerous in so advanced a pregnancy. Starting the car, Clay felt a double fear now, for both Catherine and the baby. She sat woodenly while he fastened the top button of her coat, tugged at the collar and urged, "You've got to keep warm, Cat." But she only stared straight ahead, dry-eyed, unmoving. There were no trite phrases Clay could bring himself to utter. *Don't worry* or *She'll be all right* were more . . . or less . . . than he wanted to say to the tormented woman beside him. All he could do was find her hand in the dark and lace his fingers through hers as he drove, hoping that the meager offering might help somehow. But her lifeless fingers lay inert within his hold all the way home.

He suffered an agony of helplessness, driving through the night with his thumb brushing against the back of her hand in silent communication to which she did not respond. Their hands lay upon her narrow lap, the back of Clay's resting lightly against her now fully round stomach. He thought of the pain children bear at their parents' expense and hoped his child need never suffer what Catherine now suffered.

At home he helped her with her coat, then watched as she listlessly mounted the steps.

"Catherine, what can I do? Can I fix you something?"

She had stopped, as if she didn't know where she was. He came behind her, his hands in his pockets, wishing she would say, "Make me some cocoa, rub my back, put on some music, hold me . . ." But she shut him out instead, insulated within her carefully guarded solitariness.

"No, there's nothing. I'm very tired, Clay. I just want to go to bed." She walked upstairs with rigid back, directly to the bedroom, and closed the door upon the comfort he sought to offer.

He stood in the middle of the living room looking at nothing for a long time. He shut his eyes. His Adam's apple bobbed up and down convulsively. He pictured Ada, then Catherine's face as she'd looked at her mother's still figure. He sat down on the edge of the davenport with his face in his hands. He did not know how much time had passed before he sighed, rose and made a phone call to his father. He made up his bed on the davenport and wearily took off his trousers and shirt, but when the light was out he went instead to stand before the sliding glass door, staring out at the ebony night.

He needed the woman upstairs as badly right now as she needed him.

A faint, muffled sound intruded into the bruised night, bringing him to turn from the window. He strained to listen and it came again, high, distant, like the wind behind walls—hurt wind, wailing wind—and he knew what it was before he felt his way up the stairs in the dark. He paused at her bedroom door and listened. He laid his palm against the wood, then his forehead, too. When he could stand it no longer, he found the doorknob and soundlessly turned it. In the dimness, he made out the blur of the pale blue bedspread, padded silently across to lean and explore it with his hands. He felt her curled beneath the covers, clutching them over her head. He ran his hands along the snail-shaped form, the pity in his heart a choking thing while her high keening came muffled from the womb she had crawled back into. He pulled gently at the covers but she only clung to them the tighter.

"Catherine," he began, but found his throat clotted with emotion.

She gripped the guardian covers fiercely until at last he ebbed them from her fingers to reveal her curled with her head covered with both arms, her elbows tucked between her knees. Gently he lifted the blankets and lay down behind her, then covered them both up again. He tried to pull her into his arms but she only huddled tighter, wailing in that solitary, high syllable that made Clay's eyes sting.

His voice quavered as he whispered, "Cat, oh, Cat, let me help you."

He found her fists clenched in her hair and eased them away, running a palm along her arm, then pressing his chest upon her curved back until he could bear it no longer. Bracing himself on an elbow, he leaned over the curled ball of her, brushing back her hair, assuring her throatily, "I'm here, Cat, I'm here. Don't go through this all alone."

"Mamaaaaa . . . ," she wailed pitifully into the dark, "Mamaaaaa . . ."

"Please, Cat, please," Clay begged, running his hand down her arm to find her hands fiercely knotted between her knees.

"Mama," she wailed again.

He felt her body quaking and sought to calm her by cradling her as best he could with one arm along her thigh, cupping a knee and pulling her back against him.

"Darling, it's Clay. Please don't do this. Let me help you . . . let me hold you, please. Turn around, Cat, just turn around. I'm here."

"Mama, I didn't mean to," she quailed in that same childlike voice that frightened Clay so terribly. He stroked her hair, her shoulder, braced up and rested his cheek on the back of her head, waiting for some sign that she understood.

"Please, Catherine . . . I . . . don't shut me out."

He felt the first soundless spasm, the first sob that was not yet a sob, and gently, gently, pulled at her shoulder, turning her toward him until, like a broken spring, she unwound all at once and burrowed into his arms, while painful sobs wrenched from her throat.

"Hold me, Clay, hold me, hold me," she begged, clinging like a drowning person while her hot tears scalded his neck. Her grip was like iron while she quaked wretchedly and cried into him.

"Catherine, oh God, I'm so sorry," he said throatily into her hair.

"Mama, Mama, it's all my fault."

"No, Cat, no," he murmured, clasping her to him all the more closely, as if to pull her within his very body that he might absorb her pain. "It's not your fault," he soothed, kissing the top of her head while she babbled and cried and blamed herself. All the pent-up tears that Catherine had so long refused to shed for herself came rushing out for her mother while she clung to Clay with arms and hands that could not hold tightly enough. He cradled the back of her head, pulling her cheek against the silken hair of his chest, rocking at times, lost in pity, aching with the feeling of her heaving stomach pressed at last to his, but for the wrong reason. She muttered unintelligible sounds, broken by sobs that Clay welcomed, knowing they were the cure of her.

"It's all my f-fault, all my faul . . ."

He forced her mouth hard against his chest to stop the words. He swallowed convulsively before he could speak.

"No, Cat, you can't blame yourself. I won't let you."

"B-but it's t-true. It's because I'm pre-pregnant. I should've kn-known he wa-wanted the money . . . ba-bad enough. I hate him, I h-hate him. Why did he do it . . . hold me, Clay . . . I had to get away fr-from him. I had to, but to get a-away I had to b-be those things he c-called me, but I d-didn't care, I didn't care. You're so warm. . . . They never hugged m-me, never k-kissed me. I was good, I was al-w-ways good, just that one t-time with you, but he sh-shouldn't take it out on her."

Clay's heart thundered at her pitiful outpouring. She babbled on, almost mindlessly.

"I shouldn't have le-left her. I should have stayed, b-but it was s-so awful there when St-Steve left. He was the only one who ever—"

A deep sob broke from Catherine and she clung more desperately to Clay. Now he softly encouraged her, knowing she must say these things.

"Who ever what?"

"Who ever l-loved me. Not even M-Mama could, but I n-never understood wh-why. They never took me pl-places or bought me th-things like other kids got, or played with m-me. Uncle Fr-Frank used to kiss me and I'd pretend he w-was Daddy. Steve loved me, but af-after he was gone there was nobody and I used to pr-pretend I had a baby who'd love me. I thought if only I had a b-baby I'd never be lonely."

She stopped then, having discovered this truth at last.

Clay squeezed his eyes shut hard. Her heart was hammering against his, her arms clinging tenaciously to his neck. Pity and compassion and the overwhelming need to heal her welled high in Clay. He was deluged by the desire to protect, fulfill, calm her, and to provide the missing years of love that could never be made up for. He fought against tears, holding her long and hard against his body, unable to hold her long enough, hard enough, pressing her so fiercely that at last he opened his legs to let one of hers in, high against him. And hers opened and his knee found shelter against her, too. They clung that way, sharing a new bond of warmth and comfort until, pressed between them, the baby objected to all that crowding and moved restlessly within Catherine. A wild exhilaration lifted Clay's stomach, as if he'd just reached the downhill slope of a roller coaster. And everything—the horror Catherine had suffered that day, the first feel of his child's movement in her belly, her own desperate cry for love—made his motions somehow right as his hands skimmed over her body, up her back, down her side, down her warm buttock and leg that lay over his hip. And even as Catherine cried against his chest, Clay found the hollow behind her knee and pulled her more securely into her nestling place. He ran his hand again up her hip, up her side; finding her breast and cradling it, and the side of her stomach with his forearm. She was warm and reaching and unresisting against him, and he whispered raspily against her ear, "Cat, oh, Cat, why did you wait so long? Why did it take all this?"

With a hand, he commanded the back of her head and lowered his mouth into her salt-kiss. Her mouth opened wide and took him in, and it ceased to matter that it was only in desperation she turned to him. It ceased to matter that she might later feel he took advantage of her in her weakness. His hand, warm and soft and seeking, trailed, unchecked, from her full breast to the hard, taut stomach that protruded because of him. He fondled it searchingly, awed by its solidness, by the thought of the life it carried. And as if the baby heard its father's pleas, it moved within. Clay lay stock-still then, stunned, with his palm conforming to the shape of Catherine's flesh, willing the child to move once more. And when it had, and he'd again known the feel of it, Clay reached unhesitatingly to pull Catherine's wide gown up and run his hands over the bare, firm skin beneath. He skimmed his palm again and again over the warm curve of her belly, discovering things that his body had caused in hers: the protruding navel, the engorged breasts, the widened, enlarged nipples, and—yet again—the fluttery motion of life beneath his hand. How often he had wondered. How often he had thought it his right to explore these changes of his making. How often she, too, had longed to share them but had steeled herself against him, shielded in an armor of assumed remoteness.

But what had started out as a journey of pity and compassion became one of sensuality as Clay's caressing hand moved lower, touching the crisp hair that couched the spot where Catherine's burden thrust itself sharply outward from her body. Wordlessly he slipped his hand between her thighs, covering her, swollen there, with the length of his long, closed fingers, pressing gently upward, feeling her pulse throbbing there, learning her. Thoughts of her sexuality, her pregnancy, what he knew he could not do, made him curiously callow in his exploration of her. He moved his hand once more to her stomach.

"Oh, Cat," he whispered, "your stomach's so hard. Does it hurt?"

She moved her head to answer no, amazed by his naiveté.

"I felt the baby move," he whispered almost reverently, yet his breath was warm and labored on her skin. "It moved right there under my hand." He spread his fingers over her stomach again, as if in invitation, but when nothing happened his hand again sought the intimate world between her legs.

And Catherine closed her eyes and let him . . . let him . . . let him, drifting in a myriad of emotions she'd held at bay for so long, thinking to her child, It's your father.

And the father's hand filled itself with the mother's body that readied itself for their baby's birth.

"It's too late, Clay," she murmured once.

"I know." But he kissed the hard, warm orb of her stomach anyway, then lay his face in the juncture of her legs as if he must, unable to solace himself and her any other way. The child kicked against his ear.

Catherine was drawn painfully back to reality from the secure place in which she'd allowed herself to drift. The thrum of her heart in odd spots in her body told her she had let Clay go too far to pull away from him unhurt when the time came.

"Stop, Clay," she said in a loving whisper.

"I'm only touching, that's all."

"Stop, it's not right."

"I won't go any further. Just let me touch you," he murmured.

"No, stop," she insisted, stiffening.

"Don't pull away . . . come here."

But now she resisted even more, having come fully to her senses.

He moved and tried to take her in his arms, then asked. "Why do you pull away all of a sudden?"

"Because it doesn't seem right with my mother lying in that hospital."

"I don't believe you. A minute ago you had forgotten all about your mother, hadn't you? Why did you really turn away?"

She didn't know.

Very gently he said, "Catherine, I'm not your father. I won't call you names and make you feel guilty afterward. It's not because of your mother that you turn away, it's because of your father, isn't it?"

She only shivered.

"If you keep pulling away now, he'll have beaten you just as surely as he beat her, only the marks he leaves on you won't go away like hers will, don't you see that?"

"It's my fault he beat her up, because once before I gave in to you. And now here I am again . . . I . . . you . . ." But she stopped, confused, afraid.

"He's making an emotional cripple out of you. Can't you see it, Catherine?"

"I'm not! I'm not! I feel things, I want things, I need things, just like everybody else!"

"Then why don't you let yourself show it?"

"I j-just did."

"But look what it took," he said in a pained whisper.

"Get your hands off me," she quavered. She was crying again but he would not allow her to roll away from him. "Why? What are you afraid of, Catherine?"

"I'm not afraid!" But her voice caught in her throat even as she said it.

He held her flat on her back, silently willing her to admit what it was that had held her emotionally sterile for too long, afraid that what he was doing might backfire and hurt her more.

"Of those names?"

He held her prisoner while her mind raced backward to ugly, unwanted memories that would not set her free. Clay's breath on her face brought her careening back to the present, to this man whom she loved and was so afraid of loving, of losing.

"I-I'm not," she choked, while Clay felt her pulse pounding against him in places where he held her down. The muscles in her forearms tensed beneath his hands as she repeated, "I'm not, I'm not—"

He eased his hold, prompting softly, "What aren't you? Say it, say it and be free of it. What?" She ceased struggling against him, and when he had freed her arms she flung one across her eyes and sobbed behind it. With infinite tenderness he touched her breasts, her stomach, the swollen world between her legs again, whispering urgently, "What aren't you, Catherine? Say it, say it."

"I'm not—" she tried again, but choked to a halt.

"No, you're not, you're not. Believe me. Say it, Catherine. You're not what?"

It came out in a rush, tumblewords finding voice at last as she covered her face with both hands.

"I'm not bad I'm not a slut I'm not a whore I'm not I'm not I'm not!"

He enfolded her protectively against him, pinching his eyes shut while she flung her arms around his neck and clung. He felt a shudder possess her body and spoke into her hair.

"No, you never were, no matter how many times he said it. You never were any of those things."

"Then why did he say them, Clay, why?"

"I don't know. . . . Shh. . . . The important thing is that you don't believe him, that you don't let him hurt you anymore."

They rested at last against each other, exhausted, silent. Before she slept, Catherine again pictured her mother and realized she herself had just escaped becoming the same kind of self-contained, undemonstrative being.

And for the first time ever, she felt she had beaten Herb Anderson instead of the other way around.

TWENTY-SIX

Ada opened her eye. It looked like a soft-poached egg. Her mouth tried to wince but couldn't.

"Mom?" Catherine whispered.

"Caffy?" Ada's lips were still grotesquely swollen.

"You've been asleep a long time."

"Have I?"

"Shh, don't move. Try to rest. You have a cracked rib and if you move it'll hurt."

"I'm so tired," the old woman breathed, succumbing, letting her eye slide shut again. But even in her bleary state she'd observed something that startled her eye open again.

"You've veen crying." She couldn't pronounce her *b*'s.

"A little. Don't worry about me, just worry about—" But tears stung her eyes again, burning the swollen lids. Ada saw and fluttered a hand. Catherine took it, feeling the small sparrow bones and how little strength her mother had. The same helplessness that Clay had felt the night before, now assaulted Catherine.

"I ain't seen you cry since you was a little girl," Ada whispered, trying her hardest to squeeze her daughter's hand.

"I gave it up long ago, Mom, or I would've been doing it all the time."

"It ain't a good fing to give up."

"No—no it isn't." Catherine swallowed. "Mom, you don't have to talk."

"Funny fing, you sayin' I don't hafta talk, me sayin' you don't hafta cry—least not for each other. Vut I guess we gotta do it for ourselves."

"Why don't you wait till you're feeling stronger."

"Veen waiting nineteen years to get stronger."

"Mom, please . . ."

A gentle pressure on Catherine's hand silenced her. Ada spoke with an effort.

"Time it was said. Just listen. I'm a weak woman, always have veen, vut mayve now I faid my dues. Got to tell you. Herv, he was good to me once, when I was first married to him. When Steve was a vavy you shoulda seen Herv with Steve, why, you wouldn'ta known him." She closed her eyes, rested momentarily before continuing. "And then all that vusiness started in the Gulf of Tonkin and Herv, he was in the reserves. When his unit got called to active duty, I figured he'd ve vack in no time. Vut it was worse'n we thought, and he was gone two years. He saw a mighty lot in them two years. He saw so much that he come home liking the liquor too much. The drinking he mighta got over, but what he never got over was findin' me expectin' a vavy when he got home."

Catherine wondered if she had understood Ada's distorted words correctly.

"A—a baby?"

The room was still. Ada's single, open eye stared at the ceiling.

"Yes, a vavy. That was you, o' course."

"Me?"

"I told you I was a weak woman." Ada's eye teared.

"I'm not his?"

The bruised head moved back and forth weakly on the pillow while a rippling sense of freedom seeped into Catherine.

"So you see, it wasn't all his fault, Caffy. I done that to him, and he could never forgive me, nor you either."

"I never understood till now."

"I was always so scared to tell you."

"But, why didn't you?" Catherine leaned nearer so her mother could see her face better. "Mom, please, I'm not blaming you, I just need to know, that's all. Why didn't you ever stand up for me? I thought you didn't—" Catherine stopped, her eyes flickered away from her mother's.

"Love you? I know that's what you was gonna say. It's no excuse at all, vut Herv, he was just waiting for me to show you some favoritism. Why, he'd use any excuse to vlow up. I was scared of him, Caffy, I was always scared after that."

"Then why didn't you leave him?"

"I figured I owed him to stay. Vesides, where would I go?"

"Where are you going to go now? Surely you aren't going to go back to him?"

"No, I don't need to now that you know. Vesides, it's different now. You and Steve all grown up, all I have to worry avout is myself. Steve, he's made a good life for himself in the service and you got Clay. I don't need to worry avout you no more."

A prickle of guilt traced through Catherine's veins. She rubbed the back of her mother's hand absently, then sat forward to study Ada's face.

"Who was he, Mom?" she asked wistfully.

A contorted smile tried to find its way through the swollen lips.

"It don't matter who, just what. He was a fine man. He was the vest thing that ever happened to me. I'd go through all the years of hell with Herv again if I could live those days once more with your father."

"Then you loved him?"

"I did . . . oh, how I did."

"Then why didn't you leave Da—Herb, and marry him?"

"He was already married."

Hearing all this, Catherine realized that within her mother dwelled an Ada she would never know, except for the glint of remembrance in the bloodshot eye.

"Is he still alive?" Catherine asked, suddenly wanting to know everything about him.

"Lives right here in the city. That's why it's best if I don't tell you who he is."

"Will you tell me someday?"

"I can't make that fromise. See, he went flaces. He's *something* now. You'd never have to ve ashamed of having a father like him. My—my mouth is a little dry. Do you think I could have some water?"

Catherine helped her mother drink, listened to her weary sigh as she sank back again.

"Mom, I have a confession to make, too."

"You, Caffy?" The surprised way her mother said it made Catherine wonder if Ada might not have always thought her above wrong, only she herself had been too busy looking for out-ward shows of affection to see the deeper, intrinsic feeling.

"Mom, I did it on purpose—got pregnant, I mean. At least, I think I did. I wanted to get even with Herb for all the times he'd called me names, and I wanted to get away from both of you, from that house where there was never anything but fighting and his drunkenness. I guess subconsciously I believed a baby would get me out and provide me with love. I didn't think he'd take it out on you, but I feel somehow it is part of the reason he beat you, wasn't it?"

"No, no, don't vlame yourself, Caffy. It was a long time com-ing. He said I shoulda veen at his trial, and that it was my fault he never got no money outa Clay. Vut the real reason was ve-cause you wasn't his. I don't kid myself that's the real reason, and I don't want you to go vlaming yourself."

"But I've made such a mess of things."

"No, honey. Now you just get that out of your head. You got Clay, and the vavy coming, and with a father like Clay, why, that vavy's vound to ve somevody, too."

"Mom, Clay and I—" But Catherine could not tell her mother the truth about her future with Clay.

"What?"

"We were wondering if when the baby is born, if you're strong enough then, you'd come and stay with us and help out for a couple days."

The pathetic excuse for a smile tore at Catherine's heart-strings as her mother sighed contentedly and closed her eye.

It was the day after Clay and Catherine had shared the same bed, but he'd left her asleep that morning. Returning home in the late afternoon, he was eager to see her.

She heard the door slam and her hands grew idle, the water splattering unheeded over the paring knife and the rib of celery she'd been washing. He came up the stairs, across the kitchen behind her, and laid a hand lightly on her shoulder.

"How was she today?"

A warmth seeped through her blouse at his touch, going beyond skin, beyond muscle, to the core of her. She wanted to turn, take his palm, kiss it and place it on her breast and say, How were you today? How was I? Were we happier for what passed between us last night?

"She hurt a lot, but they gave her painkillers whenever she asked for them. It was very hard for her to talk with her mouth that way."

Clay squeezed her shoulder, waiting for her to turn around, to need him again as she had the night before. He could smell her hair, fresh, flower-scented. He watched her hands as water splashed over them and she peeled green, stringy fibers from the celery.

Why doesn't she turn around? he wondered. Can't she read my touch? She must know that I, too, am afraid.

Catherine began to clean another rib of celery she didn't need. She longed to look into his eyes and ask, "What do I mean to you, Clay?" But if he loved her, surely he would have said so by now.

Last night they had been bound together by her vast need for comfort, and by the accident of her pregnancy. At the time that had been justification for the swift siege of intimacy. But he had not said he loved her. Never, during all their months together, had he even hinted that he loved her.

Their senses pounded with awareness of each other. Clay saw Catherine's hands fall still. He moved his fingers to the bare skin of her neck, slipping them behind her collar, his thumb brushing her earlobe. The water ran uselessly now, but Catherine's eyes were closed, her wrists dangling against the edge of the sink.

"Catherine . . ." His voice was thick.

"Clay, last night never should have happened," she got out.

Disappointments assaulted him. "Why?" He took the paring knife from her fingers, dropped it into the sink and turned off the water. When he'd forced her to face him he asked again, quietly, "Why?"

"Because we did it for the wrong reasons. It wasn't enough— just my mother's problems and the fact that this baby is yours. Don't you see?"

"But we need each other, Catherine. We're married, I want—"

Suddenly she put her wet hands on his cheeks, interrupting. "Cool off, Clay. It's the easiest way, because we are not going to have a repeat performance of last night."

"Dammit, I don't understand you!" he said angrily, pulling her hands from his face, holding her by the forearms.

"You don't love me, Clay," she said with quiet dignity. "Now do you understand me?"

His eyes pierced hers, steely gray into dusky blue, and he wished he could deny her words. He could easily drown in her tempting eyes, in her smooth skin and beautiful features with which he'd grown so familiar. He could look at her across a room and want to fill his hands with her breasts, lower his mouth to hers, to know the taste and touch of her. But could he say he loved her?

Deliberately now he reached to cup both of her breasts, as if to prove this was all that was necessary. Through the smock and her bra he could tell her nipples were drawn tight. Her breath was heavy and fast.

"You want it, too," he said, knowing it was true, for he felt the truth beneath the thumbs that stroked the crests of her breasts.

"You're confusing lust and love."

"I thought last night you finally agreed with me that it's a healthy thing to be touched, to touch back."

"Is this healthy now?"

"You're damn right. Can't you feel what's happening to you?"

Stoically she allowed his hands their freedom, and though she could not prevent her body from responding, she would not give him the satisfaction of moving willfully in any way suggesting acquiescence. "I can feel it. Oh, I can feel it, all right. Does it make you feel macho, knowing what it does to me?"

He dropped his hands suddenly. "Catherine, I can't exist with this coldness of yours. I need more than you put into this relationship."

"And I cannot put more into this relationship without love. And so it's a vicious circle, isn't it, Clay?" She looked straight at his face still glistening with water. She respected him if for nothing more than not lying. "Clay, I'm only being realistic to protect myself. It would have been so easy all these months with you to delude myself every time you turned your eyes on me with that certain look that makes me go all liquid, that you loved me. But I know it's not true."

"To be loved you have to be lovable, Catherine. Don't you understand that? You never try in the least. You carry yourself like you're wearing armor. You don't know how to return a smile or a touch or—"

"Clay, I never learned!" She defended herself. "Do you think things like that come naturally? Do you think it's something you're born with, like you were born with your father's gray eyes and your mother's blond hair? Well, it's not. Love is a learned thing. It's been taught to you since you were in knee pants whether you know it or not. You were one of the lucky ones who had it happening around him all the time. You never questioned it but you always expected it, didn't you? If you fell and got hurt, you were kissed and coddled. If you were gone, then came back, you were hugged and welcomed. If you tried and failed, you were told it didn't matter, they were proud anyway, right? If you misbehaved and were punished, they made you understand it hurt them as badly as it hurt you. None of those lessons were taught to me. Instead, I had the other kind, and I learned to exist without your kind. You take all signs of affection too lightly; you set too little store by them. It's different for me. I can't . . . I can't be—oh, I don't know how to make you understand. When something's in short supply its value goes up. And it's like that with me, Clay. I've never had anyone treat me nice before, so every gesture, every touch, every overture you make toward me is of far greater value to me than it is to you. And I know perfectly well that if I learn to accept them, learn to accept you, I'll be hurt far more than you will when it's time for us to separate. And so I've promised myself I will not grow dependent on you—not emotionally anyway."

"What you're really saying is that we're back where we started, before last night."

"Not exactly." Catherine looked down at her hands; they were fidgeting.

"What's different?"

She looked up, met his gaze directly, then squared her shoulders almost imperceptibly. "My mother told me today that Herb is not my real father. That frees me from him—really frees me—at last. It also gives me even better insight into what happens when people stay in a loveless marriage for all the wrong reasons. I'm never going to end up like her. Never."

During the weeks that followed, Clay mulled over what Catherine had said about love being taught. He had never before dissected the many ways in which his parents had shown him affection. But Catherine was right about one thing: he'd always taken it for granted. He had been so secure in their approval, so certain of their love, he'd never questioned their tactics. He admitted she was right, also, about his placing less value than she upon physical contact. He began to evaluate outward signs of affection by looking at them from Catherine's viewpoint and admitted that he'd taken them too lightly. He began to understand her awful need to remain free of him emotionally, to understand that the idea of loving him loomed like a threat, in light of their agreement to divorce soon after the baby arrived. He analyzed his feelings for her only to find that he honestly did not believe he loved her. He found her physically desirable, but because she had never been demonstrative toward him, it was difficult to imagine he ever would love her. What he wanted was a woman who was capable of impulsively lifting her arms and seeking his kiss. One who could close her eyes against his cheek and make him feel utterly wanted and wanting. He doubted that he could ever achieve with Catherine the kind of free-wheeling spontaneity he needed in a wife.

They bought a spooled crib and matching chest of drawers. He set it up in the second bedroom where the walls still wore that masculine paper of brown designs, totally inappropriate for a nursery.

But when the baby was born, who would stay and who would go?

Her suitcase appeared on the bedroom floor, packed, ready to go at a moment's notice. The first time he came in and saw it, he sank down heavily on the edge of the bed and buried his face in both hands, utterly miserable. He thought about Jill—willing Jill, who understood his needs so well, and wished that it was she who was expecting his child. But Jill didn't want babies.

April Fools' Day came, bringing bursting buds and the redolent scent of moist earth that marks spring's arrival. Catherine was given a lavish baby shower by Angela, whose pleasure over the upcoming arrival of her first grandchild was a burning wound to Catherine.

Claiborne surprised Catherine by stopping by one afternoon with "a little something" he'd picked up for the baby: a windup swing Catherine knew the baby wouldn't be big enough to sit in until long after she and Clay were apart.

Ada was back home and called every day to ask how Catherine was. Catherine, grown now to enormous proportions and slothlike slowness, answered, "Fine, fine, fine," until finally after hanging up one day, she burst into a torrent of tears, not understanding at all anymore what it was she wanted.

She awakened Clay in the middle of the night, hesitant to touch his sleeping form.

"What?" He braced up on an elbow, hazy yet from sleep.

"The pains have started. They're ten minutes apart."

He flung back the covers and sat up on the davenport, finding her hand in the dark and tugging at it. "Here, sit down."

She got back up immediately, if clumsily. "The doctor said to keep on the move."

"The doctor? You mean you've called him already?"

"Yes, a couple of hours ago."

"But why didn't you wake me?"

"I . . ." But she didn't know why.

"You mean you've been walking around here for two hours in the dark?"

"Clay, I think you should drive me to the hospital, but I don't expect you to stay with me or anything. I'd drive myself, but the doctor said that I shouldn't."

Her words caused a sudden stab of hurt, followed by another of anger.

"You can't keep me out, Catherine; I'm the baby's father."

Surprised, she only answered, "I don't think we'd better waste time arguing now. Do whatever you want when we get there."

They were greeted in the maternity ward by a young nurse whose name tag identified her as Christine Flemming. It did not occur to Ms. Flemming to question Clay's presence. She assumed he would want to stay with Catherine. And so, he was asked to have a seat in a well-lit room with an empty bed in it. When Catherine returned after being blood-typed, she was having a contraction and Ms. Flemming spoke in soothing instructions to her patient, telling her how to breathe properly and how to relax as much as possible. When the contraction ended she turned to Clay and said, "Your job will be to remind her to relax and breathe properly. You can be a big help." So rather than try to explain, Clay listened to her instructions, then stayed in the labor room when the nurse left, holding Catherine's hand, reminding her to keep her breathing quick and shallow, timing the length of contractions and the minutes between.

Soon the gentle-voiced nurse returned and spoke soothingly to Catherine. "Let's see how far along you are now. Try to relax, and tell me if a contraction should start while I'm checking you." It happened so fast that Clay had no time to gracefully withdraw or to be embarrassed. Neither was he asked to leave, as he thought he'd be at this time. Instead, he stood on the other side of the bed, holding Catherine's hand while her dilation was checked, amazed to find how appropriate it felt to be included in such a natural way. When the nurse finished her examination she pulled Catherine's gown back down, sat on the edge of the bed and lightly stroked the wide base of Catherine's abdomen.

"Here comes another one, Catherine. Now just relax with it and count—one, two, three . . ." Catherine's hand gripped Clay's like the jaws of a trap. Sweat broke out under his arms while beads of perspiration gathered into runnels on Catherine's temples and trailed into her hair. Her eyes were closed and her mouth was tightly shut.

He remembered what he was there for. "Open your mouth, Catherine," he reminded softly. "Pant, pant, little breaths."

And through her pain Catherine knew she was happy Clay was there. His voice seemed to calm her when she was most afraid.

After the pain was over, she opened her eyes and asked Ms. Flemming, "How could you tell it was coming?"

Christine Flemming had a pretty face with a madonnalike smile and a very patient way about her that made both Catherine and Clay feel comfortable in her presence. Her voice was silken, soothing. She was a woman well suited to her profession.

"Why, I could feel it. Here, give me your hand, Catherine."

She took Catherine's hand and curved it low around her stomach. "Mr. Forrester," she instructed, "put your hand here on the other side. Now wait—you'll feel it when it starts. The muscles begin to tighten, starting at the sides, and the stomach arches and changes shape during the height of the contraction. When it ends, the muscles relax and settle down again. Here it comes; it will take half a minute or so until it's at its peak."

Catherine's and Clay's fingertips touched, their hands forming a light cradle around the base of her stomach. Together they shared the exhilaration of discovery as the muscles tensed and changed the contours of Catherine's abdomen. For Clay, it made her pain a palpable thing. He stared, big-eyed, at what was happening beneath his hand. But in the middle of the contraction, Catherine's hand flew above her head and Clay tore his eyes away to her face to find her lips pursed, jaw clenched against the pain. He leaned to soothe her hair back from her forehead, and at the touch of his hand, her lips relaxed and fell open. He spoke his litany again in quiet tones, reminding her, and felt a curious sense of fulfillment that he had the power to ease her, even in the height of her labor.

"That one was longer than the last," Christine Flemming said when it was over. "As they get closer, it's more important for you to relax between them. Sometimes it helps to have your tummy rubbed lightly, like this. I like to think that the baby can feel it, too, and knows you're out here waiting to welcome him." With a gentle palm the nurse stroked the outer perimeter of Catherine's stomach. Catherine's eyes remained closed, one wrist over her forehead, her other hand in Clay's. He felt her grip slacken as the nurse continued those feather-light strokes over her distended abdomen. With a smile, Christine Flemming looked up at Clay and said softly, "You're doing very well, so I'll let you take over for a while. I'll be back in a few minutes." Then on silent white shoes she was gone and Clay was left to stroke Catherine's stomach.

He understood things in that time of closeness with Catherine, things as deep and eternal as the force of life trying to repeat itself in her body. He understood that nature had planned this time of travail to draw man and woman closer than at any other time. Thus the pain had purpose beyond bringing a child into the world.

When they took Catherine to the delivery room, Clay felt suddenly bereft, as if his role were being usurped by strangers. But when they'd asked if he'd taken the classes required for fathers to be in the delivery room, he'd had to answer honestly, "No."

The University of Minnesota Hospital did not use delivery tables anymore. Instead, Catherine found herself placed in a birthing chair, which allowed gravity to pull while she pushed. Christine Flemming was there through the delivery, supportive and smiling, and once Catherine even joked with her, saying, "We're not so smart. The Indians knew this secret long ago when they squatted in the woods to have their babies."

The daughter of Catherine and Clay Forrester was born with the fifth contraction in the birthing chair, and Catherine knew before she faded off into blessed sleep—lying flat now—that it was a girl.

Catherine swam upward through a lake of cotton fuzziness. When she surfaced and opened heavy-lidded eyes, she found Clay dozing in a chair, his cheek propped on one hand. His hair was disheveled and he needed a shave. He looks terrific, she thought through a crazy, disoriented fog. Her mind was still moony and wandering as she studied him. The rhythm of his breathing was lengthened by her drug-induced lethargy. Between pains, hazily she thought, I still love him.

"Clay?" The word was a little mumbled.

His eyes flew open and he jumped to his feet. "Cat," he said softly, "you're awake."

Her eyes drifted closed. "Barely. I did the wrong thing again, didn't I, Clay?" She felt him take her hand, felt the back of it pressed against his lips.

"You mean having a girl?"

She nodded her head, which felt like it weighed hundreds of pounds.

"You won't think so when you see her."

Catherine smiled a little bit. Her lips were very dry and he wished he had something to put on them for her.

"Clay?"

"I'm here."

"Thanks for helping."

She drifted into oblivion again, her breathing heavy and rhythmic. He sat on the chair beside her bed with his elbows on his knees, holding her hand long after he knew she was asleep again. Then with a heavy sigh he lowered his forehead against her knuckles and closed his eyes as well.

Grandmother Forrester's cane announced her imminent arrival. When she rounded the doorway, the first thing she said was, "Young lady, I am seventy-eight years old. The next one had better be a boy." But she limped to the bed and bestowed an honest-to-goodness kiss upon the consummate perfection of her firstborn great-granddaughter.

Marie came, laughing as ever, with the announcement that she and Joe were going to get married at last, as soon as he graduated from high school in a couple of months. She added that she'd been inspired to "give it a whirl" by Catherine and Clay's success.

Claiborne and Angela came daily, never empty-handed. They brought dresses so absurdly frilly the baby would surely get lost in all those ruffles, stuffed toys so big they would dwarf an infant, a music box that played "Eidelweiss." Although they both fawned over Melissa, Claiborne's reaction to her was heart-touching. He would stand at the nursery window with his finger-tips against the glass as if transfixed. Walking away, his head was the last to be turned forward. He even stopped on his way home from work one day, although it was decidedly inconvenient for him to do so. He said things like, "When she's old enough to ride a trike, Grampa will see that she gets the best one in town." Or, "Wait until she walks—won't that be something?" Or, "You and Clay will have to take a weekend away by yourselves soon and leave the baby with us."

Bobbi came. She stood in front of the window with her thumbs strung up on her rear jeans pockets, her feet rolled over until she was almost standing on the sides of her shoes. "Well, wouldja look at that!" she exclaimed softly. "And to think I had a hand in it."

Ada came with the news that she'd signed up for a course in driver's education so she could come to Catherine and Clay's house to see the baby now and then. Herb had disappeared.

Steve wired an enormous bouquet of pink carnations and baby's breath and followed it with a long-distance phone call in which his main message was that he'd be getting leave again in August, and when he got to Minnesota, he wanted to see Cathy and Clay and Melissa all living under one roof.

And, of course, there was Clay.

Clay, who was just across the river at the law school and

popped in at any time of day. Clay, who stood at the end of Catherine's bed when they were alone together and couldn't seem to think of anything to say. Clay, who played the father's role well when other visitors were there, laughing at their jokes about waiting until Melissa was bringing boyfriends home, turning his smile on Catherine, exclaiming over the never-ending stream of gifts, but spending long minutes at the nursery window alone, trying to swallow the lump that never disappeared from his throat.

Ada came and helped out for three days after Catherine and Melissa went home. During that time Ada slept on the davenport. It became particularly hellish for Clay, sleeping with Catherine. Each night he would awaken to the tiny sounds of suckling from the other side of the bed and he wanted more than anything to turn the light on and watch them. But he knew Catherine would be bothered by both the light and his watching, so he lay silent, pretending to be asleep. How surprised he'd been at the news that she intended to breast-feed the baby. At first he supposed she made the choice out of a sense of duty, for there was a lot of propaganda on the subject. But as the days wore on, he realized that everything Catherine did for and with Melissa was done instead from a deep sense of mother-love.

Catherine began to change.

There were times when he came upon her with her face buried in Melissa's little tummy, cooing to her, talking in soft expressions of love. Once he saw her lightly suck on Melissa's toes. When she gave the baby a bath, there was a steady stream of talking and light laughter. When the baby slept too long, Catherine actually hounded her bedroom doorway, as if she couldn't wait for Melissa to wake up again and want to be fed. Catherine began singing a lot, at first only to Melissa, but then seeming to forget herself and singing absently when she worked around the house. It seemed she had found her source of smiles, too, and there was always a ready one waiting for Clay when he got home.

But while Catherine's contentment increased, Clay's virtually disappeared. He astutely refrained from getting involved with the baby, though it was beginning to have a growing, adverse effect on him. His temper flared at the slightest provocation while Catherine's seemed as unassailable as Melissa's—for Melissa was truly a satisfied baby with a flowery disposition. As graduation neared, Clay blamed his crossness on the pressure of finals and the bar exams coming up shortly.

Angela called and asked his permission to plan a little Sunday brunch on the weekend following his graduation. When she said she'd already received Catherine's approval, Clay snapped into the phone, "Since the two of you already have the whole thing planned, why are you bothering to ask me!"

Then he had to do some fancy skirting to get around his mother's demand to know what on earth was eating him.

Clay graduated from the University of Minnesota law school with honors when Melissa was two months old. Now he held a degree, but he had never held his daughter.

TWENTY-SEVEN

The day of the brunch would have been well suited to a June wedding. The sprawling backyard of the Forresters was at its finest. The view over the flaming chafing dishes on the semicircular terrace was lush with color. The terrace itself was delineated by carefully pruned global arborvitae, which in turn were edged with alternating clumps of marigold and ageratum, the purple and gold contrast creating a stunning effect. The yard stretched in falling terraces to the far reaches of the property where a file of blue spruce marked its boundaries. The rose gardens of phalanx symmetry were in full bloom, in full scent. Shapely maples and lindens dotted the grass with vast splashes of shade. It was like a pastoral scene from an impressionist's brush: ladies in filmy dresses drifting from the terrace across the lawn, men sitting on the parapet of the terrace, everyone nibbling on melon and berries.

Catherine was sitting on the grass when a shadow fell over her and she glanced sunward, blinded at first and unable to make out who stood above her.

"All by yourself?" It was Jill Magnusson's rich, lazy voice. "May I join you?"

Catherine held up a forearm to shade her eyes. "Of course, have a chair."

Dropping to the grass, Jill doubled up her thoroughbred legs and folded them elegantly to the side—like a ballerina in a swan scene, thought Catherine. Jill tossed back her thick mane and smiled directly at Catherine.

"I guess I should apologize for not sending a gift when the baby was born, but you know how it is."

"Do I?" Catherine replied sweetly—a little too sweetly.

Jill's gaze drifted over Catherine before she smiled archly. "Well . . . don't you?"

"I don't know what you're getting at."

"You know precisely what I'm getting at, and I won't be a hypocrite about it. I'm completely jealous of that baby of yours and Clay's. Not that I'd want one, you understand, but it should have been mine."

Catherine controlled the urge to slap her. "Should have been yours? Why, how gauche of you to say so."

"Gauche maybe, but we both know it's true. I've been damning myself ever since October, but I've finally decided to lay my cards on the table. I want Clay; it's as simple as that."

Some stirring of pride made Catherine answer, "I'm afraid he's already taken."

"Taken for a fool maybe. He's told me what kind of relationship you two have. Why do you want to hold a man you don't love and who doesn't love you?"

"Maybe to give our daughter a father."

"Not the healthiest reason, you'll have to admit."

"I don't have to admit anything to you, Jill."

"Very well—don't. But ask yourself why Clay asked me to wait for him until he could get this mess straightened out." Then Jill's voice became quite purring. "Oh, I see this is news to you, isn't it? You didn't know that Clay asked me to marry him right after he found out you were pregnant? Well, he did. But my silly pride was shattered and I was totally wrong in turning him down. But now I've changed my mind."

"And what does he have to say about it?"

"Actions speak louder than words. Surely you know that while you turned a cold shoulder on him all last winter he knew where to find a warm one."

Catherine's stomach was aquiver. "What do you want from me?" she demanded coldly.

"I want you to do the right thing, turn Clay free before he falls in love with his daughter and stays for the wrong reason."

"He chose me over you. That's hard for you to swallow, isn't it?"

Jill tossed her hair behind a shoulder. "Kiddo, you didn't fool me with that trumped-up wedding of yours. This is Jill you're talking to. I was *there* that night and it's no hallucination that Clay kissed me far more intimately than grooms are supposed to kiss other women." Jill paused for dramatic effect, then finished, "And he told me he still loved me. Strange for a man on his wedding night, huh?"

The memory of that night came back to Catherine, but she hid her chagrin behind a mask of indifference. She turned now to see Clay sitting on the terrace, deep in conversation with Jill's father.

Jill went on. "There's no doubt in my mind that if this . . . mistake"—Jill's pause seemed to denigrate the word further—"hadn't happened between you, Clay and I would be planning our wedding right now. It was always implicitly understood that Clay and I would eventually marry. Why, we've been intimate since the days when our mothers plunked us naked together into our little plastic backyard pools. In October when he asked me to marry him, he admitted you were nothing more than a tragic mistake to him. Why not do him a favor and bow out of the picture?"

It was clear that Jill Magnusson was used to getting what she wanted, by fair means or foul. The woman's manner was insolent and rude. There was no note of appeal in her attitude, only brazen self-assurance.

Oh, she was as cool as Inella's tomato aspic up there on its bed of crushed ice, thought Catherine. But Catherine disliked tomato aspic, too.

"You assume a lot, Jill," Catherine said now with a little ice of her own.

"I assume nothing. I know. I know because Clay has confided in me. I know that you've thrown him out of his own bed, that you've encouraged him to live a life of his own, to keep his old friends, his old pursuits. The baby's born now, she has a

name, and Clay is financially responsible for her for life. You got
what you wanted out of him, so why don't you free him?"

Catherine rose, brushed off her skirt and pointedly raised an
arm to wave at Clay, who waved back. Without looking again at
Jill, she said, "He's a big boy. If he wants to be free, don't you
think he'd ask?"

Catherine headed in the direction of the terrace, but before
she could get away, Jill threw one last parting shot, and this one
hit its mark: "Where do you think he was while you were in the
hospital having his baby?"

Insane thoughts came to Catherine, childlike in their vindictiveness. She wished that Inella's superb tomato aspic was made
with Jill's blood. She wanted to shave Jill's head, roll her naked in
poison ivy, feed her chocolate laced with laxative. These thoughts
didn't strike Catherine as immature. She felt hurt and degraded;
she wanted revenge and could think of no way to get it.

And Clay! She felt like taking a handful of melon balls and
firing them at him like artillery. Like overturning the chafing
dishes, getting everyone's attention, telling everyone here what a
liar and a libertine he was! How could he! How could he! It
wasn't bad enough that he'd continued his sexual relationship
with Jill, but the thought of him confiding the intimate truths
about their marriage cut deeper than Catherine ever thought
possible. Painful memories came back, bolder than ever: New
Year's Eve and Clay kissing Jill with his little finger under her
spaghetti strap; the night he hadn't come home at all while she'd
fixed supper and waited; and worst of all—four nights while she
lay in a maternity ward . . .

It was several days after the brunch.

Catherine had submerged her anger until it lay at the base of her tongue like bile, waiting to be spewed. He'd known for days that she was seething and would soon erupt. What he didn't know was what would trigger it.

All he was doing was standing beside the crib watching Melissa sleep. Suddenly, behind him, Catherine hissed, "What are you doing! Get away from her!"

His hands came halfway out of his pockets and he turned, surprised by her vehemence. "I didn't wake her up," he whispered.

"I know what you're thinking, standing there staring at her all the time, and you can just get it off your mind, Clay Forrester, because it won't work! I'll fight you till my dying day before I let you take her from me!"

With a quick glance to make sure the baby hadn't been disturbed, he moved toward the hall.

"Catherine, you're imagining things. I told you I—"

"You told me a lot of things you wouldn't do, like keep your affair going with Jill Magnusson, but she certainly set me straight about that! Well, if you want her, what's holding you up?"

"What did Jill say to you Sunday anyway?"

"Enough that I know I want to see you gone from this house, and the sooner the better."

"What did she say?"

"Do I need to repeat it? Do you want to rub my nose in it? All right!" Catherine marched into the master bedroom, slammed a hand against the light switch and paraded to his chest of drawers, flinging clothes out to punctuate her words. "You've been sleeping with her all the time you lied to me and said you weren't, so why not move in with her permanently? Do you think everybody doesn't know what's been going on between you when you stood at your own wedding reception and

French-kissed her in front of everybody there? Did you tell your mother you'd stepped out for air when you disappeared with Jill on New Year's Eve? How dumb do you think I am, Clay? And why are you hanging around here like a stray dog? I'm not going to take you in and feed you and ask you if you'd like to live with me, because I want this farce to be over. I don't want your phony condescension or your two-bit psychoanalysis about my being emotionally crippled! I don't want you coming in here fawning over *my* daughter—the one I had while you were staying nights at Jill's house. All I want is what you agreed to give me. Child support for Melissa and my college education paid for. And I want you out of here—out!—so I can get on with my life!"

The pile of clothes lay in disarray between them. The air seemed thick, as if her shouting had actually raised dust.

"She told you a pack of lies, Catherine."

Catherine closed her eyes, but the lids quivered. She raised both palms up to Clay.

"Don't . . . just don't. Don't make it worse than it already is." Her voice shook.

"If she said I've been sleeping with her, it's a goddam lie. I've seen her, yes, but I told you I wouldn't sleep with her and I haven't."

"Why are we arguing? This is only what we knew was coming all along. Do you want me to go so you can stay? Okay—" she grew obstinate—"okay, fine." She started dumping armfuls of his things back in the drawers. "Fine, I'll go. I can easily go back home now that Herb is gone." She headed for her own dresser and yanked the drawers open.

"Catherine, you're acting childish. Will you stop it! I don't want you to go! Do you think I'd toss you and Melissa out?"

"Oh, then you want to go."

She marched back to the bureau and stubbornly began to empty it again. He caught her by an arm and swung her around none too gently.

"You're an adult now. Will you start acting like one?"

"I . . . want . . . this . . . over!" she said with emphatic pauses. "I want your parents to know the truth so I don't have to listen to your dad babbling about us leaving Melissa at their house. I'm sick of your mother giving her Polly Flinders dresses that cost forty dollars apiece and making me feel guilty as Judas! I'm sick of you standing over her crib plotting how you can get her away from me! Jill doesn't want her. Don't you understand that, Clay? All she wants is you! And since you want her, too, why don't we cut through all the crap and give little Jill what she wants?"

Something inside Catherine cringed at her rudeness, her gutter language so like her father's, but she couldn't stop it. The need to hurt Clay like he'd hurt her was too strong.

"I can see Jill really did a number on you. She's very good with words, but did she ever actually say I slept with her, or did she *imply* it? I have no doubt she made me sound totally conniving and guilty."

"You told her!" Catherine raged. "You told her I threw you out of your bed when it was you who chose to sleep on that davenport. You picked out that . . . that damn long davenport, I didn't! And you had no right to tell her such private things about us!"

"I told her we were having problems; she must have guessed the rest."

"It doesn't take much guessing, does it? Not when a man sleeps with one woman while another is in the hospital having his baby!"

Clay's eyebrows lowered ominously. He ran a hand through his hair. "Goddam that Jill." Then he swung around with a palm up entreatingly. "Catherine, it's not true. I saw her the second night you were in the hospital. She was waiting outside in her car when I came home, and she followed me in."

"You had her *here*?" Catherine's voice cracked into a high falsetto. "Here in *my* house?"

"I didn't *have her here*, not the way you put it. I said she followed me in. She said she had to talk to me. We didn't do anything."

But Catherine was done arguing. "If you're leaving, leave. If not, I'm going to start my own packing. Which will it be?"

In the moments during which she stood confronting Clay, waiting for him to make the move, some bereft voice seemed to be calling from within her, beating on the inside of her stomach with tiny fists, "Why are you doing this? Why are you treating him this way when you love him? Why can't you be forgiving? Why can't you reach out and beg him to start over with you? Is that pain in his face? If you don't risk finding out, he'll be gone, and you'll be left to wonder. But then it will be too late." She stood before him, aching for him to love her, knowing she was making herself unlovable again because she loved him so much that the idea of having him—truly having him—as a husband, then losing him, would annihilate her in the end.

"I'll need to know where you'll be so my lawyer can serve the divorce papers" was all he said. Then he went to the closet to get his luggage.

Catherine hid in the kitchen while Clay packed, listening to him making trips out to the car. Her stomach felt queasy. It lifted nauseatingly until she pressed it firmly against the edge of the kitchen counter. She sensed when Clay went in to look at

Melissa for the last time. In the silence she pictured him, his blond head bent over the crib, gazing down at the baby's head— blond, too—and she felt heartless and sick with herself. She swallowed back tears, pressing against the counter until her hipbones hurt. The awful need to cry made her throat ache unbearably. It felt like she'd swallowed a tennis ball.

He came quietly to the kitchen doorway, found her standing in the lightless room.

"All of my things wouldn't fit in the car. I'll have to come back for them."

She nodded her head at the wall.

"Good-bye, Catherine," he said softly.

She raised a hand, hoping that from behind, he couldn't tell what a struggle she was having to keep from crying.

A moment later she heard the door shut.

It took him two days to clear out all his belongings for good. It took another two days before a deputy sheriff appeared at her door and served her with divorce papers. It took another week before Angela called, her voice very shaken, obviously grieved by the news. It took a week and a half before Catherine worked up the courage to visit Ada and tell her.

But it took less than an hour for Catherine to begin to miss him.

The days that followed were the most hollow of Catherine's life. She found herself staring listlessly at Clay's favorite things in the house; there were so many earth tone items he loved so much. The place was more his than hers. She remembered how awed she'd been by its luxury the first day he'd brought her here. Guilt was her constant companion. She ate with it, slept with it, paced the rooms with it, knowing full well that it was she who should have gone, he who should have stayed. And though she had once feared leaving, she now feared staying, for the house seemed to echo Clay's voice, reflect his tastes and always, always, remind her of his absence. She remembered how much fun it had been to fill the cabinets with wedding gifts, to go grocery shopping together, to work in the bright, well-equipped kitchen. She hated it now. Cooking for one was decidedly the most desolate chore in the world. Even making coffee in the mornings became a miserable task, for it reminded her sharply of all the mornings Clay had sat at the counter with a cup and the early paper, often attempting to tease her out of her morning grouchiness. She admitted now how hard she'd been to get along with, and marveled at how amiable Clay had always remained, no matter how bearish her morning temper. She had the bathroom all to herself whenever she wanted it, but found she missed the occasional trace of whiskers she used to find in the sink, his toothbrush lying wet beside hers, the smell of his aftershave that lingered in the room after he was gone. One day she made popcorn, but after it was buttered, she burst into tears and threw it all down the garbage disposal.

Telling Ada proved to be a terrible ordeal. Ada, whose life was being painfully rebuilt, a day at a time, looked much like she used to when Herb raised his fist at her. She seemed to cower, her shoulders curling, shriveling before Catherine's eyes.

"Mom, please don't act that way. It's not the end of the world."

"But, Cathy, why would you want to go and do a thing like that, divorce a man like Clay? Why he's—he's . . ." But for lack of a better word, Ada finished lamely, "perfect."

"No, Mother, he's not perfect and neither am I."

"But that wedding they give you, and the way Clay give you that beautiful place and everything you wanted—"

"Mother, please understand. It was a mistake for us to get married in the first place."

"But if Melissa is his—" But Ada placed trembling fingertips over her thin lips and whispered, "Oh, she is, isn't she?"

"Yes, Mother, she's his."

"Why, of course, she is," Ada reasoned. "She's got his nose and chin. But if Melissa is his, then why did he leave?"

"We tried it for Melissa's sake, but it just didn't work. You, above all people, should understand that I didn't want to stay with him when he didn't love me."

"No—no, I guess you wouldn't want to do that. But, honey, it breaks my heart to see you give up that good life you had. I was so happy to see you settled that way. Why, you had everything that I never had. Everything I always hoped my little girl would get. And I figured I'd buy myself a little used car soon and come—come over." Then, without changing the hopeless expression on her face, Ada began to cry. She did it silently, sitting in her beaten-up living room chair that she had recently covered with a new slipcover. The tears rolled down her sad cheeks, and she acted too empty and weary to lift a hand and swipe at them.

"Mom, you can still get a little car, and you can still come to see Melissa. And I'm not coming out of this a total loser. I've got Melissa, haven't I? And Clay is going to pay for me to go back to school in the fall."

"And you'd rather have that than be married to him?" Ada asked sadly.

"Mother, that's not the point. The point is, Clay and I are getting divorced, and we have to accept that. If you're honest with yourself, you'll admit that I never really fit into his class of people anyway."

"Why, I thought you did. The way Angela seemed to love you and—"

"Mother, please." Catherine put a hand to her forehead and turned away. The thought of Angela hurt almost as much as the thought of her son.

"Why, okay, honey, I'm sorry. Only it's so sudden and it takes some getting used to when I've been feeling so good about you being fixed for life."

From then on, whenever Catherine visited her mother, Ada rambled on about all that Catherine would give up in divorcing Clay. It didn't matter how many times Catherine pointed out the ways in which she'd benefited, Ada refused to see it that way.

In late July there came an unannounced visit from Clay's father. Opening the door and finding Claiborne there, Catherine immediately felt her throat swell. He was so strikingly handsome; she knew that Clay would look much like him someday. Missing Clay as she did, there was a swift surge of bittersweet joy at seeing his father at the door.

"Hello, Catherine, may I come in?"

"H-hello. Well, certainly."

There was a moment of hesitation during which each assessed the other. And each saw pain. Then Claiborne moved to pull Catherine briefly into his arms and kiss the crest of her cheek. She closed her eyes, fighting the overwhelming sense of déjà vu, fending off the love she felt for this man because he was Clay's father, Melissa's grandfather. She felt suddenly secure and protected in his hold.

When they were seated in the living room, Claiborne stated simply, "Angela and I were decimated by the news."

"I'm sorry."

It was easier for Catherine if she didn't look at her father-in-law, but she couldn't keep her eyes from his, they were so like Clay's.

"I waited, thinking Clay would come to his senses and come back here, but when we realized he wasn't going to, Angela and I had to know how you are."

"I'm fine, just fine. As you can see, I have everything I need. Clay . . . and you . . . have seen to that."

He leaned forward on the edge of his chair, cupped his palms and seemed to study them.

"Catherine, I'm afraid I must ask your forgiveness. I made such a mistake."

"Please, Mr. Forrester, if you're going to tell me about the ultimatum you issued to Clay, I know all about it. Believe me, we're no less guilty than you. We should have known better than to think marriage would automatically solve our problems. And we weren't truthful with you, either."

"He told us about the agreement you two made."

"Oh." Catherine's eyebrows shot up.

"Don't look so guilty about it. None of us is too lily-white, are we?"

"I wanted to tell you long ago, but I just couldn't."

"Angela and I guessed that everything wasn't as calm as it appeared on the surface." He stood up and walked to the sliding door, gazing out much as Clay had often done. "You know, I've only seen this place once since you and Clay moved." He glanced over his shoulder at her. "That was one of the things that made Angela and I wonder. It hurt, the fact that you never invited us here, but I guess we had it coming."

"No . . . oh, no." Catherine followed him to the window, reaching out to touch his elbow. "Oh, God, what good are recriminations? I thought it would be best not to—not to grow to love you, too, under the circumstances, I mean, knowing that Clay and I would be separating soon."

"Too?" he repeated hopefully. She should have remembered, he was a lawyer; he picked up on slips like that.

"You know what I mean. You and Angela were so good to us, you didn't deserve to be hurt."

He sighed, turned his eyes to the summer lawn where sprinklers threw cascades of droplets out across the greens between buildings. It was a warm, lazy afternoon.

"I'm a rich man," he ruminated. "I own all this. But there's very little pleasure in the thought right now."

"Please," she pleaded, "don't blame yourself."

"I thought I could buy Clay and you and my grandchild, but I was wrong."

"I'm not going to deny you the right to see Melissa. I couldn't do that."

"How is she?" The first trace of joy crossed his face at the thought of Melissa.

"She's getting a double chin, but she's healthy and very happy. I never thought a baby could be so good. She's napping now, but due to wake up soon. I could wake her if you like."

Claiborne's smile was answer enough, and she went to get Melissa up, then brought her out to see her grandpa. From his pocket he produced a small teething toy, and his smile was far wider than Melissa's when he gave it to her.

"Listen, Catherine, if there's anything she needs, or anything you need—ever—you must promise to let us know. Is that understood?"

"You've done more for me than you should already. Besides, Clay sends us money regularly." Then she studied Melissa's head, reached to lightly ruffle the feather-fine curls there as she asked, "How is he?"

Claiborne watched Catherine's hand on Melissa's fair head.

"I don't know. We don't see much of him these days." Their eyes met above the baby. There was deep pain in Claiborne's.

"You don't?"

"No. He went to work in the legal department of General Mills as soon as he passed his bar exam."

"But isn't he living with you?"

Claiborne became occupied with the toy, trying to get the baby to hold it in her pudgy hand.

"No, he's not. He's—"

"No need to feel uncomfortable. I think I know where he's living. With Jill, right? But that's really where he belonged all along."

"I thought you knew, Catherine. I didn't mean to spring it on you."

She laughed lightly, got up and spoke over her shoulder while she moved to the kitchen. "Oh, for heaven's sake, don't be silly. He can do whatever he pleases now."

But when Claiborne was gone, it was Catherine who stood staring out the window across the lawns, hollow-eyed, seeing Clay and Jill in the prismatic colors that jetted from the sprayers outside. Without thinking, she clutched Melissa a little too tightly, then kissed her a little too forcefully, and the baby started to cry.

TWENTY-EIGHT

During that summer Melissa was Catherine's greatest joy. The love Catherine found so difficult to display toward others she could lavish readily upon her child. Simply touching Melissa seemed to heal Catherine's wounded spirit and bring it back to life. Sometimes she'd flop on her side on the bed, taking Melissa with her, and with five tiny toes against her lips, would tell the child all the hidden feelings she had. In a voice as soft as cotton candy she poured out her feelings.

"Do you know how much I loved your daddy? I loved him so much that I didn't think I'd survive when he left. But there you were and I loved you, too, and you helped me through. It wasn't as bad after a while. Your daddy is handsome, know that? You have his nostrils and pretty hair like his. I'm glad you didn't get my straight hair. It's hard to tell about your mouth yet, whose it is. Why, Melissa, did you smile at me? When did you learn how to do that? Do it again, come on. That's the way. When you smile you look like your Grandma Angela. She's a wonderful lady, and your Grandpa Claiborne is wonderful, too. You're a very lucky girl, you know, to come from people like them. They all love you, Grandma Ada, too. But I'm the lucky one. I got you, and I love you best. Always remember that, and remember, too, how much I wanted you."

Her soliloquies to Melissa were punctuated by kisses and touches while the baby lay unblinking, her eyes, of yet undefined color, wide and trusting.

*   *   *

There came a day when Melissa learned to reach. When she first reached for Catherine's face the mother knew a joy of love such as she'd never experienced before. It was pure, unconfounded by conflicts such as other loves she'd experienced. The tremendous outpouring of emotion left Catherine's eyes awash and her heart full. As the baby grew and responded to Catherine's love, there grew within Catherine the realization that she possessed qualities she hadn't known she possessed: patience, kindness, gentleness, an ease of laughter, a modicum of mother-sense and the innate knowledge of how to make a baby feel secure.

They did everything together. Sunbathed on the deck, swam in the pool, took showers—it was during a shower that Melissa first laughed aloud—ate bottled baby food (one spoon for Melissa, one spoon for Mommy), visited Ada, went grocery shopping and registered Catherine for the next quarter. But Catherine had enough sense not to fall into the habit of taking Melissa to bed with her at night, no matter how comforting it would have been to have the baby there for company. At bedtime, she resolutely tucked Melissa into the crib in her own room, facing the king-size bed alone. She never lay down on it without thinking of Clay and the few nights they'd shared it. She couldn't help wondering if he'd still be there, had she invited him into it from the beginning. Catherine now found recriminations helpful, for she was learning much from them about herself and her shortcomings. And through Melissa she was learning it was far more satisfying to be a warm, loving person than a cold, remote one.

She learned what an abundant harvest love can reap, that the old saying is true: The more love you give away, the more you have.

* * *

In late August Steve came home. He was so dismayed to find Catherine and Clay separated that he blew up at his sister, blaming her for not trying harder to hold a man who'd done his damnedest to do right by her.

"I know you, Cathy. I know how god-awful stubborn you can be, and how once your mind is made up it sets harder than a plaster cast. You don't have to tell me you didn't love him because I know different. What I want to know is why the hell you wouldn't swallow a little of your pride and fight for him!"

He was the only one who understood all the forces behind Catherine's belligerence and stubbornness, those old millstones that had ultimately alienated Clay. Steve was the first one to come right out and blame her, and Catherine surprised him by admitting he was right. By the time Steve left he realized Catherine had done a vast amount of growing up since her wedding.

In September she went back to school, leaving Melissa with a baby-sitter. Catherine had to contact Clay to let him know there would be another bill for him to pay. He asked if he could drop by and bring her a check and see Melissa at the same time.

From the moment the door opened, he could tell that Catherine was different. There was an openness about her, starting with the smile on her face. His attention was torn between it and the wide gaze of curiosity upon the face of his daughter.

"Hi, Clay, come on in."

He couldn't control the size of his smile. "Holy cow! Has she grown!"

Catherine laughed, plopped a loud kiss on the baby's neck and turned to lead the way inside. "She's got lots of chins to nuzzle, haven'tcha, Lissy?" And Catherine did so. "She's kind of getting to that shy stage, so it might take awhile for her to warm up to you. But don't feel bad, she's that way with everybody lately."

Following Catherine upstairs, Clay glanced quickly up and down her jean-clad figure. Her old shape was back, and when she turned to face him again he noticed how tan she was. Her hair seemed lighter, bleached into streaks like honey and peanut butter.

"Sit down, you two, and say hello while I bring us a glass of cola or something."

She put Melissa into the crank-up swing that occupied the center of the living room, then ducked into the kitchen. Melissa immediately realized she'd been left alone with a stranger and stuck out her lip.

"Didn't you warn her I was coming and tell her to put on her best manners?" Clay called.

"I did. I told her you were the fella paying the bills, so she'd better watch her *p*'s and *q*'s."

Melissa began to squall, but quieted as soon as Catherine reappeared. She handed a glass to Clay, cranked up the swing, then sat cross-legged on the floor beside it.

"Oh, before I forget—here." Clay dug a check out of his pocket and handed it to her.

"Oh, thank you. I hated to ask for more."

"You earned it," he said without thinking. But Catherine seemed to take no offense. Instead, she began to describe the baby-sitter who cared for Melissa, as if to put him at ease about the woman's coming well recommended.

"You don't have to reassure me about that, Catherine. If there's one thing I don't worry about, it's the kind of care Melissa will get."

"She's a good baby, Clay, really good. She's got your temperament." Then Catherine smiled, shook her head in gay self-deprecation. "Boy, I'm sure glad she didn't get mine or she'd be driving her mother nuts!"

"You had to put up with plenty of temper from me."

"Usually after I started it, though. Oh, well, water over the dam, huh? So, how's everything with you and Jill? Are you happy?"

Clay seemed startled. The last thing he'd expected Catherine to ask about was Jill, especially in that free and easy way.

"Yes, we are. We don't—" But he stopped self-consciously.

"Hey, it's okay. I mean, I didn't mean to pry."

"No, you weren't prying. I was just going to say that Jill and I don't fight like you and I used to, or give each other the silent treatment. We coexist rather peacefully."

"Good for you. So do Melissa and I. Peace is nice, isn't it, Clay?"

He sipped his drink, assessing this changed Catherine who seemed utterly satisfied with herself and her life. She reached over and tucked the baby's collar down, keeping up with the swing while she did it, smiling and saying, "Melissa, this is your daddy. You remember him, don't you? Shame on you for sticking your lip out and crying at him." Again she glanced up at Clay. "Your father came to visit us once. He brought Melissa a toy and asked how we were and said to let him know if we needed anything. But he's been so good to us already I'd feel guilty taking anything from him."

"What is it you need?"

"Nothing. Clay, you've been great about the money part. I really appreciate it. School is going to be great this year, I know. I mean, it's so much easier going to school when you're not pregnant." She flung her arms up and let them flop back down.

"I feel like I could conquer the world every day, you know?"

Clay used to feel that way; he didn't anymore. "Are you still sewing and typing?"

"Yes, now that school is in session again it's easy to find jobs. Don't worry, I'll help with the money any way I can. Mostly it goes for groceries. Baby food is kind of expensive." She chuckled and fluffed Melissa's hair as the swing went past. "'Course, I could save a lot on it if I didn't eat so much of it myself. We kind of share stuff, Melissa and I. I share my shower with her and she shares her food with me, huh, Lissy?"

"You take her in the shower!" exclaimed Clay. "At her age?"

"Oh, she loves it. And the pool, too. You should have seen her in the pool this summer, just like a baby otter." While she rambled on, she took Melissa out of the swing and sat the baby in her lap facing Clay. He noticed a new contentment in Catherine as she touched Melissa's hair or ear or gently clapped the bottoms of the tiny feet together. There was a naturalness about it that made Clay feel left out. The longer he observed Catherine with the baby the more he sensed how much she'd changed. She was freer than he'd ever seen her, talkative and happy, trying to withhold nothing about Melissa from him. It almost seemed as if she must share everything she could remember. But she did it guilelessly, shifting her attention from the baby to Clay all the while. Finally she said, "I think she's used to you now if you want to hold her."

But when he took Melissa, she immediately complained, so, disappointed, he handed the baby back to her mother.

Catherine shrugged. "Sorry."

He stood up to leave.

"Clay, is there anything you want from the house? I feel awful about taking everything from you. It seems like everything here is yours and I've ended up with it all. If there's anything you want, just say so, it's yours."

He glanced around the neat living room where the only thing out of place was the swing. He thought of the disarray Jill always left in her wake.

"Jill had everything already, thanks."

"Aren't there even any of the wedding gifts you want?"

"No, you keep 'em."

"Not even the popcorn popper?" She looked like a sprite while asking it.

"That wasn't a wedding gift. We bought that together."

"Oh, that's right. Well, I don't make much popcorn, so just say if you want it."

She seemed to have thoroughly adjusted to her life without him. She led the way to the door, opened it and sauntered out to the car with him.

"Thanks for bringing the check over, Clay, we really appreciate it."

"Anytime."

"Clay, one more thing before you go."

He stood beside the open car door, grateful for something that kept him there a little longer. Catherine stared at the ground, kicking a pebble, then looked directly into his eyes.

"Your father mentioned that they don't see much of you anymore. It's none of my business, but he seemed terribly hurt by that. Clay, there's no reason for you to feel like you've failed them or—or whatever." This was the first time she'd acted flustered. Her cheeks were pink. "Oh, you know what I mean. Your parents are really great. Don't sell them short, okay?"

"They don't exactly approve of my living with Jill."

"Give them a chance," she said, her voice quite low and musical, persuasive somehow. "How can they approve if they never see you to do it?" Then, quite suddenly, she flashed him a smile. "Oh, forget it. It's none of my business. Say good-bye to your daddy, Melissa." She backed away, manipulating the baby's arm in a wave.

Why was it that Clay, too, felt she was manipulating his heart in some obscure way?

Six weeks after school started a history professor named Frank Barrett asked Catherine to a show at the Orpheum. They returned to her house after an exhilarating live performance of *A Chorus Line*, and Frank Barrett tried to exact payment for the evening. He was handsome enough, in a rugged, dark-whiskered way, and Catherine thought of it as therapy when she let herself be pulled into his arms and kissed. But his beard, which she'd liked earlier, was less likable when his tongue came through it. His body, which had nothing to speak against it, was less appealing when it flattened Catherine's against the entry wall. His hands, which were square-nailed and clean, were too abruptly intimate, and when she pushed them away, it was with a healthy, negative feeling against him that had nothing to do with hangups. She simply was not attracted to him, and found it glorious to turn him away for such a reason.

When he apologized, she actually smiled, saying, "Oh, no need to apologize. It was wonderful."

Misreading her reply, he moved in again only to be staved off a second time.

"No, Frank. I meant *saying* no was wonderful!"

The poor, puzzled Frank Barrett left Catherine believing that she was somewhat wacky, not at all like she'd seemed when he'd first noticed her in his classroom.

*   *   *

In late November the law caught up with Herb Anderson and he was returned to Minnesota for trial. When Catherine saw him in the courtroom, she could scarcely believe it was he. His beer belly was gone, his face sallow, his hands shaky; life on the lam had obviously been unkind to him. But the same cynical expression still marred his face, the same droop of lips said Old Herb still thought he deserved a square deal from life and wasn't getting it.

To Catherine's surprise, Clay was in the courtroom, and so were his parents. With an effort, she forced her thoughts back to the proceedings, noting the satisfied smirk that crossed Herb's face when he saw that the Forresters did not seat themselves in the same row with Catherine and Ada.

The trial did not last long, for there was no one to come to Herb Anderson's defense, save two of his booze buddies from the old days, who looked even more desreputable than Herb, who'd at least been cleaned up and offered fresh clothing, courtesy of the county. Herb Anderson's history of violence was clearly presented in the testimony of Ada, Catherine and even Herb's own sister and brother-in-law, Aunt Ella and Uncle Frank. The past assault on Clay was brought up as evidence and dismissed, yet its impact remained. The doctor who had treated Ada testified, as did the ambulance drivers and Mrs. Sullivan. As the trial proceeded, Herb's usually florid face grew pastier and pastier. There were no verbal outbursts from him this time, only a quivering of his flaccid jowls and a persecuted expression when the judge sentenced Herbert Anderson to two years in the Stillwater State Penitentiary.

Leaving her seat, holding Ada's arm, Catherine saw Clay and his parents moving, also, toward the center aisle. He wore a stylish cashmere coat of spice brown, its collar flipped up. His eyes sought and held hers as she moved toward him, and wings seemed to flutter within Catherine's chest as she realized he was waiting for her. There was a welcome feeling of security about anticipating his touch upon her arm. Without a word—for the bench had called the next case—it was somehow understood: Angela and Claiborne separated to make room for Ada between them as they left the courtroom, followed by Catherine, with Clay's hand guiding her elbow. Walking beside him, she caught a hint of his familiar cologne. She gave in to the urge to look up at him again, tightening her arm and pulling his hand against her ribs.

"Thank you, Clay." She smiled appreciatively. "We really needed your support today."

He squeezed her elbow. The impact of his smile sent flurries deep into her stomach, and she looked away.

Once again Clay sensed the changes in her. She had gained a new self-assurance that was totally attractive on her, while at the same time she'd become dulcified. She was no longer skittish or defensive. He noticed that she'd changed her hairstyle and that the summer's streaks were now blending into its natural gold color. He studied it as she walked a step ahead of him, mentally approving of the appealing way in which it was caught up with combs behind her ears, falling in blithe curls down past her shoulder blades now.

They reached the corridor and found Angela waiting there, gazing at Catherine, fighting tears.

"Oh, Catherine, it's so wonderful to see you."

"I've missed you, too," Catherine got out. Then the two were in each other's arms and tears were hovering in the corners of both pairs of eyes.

Observing them, Clay remembered how Catherine had vowed not to let herself grow fond of his parents, but he saw that it hadn't worked, for from Angela's embrace she went to Claiborne's. It was the first time Clay ever remembered Catherine moving unguardedly into a hug, except that time with Steve.

Claiborne's bear hug made Catherine gasp and laugh, breaking the tension, but over his shoulder Catherine's eyes were again drawn to Clay, who was studying her with a faraway expression.

They all seemed to remember Ada then, and the reason for their being there. After they spoke of the case she had just won, the talk moved on to other things, growing a little fast and clipped, as if too much needed crowding into too little time. At last Angela suggested, "Why don't we all go somewhere and have a sandwich or a drink, somewhere we can talk for a while. There's so much I want to hear about Melissa and you, Catherine."

"How about The Mullion?" Claiborne suggested. "It's a favorite place of mine and not far from here."

Catherine glanced sharply at Clay, then at her mother.

Ada's hand fluttered to draw her coat closed. "Why, I don't know. I rode in with Margaret." They now took note of Mrs. Sullivan standing by, waiting with Ella and Frank.

"If you'd like, we'll take you home," Claiborne offered.

"Well, it's up to Cathy."

Catherine heard Clay say, "Catherine can ride with me." She slid him a look then, but he was buttoning up his coat as if it were already decided.

"I have my own car," she said.

"Whatever you'd like. You can ride with me if you like, and I'll bring you back uptown afterward to pick up your car."

The old Catherine intruded, with her impulse to fend off her feelings of attraction for Clay. But the newer Catherine was secure now and decided to go ahead and enjoy him while she could.

"All right," she agreed. "There's no sense in burning up extra gas."

Smiling at the others, Clay said, "We'll see you there then."

And Catherine felt her elbow firmly clasped and snuggled against Clay's warm side.

Outside the wind was howling, eddying in miniature twisters in the valleys between tall buildings. Catherine savored the icy sting upon her cheeks, for they were warm, almost burning. She and Clay got to a corner and stood waiting for a light to change. Catherine kept her eyes on the luminous red circle across the street, but she could feel Clay's eyes on her. She reached to turn up her collar but it caught on the long angora scarf twined around her neck, and Clay reached a gloved hand to help. Through all those layers of wool, his touch could still raise goose bumps up and down Catherine's spine. The light changed then.

"My car's in the parking ramp," Clay said, taking her arm again as they crossed the windy street, then crossing behind her as they turned the corner. Taking the outside, he brushed her shoulder. The touch made her tingle. She searched for something to say, but the only sound came from their heels on the sidewalk. He turned her into the echoing dungeon of a concrete parking ramp, its floor slick with motor oil. The heel of her shoe skittered, dumping her sideways, but she felt herself hoisted upright by that hand so secure on her elbow.

"You okay?"

"Yes. Winter is no time for high heels."

He watched her trim ankles, mentally disagreeing with her.

At the elevator he dropped her arm, leaned to push the button, and the silence seemed insurmountable while they waited, shivering, their shoulders hunched against the cold that seemed so much more intense in the concrete dimness. The elevator arrived; Clay stood aside while Catherine boarded. He pushed an orange button. Still they said nothing, and Catherine frantically wished she'd kept up a steady stream of chatter all the way because the privacy of the elevator was unbearable, yet she couldn't think of how to start.

Clay watched the light indicate the floors as they went up. "How's Melissa?" he asked the lights.

"Melissa's fine. She just loves the baby-sitter's; at least I'm told she's very content and happy there."

The hum of the elevator sounded like a buzz saw.

"How's Jill?"

Clay looked sharply at Catherine, hesitating only a moment before answering, "Jill's fine, at least she tells me she's very content and happy."

"And how about you?" Catherine's heart slammed around inside her. "What do you tell her?"

They had arrived at the correct level. The doors opened. Neither of them moved. The frigid air invaded their cell, but they stood as if unaware of it, gazing into each other's faces.

"My car is off to the right," he said, confused by the confusion in his chest, afraid of making the wrong move with her.

"I'm sorry, Clay, I shouldn't have asked that," she said in a rush, hurrying along beside him. "You have every right to ask about Melissa, but I have none to ask about Jill. I do wonder about you, though, and hope you're happy. I want you to be."

They stopped beside the Corvette. He leaned to unlock the door. He straightened, looked at her. "I'm working on it."

Riding to The Mullion they were both remembering the other time he'd taken her there. Suddenly it seemed childish to Catherine, the way they had grown so ill at ease with each other.

"Are you thinking about it, too, about the last time we went here?" she asked.

"I wasn't going to mention it."

"We're big kids now. We should be able to handle it."

"You know, you've changed, Catherine. Half a year ago you'd have bristled and acted threatened at the idea of going there."

"I felt threatened then."

"And now you don't?"

"I'm not sure of your question. Do you mean threatened by you?"

"It wasn't always against me that you put up your defenses. It was other things, places, circumstances, your own fears. I think you've outgrown a lot of that."

"I think I have, too."

"Since you asked me, I'll ask you—are you happy?"

"Yes. And do you know what made the difference?"

"What?" He angled a glance at her and found her watching him in the failing light of late afternoon.

"Melissa," she answered softly. "There have been countless times when I've looked at her and fought the urge to call you and say thank you for giving her to me."

"Why didn't you?"

He'd had his eyes on her for so long she wondered how the car stayed on the road. Catherine moved her head and shoulders in a vague way that said she did not have the answer. He turned back to watch the lane, and the familiarity struck her with a breathtaking blow: his profile there behind the wheel, the wrist draped negligently as he drove with the ease she remembered so well. She let her impulses have their way and suddenly leaned over, putting a hand on his jaw and pulling his cheek briefly against her lips.

"That's for both of us, for Melissa and me. Because I think she's just as grateful to have me as I am to have her." Quickly Catherine centered herself in her own seat and went on. "And you know what, Clay? I'm a fabulous mother. Don't ask me how it happened, but I know I am."

He couldn't help grinning. "And humble, too."

She snuggled into her seat contentedly. "There aren't a lot of things I'm good at, but being Melissa's mother is . . . well, it's great. It's a little harder since school started, but I cut a few corners of housework time here and there, let a few things stay dusty, and I still find time for her. But I have to admit, I'll be glad when school is over and I don't have to divide my time so many ways."

The kiss then had been purely a kiss of thanks. It was clearer than ever that Catherine's life was full and happy. She had it all together. Clay listened to her relating stories about it and suffered pangs of regret that she'd been unable to feel this fulfilled when she was living with him. He came from his reverie to realize she'd just said she was dating again. He submerged the twinge of possessiveness to which he no longer had a right and asked, "How does it feel?"

"Terrific!" She flung up her palms. "Just terrific! I can kiss back without the slightest bit of guilt. Sometimes I can even enjoy it."

She looked at him with an impish grin and they both laughed. But a hundred queries bubbled up in his mind about those kisses, the ones she shared them with, queries that, again, he had no right to ask.

They stayed at The Mullion for over two hours, until Angela had learned about each of Melissa's toys and teeth and vaccinations. Catherine was her new, free, easy self all the while. Clay spoke little, sitting back and studying her, comparing her to the way she used to be. And subconsciously comparing her to Jill. He wondered if she was dating only one man or several. He planned to ask her when he drove her back to her car.

But when the time came to leave, Catherine pointed out that it was actually closer to Claiborne and Angela's route to drop her back uptown, and she rode with them.

TWENTY-NINE

Clay stood at the window of the high-rise apartment he shared with Jill, staring down at the icy expanse of Lake Minnetonka in the cold, purple dusk below. The lake was a sprawling network of bays, channels and inlets in a western suburb bearing its name. Clay wished it were summer. In summer the lake was a water-lover's paradise, dappled by sails, dotted with skiers, peopled with fishermen, rimmed by intermittent beach and woodland. Its islands emerged like emeralds from sapphire waters. In spots where its shoreline was left to nature's whims, watery fingers erupted in lavender explosions of loosestrife, come August.

But now, in early December, Clay studied the frozen surface in distaste. Winds had whipped it into a froth as it froze, leaving it the pitted texture and color of lava. Rowboats and schooners alike looked bereft, overturned on the shore. Hoisted above the waterline their soiled canvas covers held dirty snow. On a spar below, a trio of dissolute sparrows fluffed their feathers against an arctic wind until they were blown off, trundled sideways as they flew. A small flock of mallards fought a headwind, then disappeared in their search of open water.

Watching the ducks, Clay wondered where the autumn had gone. He had drifted through it listlessly, free this year to enjoy the hunting he so dearly loved, yet somehow never even getting his gun out of its case. In the past he'd hunted with his father more than anyone else. He missed his father. But as winter thickened and intensified, so had his parents' disapproval over his living with Jill. Although they occasionally phoned, Clay sensed their silent chastisement, thus never called them back.

He saw Jill's car curve into the parking lot below and disappear toward the garages. Minutes later he heard her key in the door. Normally he'd have hurried to open it, but today he only continued staring morosely at the chill scene outside.

"Oh, God, it's cold! I hope there's a nice hot toddy waiting for me," Jill said. She crossed to Clay, dropping gloves, scarf, purse and coat across the room like rings from a skipping stone, only—unlike ripples—the articles would not disappear. It aggravated Clay, for he'd just cleaned up the place again when he got home. Jill crooked an arm through his and rubbed her cold nose against his jaw in greeting.

"I like it when you get home first and you're here waiting."

"Jill, do you have to drop your stuff everyplace like that?"

"Oh, did I drop something?" She looked at the trail behind her, then nuzzled Clay again. "Just anxious to get to you, darling, that's all. Besides, you know I always had a maid at home."

"Yes, I know. That's always your excuse." He couldn't help recalling how Catherine used to enjoy keeping the town house clean and neat.

"Irritable tonight, darling?"

"No, I'm just tired of living in a mess."

"You're irritable. In need of some liquid refreshment. What have you been standing here brooding about, your parents again? If it bothers you so much, why don't you go over and see them tonight?"

But it only irritated him further that she simplified it so, as if

his problems could be solved by a simple visit. She dropped her shoes in the middle of the room on her way to the liquor cabinet. She picked up a brandy decanter, swung around loosely to face him and said, "Let's have a drink, then go out and get some supper."

It was Friday night, bleak and cold, and he was tired of running. He wished just for once she'd suggest making dinner at home, doing something cozy and relaxing. The memory of sharing popcorn and studying with Catherine came back, so inviting now. He pictured the town house, Melissa in her swing with Catherine cross-legged beside it in her jeans. Looking out at the cold, icy lake, which was receding into dusk's hold, he wondered what Catherine's reaction would be if he showed up at her door. Abruptly, he walked over and closed the draperies. Before he could reach for the lamp switch, Jill moved close in the dark. She wrapped her arms around him, pressed her breasts to his chest and sighed.

"Maybe I can think of a way to coax you out of your bad mood," she whispered huskily against his lips.

He kissed her, waiting for arousal to grip him. Instead, he was gripped only by hunger pangs; he'd skipped lunch that day. It struck him that the state of his stomach overrode his bodily response to Jill. It made him feel emptier, hungrier, but for something that went beyond either food or sex.

"Later," he said, brushing her hair back, guilty now for his lack of desire. "Get your coat and let's go out and eat."

Melissa was teething and fussy and whiny these days. She resisted bedtime, so Catherine often brought her out onto the living room floor until she fell asleep there, then carried her up to her crib.

The doorbell rang and Melissa's eyes flew open again.

Oh, damn, thought Catherine. But she leaned over, kissed Melissa's forehead and whispered, "Mommy'll be right back, punkin."

Melissa started sucking on her bottle again.

Through the door Clay heard her muffled voice.

"Who is it?"

"It's Clay," he said, close to the wood.

Suddenly Catherine forgot her irritation. Her stomach seemed to suspend itself, then drift back into place in an unnervingly tentative way. It's Clay, it's Clay, it's Clay, she thought, deliriously happy.

On the other side of the door Clay wondered what he'd say to her; she'd surely see through his flimsy excuse for coming here.

The door fairly flew open, but when it swung back she stood motionless. First impression made her momentarily mute: his wind-whipped hair in a whorl of inviting imperfection above the turned-up collar of an old letter jacket; faded jeans hugging his slim hips; his hands in his pockets like some uncertain high-school sophomore ringing a girl's bell for the first time. He hesitated as if he didn't know what to say, then his eyes traveled down to her knees, then back up, then seemed not to know where to rest. Everything in her went all loose and jellyish.

"Hi, Catherine."

"Hi, Clay."

Suddenly she realized how long it had been since either of them had moved and remembered that Melissa was on the floor with the cold wafting in.

"I brought Melissa a Christmas gift."

She stepped back, let him in, then closed the door to find

herself disarmingly close to him in the rather confined area of
the entry.

Clay briefly glanced down at her attire. "Were you in bed
already?"

"Oh—oh, no." Self-consciously she tugged the zipper of her
robe the remaining two inches up her neck, then jammed her
hands into its pockets.

"I guess I should have called first." He stood there feeling
graceless and intrusive. The robe was fleecy pink, with a hood,
and pockets on the front like a sweatshirt. Her hair was pulled
back with a plastic headband and the ends of it were still wet.
Her face had that scrubbed, shiny look that he recognized so
well. With a start, he realized she'd just gotten out of the shower.
He knew perfectly well there was no bra beneath that fuzzy, pink
fleece—he remembered that untethered look of hers.

"It doesn't matter, it's okay."

"Next time I'll make sure I call first. I just bought something
on impulse, and I was driving past and decided to drop it off."

"I said it was okay. We weren't doing anything special anyway."

"You weren't?" he asked dumbly.

"I was studying and Melissa was teething."

He smiled then, a big, warm, wonderful smile, and she
hunched up her shoulders and pushed her hands as far down in
her pockets as they'd go because she didn't know how else to
contain her happiness at his being there.

Suddenly there was a loud thump and the living room was
plunged into darkness, followed by a second of silence before
Melissa's wail of panic billowed through the blackness.

"Oh, my God!" Clay heard. He groped, touched the fleecy
robe and followed it up the stairs in the direction of the living
room.

"Where is she, Catherine?"

"I left her on the floor."

"You get her. I'll get the kitchen light."

Melissa was screaming and Catherine's heart threatened to explode. Fumbling for the light switch, Clay, too, felt a stab of panic. He found the switch, then in five long-legged strides was kneeling behind Catherine, who had scooped up the baby and was muffling Melissa's cries against her neck. In the dim light Clay could see the table lamp on the floor, but unbroken. He touched Catherine's shoulder, then Melissa's head.

"Catherine, let's take her into the light and see if she's hurt." He put his hands on Catherine's sides, urging her up and felt through the robe that she was crying, too. "Come on," he said sensibly, "let's take her to the bathroom."

They laid Melissa on a fat Turkish towel on the vanity top. They could see right away where the lamp had hit the back of the baby's head. There was a tiny gash there and already it was starting to swell into a goose egg. Catherine was so upset that her distress was conveyed to Melissa, who squalled all the louder. So Clay was the one who swabbed the bruise and calmed them both.

"It's all my fault." Catherine blamed herself. "I've never left her on the floor like that before. I should have known she'd go straight for the lamp cords—she does every chance she gets. But she was asleep when the doorbell rang and I didn't think anything of it. She started sucking on her bottle again and I was just—"

"Hey, it's nothing serious. I'm not blaming you, am I?" Clay's eyes met hers in the mirror.

"But a lamp that size could have killed her."

"But it didn't. And it's not the last bump she'll take. Do you realize that you're more upset than Melissa?"

He was right. Melissa wasn't even crying anymore, just sitting there wet-eyed, watching them. Sheepishly Catherine smiled, sniffled, yanked out a tissue and blew her nose. Clay put his arm around her shoulder and bumped her up against his side a couple of times as if to say, silly girl. At that moment he understood why nature had created a two-parent system. Yes, you're a good mother, Catherine, he thought, but not in emergencies. At times like this, you need me.

"What do you say we show her the Christmas present I bought for her and that'll make her forget she even had an accident."

"All right. But, Clay, do you think this needs stitches? I don't know anything about cuts. She's never had one before."

They fought Melissa's tiny hands and caused her to start complaining again while they inspected the damage.

"I don't know much about it, either, but I don't think so. It's awfully tiny. And anyway, it's in her hair, so if there's a scar it won't show."

Finally, Melissa left the bathroom on her mother's arm, looking back at Clay with a wide-eyed look of inquiry. He set up the lamp and plugged it in again, and they all sat down on the living room floor, the baby in her yellow footed pajamas staring so silently at Clay that he finally laughed at her. Her bottom lip started quivering again, so Clay suggested, "Hurry and open that before I get a complex."

The sight and sound of the bright red, crackly paper captured the baby's attention as Catherine tore it off the white koala bear with its flat nose and lifelike eyes. At the sight of it, Melissa's mouth made a tiny "ooo," then she gurgled. The koala had a music box inside, and it wasn't long before it accompanied Melissa to bed.

Coming back down from Melissa's room, Catherine found

Clay waiting at the bottom of the stairs, his green and gold letter jacket slung over one shoulder as if he were going to leave. A throb of disappointment thudded through her. She stopped on the bottom step, curling her toes over the edge, hanging on by her heels only. Her fingertips unconsciously toyed upon the handrails. He stood before her, their eyes nearly on the same level, trying to think of something to say to each other.

"She'll sleep now," Catherine said—not quite an invitation, not quite not.

"Good . . . well . . ." He looked at the carpet while he slowly threaded his arms into his jacket sleeves. Still studying the floor, he straightened the old shapeless collar while Catherine gripped the handrails tightly. He buried his hands in the jacket pockets and cleared his throat.

"I guess I'd better get going." His voice sounded a little raspy, trying to talk soft that way so he wouldn't wake Melissa.

"Yes, I guess so." It took great effort for Catherine to breathe. The banister felt suddenly slippery.

Clay's head came up slowly, his inscrutable eyes meeting hers. He gestured with one of his hidden hands as if waving good-bye—jacket and all.

"So long."

She could barely hear it, he said it so softly.

"So long."

But instead of moving, he stood there studying her, the way she perched on that bottom step like a sparrow on a limb. Her eyes were wide and unsmiling, and he could see the way she forced herself to take shallow, fluttering breaths. His own breath wasn't any too calm. He wished she wouldn't look so stricken, but knew she had good reason to be scared, just as scared as he was at that moment. Her hair was dry now, the ends curling wispily upon her shoulders, upon the folds of the hood that hilled up around her jaw. She stood there all still, arms straight out from her sides, looking almost breastless in her robe. Face shiny, devoid of makeup, hair unstyled, feet bare. He tried not to analyze, not to think either "I should" or "I shouldn't," because he only knew he had to. He took three agonizingly slow footsteps toward her, his eyes roving her face. Then he leaned silently and put his face in the spot where her hair lay, lifted by that hood. He breathed of her remembered fragrance—soft, powdery, feminine scent that he'd always loved. Catherine's lips fell open and she moved her jaw against his temple while deep in her body things went liquid, deep in his, things went hard. Her heart scrambled to make sense of this while it seemed to take light-years of time before he straightened and their eyes met. They asked tacit questions, remembered old hurts they'd caused each other. Then, still with his hands in his pockets, Clay leaned and touched her lips softly with his own, seeing her lashes drop just before his own eyes slid shut. He kissed her with a light lingering of flesh upon flesh, letting the past slip into obscurity, yet unable to prevent it from being part of the kiss. He told himself he must go, but when he drew away her lips followed, telling him not to. Their eyelids flickered open to breach that moment of uncertainty before he moved more surely against her lips. There was a timorous, first opening of mouths, warm touch of tongue upon tongue, then Clay wrapped his hands, jacket and all, around her, pulling her inside it with him. Handlessly they embraced, for she still clutched the rails, and his hands were lost in his pockets behind her, quite afraid to pull them out and start something they certainly should not finish. But it was impossible, unbearable, this handlessness. Then Catherine seemed to lean off the steps, drifting into the warm place he opened up to her, losing her arms deep inside his jacket. He enclosed her in the cocoon of soft, old wool and leather, and hard, young flesh and blood, lifting her off that step, turning, holding her suspended against him while the kiss became reckless and she went sliding down his body. Her bare toes touched canvas and she was standing on his tennis shoes. One hand came out of his pocket and found her hair, cradling the back of her head, pulling her against his mouth. His other hand left the safe confines of its pocket and flattened itself upon the center of her back, then drifted lower, lower, to the shallows of her spine, to bring the length of her body against his. Through her robe she could feel his belt buckle and the hard zipper of his jeans, and she remembered drinking wine from his skin. Ironically, the thought sobered her and she tried to push away. But he pulled her almost violently against the thunder of his heart, crushing her.

"Oh, God, Cat," he whispered in a strangled voice, "this is where we started."

"Not at all," came her shaky reply. "We've come a long way since then."

"You have, Cat, you have. You're so different now."

"I've grown up a little, that's all."

"Then what the hell's the matter with me?"

"Don't you know?"

"Nothing's right in my life anymore. Everything's gone wrong since you and I made that damn agreement. The last year has been miserable. I don't know who I am or where I'm going anymore."

"Is this going to tell you?"

"I don't know. I only know it feels right here with you."

"The first time we met it felt right, and look where it landed us."

"I want you," he half-groaned against her hair, wrapping his arms around her so far she heard old stitches pop up the back of his jacket. She closed her eyes and swam in a warm, wet place of his making, secure enough now to take the plunge, to say that which she'd refused to say during the agonizing months she'd lived with him.

"But I love you, Clay, and there's a difference."

He pulled back to search her face, and she willed him to say it, but he didn't. He read her thoughts and knew what it was she waited for, but found he could not say it unless he was certain. Things had happened so fast he didn't know if he was running on impulse or emotion. He only knew she looked beguiling, and that she was the mother of his child and that they were still husband and wife.

He came back against her hard, and the momentum swept them to the carpeted stairs. All in one motion he pressed her down and lifted his knee, riding it across her stomach, hip and thigh, caressing her with it while he searched the neck of her robe for the zipper, slid it down and plunged his hand inside to slake it with her breast, then run it down her stomach.

"Stop it, Clay, stop it," she implored, dying because she wanted nothing more than to turn her body inside out for him.

Against her warm neck he said throatily, "You don't want this to stop, not any more than you did the first time."

"Our divorce will be final in less than a month, and you're living with another woman."

"And lately all I do is compare her to you."

"Is that why you're here, Clay, to make comparisons?"

"No, no, I didn't mean it that way." His hand swept down her ribs, down her stomach, heading again for the spot that wept for him. "Oh, Cat, you're under my skin."

"Like an itch you can't reach, Clay?" She grabbed his wrist and stopped it again.

"Don't play games with me."

"I'm not the one playing games, Clay, you are."

He felt her nails now, digging into his wrist. He pushed himself back, leaning on one elbow to see her better.

"I'm not playing games. I want you."

"Why? Because I'm the first thing in your life that you can't have?"

His face changed, grew stormy, then abruptly he sat up on the step beside her and buried his fingers in his hair. God, is she right? he wondered. Is that all it is with me—ego? Am I that kind of a bastard? He heard her zipper go back up but remained as he was, touching his scalp, which tingled at the thought of all that naked skin beneath her robe. He sat that way a long time, then pulled his palms down over his face. But in them he could smell the fragrance of her perfume, gathered from her skin like spring flowers.

She sat beside him, watching him do battle with himself. After a long time, he stretched his frame back against the edges of the steps, lying there at an angle. With his eyes closed he lifted up his hips and tugged at the crotch of his jeans. She could see the telltale bulge there. He rested the back of a wrist over his eyes, let his other hand lie limply down along his groin. He sighed.

Finally she spoke, but her voice was reasonable, not angry. "I think you'd better decide what it is you want, me or her. You can't have us both."

"I know that, I goddam know that," he said tiredly. "I'm sorry, Catherine."

"Yes, you should be, doing this to me again. I'm not as resilient as you are, Clay. When I get hurt it hurts for a long time. And I have no alternate lover to fall back on for support."

"I feel like I'm spinning in circles; nothing's in focus."

"I don't doubt it, living with her, coming here, your parents right in the middle. What about them, Clay? What are you trying to prove by rejecting them the way you have and going to work for someone else?"

She saw his Adam's apple slide up and down, but he didn't answer.

"If you want to punish yourself, Clay, keep me out of it. If you want to go on putting yourself into situations that rub you raw, fine. I don't. I've made a new life with Melissa, and I've proven to myself that I can live without you. When we met, you were the one with direction, the secure one. Now it seems we've changed places. What happened to that direction, that purpose you used to have?"

Maybe it left me when I left you, he thought.

At last he sat up, then pulled himself to his feet and stood with his back to her, staring at the floor.

She said, "I think you'd better go someplace and get sorted out, get your priorities straight. If and when you manage that and think you want to see me again . . ." But instead of finishing the thought, she ended, "Just don't ever come back here asking for me unless it's for keeps."

She heard the snaps of his jacket, like whipcracks in the silence. Clay's shoulders squared, then slumped, then he waved wordlessly, without looking back at her, and left the house, closing the door softly behind him.

THIRTY

Emotionally, Catherine found herself in that painful, bitter-sweet state she'd faced and gotten through once before when Clay left her. Again, she suffered reveries from which she emerged to find her hands idle, her thoughts and eyes meandering out the window, across the snowy city to Clay. Clay, whom she'd have on one condition only, thus would probably never have at all. The contentment she'd known from loving Melissa ceased to sustain her. Emptiness crept into her unexpectedly, in the middle of the most everyday activities: studying, folding laundry, walking across campus, giving Melissa a bath, driving the car. Clay's visage appeared before her constantly, his absence again robbing her of joy, making life seem wan and empty, at times bringing tears to her eyes. And like all lorn loves, she found reminders of him in countless places that were only illusory: in the reddish-gold hair of some stranger on the street; in the cut of a sport coat on a muscular shoulder; in the inflection of someone's laughter; in the way certain men crossed their ankles over their knees, dropped their hands into their pockets or straightened their ties. One of Catherine's professors, when he lectured intensely, had Clay's habit of standing with arms akimbo, holding his sport coat back with his wrists, studying the floor between his outspread feet. His body language was so like Clay's that Catherine became obsessed with the man. It did no good to tell herself she was transferring her feelings for Clay to a veritable stranger. Each time Professor Neuman stood before class that way, Catherine's heart would react.

She counted off the days until Christmas break when she would no longer have to be subjected to Professor Neuman and his similarities to Clay. But Christmas brought its own bitter-sweet memories of the year before. In an effort to stave them off, she called Aunt Ella and wangled an invitation for herself and Ada for Christmas Day. But even having plans didn't help much, for she never turned on the lights of her tiny tree without having to quell the soft, seductive memories of the previous year at Angela and Claiborne's house. She would walk to the sliding glass door and look out at the snow-laden world and jam her hands into the pockets of her jeans and remember, remember, remember. That magical house with all its love, lights, music and family.

Family. Ah, family. It was so much the root of Catherine's unhappiness, had been all her life. She would look at Melissa and tears would gather, for that family security the child would never know, no matter how much she herself lavished her daughter with love. She fantasized about Clay coming to the door again, only this time it would be different. This time he'd say he loved her, and only her, and they'd bundle Melissa into her little blue snowsuit and when the three of them arrived at the big house it would be just like last year, only better. Catherine closed her eyes, hugging herself, smelling again the tang of newly blown-out candles, remembering soft mistletoe kisses . . .

But that was fantasy. Reality was making it through Christmas alone, as a single parent, with no one to place gifts beneath her lonely tree but herself.

"Let's get a tree and put it up," Clay said.

"What for?" asked Jill.

"Because it's Christmas, that's what for."

"I don't have time. If you want one, put it up yourself."

"You never seem to have time for anything around the house."

"Clay, I work eight hours a day! Besides, why cultivate interests you never intend to use?"

"Never?"

"Oh, Clay, don't start in on me now. I lost my blue cashmere sweater and I wanted to wear it tomorrow. Dammit, where could it be?"

"If you'd muck the place out once a month or so, maybe you wouldn't lose track of your things." The bedroom looked like an explosion in a Chinese laundry.

"Oh, I know!" Jill suddenly brightened. "I'll bet I took it to the cleaners last week. Clay, be a darling and run over and pick it up for me, will you?"

"I'm not your laundry boy. If you want it, go get it yourself."

She picked her way across the littered floor and cooed close to his face, "Don't be cross, darling. I just didn't think you were busy right now." When she would have teasingly inserted her glittering nail into the smile line on his cheek, he jerked his head aside.

"Jill, you never think I'm busy. You always think you're the only one who's busy."

"But darling, I am. I'm meeting the project engineer for the first time tomorrow and I want to look my best." She tried to put him into good humor with a quick caress. But that was the third time she'd called him "darling," and lately it had started to bother him. She used the term so loosely it sometimes stung. It reminded him of what Catherine had said about the value of affection going up when it was in short supply.

"Jill, why did you want me back?" he asked abruptly.

"Darling, what a question. I was lost without you, you know that."

"Besides being *lost* without me, what else?"

"What is this, the Spanish Inquisition? How do you like this dress?" She held up a pink crepe de chine and swirled in a little side-step, eyeing him provocatively.

"Jill, I'm trying to talk to you; will you forget the damn dress?"

"Sure. It's forgotten." She dropped it negligently on the foot of the bed and turned to grab a brush and begin stroking her hair. "So talk."

"Listen, I—" He hardly knew where to begin. "I thought our lifestyles, our backgrounds, our futures were so alike that we were practically made for each other. But, this—this isn't working out for me."

"Isn't working out? Clarify that for me, will you, Clay?" she asked crisply, stroking her hair all the harder.

He gestured at the room. "Jill, we're different, that's all. I have trouble living with the clutter, the meals in the restaurants and the laundry that's never clean and the kitchen cabinets that are full of magazines!"

"I didn't think you wanted me for my domestic abilities."

"Jill, I'm willing to do my share, but I need some sense of home, do you understand that?"

"No, I'm not sure I do. It sounds to me like you're asking me to give up my career to push dust around."

"I'm not asking you to give up anything, just to give me some straight answers."

"I would if I knew exactly what it is you're asking."

Clay picked up a lace-trimmed violet petticoat from a chair and sat down wearily. He studied the expensive garment, rubbing it between his fingers. Quietly he asked, "What about kids, Jill?"

"Kids?"

Her brush stopped stroking. Clay looked up.

"A family. Do you ever want to have a family?"

She whirled on him angrily. "And you said you're not asking me to give anything up!"

"I'm not, and I'm not even talking about right away, but someday. Do you want a baby someday?"

"I've just put in all these years getting a degree; I have a future ahead of me in one of the fastest-growing fields there is, and you're talking babies?"

Without warning, Clay pictured Catherine crying because Grover's baby had died, then in the labor room with their hands together on her stomach as the contractions built; he thought of her cross-legged on the living room floor clapping Melissa's feet together, and the way she'd cried because Melissa had bumped her head.

Suddenly Jill threw the brush down. It cracked on the dresser top, went skittering off the mirror and landed on the floor inside an abandoned high-heeled pump.

"You've seen her, haven't you?"

"Who?"

"Your . . . wife." The word galled Jill.

Clay didn't even consider lying. "Yes."

"I knew it! As soon as you came in here complaining about the mess, I knew it! Did you take her to bed?"

"For God's sake." Clay stood up, turning away from her.

"Well, did you?"

"That's got nothing to do with this."

"Oh, doesn't it? Well, think again, buster, because I'm not playing second fiddle to any woman, wife or not!" Jill turned

back to the mirror, picked up a fat brush and savagely began
applying blush to her cheeks.

"That's part of this arrangement we have here, isn't it, Jill?"

She glared at him in the looking glass. "What is?"

"Egos, yours and mine. Part of the reason you wanted me
was because you've never had to do without anything you
wanted. Part of the reason I left Catherine is because I've never
had to do without anything I wanted."

Her eyes glittered dangerously as she swung around to face
him. "Well, we're two of a kind then, aren't we, Clay?"

"No, we're not. I thought we were, but we're not. Not anymore."

They stood with eyes locked, hers angry, his sorry, in the
meadow of strewn garments, coffee cups, newspapers and
makeup.

At last Jill said, "I can compete with Catherine, but I can't
compete with Melissa. That's it, isn't it?"

"She's there, Jill. She exists, and I'm her father and I can't
forget it. And Catherine has changed so much."

Without warning she flung the makeup brush at him and it
hit him on the cheek as she yelled, "Oh, damn you! Damn you!
Damn you! How dare you stand there mooning over her! If you
want her so bad, what are you doing here? But once you leave,
don't think your half of the bed will be cold for long!"

"Jill, please, I never meant to hurt you."

"Hurt? How could you hurt me? You only hurt the one you
love, isn't that how the song goes?"

When Clay left Lake Minnetonka, he drove aimlessly for hours.
He headed for Minneapolis proper, circled Lake Calhoun,

headed east on Lake Street past the quaint little artsy shops at the Lake Hennepin area, farther east where seedy theaters gave way to seedier used-furniture stores. He turned south, caught the strip that cut Bloomington in half and circled west again. The lights of the Radisson South split the night sky with its twenty-two stories of windows as Clay turned onto the Belt Line, unconsciously heading for Golden Valley.

He took the exit of Golden Valley Road without deciding to, and threaded through the streets that once had been his route home, passing Byerly's Supermarket where he and Catherine had first gone grocery shopping. He pulled into the lot beside the town house but let the engine idle, leaving only the parking lights on. He looked up at the sliding glass door and there, shining out onto the snowy balcony were the multicolored lights from a Christmas tree. As he sat staring at them, they blinked out and the window grew dark. Then he put the car in gear and headed for a motel.

When Clay appeared in the doorway of the study, Claiborne looked up, tried to mask his surprise, but couldn't quite bring it off. He half rose from his chair, then settled down again behind the desk with a bald look of hope.

"Hi, Dad."

"Hello, Clay. We haven't seen you for a long time."

"Yeah, well, don't tell Mother I'm here just yet. I'd like to talk to you alone first."

"Of course, come in, come in." Claiborne removed a pair of silver-rimmed reading glasses from his nose and dropped them on the desk.

"The glasses are new."

"I've had them for a couple of months, can't get used to the damn things, though."

They both looked at the glasses. The room was still. Suddenly, as if inspired, the older man rose.

"How about a brandy?"

"No, thanks, I—"

"A Scotch?" Claiborne asked too anxiously. "Or maybe some white wine. I seem to remember that you liked white."

"Dad, please. We both know white wine isn't going to fix a damn thing."

Claiborne dropped back into his chair. A log hissed in the fire and shot a tongue of blue flame sideways. Clay sighed, wondering as he had so often recently, where to begin. He sat on the edge of the leather love seat and pressed his thumb knuckles deep into his eyes.

"What the hell went wrong?" he finally asked. His voice was quiet and searching and pained.

"Absolutely nothing that can't be fixed," his father answered. And even before their eyes met again, their hearts seemed to drop burdens that each had borne for too long.

The telephone rang for the fifth time and Clay's hopes waned. He angled the receiver away from his ear, leaned his head back against the headboard and shut his eyes. Traffic roared past on the highway outside. He studied his stocking feet stretched out before him, his suitcases lying open, sighed and was just about to give up when Catherine said hello.

She stood in the dark bedroom dripping bathwater onto the carpet, trying to get a towel wrapped around her without dropping the receiver.

"Hello, Catherine?"

Her heart seemed to flip up into her windpipe and her hands
stopped messing with the towel. It slid down off her back and
she clutched it to her breast, feeling her battering heart through
the terry cloth.

At last she said, "H-hello."

He heard the catch in her voice and swallowed. "It's Clay."

"Yes, I know."

"I didn't think you were home."

"I was in the tub."

The line buzzed for an interminable moment while he wondered which phone she'd picked up and what she was wearing.

"I'm sorry, I can call back."

"No!" Then she calmed herself a little. "No, but . . . can you
wait a minute, Clay, while I get a robe on? I'm freezing."

"Sure, I'll hang on." And hang on he did, clutching the receiver in his damp palm while hours seemed to drag past and
visions of a pink hooded robe filled his mind.

Catherine flew to the closet, dropping the towel, scrambling
for her robe, frantic, impatient, fumbling, thinking, Oh, my
God, it's Clay, it's Clay! Oh, Lord, oh, damn, where's my robe?
He'll hang up. . . . Where is it? Wait, Clay, wait! I'm coming!

She tried running back to the phone and stepping into the
robe at the same time, but the zipper went only halfway down
the front of the thing, and she stumbled, arriving at the phone
breathless.

"Clay?" he heard, and the sound of her anxiousness made
him smile and feel warm inside.

"I'm here."

She released a pent-up breath, got the zipper up and perched
on the edge of the bed in the semidarkness, with only the light
from the closet easing around the corner into the room.

"Sorry it took so long."

He figured it had probably taken seven seconds. Still, he was afraid now to ask what he'd called to ask, afraid she'd turn him down, sick at the thought that she might.

"How are you?" he asked instead.

She pictured his face, the face she'd been searching crowds for ever since she'd last seen it, pictured his hair, which she'd imagined she'd seen on hundreds of strangers, his eyes, his mouth. Long moments passed before she admitted, "Not so happy since you were here last."

He swallowed, surprised at her answer when he'd expected the usual trite, "Fine."

"Me either."

It was incredible how two such simple words managed to slam the breath out of her. Frantically she searched for something to say, but her mind remained filled only with his face, and she wondered where he was and what he was wearing.

"How's Melissa's head?" he asked.

"Oh, fine. It's all healed up, no worse for the wear."

They both laughed nervously, but the strained sound ended abruptly at both ends of the wire, followed by silence again. Clay raised one knee, propped an elbow on it and kneaded the bridge of his nose, his heart thundering so loud it seemed she must hear it at her end.

"Catherine, I was wondering what you're doing tomorrow night."

She clutched the phone in both hands. "To-tomorrow night? But that's Christmas Eve."

"Yes, I know."

Clay quit kneading his eyes, took up pressing the crease of one trouser leg between his fingers instead. "I was wondering if you and Melissa have plans."

Catherine's eyes slid shut. She raised the mouthpiece up to her forehead so he couldn't hear her jerky breathing. She got control.

"No, not for tomorrow night. We're going to Uncle Frank and Aunt Ella's on Christmas Day, but nothing for tomorrow." Up went the receiver to her forehead again.

"Would you like to come out to the house with me?"

She put her hand on the top of her head to keep it from leaving her body, struggled to sound calm.

"Out to your parents' house?"

"Yes."

He felt physically sick during the interminable moments while she thought, What about Jill? Where is Jill? I told you not to call me unless it was forever.

"Where are you, Clay?" she asked, so quietly he had to strain to hear the words.

"I'm in a motel."

"A motel?"

"Alone."

Joy sluiced through every vein of her body. Her throat and eyes felt flooded while she sat there gripping the phone like some babbling idiot.

"Catherine?" His voice cracked as he said it.

"Yes, I'm here," she got out.

In a stranger's voice he managed, "For Chrissake, answer me, will you?" And she remembered how Clay swore when he was scared.

"Yes," she whispered, and slid down with a thump onto the floor.

"What?"

"Yes," she said, louder, smiling great-big.

The line grew silent for a long, long time, with only the sound of some distant electronic bleeps making music in their ears, then disappearing.

"Where are you?" he asked then, wishing he were with her now.

"I'm in the bedroom, sitting on the floor beside the bed."

"Is Melissa asleep?"

"Yes, for a long time."

"Has she got the koala bear with her?"

"Yes," Catherine whispered, "it's in the crib by her head."

The line went quiet once more. After a long time Clay said, "I'm going back to work with Dad, as soon as possible."

"Oh, Clay . . ."

She heard him laugh, but it was a deeply emotional laugh, as if it were very hard to bring from his throat.

"Oh, Cat, you were right, you were so right."

"I was only guessing."

This time when he laughed it was less strained, then she heard him sigh.

"Listen, I've got to get some sleep. I didn't get much last night or the night before that or the night before that."

"Me either."

"I'll pick you up at five or so?"

"We'll be ready."

Silence roared between them again, a long, quivering silence that said as much as the soft words that followed:

"Good night, Catherine."

"Good night, Clay."

And again, silence, while each waited for the other to hang up first.

"Good night, I said," he said.

"So did I."

"Then let's do it together."

"Do what together?"

She never knew before that you could hear a smile.

"That too. But later. For now, just hang up so I can get some sleep."

"Okay, on three, then?"

"One . . . two . . . three."

This time they hung up together.

But they were both sadly mistaken if they thought they'd get much sleep.

THIRTY-ONE

The next day crawled. Catherine felt light-headed, at times giddy, almost removed from herself. Passing a mirror, she found herself staring at her reflection long and assessingly before covering her cheeks with both hands, closing her eyes and reveling in the heartbeat that seemed to extend into every nerve ending of her body, its cadence fast-tripping. She opened her eyes and warned herself this might be a false alarm. Maybe just Clay's way of seeing Melissa, giving his parents a chance to see her, too, during the holiday. But then Catherine would remember his voice on the phone, and she knew somehow this was what she'd been dreaming of. Her thoughts flew to the oncoming evening. Hurry, hurry!

Finally, to kill time, she bundled Melissa into the car and went out shopping for something new to wear. She moved through the crowds of last-minuters in a thoroughly changed state from the previous day. She smiled at strangers. She hummed along with piped-in carols. She was eminently patient when forced to wait behind slow-moving lines at cash registers. Once she even spoke to an older man whose temper was on edge, whose face was red and quivery and impatient. A new feeling of ebullience lifted Catherine as she saw his impatience dissolve beneath her own good spirits. And she thought, See what love can do?

Back at home she put Melissa down for a nap and took a leisurely bath in an explosion of bubbles. Emerging from the tub, she stood before the wide vanity mirror blotting her skin. She felt giddily gay, childish and womanly all at once. She made a moue at her reflection, then struck a seductive pose with the towel partially shielding her nudity, then tried a different pose, a different facial expression. She leaned nearer the mirror, tugging tendrils of hair out of the hastily secured topknot, giving herself a kittenish look with loose wisps at her temples and the back of her neck. She wet her lips, allowed them to fall slightly open, lowered her lids to a smoky expression and breathed, "Hello, Clay." Then she tried standing with her back to the mirror, looking over one shoulder, saying impishly, "Hi, Clay." Next she turned, slung the towel around her neck, its ends covering the rosy peaks of her breasts, put her hands on her bare hips and said sexily, "Whaddya say, Clay-boy?"

But suddenly she dropped the charade; she was none of these characters. She was not a little girl anymore, she was a woman. What was happening in her life was real, and she must present only the genuine Catherine to Clay. The real Catherine dropped the towel at her feet. She stood straight and tall, studying her body, her face, her hair. She took up the bottle of lightly scented lotion she'd splurged on that morning, her eyes never leaving her reflection as she poured some within her palm and began applying it to her long, supple arms, her shoulders, her neck, circling it and reaching as far onto her back as she could. She cupped her hand for another cool, sleek helping, its smell—the scent she knew Clay loved—all around her now in the warm, steamy bathroom. She rubbed it into her stomach, up the cove between her ribs, her eyes sliding closed as her palms slipped over her breasts, feeling the vaguely welcome discomfort at touching the nipples puckered into gem-hard points. Standing there touching herself, she thought of Clay, of the night ahead. I want you, Clay, she thought, I've wanted you for so long. She imagined it was Clay's hands rubbing her breasts. Her eyelids fluttered open and she took more lotion, watched her palms rub slowly together before she raised one foot, resting it on the vanity, pointing her toes as she spread the scented coolness from the arched top of the foot up the calf, behind the knee, thigh, over the buttock, the sheltered spot between her legs. I'm wanton, she thought. Then, No, I'm a woman, with a woman's needs. The scent Clay loved was all over her now.

Slowly she took the combs from her hair and began brushing it, remembering that night of their blind date, then the night the girls at Horizons had played handmaiden. That was the night of her second date with Clay. She took as much care now with her toilette as the girls had taken that night. She dressed in the minuscule bra and panties that Clay had never seen on their wedding night. She worked over her makeup until it was a subtle work of art. But she kept her hair loose, simple, lightly curled back from her face much as she wore it when she first met Clay.

The new dress was of pale plum crepe de chine, a wraparound that dropped from lightly gathered shoulders to the hem in an easy looseness. It was collarless, leaving a V of skin exposed at the neck. When she tied the string-belt, the dress gained shape, accenting her hollow-hipped thinness. She buttoned the cuffs at her wrists, then stood back to study herself. She pressed her palms to her dancing stomach, then brushed back a wayward wisp of hair. The movement stirred the scent of Charlie, which was trapped now in the fabric of the new dress. Gold loops for her ears, a simple, short chain that fell only to the hollow of her throat, and sling-back shoes of black patent. She chose them because they were the highest she had, knowing how heartily Clay approved of a woman's foot in high heels.

It struck Catherine that she was, without a doubt, trying to be alluring to Clay, and for a moment she felt guilty. But then Melissa called, in her after-nap gibberish, and Catherine hurried to get the baby ready.

Clay had gone out and bought a whole new outfit as well. But now, on his way to Catherine's, he wondered for the tenth time whether the silk tie looked too formal. He wondered if he'd appear to be a spit-combed, nervous schoolboy, all trussed up and tightly knotted this way. What the hell was the matter with him anyway? He'd never had the vaguest doubt about choosing his clothing before. But as he sat at a red light, Clay twisted the rearview mirror so he could study the tie once more. He yanked the Windsor knot halfway down, then changed his mind and slipped it back into place. He glanced at his hair, smoothed a palm over it, although not a filament was out of place. Someone behind him honked the horn and he muttered a curse and proceeded through the green light. Suddenly, as if just remembering, he withdrew a tape from the deck, found another and put it in the track, filling the car with the music of The Lettermen. Too obvious! he reprimanded himself, and tucked The Lettermen out of sight again.

* * *

With more than a half hour to spare, Catherine was all ready. She pictured Clay, somewhere out there getting prepared to come for her, wondered what he was feeling, what he was thinking. Melissa seemed to pick up her mother's distraction and capitalized on it, getting into things she knew she wasn't supposed to touch: the tree decorations, the knobs of the television, the philodendron on the coffee table. Finally, unnerved further by constantly pulling Melissa away from trouble, Catherine deposited her in the playpen and continued her pacing without interference.

The bell rang.

Twice, let him ring twice, she scolded her impatient feet, while outside, Clay crammed his hand into his coat pocket to keep from ringing again too soon.

What should I say? she wondered wildly.

What should I say? he wondered frantically.

The door opened and she stood there in a loosely belted thing that made her look willowy and wonderful.

Snow fell upon the shoulders of Clay's rich, brown leather topcoat.

"Merry Christmas," he said, his eyes on her face while he took in details of her slender feet arched into high-heeled shoes, and the way the dress draped over her hips.

"Merry Christmas," she answered, smiling a small, nervous smile, stepping aside with a hand still on the doorknob to let him pass into the house. He turned around to watch her close the door, letting his eyes travel down to the backs of her calves, then up to the hair on her shoulders. When she met his eyes he said, "Nice dress."

"Thank you. It's new. I . . . well, I spent a little of your money on it."

Why did you say that! she scolded herself, but then he was smiling, saying, "I heartily approve, especially since I did the same thing."

"You did?"

"Christmas present for myself." He opened his topcoat to give her a brief glimpse of herringbone tweed the color of coffee with cream in it.

"In browns, of course."

"Of course."

"But then you always did look your best in browns." The entry suddenly seemed to grow too small, hemming them in, and Catherine moved to lead the way up to the living room, chattering. "Melissa's wearing a new dress, too, one your mother gave her that she just grew into. Come and see her."

"Hey, she'll outshine us both," Clay said right behind her. "Hi, Melissa." And for once Melissa didn't cry at the sight of him.

Catherine stooped and lifted the child, turning with her on her arm, carefully avoiding Clay's eyes as she said, "Can you say hi to Daddy, Melissa?" Their baby only gazed at Clay with bright, unblinking eyes. Catherine whispered something Clay couldn't make out and nudged Melissa's little hand. Still staring, the baby opened and closed her chubby fingers once.

"That's hi," Catherine interpreted, and briefly met Clay's pleased smile. Then she sat down on the davenport and began stuffing Melissa's hands and feet into a blue snowsuit. "Clay, would it be all right if we took my car, then we can take the playpen along."

"We won't need a playpen. Mother had one of the bedrooms redone into a nursery."

Startled, Catherine looked up. "She did?"

Clay nodded.

"When?"

"Last summer."

"She never told me."

"She never had a chance."

"Does she . . . I mean, do they know we're coming tonight, Melissa and I?"

"No. I didn't want to disappoint them if it didn't turn out."

As in a scene from a long-remembered favorite movie, the car moved through the streets while along the way streetlights eased on, signaling the arrival of dark. Catherine was filled with such an odd combination of emotions. The peaceful feeling of being again where she belonged was combined with the breath-halting sense of anticipation leading ever closer to a place where she belonged even more. She counted the hours until the end of the evening.

Clay cast careful glances her way. Christmas did things to a person, he thought, smiling appreciatively at the sight of Melissa reaching for knobs on the dash while Catherine pulled the tiny hands away time and again and gently scolded. He glanced at Catherine's profile once more, his nostrils almost flaring in the light, powdery fragrance emanating from her, and he wondered how he'd make it till the end of the night when he could get her alone again.

The driveway curved to meet them, and Catherine couldn't control the small gasp. "I've missed it," she said, almost to herself. An expression of pleasure tipped up the corners of her mouth beguilingly.

They swept up in front of the door and Clay was around the car, reaching for Melissa, taking her up and into the crook of his arm, then taking Catherine's elbow as she stepped from the car. They stood for a moment in the mellow glow splashing their faces from the carriage lanterns. The streamers of a red ribbon made a light tapping sound as they flicked against the bricks in a light, crisp wind. That wind lifted Clay's hair from his forehead, then set it gently back down as Catherine gazed at him. It toyed with the gold hoops at her ears, sending them swinging against her jawline where he wanted to bury his lips. But that would have to wait.

"Let's ring the bell," he said puckishly.

"Let's," she seconded.

When Angela opened the door she was already saying, "I wondered when—" But the words faded and she placed delicate fingers over her lips.

"Do you have room for three more?" Clay asked.

Angela didn't move for the longest time. Her eyes grew too sparkly, going from the smiling face of Catherine, in the shelter of Clay's arm, to that of Melissa, in his other arm.

"Angela," Catherine said softly. And suddenly the older woman in the pale yellow dress moved to encompass all three as best she could, unable to quite contend with everything at once, with the tears threatening to spill over her lids, with getting them all inside, beckoning Claiborne, taking Melissa—blue snowsuit and all—getting kissed by Clay and by Catherine.

When Claiborne saw who it was, he was as excited as Angela. There were more hugs, interrupted by a surprised Inella, who stopped short and broke into a pleased smile at the sight of the newest arrivals and was immediately drawn to Melissa, who was sitting on her grandmother's lap on the steps, having her snowsuit removed.

The tap of Elizabeth Forrester's cane announced her arrival from the living room. She cast a haughty eye over the assemblage in the foyer, stated to nobody in particular, "High time somebody came to their senses around here," and tapped her way back to the dining room, where she ladled herself a cup of eggnog, added a tot of rum, then mumbled, "Oh, why the bloody heck not," and tipped up the bottle again with a satisfied smile.

The mistletoe was there again, everywhere. Catherine tried neither to avoid it nor seek it, but to ignore it, which was virtually impossible, for each time she looked up she found Clay's eyes seeking her across the room. Those eyes need not stray up to remind her of mistletoe. All evening she felt as if she wore a sprig of it in her hair, so suggestive were the glances they exchanged. It was odd, Clay staying away from her, always eyeing her across the room that way. Time and again she turned from conversation on which she had difficulty concentrating to the tug of his eyes on her back. And always, she would be the first to look away. The food was laid out upon the buffet and they found themselves elbow to elbow moving down the serving line.

"Are you having a good time?" he asked.

"Wonderful. Are you?"

He thought about answering truthfully, No, I'm miserable, but lied instead. "Wonderful, yes."

"Aren't you going to eat anything?"

He glanced at his plate, realized he was halfway past the food and his plate was still empty. She stabbed a Swedish meatball out of the wine sauce and dropped it on his plate.

"A little sustenance," she said, matter-of-factly, never raising her eyes as she moved on to the next chafing dish. He looked at the forlorn piece of meat all alone on the plate and smiled. She knew as well as he did what kind of sustenance he needed that night.

Melissa let it be known immediately that she resented being left in this strange room, in this strange crib, all alone. Catherine sighed and went back into the room, and immediately her daughter stopped crying.

"Melissa, Mommy's going to be right here all the time. You're so tired, sweetheart, won't you lie down?"

She laid Melissa down, covered her, and hadn't even made it as far as the door before Melissa was standing, clutching the rail and crying pitifully.

"Shame on you, punkin," Catherine said, relenting and picking the baby up again, "you're going to hurt Grandma's feelings after she made this beautiful room all for you." It was beautiful. It had all the charm Angela could so easily bestow on everything she touched: bright patches of gingham checks in pastel pink, blue and yellow, blended skillfully into tiered curtains, patchwork comforter and an adorable padded rocker. Turning around to study the room in the glow of the small night-light, Catherine stopped short at the sight of Clay standing in the doorway.

"Is she giving you trouble?"

"It's a strange room, you know."

"Yes, I know," he said, crossing toward them to stand behind Catherine, talking to Melissa over her shoulder. "How about some music then, Melissa? Would you like that better?" And then, to Catherine, "Mother is starting the carols now. Why not bring her back downstairs? Maybe the music will make her sleepy."

Catherine turned to glance past Melissa's blond head at Clay. The look on his face made her pulse race. She realized they were alone, the sounds of the piano and voices drifted up to them from below. Clay moved, extending a hand to touch her . . .

But it was Melissa he reached for, and in the next instant the weight was gone from Catherine's arm.

"Come on," he said, taking Melissa, but never pulling his eyes away from Catherine's, "I'll take her. You've had her all night."

Melissa fell asleep in Clay's arms during the singing, but when she was returned to the crib, her eyes flew open instantly and she began to whimper.

"It's no use, Clay," Catherine whispered. "She's exhausted, but she won't give up."

"Should we take her home then?"

Something in the way he said the word *home*, something in the beckoning, wistful tone of his voice made the blood clamor in Catherine's head.

"Yes, I think we'd better."

"You get her dressed and I'll make our excuses."

All the way to the town house they didn't utter a word to each other. He switched on the radio and found that every station was playing Christmas carols. To the lull of them, Melissa at last fell soundly asleep in her mother's lap.

It was as if Catherine had played this scene before, putting

Melissa to bed, then coming down to find Clay waiting for her. He was sitting on a swivel stool this time, with his coat still on. He had one foot propped on a rung of the opposite stool, an elbow leaning nonchalantly on the edge of the counter. Something caught Catherine's eye, something he twirled between thumb and forefinger, something green. Silently he twirled it— back and forth, back and forth—and it held her gaze like the watch of a hypnotist. Then the thing stopped and she realized it was a sprig of mistletoe he held by its stem.

Staring at it, she stammered, "Th-the baby's . . ."

"Forget the baby," he ordered softly.

"Would you like a drink or something?" she asked stupidly.

"Would you?"

Her eyes were drawn to his, to the level, unsmiling study in gray. The silence hummed, enveloping her momentarily. Then without moving a muscle, he said, "You know what I want, Catherine."

She looked at her feet. "Yes." She felt as if she'd turned into a pillar of salt. Why didn't he move? Why didn't he come and get her then?

"Do you know how many times you've turned me away, though?"

"Yes, eight," she gulped.

The blood leaped wildly to her face as she admitted it. She raised her eyes to him, and he read in them the cost of each of those times. And in the silence the mistletoe again began twirling.

"I wouldn't care to make it nine," he said at last.

"Neither would I."

"Then meet me halfway, Catherine," he invited, stretching out a hand, palm-up, waiting.

"You know what my conditions are."

"Yes, I know." He held the hand as before, in invitation.

"Then—then . . ." She felt like she was choking. Didn't he understand yet?

"Then say it?"

"Yes, say it first," she begged, staring at his long, beautiful fingers, the palm that waited.

"Come here so I can say it up close." It was almost whispered.

Slowly, slowly, she reached to touch the tips of his fingers with her own. But he did not move them until she herself had traveled a share of the distance, telling him what she, too, wanted, as her cold palm slid over his warm one. His fingers closed over hers in slow motion and he pulled her toward him more slowly yet. Her heart slammed against the walls of her chest and her eyes drifted to his as he reeled her close, settling her there against his open legs, his one foot still propped wide on the rung of the other stool. There was no question then about what it was he wanted. His heat and hardness spoke for itself. He pressed her firmly, securely against his loins, then closed his eyes as his lips opened over hers. The mistletoe grew lost in the long sweep of her hair. She felt his hand, warm and forceful against her buttocks, holding her tight while his warmth and hardness branded her stomach. His kiss became all seeking and fevered, a wild crushing of tongue and lips, and she felt their teeth meet, then tasted blood, but had no thought for whose it was. His hands came one to each side of her face, and he jerked her fiercely away from his lips, looked into her eyes with a tortured expression.

"I love you, Cat, I love you. Why did it take me so long to realize it?"

"Oh, Clay, promise me you won't ever leave me again, so I know what I'm getting into."

"I promise, I promise, I promi—"

She stopped his words by flattening herself against him with such force that he grunted. He pulled the whole long, supple, welcome length of her against him. She felt his raised knee rubbing possessively against her hip and wound her arms around his neck, holding him tenaciously. Then she felt herself hoisted off the floor as he swiveled the stool around and in a single motion half leaned, half fell, pressing her back against the edge of the counter. But it cut into her shoulders, so she pushed him back, turning him, taking him with her on a brief journey together on that swiveling stool until she stood again on the floor between his open knees. They kissed, warm against each other, and somehow while they did it, the stool began twisting back and forth, back and forth, almost like the mistletoe had done twirling earlier in his fingers. And each time the stool moved, Clay's erect body brushed provocatively against hers while she rose up on tiptoe to meet it, brushing harder each time. She felt his hand leave her hair and seek the knot of her belt. Dimly she thought about helping him, but leaned against his loose hold instead, pleasured at the feel of his hand there between them, then at the touch of the belt as it glided down the backs of her legs to the floor. One-handed, he opened the dress, touching the skin of her throat first with his fingers, then with his lips, then moving lower, lower, lower, until his hand lay warm on the lowest part of her stomach. He backed away to look at her while he wrested the dress from her shoulders, and when he saw the brief garments beneath, he groaned and buried his face in the band of bareness between bra and panties, wetting the skin there with his tongue.

"Did you know I wore these on my wedding night?" she asked in a husky voice that sounded strangely unlike her own.

"Did you?" His eyes burned into hers, his hands traced the

lotus petals along the top of the bra. "But tonight will be our wedding night." Then both of his arms went around her, and she felt her bra go tight, then loose, then fall away in his hands. His head swooped forward while hers dropped back. His kiss fell upon her bare breast, and a faint growl sounded in her arched throat as his tongue circled the nipple, then the edges of his teeth rode lightly against the cockled point. Strangling in delight, she threaded her fingers in his soft hair, directing him to her other hungering breast. Carried away, his teeth tugged too hard and she flinched, her nostrils distended. With a sound of apology deep in his throat, he suckled more lightly. Deep in her body, sensations sluiced and impatiently she tugged at the shoulders of the leather topcoat he still wore. Without taking his mouth from her flesh, he freed his arms, let her take the coat from his shoulders and drop it, unheeded, behind him, followed by his sport coat. Nuzzling each other, dropping kisses wherever they chose to fall, he worked the knot from his tie while she unbuttoned his shirt. Then it joined the rest on the floor. One-armed, he brought her back where she belonged, with her naked breasts against his bare chest. He eased away from her then, to watch the sight of his hands cupping her breasts. He flattened one hand against her stomach and ran it down inside the front of her bikini until he touched her intimately.

"Do you want me to take the rest off?" he asked, nuzzling her neck, tonguing her skin there, even tasting her perfume now.

"We're in the middle of the kitchen, Clay."

"I don't give a damn. Should I take it off or will you?"

"This was your idea," she whispered coquettishly, smiling against his hair.

"Like hell." But in one swift motion he had her panty hose and bikini down to her knees, then he picked her up effortlessly and set her on the edge of the counter, hooking a stool and send-ing it out of the way with a foot. He knelt down, raised his eyes to hers as he removed first one high heel, then the other, then with a sweep of both hands had her last two garments lying in a soft heap on the floor. He moved up next to the counter and she raised her arms, looped them around his neck, opened her knees and looped them around his waist and said, "Take me upstairs to our bedroom." He pulled her off the counter until she was astraddle his waist, her ankles locked behind him. Her naked flesh was pressed against his navel and the smell of her perfume was like a cloud about them as they walked that way, kissing, up-stairs to the bedroom. He stood by the lamp and said, "Turn it on." She let go of his neck with one hand and reached.

Standing beside the bed he whispered, "Let go," into her mouth.

"Never," she whispered back.

"Then how can I get my pants off?"

Without another word she unhooked her ankles and fell backward with a bounce onto the mattress, lying there watching him while he unbuckled his belt, unzipped his trousers, never taking his eyes off her. When he was naked, he knelt above her on one knee, his hands on either side of her head.

"Catherine, I know I'm a year and a half late asking this, but are you going to get pregnant out of this?"

"But if you'd asked that Fourth of July, we wouldn't be here now, would we?"

"Cat, I just don't want you pregnant for a while. I want to enjoy you flat and thirsty for a while first."

"Flat and thirsty?"

He realized he'd given himself away, so he leaned his head down to kiss her and stop her questions. She turned her mouth aside.

"What does that mean, flat and thirsty?"

"Nothing." He nudged around at her lips, trying to get her to stop talking and touch him.

"You answer me and I'll answer you," she said, avoiding another pass of his lips against hers.

If she got mad at him now, he thought, he'd never forgive himself for opening up his big mouth. But he had to answer.

"Okay. I read your diary. All that stuff we did with the wine—that's what I meant by flat and thirsty."

She burned now, but not with anger, with embarrassment and sensuality. "Clay, I feel like I'm dying of thirst right now, and believe me, I won't get pregnant."

She could feel his muscles quivering on each side of her head. His voice was racked as he asked. "Then how long do I have to hang here before you touch me?"

No longer, she thought, no longer, Clay, and reached to touch him lightly with the backs of her fingers, measuring his ardor with feather strokes that robbed him of breath. The months of want drifted into oblivion at her first caress. The days of searching had their answer. Her hand explored, enclosed, stroked, cupped and thrilled, until Clay's elbows turned to water. He collapsed beside her, reaching, seeking her warm skin. Her stomach was a little softer now, but the old hollows were back below her hipbones. Her thigh was smooth and firm, lifting at his touch to free the spot his hand sought. As he moved toward it, her hand fell still upon his tumescence. Sensing her urgency, her expectancy, he lay his head upon her breast and listened to the thunder of her heart beneath his ear as he touched her depths for the first time. It thundered there in double time, and he could feel it lifting the weight of his head with each beat. Outwardly she lay limp and passive, but her heartbeat told the truth. He moved his fingers once, and she lurched and gulped for air. He rolled half over her, kissing her eyes, her temple, the corner of her mouth, her lips, which lay slack, as if what was happening to the inside of her body robbed her of the will to do anything but drift in the grip of pleasure. He aroused her with butterfly touches, bent again to cover her breasts with kisses, sliding his lips over her stomach, feeling it rise with each lift of her hips. Low animal sounds scraped from her throat, then his name, repeated as an accent to each thrust she could no longer control.

He spoke her name—Cat—over and over, letting her soar, experiencing a new high, a sharing of purpose with her as he brought her near climax and sent her shivering. This, he knew, was what he had not given her the first time, and he meant to make it up to her all the other times of their lives.

"Let it happen, Cat," he whispered hoarsely.

But suddenly he knew he had to share the sensation to its fullest. Easing onto her, he sought and found, entered and plunged, murmuring soft sounds; lovesounds that took on their own meaning.

She shuddered and arched first, and he was close behind her, so close that the film of dampness dried from their skins at the same time.

Into her hair he spoke weakly, "Ah, Cat, it was good for me."

"For me too."

He lay his palm on her stomach, then ran it lower, let it rest peacefully on her body, then just barely inside it. She could feel his jaw move in the hollow of her shoulder as he spoke.

"Cat, remember in the hospital when the nurse showed us the way the contractions build up?"

"Mmm-hmm," she murmured, toying sleepily with his hair.

"It felt the same way inside you a minute ago."

"It did?"

"It made me think of how close pleasure and pain are. It even seems as if the same things happen in your body during the moments of your greatest pleasure and your greatest pain. Isn't that odd?"

"I never thought about it before, but then I never—"

He raised up, leaned on an elbow and looked down into her face. He touched a lock of hair, easing it back from her forehead.

"Was that your first time, Cat?"

Suddenly timid, she surrounded him, hugged him too close for him to see her face.

"Yes," she admitted.

"Hey." Gently he removed her tight grip so he could look at her again. "After all that we've been through, are you getting modest on me?"

"How could I possibly claim modesty now?"

"Just don't ever be afraid to talk to me about anything, okay? If you don't trust me with the things that bother you, how can I help you? All that business about the past and your feelings for Herb, do you see that we seem to have conquered that already, together?"

"Ah, Clay." She sighed and leaned against him, promising herself she'd never withhold her feelings from him again. A short time later she said, "Did you know that I started falling in love with you while you were courting me at Horizons?"

"That long ago?"

"Oh, Clay, how could I help it? All those girls panting after you and telling me how perfect you were, and you coming by in your sexy little Corvette, with your sexy clothes and that sexy smile and all those sterling good manners of yours to offset all that sexiness. God, you drove me crazy."

"Idiot girl," he laughed. "Do you know how much time you could have saved if you'd just once let on what you were feeling?"

"But I was so scared. What if you didn't feel the same way about me? I'd have been shattered."

"Yet every time I made advances I felt like you couldn't stand me."

"Clay, I told you that first night that my dad made me come to your house—marriage had to be for love only. Please, let's always be this way, like we are tonight. Let's be good to each other and promise all those things that we never really promised in that trumped-up marriage ceremony."

Lying naked, with their limbs entwined, secure in each other's love, they sealed those vows at last.

"I promise them, Cat."

"I do, too, Clay."

On Christmas morning Melissa woke them up, babbling and thumping her heels on the crib. Clay came awake groggily, stretched and felt bare skin on the other side of the bed. He turned to study the woman who lay on her stomach, sleeping beneath a swirl of blond hair.

He started to creep from bed noiselessly.

"Where you going?" came a voice from under the hair.

"To get Melissa and bring her in with us, okay?"

"Okay, but don't be gone long, huh?"

They came back together, the one in aqua blue footed pajamas, the other one in nothing. When Catherine rolled over, Clay plopped Melissa down beside her, then got in, too.

"Hi, Lissy-girl. Got a kiss for Mommy?"

Melissa leaned over and sucked her mother's chin, her version of a kiss.

Clay watched with a glad expression on his face.

Catherine looked at his tousled blond hair, his smiling gray eyes and asked, "Hi, Clay-boy, got a kiss for Mommy?"

"More than one," he said, smiling. "This is one child who's going to learn early the value of touching."

He leaned across the baby then, to give his wife what she wanted.